AIRSHIP NINE

The group assembled in the lower cargo bay were dressed in every conceivable kind of heavy garment they could find, with the quality of jackets, boots and coats ranging from the designer fashions worn by Andrew and Kathleen Sinclair to the soiled workman's jacket of Floyd Robinson.

'Okay – everyone understand their instructions?' Madigan asked once more as he scanned the group.

'I have a question.' Andrew Sinclair stepped forward. 'Why can't we just plan on making ourselves comfortable in the station and wait until the weather clears completely?'

'The captain felt that we should stay together whenever possible.'

'Why?'

'In case of a sudden change in plans.'

'That concept is open to debate.'

'No it isn't, Mr Sinclair.' Madigan raised himself to his full height and took a deep breath to help keep his temper in tow. 'Okay, if everyone's ready then all we do is wait.'

The wind was picking up, and so was the snow. If they didn't get to land at Palmer very soon, it might be days before the weather cleared enough to let them have another shot at it. But before he could think another negative thought, the sight of the rocky coastline came into full view beneath them. 'There it is – get ready, put on your face masks!'

*By Thomas Block, and published
by New English Library:*

MAYDAY
ORBIT
FORCED LANDING
AIRSHIP NINE

AIRSHIP NINE

Thomas Block

NEW ENGLISH LIBRARY

The extracts from the lyric 'As Time Goes By', written by Herman Hupfield, are used by kind permission of Redwood Music Ltd, 14 New Burlington St, London W1X 2LR.

First published in the USA in 1984 by G. P. Putnam's Sons

First published in Great Britain 1984 by New English Library

NEL Open Market Edition 1984
First NEL Paperback Edition September 1985

NEL Books are published by
New English Library,
Mill Road, Dunton Green,
Sevenoaks, Kent.
Editorial office: 47 Bedford Square, London WC1B 3DP.

Printed in Great Britain by
Hunt Barnard Printing Ltd., Aylesbury, Bucks.

British Library C.I.P.

Block, Thomas H.
  Airship nine.
  I. Title
  813'.54[F]   PS3552.L634

  ISBN 0-450-05839-5

To all those who have, with sometimes no more than a few words or a quick glance, given me things to write about – not the least of whom are Ryan, Steven, Kim and the perennial EFB.

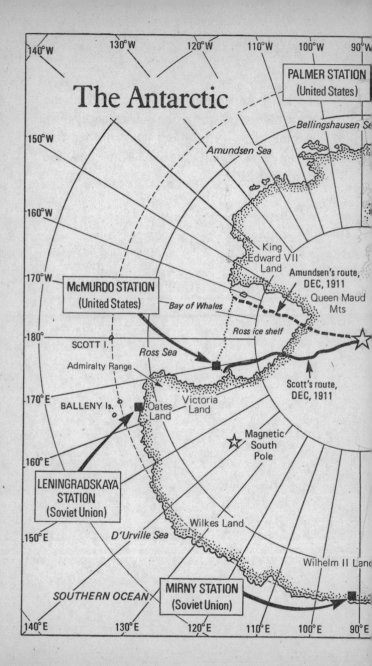

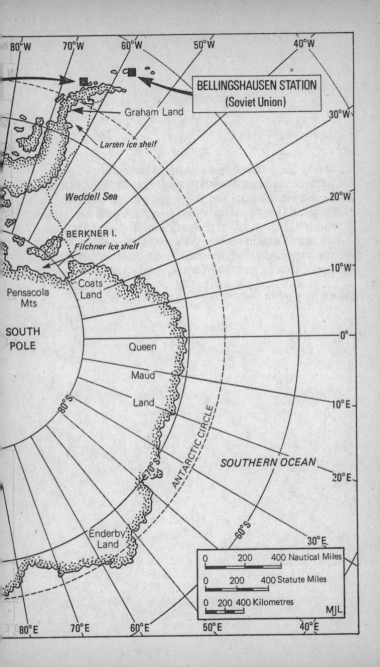

Acknowledgments

I'd like to thank the people at Airship Industries, England, for letting me pound on and fly their new Skyship. For my Antarctic experience, the following groups went above and beyond the call of duty to provide me with the things I required: the staff at Palmer and Faraday stations, Antarctica; Captain Heinz Aye and the crew of the *World Discoverer*; Society Expeditions, Seattle, Washington. A special thanks goes to Werner, Amy, Judy, Steve and all the others who photographed, noted and trekked with me while I spent time at the bottom of the world.

. . . on a full stomach, layered with proper clothes, the cold can be amusing. But for a working man, it's prime evil and torment. Men are twice as poor in such cold, thieves are craftier and robbers fiercer . . .

Anton Chekhov

. . . the fundamental things apply, as time goes by.

Dooley Wilson as
Sam, from the movie
Casablanca

Prologue

At precisely 3.02 p.m., New York time, on April 6th, the mammoth space platform GF-2 began its fifth fore-to-aft tumble on its current rotation as it maneuvered through the airless environment. At that moment the United States flag mounted on the platform's aluminum-colored center section gleamed brilliantly as it was turned to face the unrelenting sun. The earth hovered 22,500 miles below the space platform, looking like a mosaic painted on a basketball being held at arm's length. The patterns of the earth's vivid colors – blues, greens, browns, whites – continuously changed as the warm, life-filled planet revolved peacefully along its axis.

It would have been a strikingly beautiful sight to watch, except that there was no one on board space platform GF-2 to appreciate the scene. Since the last of the astronaut-technicians had departed from the huge orbiting missile platform eight months before, the functioning of that unit had been strictly automatic. Routine. No one could have prophesied that an unusual blend of circumstances would soon combine into the basis for an unthinkable accident.

A deep space quasar identified as 3C73 had been bombarding the electro-magnetic vanes of platform GF-2 with a heavy barrage of X-ray impulses for the past several weeks. It was something that the ground engineers at the California monitoring laboratory had easily recognized from their consoles. But what could not be determined from the sophisticated earthbound monitors was that this new and exotic source of energy had begun to interact with other disquieting influences.

There had been constant solar flare activity during the three previous days. In addition, the influence of the random traces of radioactivity in the layers of galactic dust which had gathered on the honeycomb structure of GF-2 from its time in orbital space had caused a massive accumulation of high frequency energy to surround the craft. At eleven seconds past 3.03 p.m. the critical charge was finally reached and the high frequency energy suddenly surged into the interior structure of the space platform. The onboard circuits – which had not been designed to accommodate a massive electrical violation – reacted in the only manner that they could. Within less than a microsecond, the electrical systems of space missile platform GF-2 had gone from routine functioning to total disarray.

Along the enormous length and width of GF-2, the four dozen missile bay doors opened simultaneously. Ten seconds later the rocket engines on each of the nuclear-tipped, multiple-warhead missiles ignited. In a soundless display of enormous energy, the forty-eight United States ballistic missiles exited from platform GF-2. All forty-eight missiles had launched themselves toward their pre-programmed targets.

A white-painted Soviet missile platform, known in the Kremlin as N-1, rode in the same geosynchronous orbit as the American platform, although it was positioned considerably further north toward the polar region. Its position gave the electronic sensors built into N-1 a clear signal that earthbound missiles had been fired from the competing United States space weapon. In accordance with the announcement that the Premier of the Soviet Union had made in a face-to-face confrontation with the President of the United States after the Soviet missile platform was first made operational, the onboard programming of N-1 had also deliberately been designed to be totally automatic. Any first strike attempt by the United States missile platform would result in a nearly instantaneous retaliation from the Soviet counterpart.

While vocally displaying their disagreement and distaste of this arrangement, the politicians of both countries had secretly agreed that the concept – known by the title of 'mutually assured destruction'; its official acronym was

MAD – would be the best preventive medicine to guard against an all-out nuclear war. But none of the aspects of the MAD doctrine would occur to the dozens of scientists and technicians in either the United States or the Soviet Union as they helplessly watched the displays on their earthbound consoles that told of the attack against the Soviet Union by the missiles from GF-2, or of the automatic retaliatory nuclear strike against the United States and its allies being launched by Soviet station N-1.

In the California monitoring lab responsible for the United States missile platform GF-2, the scientists frantically spent the last fifteen minutes of their lives in an attempt to determine exactly what had gone wrong. One of the senior scientists on duty that afternoon – Kenneth Vandergriff, a tall, thin man from Minneapolis, Minnesota – was on the right track to the correct explanation. He had already come up with part of the truth by the time the first of the Soviet missiles exploded in the vicinity of the laboratory where he worked. Vandergriff was instantly vaporized from the face of the earth, as were millions of others for hundreds of miles around him as more bombs exploded within scant moments of the first. When Vandergriff's body had been turned to dust, the last chance for mankind to understand what had gone wrong with their complex system for maintaining peace by a pact of mutually assured destruction was now gone forever.

Elwood B. Benson had just run out of car wax and had begun to walk back toward his four-car garage in a fashionable section of Pittsburgh when he heard the first of the sirens. Benson stood silently for half a minute as he attempted to figure out what the noise of the high-pitched sirens in the distance could mean. It was nothing he had ever heard before, he was certain of that much, and he wondered if this was the beginning of an alert for an approaching tornado or something of that sort.

Benson scanned the horizon to the west, but it was

cloudless as the forecast had indicated. Benson shrugged, then decided that his best bet was to listen to a radio – if there was going to be a storm he certainly wanted to know early enough so he could move his Rolls Royce into the garage before it got wet. Benson turned and stepped toward the silver Rolls Royce in the driveway, opened the car's massive door and reached across for the radio knob. What happened to him next occurred so quickly that Benson would never realize that the immediate cause of his death was a result of the impact against his body of the heavy stainless steel grillwork of his Rolls. That grillwork – now without its Flying Lady mascot since the hefty symbol had been snapped off an instant earlier – had been propelled up and backward through the car's window by the enormous force. The first nuclear explosion that detonated high above the US Steel building in the middle of downtown Pittsburgh had, within a few moments, already eliminated most of the residents of that city and its surrounding areas. The additional two nuclear weapons that would explode over the same general spot during the next half hour would be a classic example of the overkill that had often been postulated for an all-out nuclear war.

Police Officer Pierre Lesueur walked his assigned beat down the broad, treelined expanse of Cours Mirabeau in the city of Aix-en-Provence. His eyes quickly scanned across each of the shop windows and doors that he passed, but his mind was far off, hundreds of kilometers to the north, in Paris. He would be there in just another few weeks, at the apartment of his friend Jean-Claude. The trip brought the promise of evenings better spent than on patrol in a sleepy town in southern France. Lesueur fiddled with the door of one more shop – it was, as they all were, tightly shut and locked – before he paused for a moment to rub his eyes and think again about the idea of asking for reassignment to the Paris police force. Lesueur knew that the cost of living in Paris was much higher, but then again . . .

The small radio that Lesueur wore on his belt buzzed

its alarm. Lesueur reluctantly reached for the portable radio and put it to his ear. What he expected, of course, was another routine message to the effect that another of the local citizens had tasted too much wine from the overflowing vats and had allowed their auto to stray from the road and into a cypress tree. Instead, the words that poured out of the small electronic box – they were nearly incomprehensible because they were spoken so rapidly, with so much emotion – caused Officer Lesueur to freeze where he stood. Nuclear war. Paris devastated. The Brittany coast under attack. A massive explosion over the city of Bordeaux.

The sounding of the town's emergency siren was what brought Lesueur around, its sudden warbling noise slicing into the quiet night and nearly causing him to jump out of his own skin. Whoever was in charge back at headquarters had decided to activate the town's emergency siren – and Lesueur could already see that the decision had been a definite mistake.

Lights began to blink on in the apartments over the shops on the Cours Mirabeau, and, across the boulevard, in the larger homes and mansions on the far side. Within moments after that doors began to open. The first of the citizens to respond to the alarm began to pile out on the sidewalks, dressed in nightclothes and whatever else they had hastily put on. Those who spotted the policeman rushed toward him for an explanation. But before Lesueur could offer the frightful news to even the first of the men and women who headed toward him, there was an ungodly flash of light from behind him that lit up the entire southern sky.

'Get back, get inside!' Lesueur shouted as he resisted the urge to turn toward where the flash had come from and concentrated instead on the people. Lesueur began to run headlong down the street, waving his arms and shouting, 'Marseilles! They've bombed Marseilles! Get indoors!' But even before he reached the first group of people on the sidewalk, Officer Lesueur felt the hot wind at his back and knew that it was already too late.

The force of the explosion above the French Naval

facility at Marseilles was powerful enough to spread its destruction as far away as Aix-en-Provence, nearly twenty-five kilometers to the north. The destructive wind that ripped through the sleepy town went from calm to more than hurricane force in the blink of an eye and, with it, carried away most of the people and the structures. Officer Lesueur was picked up and swept away with the searing wind as if he were no more than a twig in a maelstrom. Lesueur's body impacted against the brick façade of an archway. The archway itself crumbled a few seconds later when the main force of wind proved too much for even it. One by one, nearly every person and structure that comprised Aix-en-Provence – a city of quiet elegance that dated back to before the birth of Christ – had been ground away to nothing.

Flight Leader Li Ching tapped the face of the cockpit's inert radio one more time, but he now knew for certain that the radio had failed completely. Li Ching lifted his eyes from the instrument panel in front of him and scanned the sky that he flew through. The first hint of dawn was on the eastern horizon, but the ground beneath him remained etched in deep black. Off in the distance Li Ching could make out the ground lights of Baoji and, beyond that, the larger point of light that represented Xian. Li Ching continued to fly the MiG 21 jet in a wide circle, uncertain of what to do next. He leveled the wings momentarily as the MiG 21 headed north toward the Gobi desert that separated China and Mongolia. Li Ching's feeling was that if he had any chance of locating the remainder of his group, that would be the direction he would find them in.

Tsang is an incredible fool. He was told to remain in close formation. Li Ching could not believe his misfortune – that first his wingman had managed to stray from him during the scramble to intercept height, and that now his radio had failed. Even though radio failures were a common enough experience in the older fighters that his squadron was relegated to, Li Ching knew that he would be open to a great deal of criticism from the training committee unless he somehow managed to locate his unit so he could complete whatever this unexpected exercise was.

Li Ching began to bank the MiG sharply to the west again when he spotted something up high. He leveled the wings and watched the growing smear of a contrail as it climbed in a wobble from wherever it had been launched. He watched in amazement as other contrails joined the first one, in an obvious formation of missiles being fired at some unknown target above them – a target that was headed in his direction.

This is no training exercise! What could be happening? Flight Leader Li Ching took his hand off his aircraft's throttle in order to pound his fist against the inoperable radio one more time. This time, his hand never reached the spot that he intended it to. The first of the many nuclear bombs to be detonated over China exploded a few thousand feet directly above his head. That bomb instantly removed any trace that either Flight Leader Li Ching or his MiG 21 had ever existed.

During the next quarter hour, countless millions of others were also annihilated as the unbridled rein of nuclear bombs continued to be launched and exploded. By 3.45 in the afternoon on that spring day of April 6th, not only were the United States and the Soviet Union completely devastated but so also were many of the other nations of the world. Their own nuclear arsenals had also been launched against enemies near and far, old and new. By the dozens, a growing list of nations – more than any of the professional strategists around the globe had ever dared to predict – had joined the unstoppable conflagration. Nearly every corner of the earth had become a full-scale participant in the death throes of a planet that had rotated so peacefully not a half hour before.

One

THE LARGE white airship droned on through the hazy, placid sky as it cruised above a becalmed sea eight hundred feet below. The synthetic material that gave the ship its familiar cigar-shaped blimp appearance had a wide red line painted horizontally along its midsection, and that line provided the only splotch of color against an otherwise grey and featureless sky. A large number nine was stenciled on either side of the forward part of the craft's rounded nose, and each of the large fiberglass rudders – there was one mounted above and one mounted below the rear of that envelope – had an American flag displayed prominently on its surface. The name Airship Airlines was painted in black block letters just forward of each of the flags.

The slight tremors from the ship's two engines mounted on the rear of the underslung structure were, at that moment, the only vibrations to pass through the craft. The air that they flew through was incredibly smooth. The pulses of engine power traveled forward through the ninety-foot length that made up the fiberglass and aluminum two-decked structure beneath the envelope. It was inside this underslung area – the gondola – where the passengers, crew and freight were all housed. The mild but persistent engine pulsations finally wakened a man who was sleeping in a midships cabin on the left side. He slowly lifted his head off the pillow and glanced around the tiny cabin for a few moments before he finally spoke in a voice that was a combination of sleepiness and anger. 'Dammit, we've fallen asleep. What time is it?'

Nancy Schneider had dozed off for what she thought was no more than a minute or two. When she heard Ray Madigan's voice she immediately opened her eyes. 'What's

. . . the time?' Nancy blinked a few times, then quickly rolled away from where Madigan's muscular arm had been tucked beneath her body. She turned to face the travel clock on the small nightstand next to her bed.

'I told you to be careful not to fall asleep.' Madigan glanced down at her. Nancy was naked, but the bed sheet was twisted around her body from the middle of her back and lower. Madigan hated fat women the most, ugly women second. Nancy had a little too much of a mousey appearance to be rated as any great beauty, but her good skin, tight body, thin features and ponytailed blonde hair were more than enough votes in her favor to make her acceptable.

'That was very nice,' Nancy said. She yawned.

'Right.' Madigan rolled his body to the edge of the narrow bed and, maneuvering around Nancy's naked body while being careful not to touch her – physical contact afterward was not one of the things he enjoyed – he sat himself up on the edge of the mattress. 'But you know damn well that I'm supposed to be on watch. You shouldn't have let me fall asleep.'

'A few minutes won't make any difference.' Nancy pointed to the clock and smiled. She noticed that Madigan was no longer looking at her. 'But you'd better get going, darling.'

'Sure – except that now I've got to put up with more bullshit from Whitaker.' Madigan scowled as he dressed and surveyed the horizon through the plexiglass window. 'The visibility is just as shitty now as it was an hour ago.'

'Really?' Nancy used the excuse of looking out of the window in order to brush up against him, her body rubbing against his for a few seconds until she reached for her bathrobe, slipped it on her shoulders and tied the belt. 'At least there's no turbulence.'

'Conditions are too stable for turbulence.' Madigan buttoned up his uniform shirt, then carefully adjusted the three-striped epaulets that he wore above each shoulder – the standard uniform for an airship's copilot.

'What are you going to tell the captain?' Nancy allowed herself to gently lay her fingers against the firm outline of

10

muscles along his back. Even with his shirt on, it was obvious that Ray Madigan was a powerful man.

'I'll tell Whitaker that you and I were engaged in an afternoon matinee.'

'I'm being serious.'

'So am I. It's been one hell of a show.' Madigan gestured toward the rumpled sheets on the bed.

Nancy squirmed slightly in mock discomfort, although sex and love – areas that to her sometimes overlapped, sometimes didn't – were topics she always enjoyed discussing. Reluctantly, she changed the subject. 'Are you going to be at the dinner tonight?'

'No. Like I told you, it's my watch. I think our esteemed captain has the evening's honors.'

'I wish you got along a little better with Whitaker. Airships are too small for personal feuds.'

Madigan laughed contemptuously. 'Sure, that's easy for you to say – you don't have to deal with him. I'm the one who's stuck in an eight-foot-wide cockpit with that prick for the next ten thousand miles.'

'You don't know for sure that he's the one who put in the fitness report against you.' Nancy brushed back a few of the blonde strands that had worked loose from beneath her ponytail. The fact that she was thirty years old and still wore her hair the same way she had for the past fifteen years was another distinction that she found pleasant to think about. When things worked well, there was no need to change them.

'Like I told you a hundred times, I do have a few friends in high places. They're the ones who saw the report.'

'That's not exactly what you told me.' Nancy glanced through the plexiglass window at the sea below, then looked back at the copilot. 'You told me that one of the clerks saw Whitaker's signature on a fitness report on the chief pilot's desk. That doesn't necessarily mean that Whitaker's report was the bad one.'

'Cut the bullshit, okay?' Madigan stepped over to the far cabin wall and ran his hand along a row of rivets on a gondola bracing beam. 'Fact number one is that I was next up for promotion to captain. Fact number two . . .'

'Yes, but . . .'

'Fact number two,' Madigan continued, 'is that they gave *Airship Sixteen* to Henderson. I can fly better than him with both eyes shut.' Madigan spoke in his usual brisk tones, but for a change he avoided staring at the person he spoke to. Instead, he kept his eyes fixed on the row of rivets under his fingers. 'Whitaker did it to me, all right. I can tell from the way he looks at me.'

'Then why would he have you assigned to his ship again? That doesn't make sense.'

'Sure it makes sense. All the other fitness reports were okay. All the reports except Whitaker's.' Madigan spoke off-handedly, but it was obvious that he was obsessed with having been passed over for promotion to captain. 'So the chief pilot must've asked him to give me one more try, one more look. That's what this voyage is all about, at least as far as he and I are concerned.'

'Then maybe you should put out more of an effort.'

'Maybe I should just punch the son-of-a-bitch in the mouth, for all the good my effort would do. I don't know why the hell you can't see it, but Whitaker already has his mind made up. Case closed. He doesn't like me and nothing's going to change that.' Madigan was getting himself wound up, but he had to work at keeping his voice low since Whitaker wasn't more than forty-five feet away somewhere in the confined space of the gondola. 'Since he threw his son out of the house and the boy died of a drug overdose a few weeks later, Whitaker's been even more of an asshole than ever. It doesn't make any difference to him whether I can be a good captain or not – to be in command of an airship has somehow become his private club. It's a club that he doesn't want people like me to be a member of.'

'How old was his son?'

'Seventeen. I met him once when we were leaving on a trip. It was strange how directly opposite he was from his old man – very loose and casual, didn't give too much of a damn about anything.'

'Being the opposite of your parents isn't unusual.' Growing up, Nancy had been totally opposite from her mother.

12

Now that she was getting older, she was beginning to appreciate her mother's discipline and character.

'Yeah. And Whitaker was always lecturing the poor kid on right and wrong. He threw the kid out because he had broken one of Whitaker's honor-code rules.'

'How?'

'By having pot in his room, a few joints the kid had brought home from a party.'

'Is that all?' Nancy shuddered – she suspected that over the years her parents had found a good many things in her room that were a great deal worse. She was thankful that her parents had the good sense to know when to say something, and when not to.

'For Whitaker, a few joints is reason enough to make a grandstand play – even if the result is going to fuck up a person's life. But at least he got a little of what he deserved when his wife walked out on him. Served that prick right.'

'I see.'

'Do you? Great. Well, I see some things too. I see that I'll never make captain as long as Whitaker has any influence over that decision.'

'What are you going to do?'

'When we get back to the States I'm going to insist on a different assignment. I'd quit before I'll fly another trip with Whitaker.'

'Would you really?' Nancy's first choice, of course, was that Madigan be made into an airship captain so she could be the girlfriend of the man in charge rather than the first officer. But Nancy's second choice was to have things stay exactly the way they were. Having Ray talk about quitting now that the two of them had a good relationship going was the last thing she wanted to consider.

'Damn right I'd quit. But don't worry. I don't think that'll be necessary. Once Whitaker takes his pound of flesh from me, the home office can save face by letting me escape to another airship. Eventually, I'll pile up enough good fitness reports to allow the chief pilot to graciously disregard the one from Whitaker.'

'That's good.'

'Sure, except that it'll take time. But time doesn't matter

because it'll be a red-letter day in my life when I finally get away from that prick.'

Nancy opened her mouth to reply, but then decided to say nothing. Now was obviously not the time. The strange thing about Captain Whitaker was how well respected he was by most people and how deeply hated he was by a few. As far as she was concerned, Nancy had found Whitaker pleasant to work for and easy to get along with – which made it even more of a mystery to her why Ray couldn't do the same. Maybe what he had said about Whitaker was true, maybe Ray couldn't do right no matter what. 'You look nice,' Nancy said as she took a step backward so she could see all of him. He was six foot tall and absolutely solid, with wide shoulders and a narrow waist. A thirty-three year old with a perfect body. 'Don't worry, darling, things always work out.'

'Bullshit. They only work out if you make them.'

'We worked out, didn't we?'

'You're forgetting that I'm the one who made it happen.'

'Not entirely.' It had been only the third day after joining *Airship Nine* in England that she had made love to him for the first time. Since then – for nearly four weeks now – the two of them had been together whenever she could arrange it. Being with Ray was like an addiction to her, a habit that she couldn't break. 'You should comb your hair.'

'Right.' Madigan strolled toward the mirror on the wall and took a comb out of his pocket. He began to carefully maneuver his long thick hair into the pattern he preferred.

'You're not bored with me, are you?' Nancy asked the question casually as she slipped off her bathrobe and began to dress. While she waited for his reply – he seemed to enjoy the silence that now hung between them – she looked anxiously out the cabin window toward the ocean below. The sea seemed as tranquil as the sky they flew through. She liked being an airship's stewardess. Before joining Airship Airlines she had worked for a regular jet airline – USAir – and flew as a junior flight attendant on transcontinental flights, but her current job on the airship was far more fun.

14

'Why do you ask that? Do I look bored?' Madigan turned around and faced her.

'I don't know, sometimes the question just pops into my mind. I just wondered.' Ray had a way of making her feel self-conscious; it was the part of their relationship that she hated, but a part that she always seemed to seek out in men. It was trial by fire, as one of her girlfriends in college had once said.

'Critical self-examination is a wonderful thing,' Madigan flashed a big smile. 'Look how much self-examination I've done lately. Look how good it's been for me.' Madigan reached forward and patted Nancy on her bottom, his hand lingering along the folds of the soft underpants that she had just finished putting on. 'You should keep wondering, keep doubting even those things that you think you're absolutely sure about. That's how you stay sharp – by being unsure of everything and everybody.' Madigan laughed, then stepped toward the cabin door that would lead him into the interior of the airship and toward the cockpit.

'Sometimes I wonder if you're serious when you say those things.'

'Sometimes I wonder, too.' Madigan stood expressionless, his face not giving any additional clues to his feelings.

Nancy watched the door close behind him. For several seconds she stood precisely where she was, hardly even allowing herself to breath. *He's no good for you*, the familiar thought pattern began as it played over in her mind like a broken record. Yet she knew that it was a song she had heard too many times before, too many times from her mother, from her friends, even from herself. *No good for you. You always pick men who are no good for you*. But whatever the reason was, Nancy Schneider didn't care. Even if she wanted to, Nancy knew that it would take more than just the mouthing of those too familiar words ever to get her out of her habits, ever to make her change.

Doctor Everertt Tucker leaned over the seatback and peered through the plexiglass windshield in front of him.

'So this is the zone that you spoke of? Convergence, I think you called it?'

'That's correct.' Captain Lou Whitaker turned sideways in the left front seat of the airship and faced Tucker. 'Our flight plan route puts us directly along the convergence zone for nearly four thousand miles. At this speed,' Whitaker said in a friendly, conversational tone as he tapped the airspeed gauge on the flight panel in front of him, the needle quivering at a reading slightly below one hundred miles per hour, 'we'll be laying on the convergence zone for nearly two full days.'

'It's even more complicated than that,' Steve Galloway volunteered from the copilot's seat as he glanced first at the captain, then back at the elderly Englishman who stood behind them. 'About the same time we leave the zone of convergence, we also cross the international date line. That means, calendar-wise, nearly three days on the convergence.' Galloway grinned, his youthful, broad smile showing that while the fact itself was true, he was obviously joking about its significance.

'So since today is the afternoon of April 6th,' Tucker said as he made an exaggerated gesture to check his calendar watch, 'it will be April 8th – no, 9th – before we leave this devil of a misty fog.' Tucker leaned slightly more forward and pretended to adjust his wire-rimmed glasses, as if he were trying to see through the murk they were flying through. 'I dare say I'm a bit disappointed. It's one thing to be slower than a slow boat to China, but quite another to be blinded by fog for what will go down as three full days in my diary.'

'No different than what they saw fifty years ago from the *Hindenburg*,' Whitaker said. He ran his hand across his receding hairline, pushing to one side the few hairs that remained as a brown peninsula that stuck into the deepening sea of tanned and ruddy scalp. Moving those unruly strands back and forth had become an unconscious habit a year before, shortly after his forty-fourth birthday.

'Or what they saw from the R-101,' Tucker added, getting back to the old British airship that had been his consuming passion since he'd begun his most recent assign-

16

ment for the Homeland Historical Society. 'I've read many a logbook page from the R-101 – the official, original pages, mind you. Essentially, they agree with what you've said. Except that while a North Atlantic crossing had an equal paucity of visual excitement, the airship flights on those routes also seemed to have had much worse weather to deal with than we've had on this flight.'

'It's been our good luck, nothing more. The South Atlantic – particularly here in the Drake passage – has some of the worst weather known to man. The Antarctic continent,' Whitaker added with a sweep of his hand toward the left quarter of the cockpit windshield, 'is the premier bad weather factory. We've been lucky, that's all.'

'That certainly is a quaint concept. Luck and I normally don't go hand in hand.' Tucker casually adjusted the set of his tweed jacket, then touched the large Windsor knot in his necktie to be certain that it was dead center. If all his years of being a professor of history at Cambridge had taught him anything, it was that careful planning and attention to detail usually far outweighed the factors of luck and chance.

'You should've been with us a month ago, the last time we flew this route,' Whitaker said. He brushed some lint off the captain's epaulets on his shoulders. 'All we did was get pounded, from the minute we left Africa until just a few hundred miles from Australia.'

'That was my first flight as the airship's second officer,' Galloway added as he glanced back at Tucker. Normally he would have said nothing – he certainly wouldn't have chanced a word if First Officer Madigan had been in the left seat instead of Whitaker. But Galloway liked the captain, so he attempted to assist him in whatever small ways he could, even in casual conversation. 'We wallowed around enough to make me green. This airship is a stable beast,' Galloway continued, patting the instrument panel in front of him, 'but nothing stays perfectly smooth when the sky turns into a washboard.'

'Back to my original point,' Tucker said. 'What is the cause of this mist – this convergence line – that we've been relegated to spend nearly forever in?'

17

'I was going to discuss that at dinner tonight.' Whitaker looked down at the clock on his instrument panel. Three more hours and it would be his turn, since it was Whitaker's policy to rotate the special duty of host of the evening meal among all four of the airship's operating crew, rather than keep it solely for himself as most of the line's captains did. 'I'll give you a sneak preview, but only as long as you promise that your face won't fall in the soup when you hear me repeating myself later.'

'Certainly not, captain. The soup is too frightfully hot to chance that sort of thing. I promise to remain alert.' Tucker took a long-stemmed pipe out of his coat pocket and tapped its bowl lightly against the bulkhead behind the cockpit seat. 'This convergence effect in the atmosphere is caused by temperature, isn't it?'

'Correct.' Lou Whitaker leaned back even further, in a posture of complete relaxation. He enjoyed carrying passengers on the airships he commanded. The company had added three passenger cabins on the main floor of the gondola eight months ago and so far none of the passengers that had flown on *Airship Nine* had been a problem; a few had even been quite interesting. 'Temperature is what causes the convergence zone. It's the meeting of the cold water from the Antarctic region and the warmer waters from the South Atlantic. Where the two meet, they often set up an area of fog.'

'Simply to deprive me of the view, I'm quite certain.'

'Probably.' Whitaker paused for a moment to scan the airship's flight panel. As he suspected, the gauges showed that everything on the airship was strictly routine. 'What time is your relief due?' Whitaker asked as he turned to Galloway.

'Any time now,' Galloway answered casually, even though it was already fifteen minutes past the hour – which meant that First Officer Madigan was already fifteen minutes late. That was typical. Galloway said nothing about the first officer's tardiness because he didn't want to add to the captain's problems and, besides, he knew that Ray Madigan would eventually take any problems with the captain out on him.

18

'Any time now,' Whitaker repeated, annoyed. He frowned as he remembered from the duty roster he had made up the evening before what time the first officer was due to take over the flight deck watch. 'I should've known.'

'Known what, skipper?'

'Nothing.' Even though he had promised himself not to think about it anymore, Whitaker was again aggravated by how damned near this crew was to being the finest he had ever flown with. Steve Galloway was currently the best second officer in the airship fleet – young, bright, responsive, eager to learn and technically competent. Friendly, too. Whitaker watched him in the copilot's seat: the way Galloway ran his fingers across the airship's flight controls, even though the ship was at the moment being steered by its autopilot, told Whitaker all he needed to know about the young man's feelings toward his job. 'Did Madigan give any reason why he might be late?'

'No sir. None that I recall.'

'If he's not here in a minute, I'll page him on the PA.'

'I don't mind sitting here. I like it.'

'That's not the point.' *That damned Madigan. He just keeps pushing.* With the notable exception of the airship's first officer, Whitaker was indeed very happy with his crew. David Weiss was as good a radio operator as anyone could ask for. His only fault was his extreme shyness, something Whitaker thought he might be able to help Weiss to overcome once they had gotten on a friendlier, more casual basis. Because socializing with the passengers – even though there were only four passengers on board for this flight – was so obviously painful for David Weiss, Whitaker had made an exception in the dinner hosting assignments.

'Now that I think of it, Madigan might've told me that he needed to help Nancy with something.' Galloway squirmed slightly in his flight chair.

'I see.' Whitaker could tell that Galloway had made up that excuse in an attempt to keep things peaceful among the crew. It was an admirable trait – and one that First Officer Madigan would unquestionably milk for all the mileage that he could. 'I'll wait a little longer before I go looking for him.'

'Good. I don't want to bother him if Nancy needs help. I don't mind staying on watch, really.'

'Your choice.' Whitaker thought about Nancy. She had worked out well enough as the airship's stewardess and cook, even though Whitaker had initially worried more about her than about the first officer. For the thousandth time since he had met both of them a few weeks before, Lou Whitaker wondered why Nancy Schneider was attracted to a man like Madigan.

'Excuse me, captain. But would you mind if I continue to stand here and look over your shoulder,' Doctor Tucker asked anxiously. He didn't thoroughly understand the relationship between the captain and the other members of his crew – like most of the Yanks he had known they all seemed to be terribly informal toward each other and toward the command structure – but Tucker had seen enough of the internal machinations on *Airship Nine* to realize that there was indeed some level of tension on the vessel. It now appeared as if the captain were going to discuss disciplinary matters. Good sense and discretion meant that it was either time for Tucker to make his own presence felt again, or to leave.

'We wouldn't mind at all. As I said when you first came aboard, you've got the run of the ship.' Whitaker gestured expansively toward the British historian. 'You're not in our way in the slightest.'

'If you're certain, then I'll stay. I'm beginning to make some sense of your instruments. By languishing here on the flight deck I invariably get more of a true feeling toward airships.' Tucker considered adding that by being in the cockpit he also acquired more of a feeling toward airship crews – that was certain to be one of the focuses in his historical study – but now was unquestionably not the time to add that point.

'Right.' Whitaker turned away and was quickly lost again in his own thoughts. Stewardess Nancy Schneider was an enigma to him, just like his ex-wife Marilyn had always been – just as she had been right up to the end last September when she told him that she was leaving. Marilyn's reaction to the death of their son had been an enigma, too – she refused to talk about it, although Whitaker could tell from her attitude that she held him completely responsible. It was unfair. Whitaker took a long and deep breath, then looked out ahead.

Even though it was only mid-afternoon, the combination of the southern latitudes plus the season of the year had already begun to work against them. It was nearly dark. Other than a grey glow on the murky horizon, the daylight had all but left them already. The bottom side of the airship was cast in deep shadows and, from where he sat, the front half of the giant helium-filled bag that stuck out 125 feet ahead loomed like a huge awning that effectively blocked what little daylight remained. The white coloring of the polyurethane envelope that comprised most of the mass of *Airship Nine* had lost its pleasant appearance and now appeared lifeless in the bland glow. Now there was nothing to see but the ocean below. The horizon was indistinct. They were flying through the inside of a milk bottle.

Lurkin' in the murk. Nothing to see but the flight panel. If it's not on the instruments, it's not happening. Those expressions from his past reminded Whitaker of the years he had flown jet aircraft, of the years he had thrown countless hours of his life away in an environment that was as intrinsically interesting as a grey-painted clothes closet. In the airships that he now flew – at least most of the time – he was in constant contact with the environment that he navigated across, in a continual and intimate relationship with the ground. That was why, even though he was not needed in the cockpit at the moment, he had come up anyway – he enjoyed the airship so much that it wasn't a job for him, it had, in fact, become most of his life.

Whitaker continued to scan the ocean beneath him. The features they flew over were usually no more than a few thousand feet beneath them, and it seldom went past at a speed of more than one hundred miles an hour. Whitaker thanked God that the modern airship companies had

21

convinced enough people that low-cost hauling of special-
ity freight – airships were faster than sea vessels, cheaper
than conventional airplanes – was a viable segment of the
marketplace. Now, with the addition of three passenger
cabins in the airships, they had the best of both worlds.

Whitaker looked at his panel clock again. It was now
twenty minutes past the hour. 'Five more minutes, then
I'll find him.' Madigan was probably in Nancy's cabin,
probably doing more to her than Whitaker cared to imagine. Normally, he didn't begrudge any man or woman
their right to do what they wanted with whomever they
wanted to, but there was just something about Ray Madigan . . . Whitaker looked outside again, to take his
thoughts – and his growing anger – off the first officer.

One of the few things Whitaker could still see clearly in
spite of the murkiness surrounding them were the two
dangling nose ropes as they swept back at an odd angle
through the airstream. Other than that slight display of
motion they provided – the ropes were permanent objects
on an airship, permanent mooring lines to be used by
ground personnel as they worked them in for landing – the
craft they flew in seemed suspended in the sky. Except for
the gauges on the flight panel in front of him, there was
no way to determine how much forward progress, if any,
Airship Nine was making on its long journey from South
Africa to Australia.

'Captain . . .'

Whitaker spun around in his flight chair, expecting
to see Ray Madigan behind him, expecting to hear the
beginnings of another lame excuse as to why the first
officer had chosen to do something other than his proper
assignment. Instead, Whitaker saw David Weiss, the
young man's face drawn pale, his left hand clamped in a
death grip on a sheaf of papers. The papers were visibly
trembling.

'God, man, you look ghastly. Are you all right?' Doctor
Tucker took a step sideways to get out of the way and
clear a path for the airship's radio officer to reach the
captain.

'What's happened?' Whitaker worked at keeping his

voice calm, but it still managed to crack. There was an immediate, incredible tension between them, caused by the expression on Weiss' face. 'Is that a teletype message?' Whitaker reached out toward where the radio operator's hand continued to grip the sheaf of papers. 'Is that . . . a message . . . for us?' Whitaker now had his hand on the messages. He could see the distinct red printlines that the airship's teletype machine always made along the paper's edge. But, incredibly, Weiss continued to stand rigidly in the narrow companionway that led to the cockpit seats, his eyes wide, the lines of his mouth taut, his lips slightly parted.

'Oh God . . . It couldn't . . . I can't believe . . . found them on the printer . . . I was at dinner . . . just come back . . . God . . .'

'Let go of them!' Whitaker had raised his voice enough to allow it to reverberate through the airship's flight deck. 'For God's sake, let me see them!' With great effort the captain finally managed to snatch the papers from Weiss' clenched fist.

'What on earth could have happened?' Tucker had not taken his eyes off the radio operator for a moment, yet the young man continued to remain totally dazed, totally overwhelmed by whatever he had seen. Tucker then attempted to twist his body around to look over the captain's shoulder to read the teletype message, but he quickly discovered that there was not enough room to position himself properly behind the captain's flight chair.

'God Almighty . . .'

'What is it?' Even though no one answered him, Doctor Tucker could see from the expression of horror and revulsion on the captain's face that the news was going to be bad. The news was going to be very, very bad indeed.

Two

CAPTAIN ANDREI Kollontai walked alone by the rail at the bow of the Soviet motorship *Primorye,* his eyes fixed on the tranquil sea ahead. The swells of dark water lapped over each other but barely caused any discernible churn. As far as Kollontai could tell by looking into the haziness that surrounded the ship, in no direction were there more than minor undulations in the carpet of water that they rode on. With the engines shut down and the *Primorye* dead in the water, there was not even any wake behind them. The eerie calmness made the truth of the teletype messages even more difficult to comprehend. Nuclear war and the potential end of the world were impossible to come to grips with when all around them was as quiet as Sunday afternoon in Gorky Park.

Kollontai stopped beside the anchor windlass and mooring winch on the forecastle. He ran his fingers up and down the massive chain wrapped around the takeup spool, then along the unit's gear housing. He turned and looked aft, down the *Primorye*'s starboard beam toward the fantail. Even in what faded afternoon sunlight still managed to penetrate through the thick haze, the *Primorye*'s white superstructure glistened superbly and appeared quite majestic above the bright red base of the ship's hull.

Kollontai watched for a moment as several members of his crew worked at securing a piece of outsized cargo in an area beneath the aft lifeboat davit. Beyond them, Kollontai could see the tip of one of the helicopter rotor blades. The line that secured that immobile blade to the pad – the ship carried two army helicopters on this special re-supply assignment – was taut enough to cause that blade to be bent markedly downward at its tip. 'Check the helicopter cables,' Kollontai shouted, although there was

24

no need to raise his voice very much since it carried quite well through the calm air. 'Be certain that the cables are not too tight,' he added, now that he had the attention of the men working with the outsized cargo thirty meters away.

'Yessir,' the ranking chief from the work group responded. He immediately sent two men aft to check on the helicopters.

Kollontai watched the seamen, glad that at least a few of his crew were occupied in some sort of meaningful duty to help take their minds from the incredible news.

'Captain, the cable tautness appears to be normal,' the chief of the work party announced when his men returned with their report.

'Very well.' Satisfied, Kollontai began to scan the remainder of his ship. The *Primorye* was a modern Soviet Merchant Marine transport, and it was a comfortable ship to serve on. Its twin diesel engines and enormous oil bunkers enabled the ship to range far from home without refueling. Its maximum speed was fourteen knots. With an overall length of eighty-seven meters, the ship easily supported the seventy-five crew and sixty-three passengers that were aboard her on this recovery voyage to the Soviet Antarctic stations. In fact, Captain Kollontai had hauled nearly twice that many on some of the past voyages during the sixteen months that he had been the *Primorye*'s master. After allowing himself a few more moments of harmless, insignificant thoughts, Captain Kollontai reluctantly turned and looked toward the ship's bridge.

He could see that the three of them were still up there where he had left them. Each of them was in a different section of the wide ship's bridge – the area that was, in fact, the heart and soul of the *Primorye*. Doctor Ney still stood in the center of the window-filled room, near to the steering controls and the radar screen. Ney seemed to be reading from a piece of paper that he held in his hand. On the starboard quarter of the bridge, now slightly deeper into the shadows, stood Major Zinoviev. The major appeared to be answering Ney, or vice-versa. After a moment Kollontai's eyes moved slowly across the width of the bridge to the port side. Aleksandra Bukharin had moved over to that area and now stood alone, her face averted from the other two, as she leaned against the navigation table. Her long hair formed an interesting silhouette against the metallic wall panels behind her and Kollontai watched that silhouette for quite some time. But he finally managed to bring himself around to do what he knew he had to do next. Captain Kollontai climbed the stairs that led to the ship's bridge and walked inside using the starboard hatchway.

'It is already past one hour,' Doctor Boris Ney announced in a low but firm voice as he rocked back and forth on his heels, his hands outstretched in front of him and laid against the ledge that surrounded the steering controls.

'I can assure you that I know how to tell time.' Kollontai glanced over perfunctorily at the man he spoke to, as if an apparent lack of interest from him might somehow make him disappear. Kollontai was already sorry that he had come back to the bridge, although he obviously had no choice. 'I have indeed learned something over the years, in spite of what you may have heard from Moscow.'

Ney waited several moments to respond, until the silence between them had reached an unbearable level. 'That's not what I had heard in Moscow,' he answered carefully, aware that his reply could be a turning point for the other two. Ney glanced first toward the army major on his right, then at the lady physician who continued to lean against the navigation table to his far left. Both of them were obviously waiting to hear what his response to the captain would be. 'I had heard that you were a careful and thoughtful man who had earned the respect of his crews. A true commander of your vessel, in every sense of the word.'

Captain Kollontai turned slowly. 'Is that so?' he asked without enthusiasm. Kollontai allowed his eyes to lock with Ney's. He could tell nothing from looking at the scientist, since the man's eyes remained, as always, totally expressionless. 'It's difficult to believe that they think fondly of a man who has chosen the wrong career path,'

Kollontai said, more to keep the conversation going than to get an answer. Whenever they stopped arguing with each other, the nightmare that he still had to deal with would surface again and become more than he knew how to handle.

'Captain, you do yourself an injustice.'

'I doubt it.' Kollontai continued to watch Ney closely, but the man's well-sculptured beard more than covered any hint of an honest emotion that might have come elsewhere from the lines of his face. To the uninformed, Doctor Ney would have seemed like a man without any degree of passion, a disinterested observer – except that Captain Kollontai knew better.

'The ship has remained dead in the water for slightly more than the one hour you had commanded us to wait. It was unquestionably prudent to have us sit quietly while we waited to see which way these horrid messages would go,' Ney said as he waved his hand toward the misty, becalmed waters of the Antarctic sea that the Soviet merchant ship sat in. 'But it's now time for something else.'

'I agree with Doctor Ney.' Major Ilya Zinoviev stepped forward cautiously. It was the first time he had dared to open his mouth and speak with the others on the ship's bridge after his open and hostile confrontation with Captain Kollontai less than one hour before. But now he felt he could wait no longer. 'It's time for a decision.'

'And which way are you leaning, Major – or is it stupid of me to even ask?' Captain Kollontai had again found himself raising his voice without wanting to – it was, he knew, an automatic response whenever he was forced to deal with the sort of military imbecile that Major Zinoviev so aptly represented. It was men like Zinoviev who had caused Kollontai to leave the Soviet Navy years before and join the Merchant Marine instead.

'I've changed my mind about wanting to launch an immediate attack against the American base.' Zinoviev had begun to shuffle his feet. The sound of his heavy boots against the tile floor was a welcome relief to the nerve-shattering silence on the bridge.

'Yours was an idiotic outburst, especially with so many

of the crew and support staff around.' Kollontai glared at the major.

'Possibly.' Major Zinoviev dabbed at the growing line of perspiration that encircled his clean-shaven head, then glanced toward Doctor Ney before he looked back at Kollontai.

'The people at home have paid the ultimate price for our ultimate stupidity,' Kollontai said. 'Most of the populations asleep in their beds at one moment, then turned into dust and vapor the next. Think of our families . . .' Kollontai turned from Zinoviev and faced toward the sea. Yekatrina and Lidiya were now certain to be dead, since his house was so close to the naval base at Severomorsk. *I should have known better, I should have expected this, I should have moved them to the country years ago.* Kollontai closed his eyes and attempted to blot out the image of what that house on Ryjzy Prospect must look like now that countless nuclear weapons had exploded overhead. 'The people at home have suffered incredibly,' Kollontai repeated, although he now spoke only to himself. Yet what seemed unbelievable to him was how he was taking the reality of it, how he now felt. Even though his beloved wife and daughter were certain to be gone forever, Kollontai could not focus his mind on that thought. As if it were drawn by a magnet, he could not keep his memory from locking onto the single and haunting image of the house on Ryjzy Prospect. It was a house that no longer existed, on a street and in a city which also no longer existed.

'You were correct,' Doctor Ney said after a suitable silence. 'The best course of action was for us to wait for more information.'

'And what sort of information do we have now?' Aleksandra Bukharin had spoken softly from where she stood by the navigation table. Aleksandra kept her eyes fixed toward the *Primorye*'s red-painted bow and did not bother to look at the three men who stood a few feet to her right. She allowed her left hand to play absently with the long strands of her black hair as it flowed across her shoulder and along the top of her dress.

'But we now have dozens of additional messages,' Major

28

Zinoviev protested. He reached for a stack of papers beside him, which had continued to grow in size every few minutes as the radio operator brought more of the teletype printouts to the bridge. 'We now have dozens of confirmations.'

'And each one is more a nightmare than the one before it,' Aleksandra said as she stepped forward and grabbed the top few messages from Zinoviev. 'Moscow – Leningrad – Kiev – Minsk – Odessa – Vladivostok – Irkutsk – all are destroyed . . . everyone above ground level has been burned beyond recognition . . . We are dying . . . Help us . . . Help me . . .' Aleksandra's voice had faded to nothing, but she continued to flip through the teletype messages, the expression on her face contorted by sympathy for those who had sent the messages she held in her trembling hands.

'Let us be rational. All we know for certain is that a nuclear war has begun.' Doctor Ney spoke dispassionately, as if he were commenting on some minor annoyance rather than the annihilation of his homeland. 'Our major cities have been destroyed. Communications are disrupted. We are now out of voice radio contact with all stations, probably because of the atmospheric disturbances caused by the thermo-nuclear explosions. Only the satellite teletype circuits seem to be working – and then only sporadically.'

Captain Kollontai shook his head slowly. 'And where does that leave us? Even after waiting the hour that I had insisted on, I can tell you with certainty that I still don't know what we should do next.'

'We've got to do something. For the sake of the crew.'

'In God's name, I warn you again not to lecture me about the welfare of my crew!' Kollontai had allowed himself to explode at the major again, but this time he knew exactly why. 'You didn't give a kopeck's damn about the crew when you drummed them up with that senseless shouting about the need to attack the American Palmer station!' Kollontai shot a quick glance out the starboard window, toward where one group of seamen were clustered below on the main deck. Even from this distance he could see the fear, the disbelief, the terror on their faces.

He would need to deal with them shortly, or all hell would break loose on board.

'That's not true, I only meant . . .'

'In a pig's eye! Your solution is to come out fighting, to throw another one hundred and thirty-eight people – all of them civilians I should remind you, except for those in your helicopter unit – into a senseless attack that can do nothing but add our bodies to the billions of others!'

'There are no civilians any more, we're at war!'

'We're *all* civilians, damn you!' Kollontai took two giant strides across the room toward Zinoviev. He grabbed the remaining teletype messages from the major's hands. 'Look at these – it's already over! There is nothing left but civilians – dying by the millions while you speak about the need to attack a group of foreign scientists camped on a mound of frozen white at the bottom of the world!'

'Stop this at once!' Doctor Ney made a partial move to put himself between the *Primorye*'s captain and the army major, but was relieved to see that neither of the men was ready to make a physical confrontation out of their argument. 'This is idiotic.' Ney paused, then turned to the captain. 'We've got to stop this bickering. We've got to be more deliberate.'

'In what way?' Aleksandra had also jumped into the conversation in order to keep it headed in a better direction.

'In a way that makes our group of four,' Ney said, 'into what it must become. Into an effective *nachalstvo*.' Ney eyed the three others cautiously. 'If we are to be the governing council – which was, as you recall, the captain's intention in summoning us to the bridge – we need to be certain that we speak with one voice.'

'The voice of *poryadok*,' Zinoviev said. He had partially mumbled the final word, but it had still come across unmistakably.

'Yes, law and order. That must be our first concern.' Ney nodded enthusiastically.

'I intend to keep command of my ship. I intend to keep things going as usual.' But Kollontai knew that he had just made a totally absurd statement when considered against

30

the fact that the world itself had changed so drastically during the last hour. Everything aboard the ship was also certain to change, once the initial shock of the news had worn off. That was why Kollontai had called up the leaders of each of the groups represented on the ship, rather than simply issuing whatever orders he felt were appropriate. If there was any hope of control, any hope of preventing disarray or total despair, it would come from a governing body that represented all of the 138 who were on the ship. Ney was certainly right, this *nachalstvo* could speak with only one voice – one loud and clear voice – if the situation on the *Primorye* were to remain under control. 'I intend to remain in firm command until our situation alters enough to make other arrangements in our best interest. Since we are still at sea and still on board the *Primorye*, there's no question about my being in command. Yet I agree that arguments among ourselves are senseless.'

'They are.' Ney didn't care for the idea of Kollontai as the final and absolute authority, but he knew it was far too early to attempt to change that arrangement – the ship's crew would resist any lessening of their captin's importance, and, at this point, so would most of the others. Ney would work on that problem later. 'So then let us remain rational. Enough time has gone by and we've thought about the problem long enough. Let's have each of us list whatever options we've come up with. We should also voice our opinions as to what course of action we think might be best.'

'Good.' Aleksandra smiled weakly, the first time she had managed even that much of a positive expression in the last sixty minutes. 'After that, the captain can make his decision based on what each of us thinks is best for our people.' Although she had hardly done more than speak to the man since the voyage had begun nearly two months before, Aleksandra felt comfortable with Captain Kollontai. He was intelligent, fair, and methodical in his approach to problems. He was also very well respected.

'I apologize for my errors,' Zinoviev said. He was not one to trifle with the chain of command and – even though Kollontai was technically not his direct superior since the

31

ship was non-military – the captain's right to keep control of his vessel was inviolate. 'I don't know what's gotten into me. The situation, I guess.'

'I understand completely. All of us are suffering from shock. I certainly am.' Kollontai nodded sympathetically, partially as a show of solidarity and partially from a sincere appreciation of Zinoviev's openness. For the first time since he had met the major, Kollontai thought that perhaps he had been unfair to him. The man might prove to be an asset after all. His two helicopters, strapped to the stern of the *Primorye*, were invaluable – and Zinoviev did seem to get along very well with his group of nine men.

'It's not really part of my duty to volunteer opinions, not unless you ask for them.' Zinoviev paused awkwardly. He suddenly felt like a fool for all the trouble he had caused. He glanced over at the other two on the bridge. Aleksandra was clearly pleased, but he could tell nothing from Doctor Ney's neutral expression. Zinoviev looked back at Kollontai. 'I'm here only to aid your mission with my helicopter unit. What I mean is that, as far as I'm concerned, nothing has changed. There's certainly no question that this is your ship.' Zinoviev leaned forward and tapped his finger against the brass nameplate with the word *Primorye* stenciled on it.

'Your acceptance of my command is gratifying,' Kollontai said. 'I appreciate it, honestly I do. But there's still one thing you said that's wrong.'

'What?' Zinoviev blinked, he had no idea what Kollontai was leading up to.

'That your people are here to aid my mission. I think 'it's best to remember that this is not a mission at all – it's purely an assignment. A civilian assignment.'

'I only meant that . . .'

'My friend, listen to me,' Kollontai said as he laid his outstretched arm on Zinoviev's shoulder in a gesture of friendship. *I've misjudged him. He's going to be a good man to have on board.* 'My assignment to pick up the Soviet Antarctic expedition from the Mirnyy station was purely a scientific pursuit. We were under the jurisdiction of the Merchant Marine division. Your two helicopters and your people were on loan to us from the army, but that doesn't change the nature of what we were doing. Scientific. Civilian. An assignment, not a mission. Do you follow me?' Kollontai waited for an answer.

'Yes, I do.' Zinoviev moved forward and embraced the captain in a display of acceptance and friendship. 'I'm with you. Comrade, my people are with you.'

'Thank you.'

'That's very nice,' Ney said petulantly, 'but now that it's settled, let's get on with our list of options.' Ney moved to his right, retrieved what remained of the stack of teletype messages and then took out a pad and pencil.

'How do you suggest we do this?' Aleksandra asked.

'I'll take notes as each of us speak,' Ney volunteered. 'Captain, why don't you go first and let us know how you see the situation.'

'Okay.' Kollontai began to speak slowly. 'We are out of contact with everyone of authority. We have no standing orders of battle in the Merchant Marine, so even technically speaking we shouldn't consider the *Primorye* at war with anyone.'

'But certainly in an all-out confrontation . . .'

'Let me finish!' Kollontai snapped at Zinoviev, forgetting that they had just come to terms. 'Defending ourselves is one thing, being an outright aggressor is quite another!'

Boris Ney leaned back and began to scribble odd words and phrases as Kollontai spoke. But Ney's thoughts were somewhere else entirely. *Vozhd*. Only Lenin and Stalin had managed to capture that title – great leader – from the people. The two dictators had done it with insight, courage, determination and – most of all – good timing. When the opportunities were ripe, each of them had moved without hesitation and, whenever necessary, with ruthlessness. *Vozhd*. Ney smiled to himself. He always felt that he had the potential to be a great leader, to be another Lenin or Stalin. Ney knew that he had the necessary determination to do the job, just as he also knew that he had enough skill. It now appeared as if he might also have the opportunity. *Vozhd*. If he played his hand correctly during the next few weeks, Doctor Boris Ney

33

felt that he might very well stand a chance to become the next ruler – another great leader – of whatever remained of the Soviet Union. Perhaps even of the world.

'Okay, what is it?'

'I'll do the talking. Sit down.' After he closed the door of his stateroom on *Airship Nine*, Captain Lou Whitaker pointed to the empty chair in front of his desk.

'I'll stand. I imagine that this isn't going to take very long.'

'I don't care what you imagine. Sit down.' Whitaker needed every shred of self-control he could muster to prevent himself from losing his temper. It was obvious that the belligerent son-of-a-bitch of a copilot who stood in front of him was going to keep pushing until he made that very thing happen. 'We've got a few things to straighten out. Here and now.'

'Suits me just fine,' Ray Madigan said. 'I suppose that if you're going to make another of your speeches, maybe I should sit down after all.' Madigan grabbed the chair, swung his leg over it and sat down. 'I'm all ears.'

'That's where you're wrong. You're not all ears, you're all mouth. I'm not going to put up with it any more.' Whitaker could feel his blood pressure rise even higher than it had after he had read the first of the teletype messages. Even higher than it had during the briefing he had just given the passengers and crew, with Madigan making asinine comments in the background all the while. 'The two of us don't get along, that's obvious.'

'More than obvious.'

'But now,' Whitaker said as he waved the stack of teletype messages in his hand, 'our personal dislikes are a luxury we can no longer afford.'

'That's very typical of you. Very convenient.' Madigan rose from his chair. 'That's just what I imagined you would say.'

'I don't understand.'

'I didn't expect you to.'

'For Christ's sake, stop this!' Whitaker had raised his

voice louder than he'd intended to; he'd probably been heard from one end of the airship to the other. 'We've got to come to some understanding between us. Tell me what you're talking about so maybe we can get to the bottom of it.'

'My pleasure.' Madigan flexed his arm muscles while he glared at Whitaker. The idea of hauling off and knocking that balding bastard on his soft ass crossed Madigan's mind, but all that stopped him was the idea that Whitaker had been right on at least one point – that the teletype messages about world-wide nuclear war had decreased everyone's options to zero. 'Like you said, there's no doubt about it. You drive me nuts.'

'Why? What have I ever done to you?' Whitaker fidgeted. 'All I've ever asked is that you do your job.'

'Wrong. What you ask is that everyone be exactly like you, that everyone have exactly the same set of values and priorities as you do. Nobody denies that you can drive a good ship, but somewhere along the line you got it in your head that your way is the only way. The pure religion, the gospel according to Saint Whitaker. That's where that holier-than-thou attitude comes from. But I've got a news flash for you, buddy – just because someone drinks a different brand of liquor doesn't mean they can't do the same job as a captain that you can.'

'That's ridiculous.'

'Rigid. That's what you are. Completely inflexible. When people fit in with your expectations, your mold, they can do no wrong. You can afford to give those people lots of leeway because you know damn well that they're not going to take it. That's where you build up that wonderful-guy reputation that you cultivate.'

'I'm not going to listen to this line of garbage from you.' But Whitaker made no move to leave or to restrain Madigan. He stood as if he were transfixed by the copilot's words.

'But what a lot of people don't know is how really small a man you can be, how you might use anything in your bag of tricks to stop someone once you get the urge.'

'I've never done anything of the sort.'

'You did it to me.'

'That's your real point, isn't it? I didn't feel that you were ready to be a captain, at least not yet. I made a report expressing those feelings. Since then, you've been taking shots at me.'

Madigan closed in on the captain, until he was no more than an arm's length away. 'You and I both know that, according to Saint Whitaker, I'm *never* going to be a captain. And since I'm on a roll, I'm going to tell you why. It's because I don't follow in your footsteps, it's because I don't *mirror* what you are. The trouble with me being a captain is that if I were, then every time you'd see me running a ship my way that would somehow take away from your own sense of worth.'

'Incredible.' Whitaker nervously pushed some of his thinning hair back and forth across his forehead. 'But I will give you credit for being right on one point – that you're nuts.'

'Probably. That's why I'm carrying on like this. This is the wrong time and this is the wrong place, and maybe I'm talking right now because my insides are turned upside down from what we've gotten on the teletype. All I know for sure is that this is one time you're not going to lord your authority over me – or anyone else on this ship.'

'You're not making sense.'

'Bullshit. I'm making more sense than you'll ever be able to admit.'

'I'm still the captain of this airship.' But even as Whitaker spoke he stepped back, sensing a physical threat from his copilot.

'Maybe – although I'd like to point out to you that your authority came from a chief pilot and a company that no longer exist. From the evidence I've seen, they were collectively blown sky-high a few hours ago. That means that as far as I'm concerned, your role as *my* leader has already begun to live on borrowed time.'

'You've got no right to challenge my authority.'

'That attitude of yours is exactly what gives me every right to do that – at the very least.' The words had come out softer than Madigan had intended, as if he had said

36

them more out of a sense of regret than of vengeance. 'I'm smart enough not to trust you, Whitaker,' Madigan added, his words even softer now than they had been a moment before. 'Believe me when I tell you that you'd better get honest with us and with yourself. If you don't, I'm going to take you down.'

'Get out of here.'

'Sure thing.' The copilot cleared his throat, then smiled contemptuously. 'That's the smart way to handle me, just like you've handled everyone you wouldn't allow into your private club, who wasn't up to your standards. Just like you handled that boy of yours.'

'Get the hell out of here!'

'Right.' Ray Madigan stared hard at Whitaker a few more seconds before he strode ahead, brushed past him and let himself out of the captain's stateroom. He closed the door with a slam that reverberated up and down the empty corridor of *Airship Nine*.

That boy of yours. Whitaker stood where he was in the center of his room as he looked out the window at the nothingness below. He could no longer see the ocean's surface in what little light remained. The sun — which this time of year never rose very high in Antarctic sky — had already slid below the horizon line. *Airship Nine* would be in total darkness for the next sixteen hours.

That boy of yours. Allan. Yet before any memories of his seventeen-year-old son – dead now for nearly a year, forgotten during most hours of the day but still painfully a part of him late at night and during his dreams – could grab hold of him, Whitaker erected a familiar mental fortress. As usual, his work would be his salvation. *Check the teletype circuits. Check on our position relative to the coastline. Conduct a survey of our supplies.* Given a choice, Captain Lou Whitaker would rather think about the end of the world than the end of his son.

Three

THE WEATHER was good as the four men began their journey across the ice in a northwesterly direction toward the Russian station. Eduardo Rios was happy to see the deep blue of the cloudless sky and fervently prayed that it would remain clear. Even though the Soviet Bellingshausen camp was no more than ten kilometers away at the opposite corner of King George Island, any overland journey in the Antarctic was a risk. It could be clear and mild at the Chilean station while on the other side of the island a howling blizzard could be blowing. Still, Rios knew he had no choice – radio contact with Santiago, and everyone else for that matter, had been abruptly terminated after the outbreak of war.

'Do you think it's the Argentines?' Gabriel Ungarte had leaned forward and shouted his words into Rios' ear in order to make himself heard over the roar of the snowmobile's engine as it raced at nearly top speed. Ungarte sat rigidly behind Rios, clutching him and jolting violently as the spinning threads of the snowmobile propelled them forward.

'Of course it was the Argentines. Who else?'

'But where would they get atomic weapons?' Ungarte had been as shocked as the other three over the news of nuclear war between the United States and the Soviet Union. Yet it seemed remote and distant until the last few desperate messages that told of the bombs being dropped on Chile. 'Do you really think the Russians had given Argentina those bombs?'

'I don't think the British did.' As much as he wanted to glance back at his friend, Rios kept his eyes locked straight ahead in order to keep the snowmobile on a safe route between the crevices in the ice. 'The Russians. There's no doubt about it. Those are the people we have to thank.'

'They should have known better. It would be just like the Argentines to drop bombs wherever and whenever they thought they could get away with it.'

'I can see those Argentine pigs in Buenos Aires, huddled over a strategy map of South America within minutes of getting the word about what was happening in the north.' Rios had begun to shout even louder than was necessary in order to be heard, his neck and face turning a deep red from the exertion and emotion. 'The Argentine generals saw an opportunity to take control of South America. Dropping nuclear weapons on Santiago, Valparaiso, Concepcion, Punta Arenas and Christ knows where else would be the way they would eliminate us from contention. Ten million dead would mean nothing to them – just another form of inflation, to be dealt with sometime in the future by a different regime!'

'Pigs.'

'Worse than pigs.'

'Yes.'

The two men lapsed into silence. Rios glanced over his shoulder at the other snowmobile which followed closely behind in their tracks, the two men on it also held on tightly as they careened over the rugged, jagged surface of ice and snow. 'Maybe I should've listened to Fernandez. Maybe he and Estrido should've stayed behind.'

'No,' Ungarte shouted back. 'You were right, we should stay together. The Russian station is bigger and their radio more powerful. It's the only place to get the news.'

'Yes.' Rios looked back again, this time past the other snowmobile and beyond. The path of churned snow looked like a white rope strung out behind them, a visual lifeline that connected the two snowmobiles back to their base station. *Teniente Rodolfo Marsh.* Just the name of the station caused Rios to ache inside, and it took all his willpower to prevent him from turning the snowmobiles around and heading for home. *Teniente Rodolfo Marsh.* Rios had grown very fond of the Chilean camp since he had taken over as commander nearly a year and a half before. He had looked forward to this winter-over because

39

with the cutback in funds from Santiago he would be keeping things functional with a bare crew of only four. It was the sort of challenge Rios enjoyed – the management of mundane but necessary details that most of the scientists he dealt with couldn't be bothered about. But Rios knew that there would be no scientific research in the future if someone like him didn't keep the statio fit during the off-season. *But there is no future. The Russians have given the Argentines the bomb. Chile has been destroyed.*

'What will happen next?' Ungarte shouted, as if he had read his commander's thoughts. 'What will happen to us? What will hapen to the station?'

'I don't know.'

'I pray that the Russians have some news.'

'They will.' *They'll know what happens next because they planned this. They worked hand-in-hand with those pigs in Buenos Aires.* Rios looked ahead at the outcropping of brown, angular rock that protruded up through the snow. Like an intentional obstacle mounted between themselves and the Russians at the Bellingshausen station on the other side of King George Island, the range of scarred hills lay at a right angle to their route. Rios steered the snowmobile slightly to the left to take advantage of a small clearway he knew of. Unfortunately, he did not see the new crevice that had developed in the face of the ice sheet, its opened angles obscured by a thin snowdrift.

The snowmobile, still traveling far too fast for the conditions, passed over the opening edge of the ice. The vehicle's front ski began to dip downward to follow the contour of the snow beneath it, but the snowdrift immediately gave way. The crevice, which measured nearly three meters across, was too wide for the snowmobile's momentum. With its treads still spinning at high speed, the vehicle cantered downward and then dipped to a hellish angle as it rammed itself into the far edge of the crevice.

'Jump!' Rios had barely time enough to shout that one word before his snowmobile – which hung precariously with its front ski buried into the face of the far edge of the crevice – began to pitch first backward and then sideways as its engine continued senselessly to rotate the treads at high speed. Rios could feel Ungarte's hands slip from around his waist as he pushed himself forward to get away from the teetering snowmobile.

'Help! Grab me!'

Rios lunged forward enough to get a hand-hold on the edge of the far crevice. As soon as he had hoisted himself upward, he looked back. He was horrified at what he saw.

The second snowmobile with Fernandez and Estrido had evidently been following too closely behind Rios and had also been at too high a speed. At the first sign of trouble Fernandez had attempted to swerve, but he had come too close to the unseen crevice in the ice. Fernandez' snowmobile had likewise fallen over the edge, but unlike Rios' vehicle, it had not dug into the other side. While Rios watched in horror and listened to the screams of the two men, their vehicle disappeared into the gaping crevice. For what seemed like an interminable time, Rios heard them screaming – they were both close friends and they knew they were plunging to their deaths in a dark crevice that was hundreds of feet deep.

'Help me! Hurry!'

It had been only a few seconds, but even in that time the first snowmobile had managed to slip to an even more ungodly angle where it hung in the crevice. Ungarte had managed to hang on, barely, by wrapping his left hand around the metal rail behind the driver's seat as his body dangled obscenely over the open abyss. 'I'm coming!' Rios shouted at the top of his lungs to get above the noise of the engine which still continued to run at top speed. Rios edged forward as quickly as he could, his hand outstretched toward his friend. 'Try not to sway!'

'Hurry! My leg!' Ungarte howled. 'I can't hold on!'

It was then that Rios noticed the spurts of blood that were splattered across the face of the crevice near the tilting snowmobile. It took him a moment to realize that the blood had come from Ungarte's right leg. Like a chainsaw, the rotating tread on that side of the snowmobile had pressed against his friend's flesh and quickly cut it to the bone. Even from several meters away, Rios could see the unmistakable splinters of white that were laced through the bloody mass of ripped muscles and tissue. The sight of it caused the bile to begin to rise up from Rios' stomach. 'Here! Grab my hand!'

Ungarte's right hand touched the tips of his friend's fingers, but the shift of weight as he swayed himself closer had tipped the scales of the snowmobile's balance too far out of Ungarte's favor. The vehicle tilted further left, which then allowed the jammed front ski to extract itself from the opposite crevice wall. Like an acrobat doing the beginnings of a well planned tumble from a circus high-wire, the snowmobile broke loose and plunged down.

'Jump!'

It was too late. Ungarte's eyes, paralyzed with pain and fear, locked onto his friend's face for one moment before the force of gravity took over and pulled him down and away with the snowmobile. Ungarte began to tumble over and over as he fell into the open crevice, the splatterings of blood from his gouged leg making irregular markings along the sides of the sheer ice walls as far down as Rios could see. It seemed like several more seconds before his friend's continuous screams finally ended and were abruptly replaced by a thud from somewhere at the bottom of this break in the ice.

Rios clawed his way backward from the edge of the crevice and then dropped, exhausted, into the snow. 'Oh, my God . . . Jesus Christ, save them . . .' His words, to no one other than God – the only offering he could give to his friends – were barely audible as he lay exhausted in this treacherous polar wasteland.

For some ten minutes nightmarish visions of the last hour floated through Rios' mind – the first words about the world war, the half-intelligible messages from Chile that told of the bombs being dropped by Argentina, the deaths of his three friends. Finally Rios managed to force his body to sit upright. He staggered to his feet and, without looking back at the crevice, he began to walk toward the Bellingshausen station on the far side of the jagged hills ahead. *Argentines and Russians*, Rios began, the words becoming a silent marching song that helped him to keep his legs moving methodically through the snow, up onto the ice and across the hills that would lead him to his destination. *Argentines and Russians. They did this to us. They both caused it all, they caused what happened in Chile. Everything has ended because of the Argentines. Everything has ended because of the Russians.*

The window was fogged up, as it always seemed to be whenever there was something outside he wanted to see. Once again Leonid Sergeyevich began to wonder how any society could manage to build a rocket to the moon but couldn't manage a thermo window that kept its airtight seal for more than a few weeks. He would have allowed himself to go further with this familiar line of complaint, if it hadn't been for the news. There was no need to worry about Soviet society any longer, from what they had determined so far from the scraps of messages that had gotten through to the Bellingshausen station, since most of the Mother Country had been obliterated by the Americans. 'Where the hell is Gazunov?' Sergeyevich asked as he wheeled around and face the one man who remained in the overheated room with him.

'Who knows?' Maxim Fedorchuk shrugged. 'Perhaps they couldn't find the extra wire you sent them for. Perhaps they found a bottle of vodka instead.'

'It's incredible that with five men out there,' Sergeyevich said, 'we still can't seem to get a damned thing done.'

'Not so incredible, when you think about it.' Fedorchuk had allowed his eyes to drift to the top of the table he sat at. The table was littered with maps of the Soviet Union that the men in the station had hastily opened and begun to mark an hour earlier. The circles drawn around each of those cities that had been reported as totally destroyed now covered the charts so completely that they had stopped marking long before the last radio signals had come in.

'Then it's best that we don't think about it.' Sergeyevich swore softly to himself, then turned back to Fedorchuk. 'We all agreed it would be worth the effort to try to increase the power of our radio receiver.'

'Sure. Then we can find out which of the smaller towns

are gone also.' Fedorchuk rose to his feet slowly, then turned away and faced the window. He took the arm of his dirty woolen shirt to the fogged glass to wipe it clean. 'The wind is picking up,' he said as he looked out at the white caps streaking across the endless expanse of cold sea that the Soviet Bellingshausen base was build against. 'Lowering clouds. We're in for a real blow.'

'So?'

'So that means it makes no difference when Gazunov comes back with the wire.'

'Why?' Even as he asked, Sergeyevich knew that he didn't want to hear the answer.

'Because no one can climb the radio tower in this much wind. Besides,' Fedorchuk added as he turned to face the man who was his official, designated superior, 'I don't think any of us really care. Not at this point.'

'Don't be ridiculous.'

'You stop being ridiculous.' Fedorchuk pointed across the room toward a bank of scientific instruments mounted in a large grey-painted metal cabinet. 'We all know what's going to happen to the atmosphere.'

'None of that is more than theory. Pure scientific speculation,' Sergeyevich answered as he shifted his weight nervously from one foot to the other. He glanced out the window that Fedorchuk had cleared to look out at the sea, but the window had already begun to fog again.

'Is that what you really think? Nothing but scientific speculation?' Fedorchuk ran his hand roughly against his newly grown beard. It was a subconscious reminder that even in appearance the six scientists who were to winter-over at the station were different than the man in charge, the man selected by Moscow. All six of the scientists had, in fact, begun to grow what they intended to become long and scraggly beards – a small display of defiance after Sergeyevich had mentioned his preference for having them clean-shaven. 'You forget that I'm one of the originators of that particular school of scientific speculation, as you've called it. I've spent most of my forty-seven years on this earth in an attempt to understand how the atmosphere gathers up and holds pollution.'

'Nuclear debris is different.'

'Yes, it's different. It's worse.' Fedorchuk shook his head sadly. 'From the data I've seen so far on the number of nuclear weapons dropped, I'd say that most of the northern hemisphere – and even a portion of the southern continents – is going to be uninhabitable for a long, long time.'

'Stop with your damn theories of doom – they're based on mere fragments of data.'

'In fact, now that I've had a few moments to study it,' Fedorchuk continued as if the man in front of him had said nothing, 'I'm beginning to believe that the southern hemisphere is going to make out just as badly as the north. South America, Africa and Australia have definitely taken massive hits. We've gotten that much information for certain.'

'A few intercepted radio messages – all of them spoken in foreign languages through a background of heavy static – are hardly the basis for writing off half of the world.'

'Then get me more information. Get me specific samplings of the atmosphere at various locations.'

'That's what the hell I'm trying to get the extra radio wire for!' Sergeyevich shot a quick glance across the room toward the radio. It continued to remain silent, in spite of the automatic electronic scanning that they had mounted on all the normal frequencies. He turned back to Fedorchuk. 'Don't you see that I'm frightened too? In spite of what you'd like to believe, I'm not an idiot. I know enough about the projects you were working on to see the possibilities. But none of that is *proof*. That's why I wanted extra wire and booster coils.'

'It won't work.'

'We've got to try!' Sergeyevich pounded his fist on the table and the jarring caused one of the curled-up charts to roll off the far end. He ignored it and turned back to Fedorchuk. 'What we need is information, not damned theories! How can we possibly keep our sanity unless we know for certain how much of the world is left?'

'If we go with the assumption that not much is left, we can't be too very wrong.'

45

'No. I refuse to believe that, not until I get definite information to back it up.' Sergeyevich sat himself down heavily in a wooden chair at the table in the center of the room. 'I'm going to give those five imbeciles no more than ten minutes to finish an assignment this simple. If they're not back by then, you and I are going out there to find them.'

As Eduardo Rios walked the distance between the scene of the snowmobile accident at the ice crevice and the Soviet Bellingshausen station, he had stumbled and fallen more than a dozen times. On three of those occasions he had bruised or cut himself badly against the angular outcroppings of rock and ice. On one additional occasion he had tumbled head over heels down a steep incline and painfully twisted his left ankle before he managed to stop near the bottom and begin the climb upward again. But Rios' physical condition and his state of near-total exhaustion – bad as they were – were comparatively only a small portion of the damage done to him. It was his mental condition that had suffered the most. With nothing but unthinkable memories behind him and the bleakness of unending ice and snow ahead, Rios quickly lost what little rational control remained to him during that tortuous march to the Bellingshausen station.

The Russians and Argentines. They worked together. They have destroyed Chile. As his anger built and his ability to control that anger slid further away with every stumbling step he took forward, Rios could hold onto only one agonized, frenzied thought: that he must reach the Russian station. It was there that he could do what justice demanded, what the spirits of his dead friends, family and nation would insist on. Rios knew that he owed them that much. As the wind began to pick up, Rios heard the voices of his murdered brother and father being carried with it. He knew that they must have all died in their home in Santiago not more than one hour before. They now spoke directly to him, their voices unmistakable in the wind. *Justice. You must avenge us, my son. For myself. For your brother. For all of Chile. For the world.*

Rios hunched forward and forced himself to press on against the onslaught of the chilled wind and driven snow that pelted him from ahead. A man less obsessed would have temporarily given up and taken shelter against the leeward side of any of the numerous ledges of rock, thus giving his mind a chance to mend itself. But that thought of self-preservation never entered Rios' anguished consciousness. He continued, undaunted by the impossible conditions. Rios was being driven by the irrational forces inside him, driven so impulsively that the physical obstacles of mere wind and snow couldn't stop him. Rios could not stop himself now even if he had wanted to – which he did not. *Justice. They have slaughtered innocent people and I will avenge them. I promise that with every gram of life that remains in me.*

Maxim Fedorchuk turned from the fogged-up window to face the room, but he continued to stand silently for several more seconds. 'I don't see anyone,' Fedorchuk finally announced to the man who sat at the table in the center of the small room.

'Idiots.' Leonid Sergeyevich had replied with his back still turned toward the man who spoke to him. The sound of Sergeyevich's voice was immediately covered over by the low moaning of the wind as it wrapped itself, with increasing velocity, around the corners of the small building. 'Now we have no choice but to go out and look for them.' Sergeyevich picked himself up slowly from the table.

'Are you sure that you really want to bother? The five of them are huddled in the storage shed or one of the other buildings, sharing a bottle of vodka and crying their eyes out. We should leave them in peace. Better still,' Fedorchuk added, 'we should join them. It would do us more good to share our grief openly than to spin our wheels in a hopeless attempt to do a nonsensical thing.'

'Absolutely not.' But Sergeyevich's weary tone showed that he, too, was beginning to waver. 'The radio. We should attempt to improve reception. We should try at least that much,' he said with far less enthusiasm than he had ten minutes earlier. That brief amount of time spent sitting and waiting for the others to return from their assignment of finding extra antenna wire and boosters was enough to drain him of what little positive energy he had left.

'Okay,' Fedorchuk said reluctantly. He took a step forward to where his heavy parka hung on a wall hook. 'I suppose it's good to have a direction to start in and faith in a happy outcome.'

'We need that data. Firm data. The only way we're going to get it is if we make contact with Moscow, or with one of our field offices somewhere else in the world.' Now that he had stood up, Sergeyevich took one tentative step toward the radio console as if he were going to try the radio again. He stopped short and stood his ground.

'It's good to have faith,' Fedorchuk repeated, his voice now steeped in a lifeless monotone. 'But do you realize how far from reality your expectations are?'

'I realize that there's a possibility . . .'

'Both you and I know,' Fedorchuk continued without interruption, 'that the theories about atmospheric pollution differ only in degree. They differ only in the minor points of how horrible the ultimate outcome will be.' Fedorchuk reached for his parka while he spoke and held the fur-lined garment in his hands. 'The scientific community is divided on only relatively minor questions – on whether the insect population will survive relatively unharmed, on whether the smaller invertebrates will suffer from significant mutations, on whether the orbiting layers of nuclear debris will come down gradually over a span of years or fall down relatively at once. These are the areas of typical scientific disagreement. But among scientists, there's no question about the basics. Our people, our country, are gone. So are most others. Mankind is doomed.'

'You're impossible, every damned one of you!' Sergeyevich had again tapped enough of his reserve of emotional energy to wave his finger accusingly at Fedorchuk – as if that sole gesture was enough to make the nightmare go away. 'You'd run to hell and back with your theories if you had the chance – but it's an option you don't have right now, I'm happy to say. Since I'm still in command here we're going to do things my way. That includes mounting an extra antenna cable so perhaps we can get more information – *real information*. And I don't care who has to freeze their ass off to do it!' Sergeyevich stormed toward the door that led to outside and grabbed for the handle. He had intended to shout outside for Gazunov or one of the other four men, who certainly should have come back within hearing distance by now. But when Sergeyevich yanked the door open, what stood on the threshold less than an arm's length in front of him caused him to jerk backward in horror and fear.

Eduardo Rios stood in the doorway of the Soviet Bellingshausen station, his eyes wide and glassy, his clothes torn and covered with blood. In his left hand he held a large ice axe, its blade dripping with red fluid that puddled onto the snow near his boots. In Rios' right hand he clutched a segment of iron pipe. It, too, was covered with blood – and with fragments that appeared to be pieces of human skin.

'My God . . . what happened . . .' Sergeyevich managed to utter those last words, in Russian, before Rios lunged toward him. Just as the man intended, Rios managed to catch Sergeyevich squarely in the chest with the point of the ice axe. The sharpened steel tip sliced into Sergeyevich as if his breastbone was not there to protect his innards, and the weapon instantly punctured the center of the man's heart. Leonid Sergeyevich was dead even before his body had fallen onto the building's dirty wooden floor.

Maxim Fedorchuk hesitated only for an instant before he dropped his parka and wheeled around in an attempt to escape through the cabin's rear emergency door. 'Get out – get away from me!' he shouted irrationally as he stumbled over the table and sent the rolls of charts flying off in all directions. 'Back! Back!' Fedorchuk shouted, this time using one of the words of English he had learned so he could at least partially communicate with people from the other Antarctic bases. 'Stop! Are you crazy!?

Stop this!' Fedorchuk had again lapsed back into Russian.

'Pigs, you are all pigs!' Rios bellowed in Spanish as he waved the iron pipe high above his head. With what little crazed energy remained in him, Eduardo Rios stumbled toward the last of his enemies that he could get to, the last of his enemies who still remained alive. *The Argentines and the Russians did it. I will kill them. For my friends, my people. For Chile. For the world.*

'Help!' Even while Fedorchuk shouted, he knew without a doubt that the five men who had been sent outside by Sergeyevich were incapable of helping him. Each of the men must have been brutally ambushed by this maniac. Fedorchuk suddenly recognized the man as being one of the people from the Chilean station – he remembered meeting the man once, several months before on the glacier. 'Leave me alone!' Fedorchuk reached the emergency door and fumbled with the handle, but an accumulation of wind-driven snow had formed enough of a seal on the outside to prevent the door from swinging open.

Rios pushed aside the last obstacle, a wooden chair, that remained between him and the Russian. As he did, Rios raised the ice axe again, this time with its cutting blade aimed down. He would – with the renewed strength that he knew God would give him for accomplishing this task of retaliation, of retribution, of justice – kill his last enemy with one stroke of his weapon.

Without wanting to, Fedorchuk shut his eyes after he saw the crazed Chilean begin to raise the axe. 'Please . . . no . . .' Fedorchuk whimpered as he hung onto the emergency door, his body leaned as far away from the madman as he could, his arms still pulling violently inward on the door handle.

At that moment the seal created by the wind-blown layer of snow on the outside of the emergency door finally reached its breaking point. The layer of frozen snow suddenly let go, and this allowed the wooden door to respond to the frantic tugs from the man on the inside.

At first Fedorchuk thought that he had tumbled backward because he had been hit by the axe, but then he realized that he had fallen simply because the door had sprung open. The bitter cold wind – which now carried needle-like shards of frozen ice and snow with it – bombarded Fedorchuk's face as he opened his eyes and looked up.

The blade of the axe, still covered with the blood of Sergeyevich, Gazunov and the others, was buried deeply into the door where it had struck it on the way down. Laying at Fedorchuk's feet was the Chilean maniac, the man's body sprawled across the wooden floor. For an instant Fedorchuk's spirits swelled with renewed hope because he thought that the Chilean was dead.

But Eduardo Rios had only fallen off balance when the blade of the ice axe impacted the edge of the door and then embedded itself deeply into the wood. Rios was no more than slightly dazed. He opened his eyes, looked around, then met the terrified stare of the man he was after. *The Russians gave the bomb to Argentina! They are the ones who destroyed Chile! Murdered innocent people! They are responsible!* Rios, who was responding with single-minded energy, twisted his head from side to side until he saw what he needed. His hand went for the iron pipe which lay on the floor nearby.

Fedorchuk jumped to his feet and vaulted out the opened door. His body hit the compacted snow outside quite hard and he tumbled down the slight incline. For a few seconds Fedorchuk was disoriented, but then he got his bearings and turned himself around to face the building he had just escaped from.

The Chilean was coming toward him, slowly and carefully, the iron pipe being waved in front of him in lethal sweeps as if it were a sword. Fedorchuk felt the bitter cold of the wind as it penetrated through his woolen shirt and pants, and for an instant he thought about how incredible it was that his arms and legs could be shivering, yet his forehead could be covered with sweat. He turned and began to run.

Get to the storage shed. Find a weapon. Fedorchuk pushed his legs though the uneven piles of ice and snow that were constantly accumulating between the buildings. He stared out ahead through half-closed eyes as he attempted to shield his face from the elements by raising his arm in front of him. Fedorchuk knew that the storage shed was somewhere ahead – directly into the driving wind. As he moved forward, the unrelenting bombardment from the shards of blowing snow and ice were beginning to peel off tiny blotches of skin from the unprotected areas of his face and hands. *To the left. Twenty more meters. No more than that.*

Fedorchuk tripped on a dark shape in front of him and fell, face down, against a bloodied body that lay sprawled against the snow. *Gazunov! My God!* The Russian scientist had not only been murdered but Fedorchuk could now see that he had also been brutally mutilated. His face was nearly split in half by what was apparently an axe blow. Fedorchuk pushed himself to his feet and stumbled onward, the front of his pants and shirt now covered with Gazunov's frozen blood. As he moved forward Fedorchuk could see two more dark shapes to his left – apparently the bodies of more of the murdered group of five. Fedorchuk forced the haunting images of the mutilated bodies of his friends from his mind as he concentrated totally on his goal. *Find the storage shed. My only chance.*

Just when Fedorchuk thought that he must have missed the storage shed and that he should turn back again, it suddenly appeared directly ahead of him – a dark shadowy structure against the grey background of blowing snow. It was no more than ten meters away, up a slight incline in the ice shelf that the building had been erected on. In a motion that had become more of a stumble than a walk or run, Maxim Fedorchuk reached the door of the storage shed. He put his hand on the knob.

The sounds made by the Chilean madman were easily masked by the howling wind, and the first knowledge that Fedorchuk had of the man's presence directly behind him was when he felt the iron pipe as it glanced along the side of his face. An instant later Fedorchuk felt his right shoulder cave in from the blow of the weapon – a blow that would have split his skull had he not, out of pure chance, jerked his body sideways at precisely the right time.

Fedorchuk fell to the ground and, as he did, he managed to roll into Rios' legs and knock him down also. The two men rolled down the slight incline together for a few meters before Fedorchuk managed to push himself away. Clawing his way to his feet, Fedorchuk spotted the iron pipe where it had also rolled downhill toward them. It was now within arm's reach.

Kill him. Only way. Fedorchuk attempted to grab for the pipe, but he found that his right arm hung uselessly at his side and would not respond. *Broken. My shoulder and arm.* Fedorchuk scooped up the iron pipe with his left hand and wheeled around toward the Chilean.

Rios had already gotten to his feet. The Chilean station commander was only inches away from the man that he had been chasing. In those last moments of his life Eduardo Rios clearly understood that he had been defeated in his battle against the Russian. A fraction of a second later the front of his face was totally crushed by a direct and massive blow from the iron pipe.

Maxim Fedorchuk stood over the body of the Chilean for several seconds after he had fallen to the snow. Finally, after he realized that the man was unquestionably dead, he pried open his frozen fingers, dropped the pipe, then turned himself back toward the storage shed. *Get inside. Get warm. Nothing else is possible.* Fedorchuk managed to get himself inside and get the door closed before he finally lost what little strength remained in his legs.

He crumbled to the floor. The pain from his crushed right shoulder and broken arm – which now hung at a grotesque angle from its socket – would have been nearly unbearable if it wasn't for what was happening to him. Within seconds of falling to the floor, Maxim Fedorchuk mercifully began to black out and slide into unconsciousness. *Mankind is doomed* was the last thought that worked itself through Fedorchuk's mind before he fell into unconsciousness on the floor of the warm shed.

Four

JULIE MATHEWS stood at the edge of the shoreline and looked out to sea while she waited for the others to finished. Her attention was focused on an iceberg in the center of the bay a few hundred yards in the distance. It made her think of the first time she had seen an iceberg three months before – majestic, overpowering, breathtaking with its brilliant white top and aqua-colored midsection near the waterline – as she stood on the rail of that supply ship with Richard. Both of them had gawked at everything around them, at the beauty, the desolation, the grandeur and indifference of the Antarctic. After a few more moments of memories, Julie turned and looked back at the woman behind her who was struggling with the last of the cages. 'How's it coming?'

'Damn slow.'

'Do you need a hand?'

'What I need is to have my head examined for volunteering to work with these moronic little creatures.' Annie Rizzo managed to get her hand around another of the penguins in the back of the cage and, amid the squawking and flapping of wings from it and the others still inside, she dragged the penguin out. 'Don't be such an ass, you little nurd.' Annie let the penguin go and watched as the small black and white bird stumbled to its feet and rapidly headed downslope in a clumsy gait. 'At least you could say goodbye, you asshole,' Annie shouted toward the penguin before she turned back to Julie. 'First I can't seem to get them into the damn cages, then I can't get them out. That's the story of my life.'

'Me, too.'

'And it's not right for a lady to sweat like this.' Annie wiped her hand along the ridge of perspiration on her forehead. 'I thought the Antarctic was supposed to be cold.'

'It will be. This is Indian summer.' Julie had been warned repeatedly that in just another week or two these forty degree days would be a long forgotten memory. Temperatures of thirty below zero with gale winds were what she had been told to expect. In a strange sort of way she was looking forward to it – it was the proper climate for hibernation. 'Where's Floyd?'

'He finished a few minutes ago. He's gone back to the tent.' Annie motioned over her shoulder to where the two orange tents were pitched on the beach in the distance.

'Okay. I'll go help him with dinner.' Julie pushed her long blonde hair from where it had ridden up and behind the collar of her red parka. She began to walk along the shoreline. Behind her, Julie heard Annie begin to talk to the next penguin as she reached into the cage for it. Annie's voice was chatty and conversational, as if she somehow expected the little bird to answer her back. Julie wondered for a moment if Richard hadn't been right, if the prospect of wintering over at the Palmer station wouldn't be the final vote to elect each of them to the academy of lunatics. It was probably a mistake, but it was too late now. A winter's reprieve would do her good – the prospect of spending her fortieth birthday at the bottom of the world with three men, one other woman and five thousand penguins was unique, if nothing else. It was suitable therapy for her errors in judgment and good sense.

For the first few weeks that she had been in the Antarctic with Richard, Julie had very conveniently managed to put aside the fact that the summer research field excursion would be over nearly before it had begun. After six weeks of total togetherness, everything would suddenly become just like it always had been: clandestine meetings and pretending not to know each other when their paths crossed on the campus, a few stolen hours here and there whenever Richard could find a suitable excuse to be away from home. *Richard miscalculated. Six weeks was too much of a taste.*

Julie turned away in disgust, angry at herself for having

allowed Richard's name to creep back into her thoughts again. She had no business going out with a married man, she had no business going on a summer field excursion to the bottom of the world with him and – now that it had turned predictably sour – she knew that she now had no business feeling sorry for herself. *If letting him go home by himself was such a good idea, how come it makes me feel so bad?*

When Julie had gone half the distance toward the orange tents she slowed her pace and looked back at the sea. What little ripple of wind had blown up a short while ago had subsided, and the surface of the bay was a mirrored calm. Beyond that deep and shiny blue were the rocks that stuck up into the Boyd Strait on the southwest side of Snow Island. Further to the left was the Danco coastline, its tall string of mountains disappearing in the distance as they formed the ridge that led to the tip of the Antarctic Peninsula.

As Julie had realized soon after her arrival, the atmosphere of the Antarctic was so clear that it was easy to be deceived by distances. Mountains that seemed no more than twenty miles away might in fact be eighty or ninety. In the absence of haze, the colors themselves seemed different – deeper, more striking, more vibrant than what she remembered from home. The Danco mountain range to the southeast was tinted lavender, the curving surface of the icefield at its base an enormous expanse of yellow and salmon pink. Far to the northeast, beyond the end of the Danco range, rose the peninsula's distant peaks. They seemed close, but in fact they were more than a hundred miles away. Everything in the Antarctic seemed close, but everything was always very far away, very difficult to get to – and very difficult to get back from. Julie turned back toward the tents and began to walk.

'How's Annie doing?' Floyd Robinson called out as he stepped from the tent and spotted Julie approaching. 'Are her boys cooperating?'

'Boys will be boys.' Julie forced a courteous smile as she stepped up to the campsite.

'That's what I've heard.' Robinson watched Julie's eyes

56

for a few seconds before he turned and snubbed out the remains of his cigarette on the tent post. He considered saying something personal, something that would again open up the lines of communication between them. He decided against it – it was too soon to repeat himself. For a few moments Robinson looked down at the cigarette butt that he held in his hand. Finally, he shoved it into his coat pocket. 'Sometimes I wish I wasn't a member of the Sierra Club – then I'd sure as hell drop these butts somewhere else.'

'Smokey the Penguin says that a cleaner Antarctic is up to you.' Julie took one step closer so she could begin to brush imaginary dirt from the shoulder of Floyd's parka. 'You've got to set a good example,' she said graciously, knowing that he always did. Floyd Robinson was a pleasure to work for, to work with. Julie genuinely liked him. 'Keep doing your best.'

'I'll tell you the truth, it's a great deal harder for us black folks.' Robinson pasted on an artificially broad smile, in preparation for the down-on-the-farm Negro routine that he was known for. 'You folks with da' light colored skin has it easy – like keepin' a light colored car clean. I tells you, I'm da' shiny black Cadillac dat' shows every speck.' Robinson rubbed the last remains of cigarette ashes off his hands with an exaggerated flourish.

'You're a Cadillac all right.' Julie put her arm on Floyd's shoulder and kept it there long enough to show him that she meant it. He had been so kind, so understanding during those first few days after Richard had gotten on the supply ship and sailed out of sight – sailed northbound to California, to his teaching position at UCLA, to his wife.

'Hey, do you know what they call the after-shave that a black man uses?'

'No – and I wouldn't even try to guess,' Julie answered.

'Eau d' . . .' Robinson paused for effect while he did a few steps of a Bojangles shuffle as best he could on the rocky shoreline, 'de-do-dah-day.'

Julie laughed. 'You've got to be the funniest man I've ever met.'

'Thanks.' Robinson was going to use this opportunity

to add more – to say how he felt that Julie was better off now, how she would benefit in the long run from her decision to have Richard go home alone. Robinson wanted to remind her that by using this opportunity to clear her head she was making the only realistic choice she could – when he cast his eyes toward the horizon. It took him several seconds to realize what he was seeing. 'Look! Out there!'

'What?' Julie spun herself around. As she did, her mouth dropped open.

Sitting low against a sky that the progressing darkness had already turned to the color of ash was the light grey outline of an airship. It hung majestically above the mirror-clear sea, the red horizontal line along its midsection pointed slightly away from them, one of the mounted structures on the craft's tail stuck up like the fin of a shark. The airship continued to plod along on its course, slowly but diligently.

'How far away is it?'

'Two miles, maybe more.'

'You see it, too? Thank God.' Annie had run up behind the other two and was still panting as she spoke. 'I thought I was losing my mind.' She continued to hold onto the last penguin that she had taken from the box, although the bird had wriggled enough from her grip to begin to flap its short wings violently. 'What does that blimp pilot think this is, Superball Sunday? This is a hell of a strange place to be advertising tires.' Annie shot a quick and angry look down at the penguin she held in her hand before she half-tossed the animal toward the snowfield behind them. She turned back toward the airship – which had already moved a marked distance away from them since the initial sighting. 'What's he doing here? Is he lost or something?'

'Must be.'

'Maybe he needs help. Maybe they're going down.'

'They're going to need more than help if they go down in that water.' Robinson dashed toward his tent. He came out a few moments later holding a small plastic box.

'What is that?' Julie stepped beside him and watched as Robinson fumbled with the catches.

'A flare pistol.' It took Robinson two attempts before he finally got the snap on the case to open. 'Damn plastic,' he mumbled as he tore into the wrapping that the pistol and flares were individually enclosed in.

Annie paced back and forth behind Robinson as she alternated her attention between the flare case and the airship in the distance. 'It's going away – we don't have much time.'

'Goddamn plastic . . . more damned trouble than it's worth . . .' Robinson split a fingernail as he clawed at the corner of the packaging. 'Someday the whole damn world is going to be wrapped in plastic bubbles . . . then we won't be able to get into anything . . .' Robinson finally managed to break into the package. He quickly extracted the pistol, the flares, and put them all together. 'Get back, you never know about these things.' Robinson stepped away from the two women, aimed the flare pistol at the airship and pulled the trigger.

The cartridge in the pistol exploded with more of a pop than a bang, but the flare rose unerringly toward the section of sky that it had been aimed at. A trail of billowy red smoke led up and outward from where they waited on the desolate beach.

'Do you think they'll see it?' Julie asked. Even as she spoke, the sight of the grey airship had already begun to fade into the bleakness that separated the darkening sky from the featureless sea.

'It doesn't look like it.' Robinson shoved another flare into the pistol and quickly fired it, but this one seemed to have even less chance of being seen. The grey airship had become nothing more than a smear on the horizon, its tail turned directly toward them, its nose pointed into the uninhabitable interior of the Antarctic.

The lights in the lounge at the rear of the gondola of *Airship Nine* were still off, and Frank Corbi was still glued to the seat he had occupied since Captain Whitaker had told them of the horrifying news more than an hour before. As always, Corbi had his video camera on his lap, the wire to its battery power pack strung across the top of the lounge table. 'Just a few more. Then you can turn the lights on.'

'You're wasting your time,' Andrew Sinclair replied in a contentious voice. He kept his eyes lowered while his hand continued to rest on his wife's lap. The fingers of that hand moved around in small, nervous circles. 'Hollywood was vaporized. There's no sense in filming anything. Not any more.'

'Maybe, maybe not.' Corbi continued to keep the viewfinder to his eye. Periodically he pressed the camera's shooting mechanism. The soft whirring sound from the video recorder's motor filled the quiet of the lounge. 'Like I told you before, I'm strictly freelance.'

'You were.'

'Still am. I could sell to the Fiji Islanders if I cared to. I'm not tied to any studio.'

'You're right that you're not tied to any studio.' Sinclair jerked his hand away from his wife's lap and abruptly rose to his feet. 'Your movie ties were broken on their end. Permanently.' Sinclair's words were low-keyed as if they were a statement of an obvious fact, but the strain behind the words gave his pent-up emotions away. 'As far as the Fiji Islands are concerned, they've also been dealt with. The Fijis are in the path of that nuclear debris from the bombs that went off in the Orient, the ones I learned about the last time I went into the radio room.' Sinclair glanced over his shoulder toward the front of the airship where the radio room was, then turned and nodded knowingly to his wife. As he expected, Kathleen nodded back in a gesture of automatic approval.

'That's not possible,' Corbi finally answered with little apparent interest.

'What's not possible?'

'What you said.' Corbi didn't bother to take his eye from the viewfinder. He had expected a running verbal battle with young Andrew Sinclair the minute the blueblood had waltzed into the lounge. That verbal battle was now in full swing. All of Sinclair's sudden bravado was, Corbi suspected, a pure show for that airhead of a new wife of his.

'You mean what *I* said? Is that what's not possible?'

'Yes. It's impossible to get anything to Fiji.' Corbi worked hard at resisting the urge to laugh out loud. For an educated young man – Andrew Sinclair the Third was Yale, class of '83, as he had mentioned to everyone at least ten thousand goddamn times since the trip had begun – he was easy enough to goad.

'You mean nuclear debris? But surely the wind currents from China would . . .'

'I mean *anything*, man. It's impossible to get *anything* to Fiji. Ask any travel agent.' Corbi knew that the only reason he even bothered answering Sinclair was that the sport of goading this young snob had kept his own mind partially occupied. That, alone, made the effort worthwhile.

'In the Lord's name, stop with this idiocy!' Sinclair rose to his feet and looked down at Corbi. The man was overweight, his hair was unkempt, his shirt hung out of his pants, and his thin and scruffy beard formed a grubby outline along his jaw. Corbi had represented himself as a film producer and he was everything that Sinclair had expected from the type who would pursue such a vapid profession – if film production could even be called a profession. 'You told me that you're thirty-four years old, yet you keep acting like a teenager. The world is coming to an end and you're making jokes!'

'Listen, my friend,' Corbi answered in a calm voice. 'Each of us has our own way of dealing with problems, of facing the unfaceable.' Corbi put the camera down and turned toward Sinclair. 'I make jokes.'

'Your jokes are far from funny.'

'. . . and you make speeches.' Corbi paused a few seconds to give his words a chance – an outside chance, as he well knew – of sinking in. 'The real difference between us is that I only want your attention, a little social interaction, that kind of thing. You seemed to think that even your belches and farts should be taken seriously.'

'You better watch what the hell you say to me.' Sinclair took a half step forward, his face a deep red.

'Sorry.' Corbi put on a conciliatory smile. 'I didn't mean

61

to embarrass you, especially in front of your lovely wife.'
Corbi looked down at Kathleen Sinclair, whose wide blue
eyes looked back up at him. She may have been a little
dumb – no, that wasn't fair, she seemed more bland than
dumb, an exhibition of her white-bread-and-mayonnaise
upbringing – but she certainly was beautiful. Twenty-two
years of exquisite female crowned with long red hair.
Corbi forced himself to look away from her and back
toward her husband. 'Sorry, Andy,' Corbi repeated. 'I
didn't mean to imply that proper breeding and Ivy League
schools weren't significant.'

'You can stop with your insults because I understand
perfectly well what kind of point you're trying to make.
I'm not going to ask you what school you went to because
it's perfectly obvious that you didn't bother to learn anything.' Sinclair turned away, but then quickly turned back
to Corbi again. He wasn't accustomed to direct confron-
tations of any sort and he was surprised at how stimulated
he felt by this one. 'And one more thing,' he added, now
that he was on a verbal roll, 'don't call me Andy.'

'Sure thing.' Corbi resisted the urge to add *Andy* again
but in its place he allowed a small and hollow laugh to
come up through his throat. 'I went to Carnegie-Mellon
in Pittsburgh,' Corbi said as he reached for his camera
again. The entire affair would have been hilarious if it
wasn't for what made this inane conversation necessary to
begin with. *Andy the asshole is turned from rich heir to
instant pauper. Unfortunately, the rest of the world is turned
to dust.* That was an interesting enough subject for a film,
but Corbi wondered if there were enough people left alive
on the globe to bother making it for. Maybe asshole Andy
was right, maybe the only thing that Frank Corbi had
learned how to do had suddenly become an obsolete skill
in a dying world. Corbi sighed, then put the viewfinder
against his eye and pressed the camera's trigger. He began
to slowly scan the horizon to the rear of the airship, more
out of habit than any real purpose.

'I've had enough of this stupidity. I'm turning the cabin
lights on.' Sinclair headed for the wall switch.

'Wait . . .'

'I'm not sitting in this darkness for another minute just so you can waste our . . .'

'Wait! There's something out there!' Corbi leaned forward without taking his eye off the viewfinder. 'Yes! Smoke – red smoke!'

'Where?' Kathleen Sinclair jumped up from her seat. She had reached the window beside Corbi before her husband had even turned around. She quickly knelt on the sofa next to the film producer and allowed her knees to sink into the soft cushions and her body to brush up against his. 'I don't see anything.'

Corbi shot a quick glance at her. 'Over there, by that island.' He motioned with his free hand so she could follow where he pointed. 'See it?'

'Yes, yes!' Kathleen excitedly bounced up and down on the sofa as she spotted the plume of dark red smoke against the grey-white background. 'God, look at that!' She pushed back her long red hair and turned to her husband. 'Something's out there, hurry, get the captain!'

'I don't see anything.' Sinclair leaned further forward, although he was still careful not to get too close to Corbi. 'Where?'

'Never mind that. Get the captain back here, we need to turn the ship around.' Corbi would have gone himself, except that he didn't trust either of the Sinclairs to keep the target – whatever it was – in sight. 'Hurry, I'll keep the smoke in view through the magnifier on the camera.'

'I still don't see anything.' Sinclair leaned a bit closer to Corbi as he peered over the man's shoulder.

'For Chrissake, get the captain – I'm going to lose sight of it soon!'

'I'll go.' Kathleen jumped up and nearly knocked her husband over as she dashed out the lounge door and toward the cockpit. 'I'll tell the captain to turn the ship around!' she shouted back into the lounge as she raced forward. She didn't know what the red smoke meant, but Kathleen Sinclair knew enough to hurry.

*

Captain Lou Whitaker had begun to heel the airship hard to port just a few moments after Kathleen Sinclair had burst into the cockpit with the news of the sighting behind them. Once *Airship Nine* was headed properly, it took Whitaker only a short while to see the remnants of the flare against the horizon. 'There it is.'

'Looks like they're firing another one.' As Ray Madigan pointed out ahead from the copilot's seat, another wobbly line of red smoke rose from the spot on the Antarctic coastline that they were now headed toward. The smoke traveled up into the clear sky and hung as motionless as if it had been crayon mark on a sheet of paper.

'Take out the binoculars. See if you can make out what's on the beach.'

'Right.' Madigan reached for the binoculars on the sidewall. He steadied his hands against the glare shield. 'Something there . . . hard to tell . . . tents . . . people . . .'

'How many?' Whitaker could make out a splotch of color on the coastline, but nothing more.

'Not many. It looks like a small camp.' The details were coming into focus rapidly. 'A few people, two tents.'

'Okay.' Whitaker turned around to face the crowd behind him. Everyone on the airship had rushed forward upon hearing the news and had elbowed into the companionway in order to share the view out the cockpit window. 'Weiss, try to raise them on the radio. They might be transmitting.'

David Weiss began to push backward through the crowd so he could get to his radio room. 'What frequency should I try?' He eased himself round Doctor Tucker and then between the Sinclair couple. Kathleen Sinclair's perfume floated around him as Weiss waited for the captain's answer.

'I don't have any idea. Use your own judgment.'

'I'll try the standard emergency frequencies.' Weiss' hand accidentally brushed against the Sinclair woman's arm as he maneuvered around her. Once past the crowd, he hurried into the radio room.

'They've got to be a part of the scientific community,'

Doctor Everett Tucker volunteered from his position at the back of the group. 'The Antarctic treaty prohibits anything other than peaceful research and exploration.'

'Which countries are involved?'

'As I recall,' Tucker answered as he edged his way forward, 'there are a good many signatory nations to the international treaty. But the height of the research effort is during the Southern Hemisphere's midsummer – December through February. By now, only the nations that go to the expense of wintering-over would still have a contingent here.'

'I sure as hell hope they're not Russians.' Madigan continued to look through the binoculars, but he hadn't been able to learn much more. 'I can see the people now – three of them on the beach. Might be more in the tents. No flags or markings.'

'I don't think it makes any difference who they are, Russians or Americans. They're scientists, not military.' Tucker looked at the faces of those jammed in the airship's cockpit with him. The airship's young second officer Steve Galloway stood to Tucker's right, with that pretty stewardess Nancy Schneider next to him. To Tucker's left was the film producer Frank Corbi. The Sinclair couple had already pushed their way further forward and were now directly behind the captain. 'The people on the ground won't be any threat to us.'

'Maybe.'

'I'm sure of it.' But the tone in Tucker's voice showed that even he, too, had his doubts. He could no longer be sure of anything, not since what had happened a few short hours before to the rest of the world.

'Other than the United States and the Soviet Union, what other nations would keep a wintering-over group down here?' Whitaker continued to steer the airship toward the spot from where the flares had risen while he waited for Tucker's answer. Even without binoculars, they had now moved close enough to enable him to see some of the features on the beach. The tents were orange, and the three people in front of the tents seemed to be waving their arms at the airship.

'I'm not sure. Chile. Argentina perhaps. Australia might be wintering over.'

'Not the British?'

'I'm afraid that's a sore point on the home front, captain.' Tucker shook his head sadly. 'This is the first season the British aren't maintaining a housekeeping staff at the Faraday station. Budget. The scientific community at home was in a royal stew, but there were simply no funds available.'

'Okay.' Whitaker scanned the coastline one more time before he turned back to the group. 'The approach path is clear, so we can hover above them in complete safety. We can talk back and forth to them before we decide on the next step.'

'What if they shoot at us? How vulnerable are we?' Sinclair asked.

'It depends on what they shoot,' Madigan answered before the captain could respond. He turned in the co-pilot's seat in order to face the group. 'A few bullets probably wouldn't hurt us. But anything bigger – one of those hand-held rocket launchers, for instance – and our glorious white whale would get itself involuntarily beached.'

'Jesus.'

'I don't see that we have any choice.' Whitaker watched the three people on the beach carefully, but he could find nothing ominous in their actions. They continued to stand where they were, waving their arms. One or two of them appeared to be women. 'If they meant us harm, they would've tried something already,' he said, trying to sound more certain than he really was.

'How do we talk to them?' As he asked the question, Frank Corbi took a step backward and began to unravel the cord on his video recorder.

'The old fashioned way.' Whitaker pulled the airship's throttles back, then eased the wheel forward to lower the nose. The sea below them – with the coastline now only a few hundred yards away – began to grow in detail as they lost altitude. 'In a calm wind like this we can find a point of neutral buoyancy using little or no engine power.

With the throttles back the noise level will be low enough to open the windows and shout down.'

'Great. Then I should get a good sound track for the pictures.' Corbi stepped aft in order to find a spot where he could film the episode of their approach to the beach, their engagement with the unknown group below. *This is just like the train's approach in* High Noon, *just like the airplane's departure in* Casablanca. *I'm filming a classic here.* He fumbled nervously with his battery pack as he moved away.

'Okay, here we go.' Whitaker pushed further on the control column and edged *Airship Nine* up to the shoreline. Their altitude had dropped to less than one hundred feet, which made the faces of the three people on the beach recognizable. Definitely two women and one man. They still appeared friendly enough, although Whitaker kept his right hand on the ship's throttles in case he needed to accelerate quickly and get away. With his left hand he slid open the plastic window on the captain's side. 'Where are you from?' he shouted, his voice carrying well above the low and methodical ticking from the idling engines.

'Are you in trouble? Do you need help?' the man on the beach shouted back.

'Are you Americans?' Whitaker asked, although that question had become a strict formality since he could already tell that they were Americans from the way the man spoke and from the appearances of the other two. He was a black man, and the others were two very American-looking women.

'Yes. Palmer station. Thirty miles from here.'

Whitaker paused for a moment before he asked the next question. It seemed somehow immoral to be shouting out a question so hideous. Still, he had no choice. Whitaker cleared his throat and leaned further out the window. 'Have you heard the news yet?'

'What news?'

'The news about what's happened.'

'What's happened?' The black man appeared puzzled. 'Don't know what you mean.'

Damn. 'Come aboard, we'll lower a rope ladder.'

Whitaker motioned into the cabin toward Galloway, who instantly departed for the hatchway on the lower cargo deck. The captain then turned back to the group below. 'Put only one person on the rope ladder at a time. That will give us a chance to adjust our weight and balance as you climb,' he shouted to them.

'What is the news? What has happened?' the black man persisted. He turned to the two women for a moment, then back toward the giant airship that hovered above him. 'Tell us what's happened.'

'Come aboard.' Whitaker pulled his head back inside the window and shut it tightly. He sympathized with the man below, but Whitaker knew that a few more minutes wouldn't make any difference. It had been his duty to tell the passengers and crew of *Airship Nine*, and it would also be his duty to tell the people from the Palmer station. But even though they were total strangers, he'd be damned if he was going to shout out an open window that most everything – and everyone – those three people on the beach had known from back home were now things of the past.

'What in God's name could that pilot be talking about?' Floyd Robinson asked the question out loud, but he hadn't expected an answer from the women who stood beside him. Instead, the three of them stood silently and watched the scene above their heads. The airship bobbed up and down in slow and gentle motions in the dusk sky, as if it were some sort of giant but placid creature about to loll itself to sleep.

'Maybe a storm, maybe that's why they're off course,' Annie Rizzo said.

'Maybe.' Robinson continued to watch the airship above him. Portions of the ship's layered skin flexed, the canvas-like fabric pulsing mildly in and out as a result of the few air currents that moved lazily around them. 'I wonder how that big bag of gas would ride out a day of high winds and low temperatures,' Robinson asked, to fill the time while they waited for the rope ladder to be dropped to them.

68

'Probably better than I will.' Annie Rizzo frowned, then turned to Julie. 'I don't like the sound of any of this.'

'Neither do I.'

'Now that I think about it, that storm idea is stupid. I wonder what really happened.'

'We'll know very soon.' Julie pointed up at the airship. A door on the rear lower deck had been opened and, as she watched, a man threw out a long rope ladder. It unfurled quickly and hit the sand thirty feet from where they stood. 'Who should go first?'

'I'll go.' Annie took a step forward.

'Wait.' Robinson pointed toward the airship's cockpit. 'That pilot seemed concerned about weight. Maybe we should send the lightest person first.'

'No problem, Floyd. Old thunder thighs knows when it's time to back off.'

'I didn't mean anything . . . but that pilot . . .'

'Always a bridesmaid, never a bride.' Annie grabbed her girlfriend's hand and began to walk her toward the rope ladder. 'You go first, Julie. Floyd and I will stay on the beach and have a weight watcher's meeting while you find out what's happening.'

'I'm no more than ten pounds lighter than you. I can't see how that can make any difference.' Julie put her hand on the rope ladder and her foot on the first rung.

'It can't. I think that Floyd really wants me down here just in case you fall. He figures that with my luck you'll fall on top of me.' Annie steadied the bottom of the ladder while Julie began to move up. Even though the airship's engines were at no more than idle speed, they still put out enough of a blast of air to cause Julie's blonde hair to blow out from beneath the collar of her parka. 'But the problem of me going first,' Annie shouted up as she watched Julie climb higher on the ladder, 'is that with my luck if I fell I'd land on *him*.'

'Once she's inside the cabin, you go.' Robinson pointed to the tent behind them. 'I just realized that we should probably bring the radio with us. We're supposed to check in with the base in twenty minutes. I don't want to have to climb down just to do that.'

'I don't blame you.' Annie looked nervously up the long rope ladder, which swayed slightly in the breeze as if it were a snake that had reared up to its fully extended height. 'Julie's in the cabin. Here I go.'

'I'll be right behind you.' Robinson watched Annie for a moment to be certain that she would be all right, then he turned and trotted back to the supply tent. Once inside, he grabbed the portable radio and hurried back to the rope ladder. Annie had just scampered into the airship's hatchway as Robinson reached for the rope. 'Okay for me to come up?' Robinson shouted to the young man who had helped Annie inside.

'Wait.' Steve Galloway disappeared inside the airship for a brief moment before he leaned out again. 'Yes. Come up.'

'Here I come.' Robinson held the portable radio in one hand, the rope ladder in the other. By the time he had mounted half a dozen of the hemp rungs his imbalance from having only one arm on the ladder had imparted a large swaying motion to the rope.

'Careful. Steady.' Galloway could see that whatever the man held in his free hand – it appeared to be a portable radio – had caused him to shift his weight too far to one side. 'Try to lean more in the other direction.'

'Okay.' Robinson's face was covered in sweat. He had never liked altitude and climbing under the best of circumstances, and dangling midway between a bobbing airship and the rock-strewn beach below was less than a healthy situation. 'I'll shove the radio into my belt,' Robinson shouted up to the young man in the hatchway. 'Then I'll be able to hold on with two hands.'

'Be careful. Go slow.'

'Right.' But in his desire to get himself safely into the airship as soon as he could, Robinson began to rush himself. With one quick motion he jammed the small portable radio beneath his belt as best he could with only his right hand to work with. As soon as the radio was beneath his belt he grabbed for the ladder's next rung.

'Watch it!'

The sudden shift in weight had caused the dangling rope

70

ladder to begin to right itself and spin in the opposite direction. That alteration made Robinson involuntarily lean away to keep himself upright. With both his hands already firmly on the ropes there was no chance of him falling, but Robinson's unnecessary movement had caused the plastic radio to slip up and out from where it had been hastily jammed beneath his belt.

'Your radio!'

'Damn!' Robinson watched as the radio popped out from beneath his belt and, for a fraction of a second, hovered in midair only inches in front of him. But even if he had the time he wouldn't have been able to save the radio because he was now leaning and needed both hands to keep his balance. The radio tumbled face-down as it fell. It impacted on the rocky beach a moment later with a crack that was loud enough to be heard above the noise from the airship's idling engines. 'Oh, shit.'

'Forget that radio, it's gone.' Even from a hundred feet above it, Galloway could tell that the radio had been splintered into a hundred unsalvageable pieces. 'Keep coming up.' Galloway leaned further out so he would be able to help the man into the airship once he had reached the top of the ladder.

'Okay. I'm coming.' Robinson began to climb again, slowly and carefully. *I'm a damned idiot. This airship probably won't have a radio that'll work on our frequency. The base will think that something's happened to us.* But even before he had reached the threshold of the hatchway, Floyd Robinson had already put the problem of the broken radio out of his mind. Instead, he was now wondering what it was that the airship's pilot wouldn't tell them, what sort of news could be so unusual that a commercial airship would suddenly show up in the Antarctic. Whatever it was, Robinson suspected that it wasn't something he would want to hear.

Five

THE DOUBLE set of contra-rotating helicopter blades whirled above the cabin of the Kamov Ka-25, and they set up a high enough noise level to cause something of a communications problem between Doctor Boris Ney and the man to his right. 'I didn't understand you, major. Is this the coastline that Bellingshausen is on?'

'Yes. Five more kilometers,' Major Ilya Zinoviev answered in a loud voice as he continued to steer the helicopter at a low altitude above the waves. 'We should see the navigation light any time now.'

'Fine.' Ney sat further back in his flight chair, as far as his cinched-up seatbelt and shoulder harness would allow. *The Bellingshausen staff wouldn't dare to give me a problem. They'll fall in line soon enough.* Ney was pleased at the way the initial assignments had turned out; Captain Kollontai and Aleksandra were selected to address the ship's company, while he and Major Zinoviev were headed for the Soviet Bellingshausen station.

'Look! To starboard!'

Ney followed Zinoviev's directions and soon spotted it himself. The Bellingshausen station's navigation light pulsed brightly, its alternating peaks of white punctuating the darkness every few seconds. Since they had made their takeoff from the stern platform of the Soviet motorship *Primorye*, the Antarctic sky had emptied itself of its little remaining daylight as rapidly as water flowed out from a bottomless bucket. 'Will the landing be a problem in the dark?'

'No.' Zinoviev moved one hand from the flight controls just long enough to flick on two switches on his panel. Two powerful wands of white light fanned out from either side of the helicopter and penetrated far into the blackness that they flew through. 'I know the beach well. Between the waterline and the glacier is more than enough room. Enough room for twenty helicopters.'

'I can't hear you.' Ney leaned a little closer. 'Did you say no problem?'

'No problem,' Zinoviev repeated in a louder voice before he turned slightly in his flight chair in order to concentrate on the landing. The major had selected the better of their two helicopters for the trip and, even though they were carrying a considerable fuel load, the ship was lighter than normal with only him and Doctor Ney aboard. The landing would be easier than many. *The wind is light. At least I think the wind is light.* Zinoviev was disheartened by the lack of any radio communications with the station – one of the main reasons behind their flight to Bellingshausen – but that could be explained away by any of a thousand reasons that ranged from equipment problems through atmospheric conditions. Yet without radio contact Zinoviev had to guess at the wind and weather at his destination, which fortunately appeared to be quite good at the moment.

'Still no word on the radio?'

'No.'

The Kamov Ka-25 descended lower toward the blackness of the beach. By keeping the navigation light straight ahead and by constantly consulting his compass, Zinoviev knew that he could keep the craft's approach path over the open sea. The two powerful wands of white light continued to reach a few hundred meters ahead of them, probing into the darkness. Finally the beach itself loomed into view, the dark rocks of the coastline sticking up through the narrow edge of sand and the scattered patches of snow.

'Which building do they normally stay in?' Ney shouted.

'That one, straight ahead.' Zinoviev nodded toward the Quonset-type structure that reflected brightly in the helicopter's landing lights, the yellow exterior paint causing the building to stand out conspicuously. 'They must hear us by now, keep an eye out for them.' But as Zinoviev worked the helicopter's controls to lower the machine into a hover over the beachfront, he began to frown again. 'I still don't see anyone. This is not normal. Where can they be?'

'I don't know.' Ney twisted around in his flight chair and looked at the other buildings that lay on either side of the main residence, the lights from the helicopter bright enough to illuminate some of the adjacent areas as well. 'Swing the lights to the left, I think I see something over there.' Ney peered into the shadowy darkness on his side as the helicopter followed Zinoviev's commands and swiveled its fuselage around while it hovered. The craft pointed its landing lights at an oil storage tank to their left. 'There! In front of the tank!'

'Damn!' Zinoviev pushed forward on the flight controls to edge the helicopter nearer to what they saw, although it was already obvious that the shape on the ice-covered ground was that of a man – or, more accurately, what was left of a man. 'I'll move up closer.'

'Yes, hurry!'

The forward motion of the Kamov Ka-25 jerked to a stop in midair, the man's mutilated body just forward of the aircraft's nose. The downwash of air from the whirling blades began to kick up swirls of powdery snow. 'I'll land. I'll shut down the engines,' Zinoviev announced as he began to activate the proper controls – although his eyes never left the mutilated body lying on the snow in front of them. A few moments later the helicopter thumped to a landing on the hard-packed snow. With less than ten meters between themselves and the body, the river of blood that flowed down the incline toward them cut a dark red swathe across the ice as it disappeared beneath the helicopter.

'Come out as quickly as you can. Bring a medical kit,' Ney said as he took off his flight helmet, unbuckled his seatbelt and scurried out of the cockpit. He slid open the door and was met by a blast of cold, snow-filled air from the downwash of the blades over his head. Ney stepped out carefully and edged forward, his head down to stay far below the slowing rotor blades of the Ka-25. By the time he reached the inert body laying in front of the

74

helicopter, the twin set of blades above his head had slowed down and were no longer kicking up the frozen powder on the ice sheet. Ney knelt down and carefully turned over the man's mutilated body.

'Dead?' Zinoviev had come out of the helicopter with his helmet still on, the cord from its internal microphone dangling along his side. He held tightly to the canvas bag that contained the medical kit.

'Of course.' Ney examined the body for a few more moments before he stood up. 'The interesting point is the cause of death.'

'What?'

'The cause of death. Murder. Massive and deliberate injuries. From the marks, I'd say an axe was used.'

'God Almighty.' Zinoviev had seen mutilated bodies before – helicopter training accidents when there wasn't enough left of the pilot to give him a proper burial – but this was far worse. Entire sections of this man's body were perfectly intact while other parts of him were hacked apart as if he were no more than a soup chicken being cut up for dinner. Zinoviev could feel the bile rising up from his stomach and into his throat. 'The landing lights . . .' he said through a choked-up voice as he pointed tentatively toward the two bright beams from the helicopter that he had left on in order to illuminate the body, '. . . need to shut them down . . . save the batteries . . .' Zinoviev turned without waiting for a reply from Ney and hustled back to his aircraft, barely holding down his reflex to gag.

'Bring each of us a flashlight,' Ney said as he walked back to the helicopter door. As he waited for Zinoviev to come back out and during the last few seconds before the helicopter's lights were extinguished, Ney searched the horizon as far as the fixed beams would allow. To the left were what appeared to be two more bodies lying on the snow. To the right, at the entrance to a squat building, there appeared to be yet another body. Now that the engines had wound themselves down, Ney could finally hear the sounds of the Bellingshausen station itself. The air was calm and quiet, but the sea continued to smash noisily against the rocks behind them. The steady hum of a diesel generator came from one of the buildings ahead.

'Here's a flashlight.' Zinoviev had come back from the cockpit without his flight helmet on, his bald head glistening with perspiration. Zinoviev handed Ney one of the portable lights as he climbed down from the doorway. 'What do you think went on here?'

'A massacre.'

'Who could have done it?'

'The Americans,' Ney said without hesitation. He rubbed two fingers along the side of his trimmed beard as he thought about what he would say next. Ney's instincts had told him to blame the massacre on the Americans, even though he had no real belief in that notion himself. What Ney did have now was a plan or, more accurately, the beginnings of a plan.

'Incredible.' Zinoviev was still in shock, still unable to deal with what he had seen in he last few minutes.

'You go in that direction,' Ney said as he took the canvas medical kit and one of the flashlights from Zinoviev.

'Over there?'

'Yes. Toward the base of the navigation light.' Ney gestured in the direction of the white beacon that continued to rotate, its broad beam sweeping high over their heads once every several seconds and providing a measure of illumination to the features of the otherwise blackened beach. 'I assume that those two dark lumps laying on the ground are bodies.'

'I see them,' Zinoviev answered nervously.

'I doubt if they could be alive, but check and see anyway.'

'Right.'

'I'll be heading this way.' Ney pointed his beam of light toward the lump on the snow in front of the small building.

'Where will we meet?'

'At that building in ten minutes. Then we'll investigate the other buildings together.'

'Okay.' Zinoviev stepped forward tentatively in the direction that Ney had pointed, his flashlight sweeping back and forth across his path. It was as if he suspected that something even more horrible than two mutilated bodies could be lurking just outside the narrow beam of his flashlight.

Boris Ney went in the other direction. The thin layer of snow on the surface of hard-packed ice crunched noisily beneath his feet as he moved up the slight incline toward the building, his own flashlight pointed steadily at what appeared to be the fourth body. Even before he had reached the sprawled out figure on the snow, he could see three things: first, that it was a man; second, that the man was unquestionably dead since his face had been completely smashed in – probably by the iron pipe that lay not far from his feet. The third thing Ney noticed was that the dead man was dressed in different garments from the normal Soviet issue. Ney kneeled down and turned the man's body slowly from side to side in order to examine it more closely.

Even through his injuries it was obvious that this man was not Russian. He appeared Spanish – Chilean, most probably, since Ney knew that the Chilean base was on the far side of this very island that the Bellingshausen station was on. Ney glanced behind him; Zinoviev was nowhere in sight. Ney turned the body face-down. *Zinoviev won't notice the clothes. He certainly won't touch the body. He'll think it's another one of the Bellingshausen staff.* Satisfied, Ney stood up and walked toward the door of the small storage building. He opened the door slowly. He was not surprised by what he saw inside.

Lying in the middle of the wooden floor and surrounded by boxes and crates that were stacked to the ceiling was yet another man. But this man was different from the rest. He was alive. Ney searched the wall until he found a light switch, then flicked it on. One low-powered bulb in the center of the ceiling came on. Ney walked up to the man, stooped down and felt for his pulse. Weak but regular. He could see and feel the man's heaving breaths as he began to stir himself back to consciousness. 'Can you hear me?' Ney asked, in Russian, as he lifted the man's head.

'. . . yes . . .' That one word was faint but unmistakable as Maxim Fedorchuk opened his eyes for the first time since the nightmare of a battle with the crazed Chilean had ended. '. . . help me . . .'

'Of course. Very soon. You'll be all right.' Ney laid the man's head back down, then fumbled with the canvas medical kit until he found what he was looking for. It was the special syringe that Aleksandra Bukharin had given him, the powerful sedative that she had placed inside the medical kit in case some of the men at Bellingshausen might be in a bad state. 'But you must tell me first, what's happened here? Was there more than just the one man, the one lying outside on the snow? Were the Americans involved?'

'Americans?' Fedorchuk rolled his head slowly from side to side, his eyes hardly able to focus on the man kneeling over him. 'No . . . one man . . . him . . . crazy . . . killed all except me . . .' Fedorchuk closed his eyes again, this time because of the intense wave of pain that suddenly pulsed through him from his shattered right shoulder. 'Help me . . . please . . .'

'Certainly.' Ney held the syringe up to the light to examine the markings on the plastic vial. Along each two millimeters of length there was a red line. Aleksandra had carefully explained to Ney that he must use no more than one of the gradations on any person, even a heavily injured one. The drug was very powerful and it would, within two or three minutes, progressively slow down all the bodily functions while it reduced the sensations of pain. 'But surely there were Americans with that man. The Americans must have helped him. The Americans must have escaped.'

'No . . . help me . . . my shoulder . . .' Fedorchuk had trouble speaking in even a low voice as the muscle spasms from the intense pain traveled through his body. He had no idea what this man was talking about, and he didn't care. All Fedorchuk wanted was relief from his pain.

'Lie quietly. Save your energy. This will help you.' Ney began to roll up the man's shirt sleeve. 'Just lie quietly.' Ney concentrated on his actions with the syringe, carefully holding the man's arm in one hand while he aimed the long needle with the other. The sharp point of the needle pierced into the soft spot above the man's forearm. When Ney was satisfied that he had indeed found a vein, he began to push slowly inward on the plunger. 'The Americans. They were here also.'

'No. I don't . . .'

'Yes. I'm sure of it.' Ney watched the bottom edge of the plunger as it approached the first gradation mark on the vial. 'I saw them. Dozens of them. Americans.' The plunger passed the limits of the first mark. Ney continued to push. 'Americans. They were Americans.'

'Americans?' Fedorchuk could feel the sensation of something inside his left arm, even above and beyond the flood of pain that came continuously from his crushed right shoulder. But this sensation was different, as if the insides of his arm had been suddenly hollowed out and there was something warm in there, a warm and furry creature of some sort that was crawling up from his arm and into his shoulder, then into his neck and chest. 'You saw . . .?'

'Yes. I saw them.' Ney kept his steady, unrelenting pressure against the plunger. It was past the second gradation mark and well into the third. 'You saw them, too. Americans. They led the attack on the Bellingshausen station. There's no question about it.'

'Question . . . no question . . . Americans . . .' Fedorchuk felt the overpowering numbness as it reached the base of his skull and then spread itself inside his head. There was no more pain, there was nothing, there was the wide expanse of an open field, a field of snow, a field of wheat, a field of grass in front of him. Fedorchuk could see it clearly, nearly touch it. He could also hear a voice from far away. A voice that told him what he had seen. A voice that told him what he knew. *Americans. Americans have attacked the Bellingshausen station.*

Boris Ney pushed further on the plunger of the syringe, until it had bottomed out. Empty. Ney had injected the injured man with six units of the powerful sedative. 'Now you'll sleep better,' he said as he pulled the needle from the man's arm. Ney examined the empty plastic vial for a few moments before he looked around the dimly lit storage room to pick an appropriate spot. Once he had found one, Ney tossed away the empty syringe. The syringe landed on top of a stack of crates, then bounced off the crates and tumbled down behind them and out of sight.

Ney got up, walked to the door and opened it. 'Zinoviev, hurry!' he shouted out across the open expanse toward where he saw the major's flashlight in the darkness outside. 'I've found someone – and he's alive!' Once he had seen the major's light begin to move toward him, Ney stepped back toward the man who lay on the floor of the storage shed.

'Listen to me,' Ney said in a firm voice as he once again knelt down and picked up the man's head. 'Tell me again about the Americans. Tell me about how the Americans attacked you.'

'Americans,' Fedorchuk answered. He opened his eyes but he could no longer see anything beyond a few grey shadows. Bright red and white splotches had also developed in his vision, and those splotches failed to go away after he closed his eyes. Fragmented thoughts ran through Fedorchuk's head like the eddying currents in a rapid stream. 'Americans . . . attacked . . .'

Major Zinoviev had reached the door of the storage shed in time to hear those choked-off words being spoken by the man on the floor. 'What's he saying?' Zinoviev asked as he rushed over and knelt beside Ney.

'That the Americans attacked them. Murdered them.' Ney shot a quick glance at Zinoviev, then looked back at the dying man's face. The sedative had obviously taken hold. The massive overdose would bring his bodily functions to a critical point in another minute or two at the most. 'I don't think he's going to make it.'

'Where did the Americans come from?' Zinoviev leaned closer to the man's ear as he spoke – he, also, could see that the man was dying.

'Americans . . . saw them . . . you . . . they . . . attacked . . .' Maxim Fedorchuk could hear the sound of his own faltering heartbeat and, beyond that, something in the distance. Something melodic. Music from his past – a song that his father would sing to him at bedtime. The open field of snow appeared again, and this time he recognized it at once. Home. On the horizon was the farmhouse at Izevsk where he had spent the remainder of his childhood after his father had died. Standing in front of the small house were his mother and his grandparents. They were waving at him. Waving at him to come home. *I'm coming, mother. I'm coming.* Maxim Fedorchuk's heart would beat just a few more times before the overdose of sedative caused it to stop altogether and his muscles to go limp.

'I think he's gone.' Boris Ney laid the man's head back down on the wooden floor. He felt for the man's pulse. 'Nothing. I'm afraid that he's dead, too.'

'Are you sure?'

'Yes.' Ney shook his head in sorrow. 'I tried, but there was nothing I could do.'

'Don't blame yourself. He was too far gone.' Zinoviev laid his hand on Ney's shoulder.

'Internal injuries, I suppose.'

'Probably. Just look at his shoulder.' Zinoviev moved his hand down and gingerly touched the dead man's shoulder for a moment before he realized what he was doing. He quickly yanked his hand away. 'The Americans,' Zinoviev said as he stood up and edged his way toward the storeroom door. Even though the overhead light was still on, Zinoviev had kept his flashlight on continuously and now used that beam to lead him out of the room. Darkness was another thing he wasn't fond of. 'I don't understand this – why would the Americans do this?'

'Because they want to continue this war that they've started, even down here.' Ney also stood up and headed for the door. 'They want to conquer the world.'

'Could there be anyone else still alive at the station?'

'No. This man was the last, he said so himself. The Americans had apparently left him for dead.'

'Bastards. Murderers.' Zinoviev spat out the words as he stepped outside and headed in the direction of the helicopter. His flashlight made continuous broad sweeps across the ice and snow in front of them. 'They've killed innocent people for no reason. Scientists who didn't even have a weapon to defend themselves with.'

'Yes, that's what they did.' Ney smiled to himself at how quickly the major had forgotten his own words from a few hours before. It was Zinoviev who had originally suggested that the *Primorye* launch an immediate attack on the American Palmer station soon after the first news of the nuclear exchanges had reached the ship. Now the major seemed to be looking at things differently. Once again Ney saw the truth behind the adage that all great leaders seem to know instinctively: that any delay was dangerous in the science of making war because most men would change their minds too often and too quickly.

'We can't let them get the upper hand. We've got to do something right away.'

'You're absolutely right.' *Let Zinoviev do all the talking, he'll get himself worked up and that'll be more convincing.* Boris Ney fell in step directly behind the major, his own flashlight aimed straight down to illuminate the area that they walked on. 'We'll head back to the ship immediately. Then you can give your report to Captain Kollontai.'

Michael Starr had jogged quickly up the glacier at the Palmer station with no difficulty because it was a route that was a common one for him. The difference this time came from the fact that his jogging was taking place well into darkness and that, on this occasion, his goal was not the exercise itself but the destination. Starr arrived at the plateau of the ice field without being winded, the powerful flashlight he held in his right hand aimed straight at the pole in front of him. 'Hello, John, I've arrived,' Starr said as he placed the mouthpiece of the portable radio to his lips and pressed the transmit button.

'How does it look?' came the reply from the receiving end of the radio. 'Is everything together?'

'It sure as hell looks that way.' Starr ran the light up and down the large radio mast. 'Nothing wrong that I can see. Even our sign is still in place.' Starr stepped up to the metal tower and shined his flashlight on the blue and white sign that he had brought from California with him, the road sign that said *Huntington Beach, population 151,500.*

'Is the ground wire still intact? Maybe it worked itself out.'

'Nope.' Starr knelt down and examined the ground wire more carefully, but it was obvious that everything on this end of the radio network was in exactly the same condition that it had been before communications had turned to shit. 'Nothing's out of the ordinary. I guess our problem's not on this end.'

'That's what I figured, but it was worth a try. Come on back.'

'Okay. See you in five minutes.' Starr let go of the transmit button, flipped the switch and put the radio back into the pocket of his parka. But instead of rushing down the glacier toward the Palmer station buildings a half mile away, he stood where he was, pointed the flashlight straight ahead and stared at the blue and white sign again.

Huntington Beach. Except now, the population is zero. Just like most Californians, Michael Starr had been born somewhere else – in Carbondale, Illinois, twenty-nine years before. But he had lived in Huntington Beach with his parents for the last twenty years and had watched that area grow enormously. Huntington Beach had gone from a casual spot on the southwest side of Los Angeles into an area of wall-to-wall people, cars and fast food restaurants – at least until a few hours ago. Starr had managed to hear enough of the long distance radio signals at their set at the Palmer station to discover what was happening to the world. Now that those incredible radio messages had stopped coming in, Starr was in many ways relieved. He reached up and touched the blue and white sign, but did not allow himself to think about his parents, his neighborhood, his town. He would not allow himself to think about anything.

Michael Starr scanned the radio mast one more time, then he turned and began the downhill jog back to the camp. The path along the glacier paralleled the antenna cable as it snaked from the radio mast to the main building. Starr kept his flashlight on the continuous run of black pipe – the wire itself had been housed inside a plastic pipe to protect it from the elements – but everything appeared to be exactly in the same condition as it always was. By the time he had reached the last icy knoll that would descend another hundred feet to the rocky coastline where the Palmer buildings were, Starr was convinced that their radio problems were definitely not of their making, that something else was preventing the long range radio signals from reaching the Antarctic.

The lights of the main building were on, and they cast long plumes of brightness into the otherwise impenetrable black that surrounded the base. Starr stood his ground for a moment and rubbed his hand along the tight, angular features of his clean-shaven face. As he stood on the ice he allowed a chill to begin in his muscular calves and work its way upward slowly through his entire body, even though the air temperature was relatively mild and the wind was calm. *What could be happening at home? God help them. God help everyone.* From where he stood, it was difficult to believe that most of the world he had known was already dead or dying. For that matter, from where he stood on the edge of the glacier that overlooked the Palmer Antarctic station it was difficult to believe that anyone beyond him and John O'Conner had ever existed – it seemed so easy to believe that the two of them were somehow the only humans to ever inhabit the face of the earth.

Starr looked up into the black sky. A hint of the rising moon was just beginning to make itself apparent at the edge of where Flanders Bay met the Danco Coast, and Starr knew that in another half hour the eerie glow of the rising moon would begin to play along the ridges of snow and ice. The moon would illuminate the nothingness that surrounded Palmer and finally give the scene in front of him some measure of reality. But until that moment, the scene in front of him was a surrealist canvas of the first order, a stoned trip, a far and way-out ride that would easily rival any of those acid highs that Starr had participated in back home with his buddies in LA. *Keep cool, keep cool, don't let it get to you.* Standing on that icy knoll and looking down at the half-dozen metal buildings that were huddled below him in a cramped grouping on the shoreline, Michael Starr felt far more alone and vulnerable than he ever had before in his entire life. The urge to scream out in terror welled up in him, and it was only through an enormous effort of self-control that Starr managed to keep his mouth from dropping open and the primeval scream from pouring out into that soundless night sky. *Keep cool. Don't let it get you.* Starr shivered involuntarily once more, then began to sprint rapidly down the glacier and toward the main building. When he reached the door he quickly opened it.

'What the hell took you so long? Why didn't you answer the radio?' John O'Conner had met Starr at the door and was attempting to sound angry – a trumped-up display to cover his own rising sense of terror. 'I was just getting ready to go out looking for you.'

'Sorry.' Starr shrugged, laid his flashlight and portable radio on a bench near the door, then took off his parka. 'Guess I must've shut the radio off by mistake when I started back. I stood outside a few minutes.'

'For Chrissake, don't do that any more.' O'Conner reached out and swiped his hand against Starr's shoulder, a gesture that was a combination of a friendly touch and a punitive slap. 'You scared me half to death. I don't want to be the only one left here.'

'You're telling me.' Starr fell in step and followed O'Conner into the main living area of the station and, beyond that, down the corridor that led to the radio room. 'Anything else come in on the radio?'

'Sure. Lots of things. Static. An odd word or two. Different languages, most of it completely indecipherable. What little bit I did pick up a while ago was more bad news – cities and whole countries completely destroyed, clouds of nuclear debris floating everywhere.'

'Great.'

'Yeah.'

'Any word from Floyd and the girls?' They had reached the radio room and Starr moved into the far corner, allowing O'Conner to take his customary seat at the control panel.

'No.' O'Conner said nothing else, but his eyes more than gave away his concern. 'Why the hell did they have to be out when this happened? Why don't they answer the radio?'

'Search me.'

'It's one of two things, I figure.'

'What?'

'Either this atmospheric disturbance has disrupted their signal, or something has happened on their end.'

'What do you mean by atmospheric disturbance?'

'I've been doing research while you were gone.' O'Conner rose from his seat and walked across the room toward a work table where he had laid open several books. As he passed a small mirror on the wall – it was actually a Budweiser Beer sign with an oval mirror in the center of it, the company's stylized logo in red plastic letters riding along the top edge – O'Conner caught a glimpse of himself. *You look like shit.* His long hair was wild and oily looking, his eyes were hollow and ringed with dark circles and his beard and mustache were scragglier than ever. *Clean up your act. No wonder you can't think straight.* 'Here's what I found,' O'Conner said as he turned from the mirror and pointed to a book on the table.

'Don't give me the volts and ohms crap, just tell me what it means.'

'Right.' O'Conner tapped his finger against the open page. 'It's pure theory, of course, since we've never had any way to test the concept of what an all-out global nuclear war would do to the earth's atmosphere and the electro-magnetic field . . .'

'Of course.' Starr swayed from side to side nervously. He liked John a great deal, but he always hated his preambles.

'. . . so it's difficult to say with certainty. But small scale research has shown that in addition to the obvious destruction – thermo shock and fireballs, expanding areas of lethal radiation – the earth's electromagnetic field would become completely distorted. Radio waves, especially in the frequency bands of the long range ones, would act differently.'

'How?'

'I don't know. I don't think anyone does.' O'Conner

nodded toward the book on the table, as if he expected that technical journal to stand up and join in on the conversation to support his point. 'But that probably explains why our long range signals have steadily gotten worse. They have gotten worse as more and more bombs were being dropped.'

'Because the electromagnetic field goes more haywire with each bomb?'

'Yeah, that's what I think. Just look at this.' O'Conner turned around to face a world chart mounted above the work table. 'The last messages I received that were of decent quality were scattered – Alaska, Kansas, Canada, Africa, India, Central America. At the same time I was speaking clearly to both the South Pole and McMurdo stations. They reported similar communications patterns.'

'Yes, I remember that.' Starr's voice had perked up at the mention of the two other American bases in the Antarctic – if there was any chance at all of joining up with other people in the immediate future it would be with those groups, even though McMurdo was nearly 2000 miles down the coastline and the South Pole station was about 1500 miles directly inland. There were, as he recalled, about a dozen people wintering-over at McMurdo, half a dozen at the South Pole. 'Did you speak to either McMurdo or the South Pole while I was outside?'

'No, I couldn't raise them again. That's the point. We're being slowly cut off from our long range communications ability – at least in the frequency spectrum of our equipment – because the earth's electromagnetic pattern is being screwed up.'

'I see.' Starr didn't see at all, but he knew enough to trust O'Conner with the radios and electronics just as O'Conner trusted him when it came to the diesel generators and the maintenance of their other moving stock. 'But what about Floyd, Julie and Annie? Their transmitter is a short range one. They're no more than fifty miles away.' Starr glanced at a wall map of Antarctica that was pinned up beside the world chart, then he looked back at O'Conner.

'I don't know. I can't really answer that.' O'Conner sat

himself on the edge of the table and looked back toward the Budweiser sign. From the angle where he sat he could see the reflection of the window on the far side of the radio room. Its image remained impenetrably black, as if there was nothing outside the window at all, as if nothing existed beyond the confines of the room where he and Starr waited. He had volunteered to be part of the team of five who would winter over at the Palmer station primarily because he had wanted to experience a sense of isolation from the world at large, felt that it would be a good opportunity to build character. Now the joke was on him; the world he had intended to walk away from for a few months wouldn't be there when he got back – if any of them ever got back. 'Floyd's had radio trouble, I guess. Maybe something worse.'

'What should we do?'

'Wait a while longer.'

'Then what?'

'Then . . .' O'Conner slid off the edge of the table and walked across the room, his eyes fixed to the radio that was monitoring the channel that Floyd Robinson was supposed to call in on nearly two hours ago. Other than the ambient hum of the electronics, the radio remained silent. 'Then I don't know,' O'Conner finally answered as he eased himself into the chair in front of the radio. He leaned back in the chair and closed his eyes, as if he could somehow make the incredible nightmare that had begun that afternoon disappear as easily as the sight of the silent radio in front of him. 'Maybe we should think about looking for them,' O'Conner said in a low voice.

'It won't be light enough until 9.30 tomorrow morning.'

'That's fifteen hours from now.'

'It's suicide to go out in the dark. I sure as hell can't make the sun come up any faster.'

'I guess you're right.'

'We should take turns at the radio while we each get some sleep. I'll try to lie down now, come and get me in a couple hours.'

'Do you want any dinner?'

'No. For some reason, I seem to have lost my appetite.

I'll grab something later.' Starr touched his friend's shoulder, then turned and walked out the radio room door, down the corridor and toward his bedroom. Even though he had been completely drained by mental and emotional exhaustion, Michael Starr knew that there was no way he would be getting any measure of restful sleep for quite some time. He was going off to be alone in order to think, and in order to cry for all those people he had lost in the last few hours.

Six

'WE'VE DECIDED to do the dinner in two sittings since we've got so many people to feed.' Captain Lou Whitaker climbed into his cockpit seat on *Airship Nine*. Once he had made himself comfortable, he glanced over at the young second officer who sat to his right. 'Since we're going to orbit out here for the night, we might as well get started right now. You go back and help Nancy serve and clear for the first group.'

'Should I eat with them or wait until later?' Steve Galloway kept his hands on the flight controls, even though the autopilot was doing the actual work of keeping the craft on its selected altitude and heading.

'You eat with the first group. I'll grab a bite later.' Whitaker motioned with his hand to indicate that he was officially assuming command of the airship, although he also continued to allow the autopilot to do the actual steering. On top of everything else, Whitaker's experience at lunch that afternoon – tepid lamb stew served over mushy noodles – had been the final salvo that killed his appetite for the dinner meal.

'Is there anything you want me to tell the rest of the crew?'

'Stop in at the radio room to see Weiss. See if he wants dinner sent to him. He intends to stay at the radios.'

'Sure thing. What about Madigan? Should I tell him to eat at the first sitting or the second?'

'Let him suit himself.' Whitaker glanced over his shoulder and caught Galloway's eye for an instant, then turned away. 'Madigan is on the lower level. He's taking inventory of the cargo. Then he's supposed to do an inspection of the engine room.'

'Problems?'

'No. Purely a precautionary check. I felt we should utilize this time to make sure everything is working right.' Whitaker kept his eyes locked on the flight panel in front of him.

'Okay. I'll come back to relieve you when I'm done with my meal.'

'Fine, but there's no rush. I'm not very hungry tonight.' Whitaker continued to busy himself with monitoring the airship's controls and equipment. After a few moments he heard the sound of Galloway's diminishing footsteps as the second officer began to walk down the corridor that led to the rear of *Airship Nine*. When the sound of the footsteps faded away, Whitaker glanced over his shoulder to verify that he was alone.

Madigan is on the lower level. The only thing that Whitaker was pleased about was that his bastard of a copilot was as physically far from him as possible. Whitaker had watched Madigan enter the lower deck of the gondola by going through the floor-mounted hatchway near the kitchen – but not before that bastard had one more quick and hushed conversation with the stewardess. It was a conversation that Whitaker knew had undoubtedly centered around him. *Don't let that bastard get to you. He's no good. He was totally wrong.*

But something inside told Whitaker that First Officer Madigan had been at least partially correct. *Saint Whitaker. Get honest with us. Get honest with yourself.* Whitaker flipped on the readout of the electronic navigation equipment and verified that *Airship Nine* was precisely where it was supposed to be. After that, he ran a quick fuel endurance check to see how many hours at differing power settings he could continue to fly the ship. *Handle me just like you've handled everyone. Just like you handled that boy of yours.* As much as he tried, Lou Whitaker could not get Ray Madigan's accusations out of his mind.

The lights from the aft deck of the Soviet motorship *Primorye* were visible from a distance of at least ten kilometers through the clear night sky and that allowed Major Ilya Zinoviev to steer the Kamov Ka-25 helicopter directly toward it. 'I repeat, the wind is six knots across the bow. The deck is clear,' Zinoviev answered as he pressed his transmit button and spoke to the ship's radio officer. 'We will be landing in two minutes.'

'You didn't say anything about what we saw at Bellingshausen, did you?' Boris Ney leaned slightly to his right so he didn't need to shout as loud to make himself heard over the racket from the twin turbine engines and the double set of whirling rotor blades. Their trip back from the Bellingshausen station to the *Primorye* had been done at a faster speed than the speed out there – but that had necessitated extra engine power and, of course, had added measurably to the cockpit noise level. He and Zinoviev had not spoken more than twenty words to each other since the return flight had begun a half hour before.

'Of course not.' Zinoviev kept his attention on his duties as he manipulated the controls. 'Before we left we agreed that there would be no transmissions except for landing instructions.'

'Right.' Ney waited a moment before he asked his next question. 'Are conditions good for the landing?'

'Everything is fine. That's the ship, straight ahead. We land in two minutes.'

'I see it.' But all Ney could actually see was the ship's white stern light as they headed toward it, since the vessel itself was completely invisible against the black sky and sea. Even the surface of the ocean was no more than a mere promise at the lower end of the altimeter since the sea, too, remained invisible beneath them. 'How can you tell where we're going?'

'Instruments.' Zinoviev nodded toward the panel in front of him.

Ney looked down at the array of needles and dials. Except for one or two of the more elementary ones, he had no idea what any of them meant. 'How high are we flying?'

'What?'

'How far down is the water?' Ney pointed toward the

92

floor of the helicopter to emphasize his point. He guessed that their clearance above the ocean was dependent on the helicopter's altimeter and he wanted to assure himself that there was no possibility of an error. Ney suspected that Zinoviev, like most overly-specialized technocrats, was not especially resourceful or intelligent.

'Far down?' Zinoviev took his eyes off the instrument panel and glanced over at Ney for a brief moment before he realized the intent of the question. He broke into a broad smile and began to laugh, the first time he had done so since they had touched down at the Bellingshausen station an hour earlier.

Ney glared at the man to his right. 'What are you laughing at?' He fidgeted in his flight chair. 'Your eyes are no better than mine. The water is invisible.'

'And damn cold, too.' Zinoviev laughed again, but this time not as long or as loudly as at first. Something in Ney's manner had told him that he had better not. 'I'm willing to trust you to know your scientific business. Why don't you trust me to know mine?' Zinoviev had again faced forward, this time toward the stern light of the *Primorye* which had grown measurably in size and brilliance. The light was nearly to the point where the ship's structure surrounding it would be visible. Everything appeared normal.

'How far down is the water?' Ney asked again, this time in a firm and uncompromising voice. He had no intention of allowing an aerial bus driver – that was all Zinoviev and his gang of army buffoons were, after all was said and done – to get away with verbal jousting at his expense.

'See for yourself.' Zinoviev reached up and flicked on a switch on the control panel. A broam beam of light fanned out beneath the helicopter's nose.

'Fine.' Ney turned slightly to his left and studied the sea beneath them. It appeared to be approximately fifty meters below the helicopter, although it was difficult to say for certain because the water was so calm and clear. If it weren't for a minor cross current of overlapping un-dulations that moved from right to left – slight swells that were probably a result of an ocean disturbance that had traveled for many hundreds of kilometers – Ney saw that it would have been impossible to tell their height by looking straight down into such mirror-like conditions of blue water.

'*Primorye*, we are approaching the stern. Prepare for the touchdown,' Zinoviev transmitted as he pressed the button on the control stick. After he had heard the reply from the ship that everything was still in readiness, Zinoviev turned on the two landing light beams and began to concentrate on the approach and touchdown.

As the groping white beams of the landing lights reached out ahead, they finally made firm contact with the stern of the ship and the flat landing platform mounted above it. The red of the *Primorye*'s hull reflected in the harsh light of the approaching helicopter and gave sudden and vibrant life to a scene that had appeared no more than one dimensional a few moments before. The white paint that covered almost everything on the ship above its red hull also stood out conspicuously, especially against the black surface that the helicopter touchdown pad was made of. The second of the army Kamov Ka-25 helicopters in Major Zinoviev's unit – its brown paint the only odd color on the stern of the ship, its red army star facing them – was parked at the far forward end of the landing pad, still firmly lashed to the landing deck with long stretches of cable.

'There they are.'

'I see them.' Zinoviev recognized Captain Kollontai and Aleksandra Bukharin the instant the helicopter's lights illuminated them where they stood near to one another at the left corner of the landing platform. The captain held his cap in his hand and Aleksandra pressed down on the strands of her long hair while the helicopter generated a substantial breeze that swirled all around them.

'Don't say anything. Not until we're inside.' Ney wanted to capitalize on what he was certain would be the major's ability to convincingly convey the news about what had happened at Bellingshausen – news about what he had seen, what he had been told – but he didn't want to preempt any of its impact by allowing Zinoviev to mouth off too soon.

'I understand.' Zinoviev worked the Ka-25's controls

carefully as he maneuvered the helicopter to a gentle touchdown on precisely its allocated spot. Even before the wheels had fully compressed and the major had begun to shut down the controls and switches, the ground crew had rushed forward and begun the job of securing the helicopter to the deck. By the time the noise from the twin turbine engines had begun to unspool and die away, the door to the helicopter had been opened from the outside. 'Let's go.' Zinoviev took off his flight helmet, unbuckled his shoulder harness and eased himself out of the cockpit.

'Lead the way.' Ney followed quickly, near enough to be able to overhear but not near enough to be a necessary part of the first exchange.

'What's the situation at the station?' Captain Kollontai had asked the question without preamble as he met the major at the door of the helicopter, the Bukharin woman a few steps behind him. Kollontai's voice carried easily above the lessening noises from the slowing rotor blades.

'We have much to talk about.' Zinoviev could see that his ground crew were pretending to work on the cable lashings, but what they were actually doing was listening to his every word. 'But I'll need my notes for reference. We should talk on the bridge where I can read them.'

'Very well.' Captain Kollontai wheeled around and led the way as the procession of four worked its way forward along the starboard quarter of the *Primorye*. He glanced backward once to be certain that the other three members of their *nachalstvo*, their governing council, were still behind him. Seeing that they were, Kollontai continued on in silence. They brushed past countless sailors and civilian personnel who watched them carefully, but none of them said a word. When the group of four finally reached the ship's bridge, Captain Kollontai dismissed the officer on duty with a wave of his hand. After the officer had left the bridge and closed the door behind him – there was no helmsman at the ship's wheel since they were still lying motionless in the water – Kollontai turned back to Zinoviev. 'What was the situation?'

'Very bad. Critical.' Zinoviev took a deep breath, glanced at Ney, then turned back to face the captain.

Aleksandra had quietly moved beside Kollontai so that the major would be speaking to the both of them. 'All the personnel at the Bellingshausen station are dead. The Americans attacked them. Murdered them.'

'What?'

'Are you sure?' To Aleksandra, that type of news would once have been beyond the incredible – as if Zinoviev had reported that people from another galaxy had landed at Bellingshausen while he stood there. But she had learned a few years ago that people would sometimes try to murder one another for hardly any reason at all – she had seen countless examples of exactly that sort of behavior in her two years as resident doctor at the Slobodskoi prison camp near Kirov – and that had become evidence enough to make her accept almost anything without surprise.

'Yes. I'm sure.' Zinoviev began to tell the story about what he and Ney had seen. He worked his way slowly up to the part about finding the one who was still alive.

'I should have gone with you.' Aleksandra shook her head remorsefully. 'I might have been able to help him. What were his injuries like?'

'It's difficult to say,' Ney answered. It was time now for him to take the lead. 'The man had been smashed up pretty badly. I found a lead pipe near him, it must've been what they used. His shoulder and side were crushed. Hips, too. Maybe his back.' Ney let his words trail off, as if what he was saying were too painful to say out loud.

'Did you try to treat him? Did you use any of the drugs I gave you?'

'I was going to give him that pain killer, but I'm a scientist, not a physician. I was nervous and I dropped the syringe. It broke on the floor. But that didn't make any real difference because he died a minute or two later.'

'And he was in great pain when he died?' Captain Kollontai's voice was calm and matter-of-fact, but his eyes betrayed the fury and turmoil that ran through his soul.

'Yes.' Ney nodded slowly, then turned to Zinoviev and gestured for the major to add more, as if Ney couldn't bare to add any more himself.

'But not before that poor bastard told us what happened.

That's how we knew for sure.' Zinoviev smacked his hands together loudly. The noise echoed around the otherwise silent ship's bridge. 'The Americans are murderers. They attacked an unarmed camp. They massacred everyone. Bastards!'

'Where did they come from?'

Ney stepped forward to answer – the last thing he wanted was for Zinoviev to get too emotional, too carried away. 'One of two places.' Ney pointed to an Antarctic chart that lay across the navigator's table. 'The Americans have one outpost near Bellingshausen, at their Palmer station. As you can see, the distance between their station and Bellingshausen is less than 250 kilometers.'

'And only 150 kilometers from where we are now.'

'Correct.' Ney nodded in agreement with Kollontai's remark, since it was along the lines that he hoped to steer them. 'The American Palmer station is well within our range. That means we'll be able to do something about this situation.'

'Where's the other place that the Americans could have come from?' Kollontai spoke without taking his eyes off the Antarctic chart in front of him.

'Their McMurdo station. It's a much bigger facility, but on the other hand it's nearly 2500 kilometers from Bellingshausen.'

'I see. But that would take a much bigger operation on their part – aircraft or helicopters, probably with support ships. Did you see any indications of that much activity?'

'None.'

'Then they must have come from Palmer. Nothing else makes sense.'

'That's a good point, I think you're right.' Ney was happy to give whatever credit was necessary, just so he could get all of them to ultimately agree with the plan in the back of his mind. 'We should probably operate on the premise that the actions against Bellingshausen were launched from the American Palmer station. As you said, that's the only logical choice.'

'But what are you proposing?' Aleksandra had attempted to sound neutral, but her words had come out

97

harsher than she had expected. She was a young doctor dedicated to saving lives, and she knew too well the sort of action that Ney would think was best.

'They were the first to attack. I think it's obvious that we must retaliate.'

'To what purpose? To eliminate a few more of what might be the world's only survivors? We haven't had a chance to tell you about the additional messages we've received.' Aleksandra gestured expansively toward both Ney and Zinoviev. 'And there's another thing you don't know yet – you don't know about the studies your own people have done while you were gone.'

'Messages? Studies?' Ney eyed Aleksandra carefully – he didn't like the idea that she had been talking to anyone in his group without him being around, but there was nothing he could say about that for the time being. 'What have they learned?'

'Simply this.' Aleksandra retrieved a sheaf of papers that lay on a cabinet at the rear of the bridge. She handed them to Ney. 'Our long range communications are nearly in total disarray, although we did manage to get a few more messages in – messages which are in the stack I just gave you. Every message, regardless of where in the world it came from, spoke of enormous clouds of radioactive debris, of nearly total failure of their electrical equipment.'

'We should expect much of that sort of thing.'

'But many of those places were far from the fighting, far from what we expected would be the limits of the areas of danger. Those people are sending out messages to the effect that they're receiving radiation far in excess of a lethal dose.'

'None of that means . . .'

'Let her finish.' Captain Kollontai raised his hand until Ney stopped talking. Then Kollontai began to speak himself. 'In many ways we're fortunate to have some of the best scientific minds in the Soviet Union on board this ship. What they've done while you were gone was to analyze the situation and come to the conclusion – it was a unanimous conclusion – that the radiation situation is far beyond what any of the global war scenarios had calculated. They tell me that the disarray of communications is another measure of how bad things are, of how severely the earth's electromagnetic patterns have been altered.'

'Did they say anything about the ozone layer?' Ney had phrased his remark as a question but his intent was to show them that he, too, understood the peculiarities of nuclear war.

'Yes, they did.' Kollontai took the stack of papers back from Ney and shuffled through them. 'Here it is.' He handed the single sheet to Ney, who took it and began to look it over. Kollontai allowed the chief scientist a few moments to read through the paper before he spoke again. 'As you can see, your atmospheric specialists have calculated that the layer of ozone in the upper regions has been critically reduced.'

'Yes. And I agree that the ozone condition would certainly be at its worst in the Northern Hemisphere. With more ocean areas and fewer of the major political powers on this end of the globe, there was bound to be less effect on the ozone layers further south.'

'Wait.' Zinoviev stepped forward. He took the paper from Ney's hand but didn't bother to give it more than a cursory glance. 'You'll have to explain what this ozone layer means. It sounds strategically important. I don't need to remind you that very few humans are further south than we are at this moment. If our location becomes an important consideration, we all need to understand exactly what kind of advantage that might translate into.'

'An excellent point, major.' Ney dabbed a small bead of perspiration from his forehead, then shoved the handkerchief into his pocket. 'Let me explain.'

'Yes.'

'From what I've seen on these papers from our scientific people, every yardstick has convinced them that enough nuclear energy has been released into the atmosphere to totally annihilate nearly every living creature on the face of the earth.'

'That's impossible.'

'Unfortunately, no.' Ney frowned, then continued. He didn't know for certain how much of what he was about to say would be true – a portion, perhaps, since it all made a morbid sort of sense – but he quickly saw how nicely it would fit into his own master plan. Just as Lenin and Stalin had done, it was necessary for him to have a fixed base for his power to develop from. Then he could move on from there. That meant that he needed to convince this *nachalstvo*, this governing council, that all the survivors in the Antarctic should be consolidated at a single point. Once they had been, Ney would then make his bid for total control of the entire group.

'Then what's going to make our fate any different?' Kollontai looked at Aleksandra for a brief moment before he turned abruptly away to face Ney again. 'How are we going to be saved from what's happened everywhere else? Are we wasting our time with this kind of talk?'

'No.' Ney walked partway across the *Primorye*'s bridge, to a spot near the radar controls where he could be more on stage for the three of them. 'The first cause of massive death in a thermonuclear confrontation comes from the direct effects of the blasts themselves.'

'Obviously.' Kollontai waved his hand in annoyance; he certainly didn't need to be reminded that any living crea-ture within the zone of an actual nuclear explosion – as his family had been by living just outside the Severomorsk naval base – would have been instantly vaporized. 'But we're talking about a great deal more death than what could've been caused by even thousands of direct ex-plosions. That's your point, isn't it?'

'Correct.' Ney brushed his hand nervously against his beard, then began with his presentation again. 'The nuclear clouds of radiation and debris, particularly from the more archaic weapons used by the second and third level world powers, are certain to be joining up and sweeping across much of the globe as they follow the patterns of general atmospheric circulation. They will blanket most of the Northern Hemi-sphere and much of the south very shortly.'

'And us?' Aleksandra winced at the thought that a cloud of poisonous nuclear debris was somewhere just over the far horizon and headed their way – like a swarm of locusts about to descend and devour the last of what was left.

'The nuclear debris might get this far, it's conceivable.' Ney stood silently as he waited for someone to ask the next question, the obvious question.

'Are you saying that there's somewhere else we should be?' Zinoviev glanced out at the blackness that surrounded the bridge of the *Primorye*. 'Is there a safer spot than where we have the ship right now?'

'Yes.' Ney stepped over to the Antarctic chart on the navigator's table and motioned for the other three to join him. When they had all gathered around, he began by laying his hand on the center of the chart. 'Here. This is undoubtedly the safest spot on earth, simply because it's the furthest from the holocaust in the north and the resulting patterns of radioactive debris. It's also the spot that would be furthest from the major effects of the depletion of the earth's ozone layer.'

'What are you pointing at?' Aleksandra peered over Ney's shoulder but couldn't quite read the chart symbols where he had laid his hand.

'The American station at the South Pole.'

'Damn.' Zinoviev edged forward to scan the chart more closely.

'I can see that the major understands our predicament.' Ney waited in silence while everyone studied the chart.

'Then what you're telling us is that the Americans have a clear advantage – that they've got control of the best spot on earth in terms of ultimate survival.' Kollontai shook his head, all of this had been an incredible, nonstop barrage of insanity from the very beginnings of the first message from Moscow – and now this. For a brief instant Kollontai felt a profound regret that he, too, hadn't been sitting in his house on Ryjzy Prospect beside his wife and daughter, that he hadn't had his problems solved for him as quickly and as painlessly as he hoped they had.

'Yes. The Americans have the best spot.' Ney pointed to various locations on the chart as he began to lecture the group again. 'Remember that we're about to start the winter season down here in just a few weeks – that'll effect the wind and weather patterns drastically. The entire Antarctic region will be climatically isolated from the rest of the world by the dome of frigid air that sits above it for the next few months. Add to that the deadly effects of the lack of a suitable ozone layer most everywhere else on the planet, and I think you can see the outcome for anyone but the few who are inland in Antarctica.'

'What about the Bellingshausen station? Couldn't we dock near to it and still be safe?' As he spoke, Captain Kollontai studied the chart to see what kind of anchorage he could find near Bellingshausen when the expanding icefloes were taken into consideration.

'Not very likely. It's too far from the Antarctic plateau to get any advantage from the wind coming down the slope. That steady downslope wind will help to keep the nuclear debris away. I also think that the entire Antarctic Peninsula is far too close to the hostilities in South America to avoid being contaminated by radioactive fallout.' Ney passed his hand over that end of the chart and swept his fingers across the blank spot that represented the 800 kilometers in distance between the northernmost edge of the Antarctic and Cape Horn at the tip of South America.

'But you still haven't explained what you mean by the ozone layer.' Aleksandra had moved beside Captain Kollontai while she spoke to Ney – an action on her part that she quickly realized was exactly the way she felt toward the men in the room. She and Kollontai represented one point of view, Ney and Major Zinoviev the complete opposite.

'Sorry, you're right.' Ney picked up a pencil and made a quick sketch on the back of one of the teletype messages while he spoke. 'The best study on the thermonuclear effects on the ozone layer was done by the Americans in 1975. As I remember, their postulations were based on far fewer bombs being dropped than what we think actually were.'

'So the actual conditions will probably be worse.' Zinoviev didn't bother to look up as he spoke, he continued to study the terrain features for the interior regions of the Antarctic.

'Probably. But even assuming the Americans' figures, they had calculated that three-quarters of the earth's ozone in the Northern Hemisphere would have been destroyed, and nearly fifty per cent of the ozone in the south. As I'm sure you probably remember, ozone is crucial to life on earth because it shields the planet from lethal levels of ultraviolet radiation from the sun. The point of their study was that nothing could survive any direct contact with the sun for any period of time once the ozone layer had been depleted.'

'How long would it take for this ozone layer to be built back to a safe level?'

'Difficult to say. It could take as much as five years for the worst areas in the north to be safe again.'

'Five years!' Kollontai shook his head.

'Yes, but that's for total recovery of the worst areas. A year or two for most regions would be enough – even less down here.'

'I see.' Kollontai nodded, then looked down at the crude sketch that Ney had drawn and laid in front of him. 'What does this represent?'

'The changing angle between the sun and the earth.' Ney pointed to the paper where a series of circles and lines showed a progressive change.

'Is this the pattern for the next few months?'

'Yes. Notice that the South Polar region has two distinct advantages as far as this ozone layer depletion is concerned.' Like a good salesman, Ney paused for a moment to allow his audience to catch up with him. 'The first is, of course, that the ozone layer directly above the South Pole would be least affected and would thereby provide the maximum protection. The second is that . . .'

'The second is that the South Pole is about to enter into nearly total darkness for half a year.' Aleksandra surprised herself by speaking her thoughts out loud, but the conclusion was obvious from Ney's sketch. 'And by the time the sun comes back up again next spring, the ozone layer will probably have recovered some.'

'Yes. Exactly.'

'So what are our choices?' Kollontai backed away from the chart and looked out across the bow. Beyond the floodlights that played across the anchor winches and rolls of cable on the front edge of the ship, there was nothing.

Serene and total blackness. Immense and total death.

'We've got more than one hundred people with us whose lives will soon depend on getting them further inland. We don't have time enough to set up a base of our own, so our only chance is to occupy something that already exists.'

'The American station at the South Pole?'

'Precisely.' Ney wanted to quickly add more, but an inner sense – the sense of *Vozhd*, of a great leader – told him to let the others play up to him rather than vice-versa. Ney waited.

'And from what I've seen of the Americans, I can't imagine that they'll allow us to simply show up at their front door.' Major Zinoviev spoke without taking his eyes off the Antarctic chart, which he had already begun to study for the battle tactics that he was certain he would soon need.

'Probably not, but I think we should try to work some-thing out with them first.' Captain Kollontai motioned wearily for the group to follow him as he stepped toward the door at the rear of the bridge. 'Let's go to my cabin where we can sit down and talk this over. We can't afford to do anything hasty, to do anything without first giving it a great deal of thought.'

'I agree with the captain.' Aleksandra stepped alongside of him. 'Please, let's try to avoid any more war and death. We've all seen enough of that already.'

'You're right, of course.' Boris Ney followed the three of them as they stepped out of the bridge and into the short corridor that led to the captain's quarters. 'But I wonder if the Americans will listen to reason.'

'They've got to.'

'Not necessarily.' Before they had even reached the entrance to the captain's stateroom, Ney had come up with a plan for eliminating those few Americans who still remained in the Antarctic region. Boris Ney suspected that without the Americans around to complicate matters, he would quickly become the only natural choice to be leader of their group – to be leader of a group that could easily become the last of the world's survivors.

Seven

JULIE MATHEWS quietly stepped into the rear of *Airship Nine*'s cockpit. At the moment there was only one pilot up front, the young second officer who had been introduced to her earlier as Steve Galloway. He sat in the right side pilot's seat as if he were in a trance, his hands laying inertly on the ship's controls, his eyes locked straight ahead. 'It's pretty quiet up here,' Julie said in order to break the silence.

'Yes, sure is.' Galloway answered without turning around. He was aware of the woman's presence because he had seen her reflection in the glass face of the radar screen mounted in front of him. 'There's not much to do. All I have to do is keep us on station.'

'Exactly where are we?' Julie leaned forward to look out the cockpit window. As she did, her long blonde hair brushed against the young pilot's shoulder. 'I don't see anything.' Outside, the sky had turned an impenetrable black.

'There's nothing to see.' Galloway turned slightly in order to face her, just as glad not to be thinking over the same things – his parents, his friends, his home in Nebraska. 'We're hovering over the ocean about three miles from the shore where we picked you up. Like Captain Whitaker said, it's dangerous to try to go anywhere inland now that it's turned dark. I'm using just enough engine power to keep our position steady in the wind.'

'Oh.'

'Like the captain said, we're going to head for your base at first light to join up with the two men you left there. What was the name of your base?'

'Palmer station. Mike and John will certainly be surprised when we show up in a blimp.'

'Shocked is a better word.' Galloway looked at the woman – she was very pretty, but up close you could see that she wasn't particularly young. Her hands gave away her age, as did the few lines around her face. 'I understand that you work for a university.'

'That's right. UCLA at Los Angeles. The biology department.'

'How long have you been with them?'

'A few years.' *Too many years. I should've stopped it a long time ago.* 'I help with their research projects. You get sort of focused in on a specific topic and the next thing you know you're doing all sorts of weird things.'

'I see. What was your topic?'

'It wasn't mine. Like I said, my job was to help other people.'

'One of the men back at Palmer?'

'No.' That single word had come out more emphatically than Julie had wanted it to. 'Animal behavior in extreme conditions of cold climate. That was the current paper we were working on.'

'Penguins?'

'Mostly.'

'Do you need to be with a university for a long time to get these kind of trips?'

'Yes,' Julie said as she correctly guessed what he was thinking about. She had seen that look a million times from countless undergraduates. 'But this type of field trip is usually more a matter of . . . who you . . . know.' She gently tapped her fingers against the airship's wall panel. 'I guess I knew the right person.' Julie smiled weakly, then looked again at the blackness outside.

'I guess you must have.' Galloway blushed for a moment after he realized from her tone that he had obviously asked a sensitive question. He had only intended to make conversation. 'What about their radio receiver at Palmer?' Galloway wanted to change the subject. 'Is there any chance we'll be able to contact them tonight?'

'Not according to your radio man. We've already asked, because Floyd dropped our portable transmitter as he was coming up the ladder.'

'I was watching him – he was lucky he didn't fall himself.'

106

'Yes, he was. Anyway, your equipment doesn't work on our frequency.'

'Too bad.'

'Yes.' After a few moments of silence, Julie began to look around the airship's cockpit again. She motioned toward the empty captain's flight chair to the left of where the copilot sat. 'Would you mind if I sit in the other pilot's seat?'

'Go ahead.'

Julie slid into the seat gingerly, careful not to touch any of the controls around her. California. UCLA. All of it was gone forever. So were all the people she had known. *Richard is dead. Richard's wife is dead. Richard's children are dead. Accept it, there's nothing else you can do.* 'Where are you from?' Julie asked.

'Nebraska. Omaha. How about you?'

'I've been living in California for so many years that sometimes I forget that I was born in Philadelphia.'

'I see. That's the city of brotherly love, right?'

'That's what they call it.'

'I wonder what the Chamber of Commerce thinks about its brothers now?' Galloway fumbled with one of the knobs on the autopilot control panel, more out of a sense of frustration than for any real purpose. After the briefing that the captain had given to this woman and the two others they had picked up from the beach, after all the talk at dinner and all the plans they had gone over at the group meeting afterward, there was nothing left to say. It was strange that, no matter how hard a person tried, any kind of normal conversation invariably led back to the past. It led back to something that no longer existed. Nebraska. California. 'Christ, I wish to hell that I knew what to talk about that wouldn't remind me of home.'

'Me, too.' Julie shook her head in sympathy with the young pilot. He suddenly looked even younger to her. 'I suppose that we're lucky. We've at least still got a chance. None of them did.' *I hope Richard was home with his wife. I hope they were all asleep when the bombs hit.*

'I suppose.' Galloway turned away from her because he could feel another set of tears as they began to well up inside him. 'I need to take another position fix,' he said in a choked voice as he hurried to busy himself with one of the technical jobs the captain had assigned to him. Galloway knew that the only way he could deal with his own emotions was to hide from them by staying totally immersed in his work.

'Sure thing. I'll talk to you later.' Julie took the clue, rose from the pilot's seat and eased herself out of the cockpit. On her way out she put her hand on Galloway's shoulder. He didn't turn around and she didn't want him to. The two of them stood there for a full minute, his hand on the navigation controls in front of him and her hand resting gently on his shoulder. Both of them continued to face the blackness of the cockpit windows and neither said a word. After a while, Julie slowly slid her hand off his shoulder and moved a few feet further aft.

The slow, wallowing flight of the airship was hardly discernible in a calm night sky where nothing beyond a few stars could be seen, but a slight amount of the craft's motion could still be detected. The movements of the machine seemed docile and friendly – like the slow rocking of a baby's cradle. There was no jumpiness, no bouncing, only a pleasant and methodical rhythm. This was, Julie realized, a very pleasant way to travel. *Richard would've liked this. Richard would've . . .* Julie abruptly stopped her thoughts in mid-sentence, before they had a chance to get away from her again. She whirled around and began to walk down the seventy-foot corridor toward the lounge area at the aft end of the airship. As she approached the lounge she could see that most of the others – apparently everyone but Captain Whitaker and the radio operator David Weiss – were in the lounge. They were having some kind of meeting.

'The world has come to an end, and you want to watch a movie?' Andrew Sinclair stood at the entrance to the lounge, his hands on his hips, as he glared down at the bearded heavy-set man in the center of the room.

'Wrong, Andy. What I want most to do is wake up and find out that it's all been a bad dream, that it's all been a bit of undigested cheese – right, Jacob Marley?' Frank Corbi waited to see if Sinclair was going to pick up the book-and-movie reference. After a few seconds of strained silence it was obvious that Sinclair wasn't. 'Okay, Tiny Tim, let me put it to you another way.'

'What the hell are you talking about?'

'Forget it. My point is that it's now nearly midnight and we've been hashing over this end-of-the-world scenario for the last seven hours.' Corbi pointed to his wristwatch, as if he needed it to prove his point. 'I think we've just about said it all, based on what we know so far. There's sure as hell nothing else we can do, nothing else tonight. How about the rest of you? Do you agree?'

'I can tell you quite candidly that I'm in definite agreement.' Doctor Everett Tucker leaned back in the corner lounge chair, pulled out his pipe and began to stoke it. 'Our plans are made. We can't make a safe move toward the Palmer station until first light in any event.'

'And we're all getting tired. Too tired to think clearly.' Floyd Robinson watched Tucker with his pipe and responded automatically by reaching into his pocket for his own pack of cigarettes. He had three left. He took one out, put it in his mouth and quickly lit it. 'If I don't find a way to get onto something else before I run out of cigarettes, I guarantee you that I'm going to be in big trouble.' Robinson made his statement as a joke, but deep down he suspected that there was at least an element of truth to it.

'And I sure as shit can't sleep.' Annie Rizzo hadn't meant to say what she did, but as she glanced around the group she realized that no one had noticed her language – no one except perhaps that young Sinclair guy. He was frowning his disapproval. 'What I mean,' Annie added, 'is that I need some way to unwind. That briefing we got a few hours ago is a tough act to come down from.'

'So then maybe a movie isn't such a bad idea?' Corbi moved toward the rear of the lounge without waiting for their answer because he could read it in their eyes. 'We can set the movie up to run continuously – my video equipment can do that.'

'I like that idea,' Ray Madigan announced as he asserted his authority. He knew that his status as the airship's first officer carried all the weight necessary to end the argument. 'Is there anything you need?'

'Only a place to plug in. To charge the batteries.'

'I'll set that up.'

'Fine. But like I said, I don't have any selection. Exactly one movie, to be precise. I brought this particular movie along because I needed to review some of its scenes. We were going to work some of those visual concepts into the project I was doing in Australia.'

'I'm almost afraid to ask. What is it?'

Corbi ignored Madigan's direct question. 'I was going to do something along the lines of what Woody Allen did in *Play it Again, Sam*. Pieces of the old movie set against the storyline of the new movie that I was intending to shoot in Australia.'

'I don't remember seeing a Woody Allen picture by that name.'

'Well, you'll probably remember having seen this one.' Corbi held the video tape up in his hand. 'A 1942 classic. Humphrey Bogart and Ingrid Bergman. *Casablanca*.'

'Oh, no!'

'Please, Andrew, it'll be fun!' Kathleen Sinclair flushed with embarrassment when her husband glared at her.

Sinclair folded his arms across his chest and looked first at his wife, then the rest of the group as he took the obvious verbal shot that was too tempting for him to resist. 'It's a little strange to consider having fun while the world is dying.'

Corbi brushed past Sinclair and began to set up his equipment. 'Since there's not a damned thing we can do about it, we should try to have a little fun if we can.'

'I can make coffee. Snacks.' Nancy Schneider glanced over at Ray Madigan and, seeing that she had gained his approval, beamed with a broad smile. 'I'll leave the kitchen open. Everyone can come and go as they like. When you get tired, go into one of the cabins to get some sleep.'

'Since we're going to leave it on, I won't bother to rewind the tape – it'll start wherever it's sitting. You've all probably seen *Casablanca* anyway.' Corbi hunched down and worked on his machine for a few more moments so that the portable camera and playback machine with its six-inch black and white monitor was mounted on a table that commanded the best view from most of the seats in the lounge. 'Here we go.'

Corbi pressed the appropriate buttons and the screen filled with a clear image of Humphrey Bogart sitting alone at a table in a dark cafe, a half-empty bottle in front of him. The actor's eyes were bleary, his expression unmistakably sad, and his head drooped low in the universal gesture of a man who has been emotionally drained. Bogart fumbled with a glass, drained it again in one long swallow, then quickly poured himself another. He was staring straight ahead but seeing nothing. Dooley Wilson, the piano player, entered the rear of the cafe and, seeing his boss at a table in the darkness, walked toward him. Wilson was obviously concerned about Bogart, obviously sympathetic. The two of them talked. Wilson sat in front of the piano and began to play a soft, random melody.

'This is where everyone thinks Bogart says "Play it again, Sam",' Corbi announced to the group. 'But he never does.'

'Be quiet so we can hear,' Sinclair said, even though he wasn't bothering to watch the movie himself.

Dooley Wilson began to play *As Time Goes By* as the scene on the small TV did a slow dissolve into Bogart's remembrance of Paris the way it was, of the way it had been with *her*.

The radio room in *Airship Nine* had one small window on its port sidewall, but the view was of absolutely nothing, as if someone had pulled a black velvet curtain down on the outside. David Weiss turned away from the window and looked at Captain Whitaker, seated on the edge of David's bunk on the far wall. Whitaker's long legs stretched out in front of him and nearly touched the legs of the chair where Weiss had stationed himself for the last several hours in front of his radio gear.

'Let me make myself clear on this,' Whitaker said in a calm, low voice. He wanted to be as supportive to Weiss as he could in order to give the young man a firm set of ground rules to operate from. 'My intention isn't to deceive anyone. I just don't see any need to give all of them every hideous detail that comes in.' Whitaker pointed to the radio set and teletype printer with disdain, as if the gear itself were responsible for the news that it continued to provide.

'I guess you're right.' Weiss ran his sweat-soaked fingers through his hair. 'It's pretty horrible. I can't believe some of this stuff.' Weiss glanced down at the stack of messages that lay in the wire basket on his desk.

'I know it's worse for you because you know most of those guys.' Whitaker allowed the silence to hang between the two of them for a moment before he went on. 'If anyone else in the crew knew how to operate your equipment I'd have them take on the job for a while to give you a break. But like you said, conditions are erratic enough to require an experienced radio operator. That narrows it down. Strictly to you.'

'Right.' Weiss shook his head in reluctant agreement. 'I don't mind,' he lied. Weiss glanced down at the wire basket and his eyes locked on the last of the messages he had managed to receive before another burst of atmospheric disturbance had succeeded in silencing the few incoming signals on their company frequency. It was from Paul Gordon on *Airship Three*. Gordon had reported that they had been westbound over Nova Scotia when Montreal went up, and they had been caught inside the thick of the spreading nuclear debris within a few hours. *Radiation sickness. Bleeding from nose, ears, intestines. Vomiting blood. Much pain. All on board in same condition. Now unable even to stand. Can hardly focus on keyboard. Please, God, let me die.*

'Let's get rid of these.' Whitaker had sat silently and watched as Weiss read over the message laying on the top of the wire basket, and it was obvious within a few seconds that Weiss was reacting badly to it. 'Give me that stack – there's nothing there that'll help us in any way. There's no sense in keeping it. I'll burn them.' Whitaker surprised himself by sounding angry, although he didn't exactly know who he was mad at or why.

'No.' Weiss stood up and took the top message, the one from Paul, off the pile. He held it in his trembling hand.

112

'We should keep them, all of them. You never know, we might need them.' Weiss pulled the printed message from *Airship Three* closer to his body. The corner of the teletype paper rubbed back and forth across his shirt where the steady flow of his perspiration had thoroughly soaked and stained it. The dark splotch had grown measurably over the last thirty minutes.

'I don't know.' Whitaker stood up. He didn't want to cause a confrontation with Weiss over the papers, but it was obvious that the young radio operator had been shook up pretty badly. Whitaker didn't know what to say next. 'Who's the radio operator on *Airship Three*?'

'Paul Gordon.'

'Friend of yours?'

'Yes.' Weiss said nothing further, but all he could think about was the last time he had seen Paul, those two days in London when Paul had taken him to that whore. That girl – David couldn't think of her any other way than just another girl, she was no more than nineteen or twenty – had been very nice. *David, are you having a good time?* she had kept asking him. All the while Paul waited outside until the two of them were done. *Your friend really likes you* she had said, just before they walked down the steps to meet Paul. The girl had refused any money from him, and Paul wouldn't discuss the matter. *It's all been taken care of. I'm glad you enjoyed it*. He and Paul then went to dinner and a movie, some incomprehensible French film about two nearly-divorced couples riding on a train. Paul had allowed him to pay for at least that part of their evening.

'Okay, but listen to me – I want you to relax.' Whitaker patted Weiss on the arm in a calming gesture. 'We all feel the same way. There's nothing we can do for them. Don't let it get to you.'

'Right.' Weiss blinked several times, his eyes on the verge of tears. Somehow he managed to hold his tears back.

'Okay. Just relax.' Whitaker turned and started to leave. Just before he reached the door he turned back. 'I want you to get some sleep. Unwind. Maybe you should join the rest of us. Maybe you should have a drink or something. It'll help you.'

'Maybe.' *I'll never be able to sleep, not now. Paul is dying. The girl in London is already dead. I can't remember her name.* 'Don't worry about me, I'll be okay. Like you said, I'll try to lay down. I'll get a few hours' sleep. It'll probably be a few hours before atmospheric conditions make radio contact possible again anyway.'

'Okay. Fine.' Captain Whitaker hesitated at the door for another moment. Finally, against his better judgment, he opened the door and left.

David Weiss sat back down at his desk. He laid the message from Paul Gordon on the table in front of him, face up, and began to study every word. *Please, God, let me die . . . bleeding from nose, ear, intestines . . . Please, God, let me die . . .* The next time Weiss looked up at the digital clock on his panel, he saw that nearly one hour had elapsed since the captain had left the room.

Weiss' eyes were heavy with fatigue, yet when he closed them his head seemed to spin in wide and concentric circles. It was, he knew, strictly a result of the emotions that raced through his mind, emotions that seemed to go in every direction at once. He laid his head into his hands and tried rubbing his temples, but that only seemed to make the frantic commotions inside his skull even worse. David, who had always been a sensitive and solitary person, had allowed his friendship with Paul Gordon to become indispensable to him. David loved Paul Gordon.

Need something. Can't put if off any more. Even though he didn't want to, David Weiss watched his hand reach for the desk drawer. His fingers opened the drawer and shuffled quickly through the stack of papers until they reached the deepest corner. Weiss wrapped his fingers around the plastic vial that contained the powerful sedatives he had picked up on the back streets of Barcelona during his first tour of duty nearly a year before. Weiss pulled the vial out and held it up in front of him.

I promised. But this is different. His fingers fumbled with the plastic cap on the vial until it finally popped off. Weiss had allowed himself to buy the drugs after he had convinced himself that he would use them only sparingly – and only when he was off duty and off the airship. The small

114

yellowish-colored pills – he didn't know what they were called, and he didn't really care – had calmed him down and made him able to do things socially with other members of the crew. The pills had even allowed him to meet strangers, to have a good time. If it wasn't for the pills, he never would've been able to go into London with Paul to meet that girl – the first girl, the only girl he had ever been to bed with. He knew damned well that he just wouldn't have had the nerve without the help of one of those pills.

Weiss turned the open vial over and dumped the pills that remained onto his desk. There were eleven of them left. With his hand shaking so much that it took him several seconds to get one of the tiny pills firmly between his fingers, he put first one and then quickly one more into his mouth and swallowed it. He had never taken more than one at a time before, but he had never experienced such an intense feeling of total disarray, loneliness, despair inside his head before, either. Weiss laid his head down on the desk and listened to his own heartbeat as it marked the moments until the pills would finally take effect and enable him to think clearly again, to stop himself from feeling on the verge of hysteria, of having his skull split itself open from the inside.

It was the soft clicking of the teletype that caused Weiss to finally pick his head up. He looked over at the highspeed printer and watched the paper crawl up and out of it with yet another message. Although he didn't want to, Weiss couldn't stop his eyes from reading the cold and black words that were etched into the scroll of white paper.

LAST ONE ALIVE ON AIRSHIP THREE. HAVE FOUND CAPTAIN'S PISTOL. NO CHOICE. GOD FORGIVE ME. SIGNED GORDON.

Weiss ripped the message off the printer. He looked at it for one more moment, then pressed it up against his heaving chest as the deep sobs from his mounting hysteria began to take control of him. Before he even realized it, David Weiss was crying uncontrollably, the tears flowing freely down his face. *Get hold of yourself. You've got to stop.* But Weiss' rational thoughts were no more than a fragile dam set against the flood of emotions that were churning through him.

Weiss suddenly flung the crumpled teletype message that he had held against his chest across the room. Before any conscious thoughts could prevent him, he scooped up a half dozen of the yellowish-white pills from his desk. The pills were the only thing that helped him, the only chance he had to stop himself from losing control, to stop himself from going totally crazy, to stop his head from exploding from the inside. Weiss shoved the handful of pills into his mouth and swallowed them. *Paul . . . No . . . Don't die . . . Please . . . No . . . Don't leave me . . .*

Weiss laid his head on the table for what seemed like less than a minute but was actually more than ten. He finally picked his head up and that motion caused a shiver to run through him. In its aftermath, David Weiss seemed more settled to himself than he had a moment earlier. *Paul . . . The two of us again . . .*

Weiss stood up from the chair at his desk. His legs were wobbly and his vision seemed narrow and blurred, but the pressures inside his skull had definitely lessened. *Calming down . . . Paul, I'm calming down . . .* Weiss staggered across the room until his shins bumped into the edge of his bunk. He allowed himself to crumble slowly onto the bed, his body sprawled at an odd angle across it, his legs stretched toward the desk that he had sat at a short while before. *Paul, I'm calming down . . .*

Weiss attempted to open his eyes but found that he couldn't. In a short while he lost any further desire to try. The thoughts that flowed through his head were now no more than disjointed and subdued fragments as the chemical overdose in his system began to take its irrevocable toll. As quickly as his bloodstream could deliver it, the ingredients in the yellowish-white pills began to cause his bodily functions to slow down. His brain cells were being systematically eradicated at a pace that was too rapid for his bodily safeguards to prevent. *Paul . . . Two . . . Us . . .*

Fifteen minutes later, David Weiss slipped over the thin line between life and death.

Eight

WITH HIS hand resting on the wooden rail outside the Palmer station door, John O'Conner watched as his friend rode over the first rise of the glacier on his snowmobile and disappeared from view. The diffused glow from the morning sun was along the Danco coastline to the east, its presence suitably obscured by the clouds that had moved in during the night. O'Conner glanced at his wristwatch. Nine twenty-two. By ten-thirty his friend Michael Starr would be on the far side of Anvers Island and, if radio communications weren't established with Floyd and the girls by then, the plan was for Michael to use one of the motorboats on the east beach and head for Snow Island.

O'Conner took a few deep breaths. The air was still warm, but the direction and strength of the wind told him that bad weather was not far away. He looked up at the sky again. The clouds to the west were heavier and lower than the ones to the east, which further confirmed his guess on the weather. They had no more than eight hours to get Floyd and the girls back to Palmer before this new weather system arrived in full force.

Try the radio once more, then shave and shower. O'Conner stepped back inside the building, its stale odors overwhelming him as soon as he opened the door. *We've got to clean this place up. If we keep living like animals, then we'll start thinking like animals.* O'Conner went directly to the radio room.

The main radio was still on, as it had been all night. O'Conner sat down at the console and began to methodically turn the dials and flip the appropriate switches. Still, all he could get out of the equipment was irritating static. They had been totally out of touch with all stations since that last signal from South Africa had come in – Johannes-

117

burg and Cape Town gone, the area between them in flames, most of the population already dead – at three in the morning, nearly seven hours before.

O'Conner swiveled his chair to the left and began to toy with a second receiver, the one he expected to hear from Floyd and the girls on. This was also the radio that Michael Starr would call in on once every hour. O'Conner glanced at the clock. 9.57. Michael wasn't expected to send his first message until 10.30. Their agreement was that he would check in every sixty minutes after that. Reluctantly, they had both agreed that it would be best if Michael kept his receiver off at other times, in order to conserve its power. O'Conner didn't like the idea of not being able to talk to Michael whenever he wanted, but he also knew that the temptation would be too strong to keep Michael on the radio constantly.

O'Conner put his hands up against his face and ran his chewed-up fingernails roughly through his scraggly beard. *I need a shave and shower. It'll clear my head.* O'Conner rose slowly from his swivel chair, his muscles sore from sitting, his body drained. He had gotten, at the most, two hours of sleep the night before. Even after Michael had taken over in the radio room, O'Conner could hardly quiet his thoughts enough to let his eyes close. Yet lying in his bunk had been something of a relief, just like a shave and a shower right now would have been. *Time to clean up my act. It'll help me think straight.*

He had gotten as far as the corridor when O'Conner heard the first sound, a high-pitched whistling that he subconsciously dismissed as nothing but the wind. Within a few moments he realized that the noise had increased. It had become far louder, far more distinctive. It was a pulsing, mechanical sound. A throbbing noise mixed with a background of whirling, swishing air. An engine. Rapidly slewing blades. *Helicopter – it's a Goddamn helicopter!* With a response of unbridled amazement, John O'Conner reversed his direction and rushed headlong down the corridor that led to the door outside.

*

'Then you're certain there was no hope for Irkutsk?' Lieutenant Viktor Chemiakin glanced over from the co-pilot's seat of the Kamov Ka-25 helicopter. He looked first at the major who sat in the pilot's seat, then at the civilian scientist who stood in the aisle between them.

'Can't tell for sure,' Major Ilya Zinoviev shouted back as he continued to concentrate on his flying. They were leaving the open sea behind and, in the light of dawn, the coastline was easy to see even at their current distance of ten kilometers. Zinoviev glanced periodically at the chart on his lap. The American Palmer station would be on the coastline behind the next peninsula.

'How much longer?' Doctor Boris Ney had shouted his question directly to Zinoviev. The infernal noise from the helicopter was getting to him and, if it weren't for the absolute necessity of this trip to the American base, he never would have consented to go up again in the Ka-25.

'Five more minutes, just around that point of land.' Zinoviev gestured to the right with his head, since both hands were on the helicopter's flight controls.

'Good. Hurry.' Ney took one hand off the seatback in front of him and fingered the weapon in the pocket of his parka. The pistol was small, but it would do nicely for what he had in mind. His only regret was that he had been unable to talk that woman member of their *nachalstvo*, their governing council, into being the third member of this liaison and negotiating team. Aleksandra Bukharin would have been the perfect choice for what he had in mind – far better than the idiot they had wound up taking with them.

'Tell me, doctor, do you think that Irkutsk has a chance?'

'Definitely not.' Ney frowned as he answered the tall, gawky man who sat less than a meter to his left in the copilot's seat.

'Why not?'

'Because . . .' Ney could hardly believe that he was allowing himself to talk to this imbecile, yet he knew that it would probably be best if the two of them stayed on civil terms for the time being. '. . . because the regions to

119

the west of Irkutsk were unquestionably a prime target for the Americans. Novosibirsk. The precious metal mines and factories at Krasnoyarsk.'

'I see.'

'I'm sorry.' The more Ney thought about it, the more he realized that he would need this man's trust if he were to pull off his plan without a problem. Ney searched his memory in an attempt to recall the idiot's name. 'Viktor, I'm really sorry. I suppose this nightmare is easier for me to cope with because I have no immediate family. Is Irkutsk where your family was?'

'Nearby, in Zima. My father has a shop near the Oka River.'

'What sort?'

'Repair of specialty tools.'

'Oh.'

'We would hunt together every weekend when I was a boy. He and I hunted in the Sayan Mountains the last time I was home on leave.'

'How long ago?' Ney allowed his eyes to drift toward the cockpit window. The shoreline lay no more than a kilometer in the distance. Another two minutes, at the most, before they reached the Palmer station.

'Three months. Just before our unit joined the *Primorye* for this cruise.' Viktor Chemiakin felt his lower lip begin to tremble again, and he bit down on it to stop himself from crying. His father wouldn't want him to cry.

'Try not to think about it.' Ney laid his hand on Chemiakin's shoulder. 'Put it out of your mind.' Ney was still annoyed that he had been saddled with another army buffoon simply because Chemiakin happened to speak a few elementary words of English – a factor that Captain Kollontai felt could be important and one which, in itself, could be a complication that Ney didn't need. Fortunately, Major Zinoviev spoke nothing but Russian.

'There it is!' Zinoviev jerked the helicopter's controls and the Ka-25 responded by turning its nose directly toward the blue buildings on the rocky beach.

'I see it.' Yet now that they were near their destination, Ney realized that having Lieutenant Chemiakin on board would make his plan run more smoothly. There was no question that he and Aleksandra Bukharin did not get along a kopeck's worth. The tensions and suspicions between them could easily have caused a different sort of problem, could have caused a hesitation. Ney's plan could least afford a problem of that kind. 'Viktor, keep your eyes open.'

'I will.' Lieutenant Viktor Chemiakin reached for his rifle which lay on the floor to his left.

'Good. I don't need to remind you that these are Americans. Americans killed your family.'

When John O'Conner shoved the Palmer station door open he saw the helicopter skimming no more than a hundred feet above the ocean. It was headed directly for him. *A Goddamn helicopter!* O'Conner ran down the wooden steps and along the boardwalk above the rocks and mud between the station's buildings and the flat area near the beach. Just before he reached the spot where he figured the helicopter would land, O'Conner noticed the red star. *Russians. Christ Almighty.* Yet O'Conner didn't back away. He stood where he was and continued to wave his arms as he motioned for the helicopter to land on the flat area in front of him.

The helicopter maneuvered obediently. In less than half a minute it had touched down. O'Conner could see three men in the helicopter's cockpit. He heard the engine begin to wind down and watched the twin set of rotors slow. About that time the cabin door opened. Two men jumped out.

O'Conner walked toward them slowly, his hands raised slightly in an open and friendly gesture. One of the men who came toward him – tall, thin, dressed in a brown military fatigue outfit – held a rifle in his arms. The rifle was pointed forward but down. The other man was heavier, older and wore a neatly trimmed full beard. He seemed to be smiling. 'Do you speak English?' O'Connor asked as soon as the distance between them and the diminishing noises from the helicopter permitted.

'Certainly. Do you speak Russian?' Ney held his breath

for a moment because everything in his plan depended on the proper answer.

'No.'

Ney smiled. 'That's all right, because I speak English fluently.'

'I can see that you do.' O'Conner took another step toward them, although he kept his eyes predominantly on the man with the rifle.

'The lieutenant here speaks only a few words of English,' Ney continued as he pointed to the man on his left. 'Unfortunately, Major Zinoviev speaks none.'

'Where is this major?' As he asked the question, O'Conner watched another man in an army uniform step out of the helicopter. That man shouted something at them in Russian, then turned and walked toward the rear of the helicopter.

'He'll join us shortly. He says there's something mechanical he needs to inspect.' Ney then turned from the helicopter and faced the group of buildings on the rocky beach, gesturing toward the largest one. 'Is that the main facility?'

'Yes.'

'And I presume that the smaller buildings around it are for housing the generators, the workshop and that sort of thing?'

O'Conner didn't want to answer those questions, but he didn't see any way to refuse. The Russians could find out easily enough for themselves by just walking over and looking inside. There was no way in hell that he could have stopped them. 'That's right. Miscellaneous storage in that building at the back. We keep most of our food in the main building, although we do keep emergency supplies at each of the others.'

'I understand.' Ney looked carefully at the haggard young man, attempting to size up his potential for resistance. 'How many are here at this Palmer station?'

'Do you mean how many people?' O'Conner glanced over his shoulder at the building. For some reason – probably because of the way the conversation was going with this bearded Russian who had somehow turned into the Grand Inquisitor – he didn't like the idea of admitting that he was the only one left at the station.

'Yes. The number of people.' Ney shifted his weight nervously; he wanted an answer before Zinoviev finished whatever stupid thing he was doing at the helicopter and finally decided to join them. 'The number in your staff.'

'Normally, for the winter season it's five.'

'Five.' To Ney, that number was acceptable. He figured that he could handle just about that many if he was careful how he went about it.

'Yes. Normally five. But at the moment . . . it's just me.' O'Conner decided to dismiss his fears as imaginary – he would need to trust them. 'One man left this morning to look for the other three. We hadn't heard from those three since . . .'

'Since you received word that your country and mine began a senseless war. A war between pigheaded factions in the Soviet Union and the United States that quickly spread to the remainder of the world. The holocaust has become uncontrollable. It's hopeless for most of the world – and it could very well already be too late even for us.'

'Right.' In spite of the bearded man's conciliatory words, something about him made O'Conner uncomfortable. He turned toward the soldier. 'You speak English?'

'Dah. English. Small.' Lieutenant Chemiakin picked his rifle up by the barrel and cradled it inoffensively in his arms. 'Dah. Learn. Many times ago.' Chemiakin smiled, although he felt foolish doing so. He didn't know how to feel about this American. On the one hand he had his family and all of the Irkutsk region to take revenge for, but on the other hand this American seemed hardly an enemy – he looked to be just about his own age, and just about as tired and confused as Chemiakin himself felt.

'Your English is lots better than my Russian.' As O'Conner spoke, the second Russian officer finally walked from the rear of his helicopter and toward the group. Although smaller than the man with the rifle, he had infinitely more military bearing in the way he stood, the way he walked. His bald head had obviously been purposely shaved clean. If he had shaved his head to make himself look more formidable, then as far as O'Conner was concerned that man had succeeded magnificently in his intent.

As the major stepped up to them, Ney turned to Zinoviev and told him – in Russian – that there were five Americans stationed at Palmer. Ney was careful to omit the fact that the other four were at that moment somewhere else.

'Five, you say?' Major Zinoviev eyed the young American carefully as he spoke to Ney. 'Then where are the other four?' Without even realizing it, the major had laid his hand casually on the pistol that was strapped to the holster on his belt – a holster that already had the leather safety strap unfastened so it would yield its weapon quickly if it were needed. 'We should have all the Americans together so we can see their situation clearly. Then we can begin our talks.'

'Good idea.' Like the good chess player that he was, Ney had the next series of his game-plan moves already in mind. 'The American tells me that one of his men went to the storage shed in that direction,' Ney said as he pointed toward the glacier in the distance. 'The shed is just over that first rise. Why don't you get that man while Chemiakin and I round up the other three. Then we'll meet in the main building.'

'Are you sure that you want us to separate?' Zinoviev scanned the direction that Ney had pointed in, yet he could see nothing – no tracks in the snow, no crevices to indicate travel back and forth to a storage shed beyond the rise. 'This could be a trick.'

'It's no trick. That building is a considerable distance away because it's where they keep their explosives. It's probably a good idea for you to take a look at it, to see what they have.'

'How can I tell that American to come with me when I don't speak his language.'

'Use hand signals.' *What an idiot. I'm surprised he's not a general by now*. 'I'm pretty certain that the American will

124

realize that you're not here searching for the Leningrad trolley.'

'Okay, I get your point.'

'What's he saying?' O'Conner could tell from the tone of the words in their exchange – even though they were in Russian – that this major wasn't happy about what the bearded guy was telling him.

'The major wants to look the area over,' Ney lied as he reverted back to English. 'If you have no problem with that, he'll look around the camp while the three of us go to the main building. The major will join us shortly.'

'Okay with me.' O'Conner fidgeted. None of it made any sense to him. He wished to hell that Michael hadn't left before the helicopter arrived.

'Incidentally, the American tells me that there are no tracks in the snow because they usually walk toward the building over the rise by using a path at the rear of their camp.' As Ney snapped out his fabricated comment in Russian to Zinoviev, he waved his hand in the direction of the furthest building. 'But you can go straight across from here if you like – the ice is solid enough.'

'It had better be.' Major Zinoviev began to move away cautiously, his attention focused on the snow and ice in front of him.

'See you soon.' Satisfied that Major Zinoviev was taken care of for the time being, Ney turned back to the American. 'Lead the way to your building, if you please,' he said in English. 'We'd like to sit down with you to talk about the situation, to talk about the options left to those of us down here.'

'Okay.'

'Comrade,' Chemiakin said in a low voice as he put his hand on Ney's arm and spoke in Russian. 'I'm afraid I didn't follow any of this. I know that I don't understand very much English, but I didn't pick up any of what you told Major Zinoviev that the American had said.'

'Then I suppose your English is even worse than you thought.' Ney smiled solicitously, as if he were sharing an insider's joke with the lieutenant. 'Why don't you practice while we walk toward the main building?'

'I will.' Chemiakin picked up his pace and then fell into stride beside the young American as the three worked their way across the rocky beach. While Chemiakin spoke in heavily accented sentences of nearly-incomprehensible English, the three men stepped onto the wooden board-walk and headed toward the building's entrance.

Boris Ney looked over his shoulder one more time to be certain that Major Zinoviev was still safely tucked away beyond the ridgeline. Satisfied, he put his hand back into the deep pocket of his parka and wrapped his fingers around the pistol that he carried. As the young American opened the door and stepped across the threshold of the main building, Ney withdrew the pistol from his pocket. He stopped moving forward and held the pistol steadily. *One less idiot to deal with*. Ney pointed the pistol. He squeezed the trigger.

Two rapid shots banged out of the small black revolver. Both bullets found their mark – the dead center of Lieutenant Viktor Chemiakin's back. He let out a short bloodcurdling scream, then fell immediately. He hit the floor face-down, his body straddled across the width of the corridor that he had just stepped into.

'Are you crazy – what in God's name are you doing?' O'Conner had spun around at the sound of the shots and he now stood with his back to the wall, his mouth open, his eyes darting back and forth between the black pistol in the bearded man's hand and the sprawled-out body of the Russian officer he had been talking with a few seconds before. A gusher of blood had already erupted from the center of the man's back, and it flowed across his uniform and then puddled onto the dirty tile floor.

'I don't have sufficient time to explain. Turn around.'

'Stop this!'

'Turn around and face the wall immediately. If you don't, I'll shoot you.' Ney raised the black pistol and aimed it at the young American's chest.

John O'Conner hesitated only briefly, then turned around to face the wall as he had been instructed. His hands had already been raised and he could feel a wave of overpowering fear as it spread quickly through him.

'Stay where you are and you won't get hurt.' Ney took the few remaining steps between him and the American, raised the butt of the black pistol high above the man's head, then brought it down swiftly. The impact of the pistol's metal butt made a loud cracking sound as it smashed hard against the young man's skull. The American slumped to the floor. His unconscious body lay a few meters to one side of where Lieutenant Chemiakin's body was.

Boris Ney bent down and scooped up the rifle that lay beside Chemiakin's body. He put the weapon against his shoulder, aimed it down the corridor and pulled the trigger four times. As he did, he continued to back away from the corridor and toward the open door behind him. Once the forth shot had been fired from the rifle, Ney dropped the weapon and stumbled backward out the door. He looked up and, as he suspected, saw Major Zinoviev racing across the glacier toward him. 'Get down! They've gone outside! They went out through the back of the building!'

'How many of them!' Zinoviev crouched down as he moved forward as quickly as he could. He had already pulled his own pistol out of its leather holster and had pointed it in the direction that Ney had indicated. Zinoviev saw nothing. 'Where are they?'

'I don't know. Hurry.' Ney motioned for Zinoviev to continued toward him, all the while pointing his own pistol toward where the imaginary Americans would have gone. 'They've shot Chemiakin.'

Zinoviev vaulted over the wooden boardwalk's handrail and raced to the door. 'Is it bad?' he asked, but the words were hardly out of his mouth when he saw for himself. Chemiakin was awash in his own blood – there was a liter or more of blood already on the floor, and still more of it coming out of his massive wounds. 'Damn! How could this happen!' Zinoviev bent over his lieutenant to confirm what he already knew for certain. The man was dead.

'Three of them jumped out as we entered the building. They fired without warning, without giving us a chance. I was lucky, but Viktor was not.' Ney leaned against the doorway as if he no longer had the strength to stand. 'I grabbed Viktor's rifle and swung it at the American who had lured us in there – he hadn't had a chance to escape down the corridor yet.'

'Good.' Zinoviev looked down at the body of the young American laying on the floor. 'Did you kill him?'

'I don't think so.' Ney kept looking out across the glacier, as if he expected that imaginary gang of Americans to come toward them from that position. 'We should take him with us.'

'We should kill him.' Zinoviev raised his pistol toward the inert body of the American.

'No. We need information.' Ney understood that the potential for controlling and neutralizing the Americans – a necessary aspect of his overall plan to acquire and maintain power over all the survivors – was dependent on knowing where the Americans were and what their potential for resistance was.

'What sort of information do you need?'

'When this man regains consciousness, we'll make him tell us where the others could have gone. That way we can meet them head-on – and this time with sufficient strength to avoid another massacre.'

'I told Captain Kollontai that we shouldn't trust these people.' Zinoviev stooped down toward Lieutenant Chemiakin's body, gently rolled the man over and snatched off the identity tags that hung around his neck. 'Rest your soul, Viktor.' Zinoviev then moved the man's body back to what would have been a more comfortable position had he still been alive.

'I think we should get out of here. I imagine that the only reason the Americans fled was that they weren't certain how many of us there were and how well-armed we might be.' Ney continued to scan the glacier cautiously while he spoke, his back to the major. 'When they see it's only the two of us and only one rifle and two pistols between us, they might decide to attack.'

'Okay.' Major Zinoviev took a step toward the young American. 'What about him?'

'Drag him along. I'll cover you.'

'Okay.' Zinoviev grabbed the body and dragged the

128

man backwards. With Doctor Ney leading the way – while sweeping his rifle back and forth across where the mythical Americans might emerge from – the three of them made their way down the wooden boardwalk, across the rocky beach and toward the waiting Ka-25.

'I'll get us out of here,' Zinoviev said after all three of them were aboard the helicopter and Ney had slid closed the cabin door. 'You take care of him.'

'Right.' Ney reached for a coil of rope from a storage box on the left sidewall, then turned the man's body over. He quickly tied the man's hands behind him – his motions told Ney that the young man was on the verge of regaining consciousness – and then coiled the rope around his legs and body, firmly binding him in a makeshift harness. About the time he had finished, Zinoviev shouted back that they were ready to take off.

Ney held on as the helicopter jerked off the ground, the sight of the Palmer station buildings rapidly falling away as they hurriedly turned toward the sea. 'Stay low. I want you to head straight out over the water, but keep the speed down to fifty kilometers or less,' Ney shouted up to Zinoviev.

'Why?'

'Because we need information. Here and now is the best time to get it.'

'Make it fast. I want to get back to the ship. We need to plan our attack against these bastards.'

'This won't take long.' Ney leaned toward the young man, who had just opened his eyes. 'Can you hear me?'

'What . . . where am . . . what happened . . .' John O'Conner blinked several times, then tried to move. It took him several seconds to realize that his hands were tied behind him and his feet were bound together. 'Let me go – what do you want from me?'

'I'll let you go soon. I need information.'

'Let me go.'

'Where are the other Americans from Palmer? How soon will they be back?'

'I don't know.'

'I don't believe you. I think with the proper incentive

you might be happy to tell me.' Ney stood up and walked to the cabin door. He slid the door open. The roar of the outside air and the biting cold of the Antarctic wind swept into the interior of the helicopter.

'Let me go!'

'Soon.' Ney gathered up the end of the rope harness he had bound the young American in and fastened the end of it to the wire sling that hung at the entrance to the cabin door. Once the connection was firmly made, Ney stepped to the controls of the electric winch. 'You're going for a short, refreshing ride. It might be a stimulating enough experience to encourage you to tell me what I need to know.'

'I don't know where any of them are! God, stop this . . . let me go!' O'Conner attempted to free himself from the ropes, but he had been bound too tightly. 'Let me go!' he shouted as he watched the electric winch coiling in the loose end of the rope he was bound to.

'Soon.' Ney pushed the young American's body until he was poised at the opening of the helicopter's door. 'Do you have any supplies stored anywhere beyond the Palmer station?' Ney had shouted his question in order to make himself heard above the incessant wind. Both he and the young man had begun to shiver from the cold.

'I don't know anything! I don't know where the others are!'

'Perhaps, but I can't take that chance.' Without further preamble Ney pushed the American out the open cabin door. He watched as the young man jerked to a sudden stop several meters below the helicopter after all the available rope had played out. Satisfied that his plan was working, Ney pushed the appropriate button on the control panel and the winch began to wind the extended rope upward.

'Help me . . . let me go!' O'Conner could no longer feel his hands and feet because he had turned so cold. He watched in agony as he was hoisted upward on the tethered rope until he was directly opposite the cabin door. He twisted slowly in the wind for what seemed like hours but was in fact only a few minutes. The wind ripped at his clothes – he had worn woolen pants and a medium-weight nylon jacket that morning because he hadn't expected to spend more than a few quick minutes outside.

'Do your friends have any supplies stored elsewhere besides the Palmer station? Do they have any weapons?'

'No . . . they have nothing . . . a few supplies . . . tents . . .' O'Conner could hardly open his mouth as the biting, slicing wind quickly froze the skin around his jaw. His eyes watered and the tears froze to his scraggly beard. His entire body seemed to be shriveling inward. '. . . tents . . . few days . . . no more . . . no weapons . . .' O'Conner could no longer keep a straight thought in his mind.

'What about supplies? Are they stored anywhere else? Is there a place your friend could go if the Palmer station were destroyed?'

'No . . . Michael . . . No . . .?' O'Conner's eyes had watered themselves frozen shut and the wind and cold had caused his eardrums to tighten to the point where he could hardly hear the voice that was shouting at him. In place of the actual sight of the bearded man who stood in the doorway of the helicopter a few feet away, John O'Conner began to see a vision. A vision of himself.

'Are you certain that your friends have no weapons?'

O'Conner did not hear the question, and if he had he would not have been able to answer because his muscles were now immobile from the paralyzing cold. *Clean up. Think straight.* What O'Conner saw in his vision through his mind's eye was the sight of himself, his eyes ringed with dark circles, his beard overgrown and unruly, his hair wild, his skin puffy and blotched. What he saw was himself as he would have looked in the mirror of the Budweiser sign in the radio room, as he would have looked if he could have gotten himself into that warm room, if he could have gotten to the radio to call Michael and the others. *Shave. Hot shower. Think straight.*

Satisfied that he had gotten all the information that he could, Doctor Ney picked up the emergency hand axe from its mount on the helicopter wall and leaned forward. With two quick blows he severed the connection where the prisoner's rope was tied to the sling of the electric winch. Ney watched as the young American tumbled head over heels into the Antarctic sea a hundred meters below them. The man instantly disappeared below the waves. 'Zinoviev, head directly for the *Primorye*,' Ney shouted as he turned to face the cockpit. 'Full speed.'

Zinoviev looked back. He was surprised to see that Ney was alone in the cabin. 'What happened?'

'The rope must have broken.' Without giving it another thought, Doctor Boris Ney put the fate of that young American out of his mind. Instead, he began to concentrate on his next plan. He now had, Ney felt, enough solid information to guarantee the elimination of the four Americans from the Palmer station who still remained free.

Nine

WITH THE exception of Steve Galloway who remained in the cockpit, everyone else aboard *Airship Nine* moved down the staircase to the lower deck when Captain Whitaker gave the signal. As they assembled, one by one, on both sides of the opened hatchway door they all stood quietly and waited, each of them hardly looking at any of the others. The hatchway had been opened long enough for the cold mid-morning Antarctic air to chase away the effects of the heating system. Yet the nine men and women gathered inside the lower deck cargo area remained relatively comfortable because there was hardly any wind blowing through the open hatch.

Captain Lou Whitaker was the last to come down the staircase. As he entered, all eyes turned toward him. Whitaker avoided looking back at any of them and, instead, glanced through the opened hatchway at the sea below. Several small and widely separated icebergs floated on the choppy blue water, their presence trivial and insignificant on such a vast and expansive sea. The airship had turned during the night as the shifting breeze had moved northeast, and that had caused the opened hatchway to face away from the range of mountains and frozen coastline that they flew parallel to and toward the open ocean. 'I guess everyone's here,' Whitaker announced to no one in particular. No one in the group answered.

Whitaker cleared his throat as he looked around. Frank Corbi stood at the far left corner, his video camera held as inconspicuously as possible at his side, the battery pack slung over his shoulder. Whitaker nodded toward Corbi, then addressed the group. 'I expect that none of you have any objections to Mr Corbi using his video tape machine,' Whitaker began, in a voice that left little doubt that he wasn't actually asking any of them for permission. After Corbi had brought the subject up a short time before, Whitaker had briefly thought it over and decided that recording what was happening to them wouldn't do any harm.

'Wait a minute.'

'Yes, Mr Sinclair?' Whitaker's heart sank even lower than it had been – other than his copilot Ray Madigan, young Andrew Sinclair was the last person in their group that he wanted to deal with at the moment.

'Filming a funeral doesn't seem appropriate to me,' Sinclair announced. This time, he didn't step forward as he normally did whenever he made a calculated statement against whomever represented the designated authority – that was the way they had taught him to do it at Yale – but instead he continued to stand next to his wife, as if he intended to use her as a shield. Sinclair ignored the angry stares he was getting from Kathleen since he could deal with her later. As far as that blonde bitch Julie was concerned – she was also staring at him from across the room, with a less than sympathetic expression – Sinclair intended to ignore her completely. After spending four years at Yale he was damned if he was going to talk to a grown woman who counted penguins for a living. Sinclair continued to look, undaunted, at Whitaker.

'Corbi says it's just for the record.' Whitaker shrugged as he spoke, since he didn't want to get into any of it.

'Record? What kind of record?' Sinclair adjusted the zipper on his designer ski jacket – he was the only man in the room who had not put on a tie for Weiss' funeral – then waved his hand disdainfully at the group. 'Other than us down here and that one pilot in the cockpit, there's no one left in the world to give a damn about any of this.'

'We don't know that for sure. We don't know anything for sure. Making a video tape of what's happening won't make any difference,' Whitaker answered.

'That's exactly what I'm saying. Why should we bother?'

'Why don't you let *me* decide what I want to be bothered with?' Corbi took one step forward from the rear of the

134

room where he had been trying to remain inconspicuous. It was already too late for that.

'You media people may not realize this, but life isn't a series of half-hour sitcoms,' Sinclair replied smugly.

'Don't you start telling me what life is about – I don't think you've seen many of life's details from the height of that pedestal that you're perched on.'

'I want both of you to stop this.' Whitaker was sorry that he had let this business go so far. He never should have asked the group if the filming was okay, but it was too late to keep them out of it. 'Okay, we're going to take a vote. Majority rules.'

'Listen, if there's a problem with me doing this, Captain, then I won't bother,' Corbi volunteered. 'I'll put the equipment in the corner. I'll pick it up later.'

'We're not going to debate this,' Whitaker announced to the group as he ignored what Corbi was saying. 'A simple yes or no vote. All I'm going to say is to repeat what I was told. It made good sense to me. Video-taping a record is better than keeping a written diary – and maybe we have an obligation to record what's happening to us.'

'An obligation to whom?'

'All in favor of a video-taping, raise your hand,' Whitaker said as he ignored Sinclair's interruption. One by one, each member of the group put up a hand. Kathleen Sinclair was, other than her husband who kept his arm steadfastly lowered, the last one to vote yes. When she did, she seemed to raise her hand even higher than the others.

'Looks like we won't need a recount,' Julie said as she looked around the group.

'Nine are for it, and one is opposed.' Whitaker gestured for Corbi to pick up his camera. 'Whenever you're ready,' he said as he turned away. Whitaker stood silently while he waited for Corbi to get his video equipment back together. *I wish I had a video tape of Allan. I wish he could be here with me. God, please take care of him.*

'I'm ready.' Without waiting for an answer, Frank Corbi began to pan his camera across the group. The soft whirring sound of the tape machine filled the small and quiet lower cargo bay.

Whitaker continued to look out the opened hatch, first at the sea below him, then at the solid overcast a few thousand feet above. *There's no point to any of this. This is worse than a nightmare because there's no waking up.* Finally, after what seemed like an eternity to the others, the captain turned around and stepped up to the cloth-covered body that lay spread across a platform of shipping crates they had put in front of the opened door.

'I knew David Weiss better than anyone on board. Unfortunately, I didn't know him very well,' Whitaker began. He allowed his eyes to move across the length of wrapped sheets that covered Wiess' body, then slowly looked at the row of mourners. 'He was a quiet man, a very private man.' Whitaker stopped talking and coughed into his hand. Finally, he looked back at the group. 'David was hit hard by the radio messages, like we all were. But David's job was to stay in front of his radio. He did his job well, but it proved too much for him. It probably would've proved too much for any of us. I should've realized that David had already reached his breaking point . . .'

'There's no sense getting into that,' Julie Mathews said softly, her words barely audible above the low but persistent humming of the video camera. She motioned with her head to indicate that, just as they had agreed earlier, the captain shouldn't dwell on that subject. He should move on to the next thing.

Whitaker looked back at Julie. He knew that she was right, that there was no sense getting into it, that it was too late now to worry about David – just like it was too late now to worry about his son Allan. *When the hell am I ever going to learn?* Whitaker unfolded the paper that Julie had written out for him. 'I've got a short reading – that'll be our service for David – before we commit his body to the sea.' Whitaker waited a moment but no one spoke. Finally, he looked back at the paper that Julie had given him just before they came downstairs, her flowing, measured handwriting filling the page. Whitaker scanned the paper once more while the group waited.

'What's the reading from, captain?' Doctor Everett Tucker asked, more to fill the uncomfortable silence than to get an answer. He stood bolt-erect at the head of the makeshift cloth casket, his two hands clasped in front of him. As always, Tucker wore one of his three-piece suits. Other than the lack of his pipe, which he had left in his room, he appeared as dignified and venerable as he always did.

'I'm not prepared for this sort of thing . . . I asked Julie to help me.' Whitaker looked toward Julie.

'It's from John Donne,' Julie volunteered.

'Ah, yes.' Tucker nodded; he had a notion of what it would be.

'Okay.' Whitaker cleared his throat once more, then held the paper in front of him. He put his left hand down on the white sheet in front of him and could feel David's cold arm through the thin cloth. Whitaker looked across the group one more time, allowing his eyes to drift slowly from face to face. Floyd Robinson stood rigidly between Julie Mathews and Annie Rizzo, the three of them making an obvious effort to keep a firm hold on their emotions. Nancy Schneider leaned slightly against Ray Madigan, his arm wrapped around her shoulder, her eyes wet with tears. Kathleen and Andrew Sinclair had stepped closer together. Everyone was going to be affected by what they were about to do. Finally, Whitaker began to speak in a low voice that cracked under the strain of the emotions that welled up in him.

'No man is an Island entire of itself; every man is a piece of the Continent, a part of the main. If a clod be washed away by the sea, Europe is the less, as well as if a promontory were, as well as if a manor of thy friends or of thine own were . . .'

Whitaker paused. He wished he could stop to get himself a glass of water to help his parched throat. Finally, he continued. '. . . Any man's death diminishes me because I am involved in mankind . . .'

Nancy Schneider was crying openly. Madigan's arm wrapped even more tightly around her. Floyd Robinson had taken both Annie and Julie's hands into his own and held them both to his chest, his head bowed slightly. The Sinclairs stood without movement, although a steady flow of tears ran down Kathleen's cheeks.

Frank Corbi kept the lens of the video camera up to his eye while he continued to pan slowly across the scene, but the sound of his own sobs carried over the undercurrent of mechanical noises from the camera. Below the camera, his abundant belly strained the buttons on his shirt even more than usual as his diaphragm expanded and contracted with each sob. Doctor Tucker had removed his eyeglasses so he could dab discreetly at the tears that had appeared in the corners of his eyes. After needing to stop for another moment in order to rein in his own racing emotions, Captain Whitaker picked up the paper and continued.

'. . . Therefore, never send to know for whom the bell tolls. It tolls for thee . . .' Whitaker put aside the paper that he had read from. 'God bless you, David.'

The final phrase in the reading was enough to undo what little composure was left in the group as everyone began to cry openly. Whitaker realized now that they were not only mourning David Weiss, they were grieving for themselves and for the loss of everyone they had known. They were mourning an entire civilization.

Now that he had finished, Whitaker nodded toward Doctor Tucker, then took hold of one side of Weiss' body. Tucker had earlier volunteered to assist the captain from the other side. But as Tucker stepped forward, he surprised Whitaker by speaking.

'If you don't mind, captain, there's something I'd like to add.' Tucker used his handkerchief to dry his face, then turned half around so that he was facing the group. He could see that Corbi had swung the video camera toward him but Tucker refused to allow the camera to become any kind of distraction. He knew exactly what he had to say.

'Go ahead.' Whitaker stood his ground while he waited to see what Tucker wanted.

'There are actually two statements that I'd care to make.' Tucker reached for Weiss' body and gestured for Captain Whitaker to do likewise. 'An old English proverb

138

serves David's situation – and ours, I might add – quite well.' Tucker waited for Whitaker to take hold of his side of the body. With Tucker giving visual cues, the two men began to move the body down the length of the packing crate and toward the opened hatchway. 'Death usually comes too early – or too late.' In one motion, the two men lifted the body across the far edge of the packing crate. They let go of their grip and allowed the weight of the body to pull it quickly out of the opened hatch. In an instant it was gone from view as it tumbled rapidly toward the Antarctic sea below.

'But I still have something else to add, something that applies to each of us.' Tucker took a step away from the hatchway and toward the group. 'The quote comes originally from the Bible, New Testament, Matthew – but you'll indulge me if I provide it to you in the manner that William Gladstone did when he addressed Parliament in 1893.' Tucker paused for a moment to peak the group's interest – a tactic he had learned from his many years of teaching at university level – in hopes of getting a unanimous response.

'Let me entreat you to let the dead bury the dead, and to cast behind you every recollection of bygone evils. Cherish, love, sustain one another through all the vicissitudes of human affairs in the times that are to come.' Tucker allowed his eyes to lock with each of the nine members of the group before he opened his mouth to add one more line. 'The funeral service for radio operator David Weiss is now officially ended.'

Doctor Everett Tucker turned quickly on his heels and strode purposefully up the staircase. He led the procession of survivors as they headed back to the main deck and warm interior of *Airship Nine*.

'The rope broke. I told you that already.' Doctor Boris Ney stared directly at Aleksandra Bukharin as he answered her question, all the while working very hard at keeping his temper under control and his dislike for the woman doctor less than obvious to the others in the group.

139

'Ropes simply don't just break.' Aleksandra glared back at him, then glanced over at the sofa where Captain Kollontai sat with Major Zinoviev.

'This one did.'

'Not likely.'

'Neither was a full scale nuclear war, or the massacre at the Bellingshausen station.' Ney stroked his beard gently while he kept his eyes locked with Aleksandra's.

'The rope question is beside the point, although I do agree with what Aleksandra said before.' Captain Andrei Kollontai rose from the sofa and stepped over to the brass-encased porthole on the wall of his stateroom. He looked out at the choppy Antarctic sea for a few moments before he turned back to the others in the room. 'You had no business doing what you did. Regardless of what the Americans at Palmer did, you're not a field man for the KGB. Once you were out of danger, there was no need to take any chances.'

'Of course you're right,' Ney said. He was willing to admit to anything short of murder in order to change the subject, to get the four of them back to the topic at hand, the topic he needed to discuss next. 'I suppose it was the shock of seeing Viktor killed right there in front of me – and of nearly being murdered myself, I might remind you. I guess I may have overreacted in attempting an interrogation before we arrived at the ship . . .'

'You certainly did.' Aleksandra could see that the captain didn't want her to continue badgering Ney, but she couldn't help herself.

'. . . but what happened to the American was an accident.' Ney glanced over at Major Zinoviev to see if there was going to be any disagreement from him. The major sat stone-faced, as if none of the ongoing conversation had any bearing on him whatsoever. Either he had seen nothing, as Ney had suspected, or the major had decided that what had happened to the American prisoner was fine with him.

'All right.' Kollantai waved his hand in a motion of dismissal to show the three of them that the subject was now behind them. He would have liked to have told Ney that he understood, that he believed his story about the American's death being accidental – those conciliatory words had actually formed in his thoughts and had nearly risen up through his throat – but something had stopped him from saying so. In his heart, Kollontai knew that there was more to the American's fate than Ney was admitting – but Kollontai also understood that all they could do at that point was to go on. 'Then the four of us are in agreement about the next step?'

'We have no choice,' Ney said, then quickly frowned. He had again spoken too soon, since he should have allowed one of the others to answer first. That was what Lenin would have done.

'You're wrong. There are always choices,' Aleksandra said. 'Are you saying that we're committed to fighting with the Americans at the Palmer station?' She had addressed Kollontai, since she already knew Ney's answer and suspected that she knew Major Zinoviev's as well.

'We can't take any more chances. We can't expose our people to the sort of risks that we exposed Viktor Chemiakin to.' Major Zinoviev was the last one to rise up from the sofa and join the other three. By standing, each of them was signaling that a decision was nearly at hand, or at least that it should be. They couldn't put it off any longer. Zinoviev also knew that he owed Viktor Chemiakin the vow that the Americans wouldn't get away with what they had done to him, no matter what. He intended to make that point perfectly clear to the other three members of this *nachalstvo*.

Kollontai put his hand on Zinoviev's shoulder. 'I understand what you're saying, major. My sincerest sympathies to you and your men at the understandable loss you feel for Viktor. I understand your anger, too.'

'Viktor was murdered without the slightest provocation. He was a good soldier, doing exactly what he had been told to do. As far as I'm concerned, enough is enough. I know exactly how we should act next.'

'I agree with the major.' Ney decided that it was time to jump in unequivocally, now that the necessary decision was nearly within reach.

141

Aleksandra shook her head. 'None of the American reactions at Bellingshausen and Palmer make any sense. I still think we'll be able to reason with them.' She pushed back her long hair, then turned to Kollontai with pleading eyes. 'Please, let me go by myself to negotiate. They may listen to me if I show up alone and with no weapons.'

Kollontai paced back and forth as much as the crowded confines of his stateroom would allow. 'No,' he finally answered. Kollontai reached out and laid his hands gently on Aleksandra's shoulders. 'Your offer is a brave one, and certainly well motivated. We're proud of you for having made it. But it's far too much of a risk.'

'No, it's not.'

'Yes it is,' Kollontai answered firmly. As the chairman of their *nachalstvo*, it was ultimately up to him to spell out their plan of action. He would listen to the advice of the governing council, but he would ultimately make the decisions. 'While you've convinced me that we should attempt one more negotiated settlement, I'm also convinced that we must take absolutely no unnecessary chances while we do it.'

'That sounds reasonable.' Ney didn't know exactly what Kollontai was leading to, but he felt he would still be able to steer him along acceptable lines. 'What do you propose?'

'I think a show of strength rather than weakness might convince the Americans to sit down and talk.' Kollontai turned to Zinoviev. 'How do you feel about taking both helicopters – fully equipped with armament – to Palmer? I think that when the Americans see that we have that sort of firepower available to us, they might be more reasonable.'

'I'm all for it.' Zinoviev was smiling broadly. 'It's exactly what my men want. I'm sure we can be successful.'

Kollontai shot a quick glance at Aleksandra. It was obvious that both of them shared the same thought. 'But let me remind you,' Kollontai added to the major, 'that success would be measured by how quickly we convinced the Americans to negotiate peacefully – not by how many bodies you managed to lay out along the beachfront.'

'Of course.' Zinoviev pursed his lips and nodded quickly. He, too, wanted a peaceful solution if it were at all possible – but the memory of what the Americans had done to Viktor Chemiakin was a difficult one to dispense with. He would just have to see how it went once they arrived at Palmer.

'Then it's settled. I assume, of course, that I'll go along in order to negotiate.' Ney worked hard at stopping himself from looking as triumphant as he felt – things had worked out as well as he could have possibly expected. A few en route words to Zinoviev once they were on the helicopter would guarantee that the major's trigger finger would be itchy enough to prevent any unnecessary discussions between themselves and the Americans.

'When do we go?'

'Not you.'

'What?' Ney could hardly believe what he was hearing.

'I think Aleksandra should go this time. She speaks English well enough to get by. Maybe she was right about having a woman to negotiate.' Kollontai glanced toward her. She was a rare combination of intelligence, earthy beauty and sincerity. Surely the American leader at the Palmer station would see that also. Aleksandra's presence might provoke a feeling of trust between the two groups.

'That's crazy. It's too dangerous.' Ney knew that he was also on dangerous ground, that he could ill afford to seem too negative to any plan that might promote harmony between themselves and the Americans. His motives had to remain above suspicion. Ney's mind raced ahead while he fumbled with appropriate words to fill the gap. 'What I mean . . . it could turn rough very quickly . . . I'm more experienced in these situations . . .'

'Let's leave it up to the major.' Kollontai turned to Zinoviev. 'Do you think you can protect her?'

'Certainly. We'll go in as two separate units, with Aleksandra in the second helicopter. I'll have them hover within sight but far out of small arms firing range until I get a good feel about how things are going. And once we've landed both helicopters, we'll be certain to keep ourselves out of any vulnerable positions.'

'Then it's settled.' Aleksandra beamed. She was happy to finally be doing something positive to stop the bloodshed and senseless fighting. 'When do we go?'

'As soon as possible.' Kollontai turned to Zinoviev.

'I'll need a little time to prepare my men,' the major answered without being asked. He glanced at his wristwatch, then turned to Aleksandra. 'Be on the helicopter pad at exactly noon – that'll give me sixty-five minutes to get ready.'

'I'll be there.'

'Dress warmly.'

'Of course.'

'If your mind's made up, captain,' Ney said, attempting to sound nonchalant.

'It is.'

'Then, of course, I'll support your decision. I would have liked to go myself, but I understand your reasoning.' Boris Ney knew enough not to try to swim upstream.

'Thank you,' Kollontai answered sincerely. Whenever it was humanly possible, he wanted all of them to agree. Unless the survivors from the *Primorye* stuck together, all would be lost.

'No thanks are necessary.' Ney began to formulate an alternative plan. He would simply have to brief Zinoviev thoroughly by incessantly drumming into him those two stories that Ney had gotten all of them to believe – that the Americans had massacred the unarmed Russians at the Bellingshausen station and that they had then killed Vicktor Chemiakin with no provocation whatsoever. All Ney could do after that was hope for the best. Not a good solution, but the only one that was available to him at the moment. 'If you'll excuse me, then, I'll leave with the major to help him prepare.'

'Certainly.' Kollontai stood beside Aleksandra. The two of them watched in silence as Doctor Ney and Major Zinoviev left the stateroom. After the door had closed behind them, Kollontai turned back to the woman doctor. Up until a few hours ago, he had hardly noticed her – and now she had become the most important person on the *Primorye* as far as he was concerned. 'I can't tell you how important your opinions were during our meeting. Without them, I don't think I would've been able

144

to come up with this plan on my own.'

'Thank you – but I don't believe you. I think you would've come up with your own reasonable way of handling this. You were kind enough to let me have the floor, that's all.' Aleksandra looked at the smooth lines of his face, the friendly warmth of his dark eyes, the way the corners of his mouth moved outward a fraction of a second early as a tip-off that he was about to smile. Andrei Kollontai was all the good things she had heard. He was that, and more.

'Don't believe it for a minute.' Without even realizing that he had done so, Kollontai reached out with his right hand and touched her again on the shoulder. He then allowed his hand to rest gently on the folds of the patterned dress she wore, his fingers spreading open and extending from her shoulder to the top few centimeters of her delicate arm. He looked at her for quite a while, neither one of them daring to say another word. Finally, Kollontai spoke. 'In one way, I don't know anything about you. In another way, it seems as if I've known you forever. I know it's a trite thing for a grown man to say, but I can't think of anything else.'

'That's the way I feel, too.' Aleksandra hadn't taken her eyes off him. She ached inside for him – for him to wrap his arms around her, to kiss her, to caress her – but she didn't know what to do about it. 'We've all been through an enormous emotional shock. We're reacting to it. It's only natural.' Even as the words were coming out, Aleksandra was disgusted with herself, disgusted with her nonstop clinical patter. This was not the ship's sickbay, and the man in front of her was certainly not one of its patients. She had to stop always being a doctor and begin to become a woman again.

'The shock . . . you're right about the shock.' Kollontai kept himself motioness, although his facial muscles quivered slightly. 'My family is definitely gone, there's no question about that. My wife Yekatrina. My beautiful daughter Lidiya. Gone . . .' Kollontai closed his eyes for a moment, then allowed them to open again.

'Andrei . . .'

'I know. Don't say it, not yet.' Kollontai had surprised himself by the manner that he had replied to her, yet he knew that it would be wrong to change how he felt, to force himself to do something that he might not be ready for. He believed that his intuitions had always been good to him. Deep down, Kollontai felt that whatever way his heart led him was the right way to go.

'If that's what you want.' Aleksandra's face was etched by a small frown, a mark of discouragement and disappointment – but that was the only change between them. Neither she nor Andrei Kollontai moved, as if their bodies were completely disconnected from the things that they were saying to each other, from the thoughts that were going on in their minds.

'Don't say anything yet.' Kollontai had repeated himself, but he wasn't certain why. He suspected that he was looking for time, time to decide, to accept, to adjust. 'It's as if there's a thousand horses pulling me apart.'

'I know.'

'. . . pulling me apart in a hundred different directions.' Yet his eyes remained locked with hers, she was still looking up at him, her long, dark hair framing her oval-shaped face, her eyes and mouth, the shape of her features and the richness of her skin conspiring to create as beautiful a picture as he'd ever seen. That image of her and what she represented as she stood there was becoming as necessary to his personal survival as water to drink, as air to breathe. He loved Yekatrina and Lidiya, but they were dead. She was alive and his wife and daughter were dead. She was alive.

'Andrei, please let me speak.' Aleksandra could feel the tears begin to form in the corners of her eyes. She took Kollontai's hand – which had remained on her shoulder all that time – and held it tightly in her own. 'I had no husband or family. My father died years before, and my mother passed away this time last year. I had many close friends, but no family . . .' Aleksandra felt her resolve to not do anything illogical begin to melt and, at the same time, could feel the arc of her descending tears as they ran across the angles of her face.

'No, you're wrong. This thing hurt us equally. Everything is gone – all the memories, all the people, all the places. No one was hurt any more or any less because of an accounting of the number of children they've lost, or whether their wives, mothers or fathers had died yesterday or years before that. We've all lost everything. Everything. In that respect, all of us who have lived to see today have become equals.' Kollontai could hardly finish speaking before he began to choke on his own words. Slowly he pulled Aleksandra toward him, engulfed her in his arms and held onto her tightly.

Aleksandra raised her head and pressed her face against his. The warmth of their skin mixed together and so did the wetness of both their tears.

After a few moments, and without a spoken word between them, they pushed themselves apart. Without hesitation she began to undress first. The dull mid-morning light that filtered through the overcast Antarctic sky entered the stateroom through the two small portholes on the far wall and washed softly over the milky-white skin of her exposed body. He soon followed her lead and also began to undress. Neither of them dared to take their eyes off the other, as if the source of the physical strength to go ahead with this, to hold each other as close as a man and a woman could, would be coming from the power of their eyes. Both of them were afraid that the whole thing would end if one or the other of them turned away for even a brief instant. But neither of them turned away.

When they were both completely naked, he led her to the bed. Slowly at first, and then with their passions and emotions leading them on, they began to make love. They had allowed themselves the freedom of letting go, the freedom of dropping the chains that had been pulling at them from inside. Because of that, Andrei Kollontai and Aleksandra Bukharin were making love not only for themselves but also for all the people they had ever known, ever felt compassion for, ever loved. They were making love for all those people who' had not been fortunate enough to survive to see that dully grey Antarctic daylight as it poured through the portholes of the *Primorye*.

Ten

MICHAEL STARR could tell from the clouds above him that the bad weather had nearly arrived. He stopped his snowmobile for a moment to get his bearings to make sure he was heading directly back to Palmer. After checking his compass and glancing at the chart, he shoved both of them back into his pocket and took the portable radio out of its holder.

Starr took his glove off so he could work the switches properly – he wanted to be damned certain that this communications blackout had nothing to do with his end of the radio link. 'John, do you read me?' Starr asked for the hundredth time since he had decided to turn around and come back. 'Mobile Two calling Palmer station . . . Mobile Two calling John . . . Mobile Two calling Mobile One . . .' After each transmission Starr paused and waited briefly for an answer – an answer that hadn't come for more than two hours, and one that he hardly expected any longer. '. . . answer me, you bastards. Floyd, John, where the hell are you people? Mobile Two calling anyone, dammit, answer me . . .'

Starr had to fight the urge to fling the radio over one of the ice crevices. Instead, he studied it again to be certain that he had set it up properly. Of course he had, since the radio was a simple affair with two control switches, a volume knob and two indicator lights. He and John had tested it thoroughly before he had left Palmer a few hours before. The indicator lights still worked just as they had back then – yet Starr had not made even one radio contact, had not been able to speak to a single person. He hadn't really expected to be able to raise Floyd and the girls this early in his search, but it was inconceivable that John hadn't answered his first hourly check-in, or the second.

I should've turned back sooner. Something's wrong at the base. Starr was upset with himself that he had decided to press on with the search for Floyd and the girls after his first call to John at 10.30 went unanswered. He had decided that it must have been caused by an isolated patch of interference, some terrain blockage, or maybe that John had business out of the radio room and had simply missed the call. But there was no way in hell that John wouldn't have been inside and waiting for the second scheduled check-in at 11.30 – and that one also went without a response. Starr had immediately turned around, pressing the snowmobile as much as he dared considering the variable conditions on the ice pack, making good time as he headed directly back to Palmer.

Starr gave up on the radio, turned the switches off and shoved it back in its holder. Then he gunned the engine of the snowmobile and took off. The treads of the vehicle spun wildly as he kept the accelerator turned up. Long plumes of white powdery snow kicked up behind him as the treads dug in, the blowing residue also mixed with odd chunks of stone and ice.

Starr turned the handlebars of the snowmobile and the vehicle responded obediently. Now that he had gone beyond the crevice line and past the sheer vertical drops of glacial ice, Starr could safely turn to his right and head toward the coastline. Another few minutes passed and, even though he was nearing it, Starr couldn't tell exactly how close he was to the waterline because all his visual clues were distorted by varying degrees of mirage. *Slow down, dammit. Don't drive into the ocean.*

Starr backed off on the snowmobile's throttle, knowing full well that visual deceptions anywhere in the Antarctic were common enough, and near to the shoreline they were ungodly. He could feel the sudden rush of warmer air as he approached what he suspected was the shore itself – it was that drastic temperature change between cold, rocky coastline and the warmer sea that caused the mirages: it was impossible to tell where the clouds ended and the snow began. Starr throttled back even more. Suddenly, as if a cameraman had just at that moment decided to focus

149

in, the view in front of him changed dramatically from a soft blur of whites, greys and black to a recognizable form. The Cape Monaco coastline.

Ten more minutes. Starr wheeled the snowmobile to the left, parallel to the beach. To the right, between himself and the irregular scattering of rocks that made up the coastline, were a colony of Chinstrap penguins. Starr knew that if it wasn't for the roar of his snowmobile engine – something that didn't seem to bother most of the penguins and the small and boisterous Chinstraps in particular – he would have been overwhelmed by the noises from the birds. Their endless squawking rose and fell rhythmically. Predictably, their chorusing would begin with the sounds of a few solitary voices scattered throughout the rookery and then become, all at once, a deafening and unified ensemble.

Starr watched the nearest of the black-crowned birds for a moment as he sped past them. The odor from the birds' droppings, which covered nearly every rock on the narrow beach, hit him quite suddenly as he drove through on the downwind side. As always, Starr simply held his breath for a few moments as he attempted to ignore the odor. Rank aromas mixed in with pristine beauty – the Antarctic was a constant combination of extremes. Finally past the penguins, he turned his attention back to the mound of snow ahead.

Any time now. Starr was edgy to see the first sight of Palmer's buildings – the white roofs and doors, the bright blue wall panels – as the snowmobile continued to climb the last remaining obstacle between himself and the station. It was almost as if he had expected Palmer to be gone also, just as he had been told that much of the rest of the world was now gone. Nothing would have surprised him.

What he saw first was not a building at all – Starr had come out slightly left of the position that he had assumed he was at – but rather the stark black outline of the transmitting antenna. Its metal gridwork was visually etched against the grey of the deepening overcast, and Starr twisted the snowmobile handle to the left in order to head directly toward it. For the second time in two days, he was hoping to find that the antenna itself was somehow damaged – this time he needed the damaged-antenna explanation as the reason behind the lack of communications between himself and John – but Starr knew in his heart that the antenna would again be in fine shape. The Huntington Beach sign mounted on the antenna flashed by as he passed, but Michael didn't bother to look up at it. He was looking straight ahead because the roof of the first building was just coming into view.

No fire. Thank God. Like everyone else who had spent time in the Antarctic, Michael Starr was deathly afraid of fire. Even if you and your campmates survived the flames in the dry and wind-swept environment, an uncontrollable fire would force you outside and into conditions where you couldn't hope to stay alive for very long. That was why every Antarctic station was made up of several buildings and why the buildings were scattered far apart with nothing flammable linking them. Fear of fire was also the reason why the camp's net array of supplies was divided up equally and stored throughout all the buildings – this way, any fire might leave you somewhat short but not in a critical condition to survive through the remainder of the long winter. Starr pulled alongside the entrance to the main building and shut down the snowmobile.

'Christ Almighty.' The heavy, insulated door was wide open. Just inside the entrance lay the sprawled body of a man. Even before he had gotten his stiff and cold-soaked legs to dismount the snowmobile, Starr could see that the body wasn't his friend John. A pool of blood had come from a wound in the middle of the man's back and had blended together with the rivulets of muddy water on the dirty floor. The blood-and-mud mixture covered most of the entranceway and the far edges of the puddle had already begun to freeze in the cold Antarctic wind. Starr rolled the man over and looked at him. He could tell nothing, except that the dead man wore what he took to be military fatigues. 'John, are you here – can you hear me!' Starr shouted as he rummaged through the man's pockets. He could find nothing on the dead man to identify him and, after he stood up and listened, he could hear nothing from inside the building. 'John, can you . . .'

What stopped Michael this time was a distant noise, a vibration, a pulsing sound that came at him from behind. Starr stood up and wheeled around. The noise was coming from outside. He dashed out the entranceway, around his parked snowmobile and stopped on the bank of snow midway between the main building and the next. He held his breath and waited to hear more. Within moments Starr had heard the sound again and, within moments of that, had matched the sound with a visual sighting across the beachline. *Helicopters!* Two helicopters headed toward him, one laying back, hovering over the open sea, the second coming straight and fast, growing in size. Even though he had watched them for only a few moments, the nearer helicopter had gotten close enough to make its brown color and red insignia more than obvious.

Without really understanding what he was about to do or why he was doing it, Michael Starr spun around and ran back toward the entrance of Palmer's main building. He had no idea where John was, why a dead man was laying in the entranceway or why the Russian helicopter was bearing down on him – but he had no intention of staying put while he found out those answers.

'Look, he's running! Stop him!'

Major Ilya Zinoviev glanced quickly to his left toward his copilot, then out the helicopter's front windshield again. He squeezed hard on the flight controls as he continued to steer them toward the American Palmer station, toward the very building that Viktor Chemiakin had been murdered in. 'Unit two, maintain your position!' Zinoviev shouted into his helmet microphone as he pressed the transmit button on his control stick. 'Maintain a minimum distance of one kilometer from the shoreline, we are going in!'

'This could be a trap, we're too easy a target,' the copilot said nervously on the helicopter's interphone. He squirmed in his flight chair as he watched the events unfold in front of him. The unknown man on the ground had already run most of the way to the building's entranceway and would soon be safely inside. The major was pressing on straight ahead, in a low, swooping dive, as if he intended to attack. 'Are you going to shoot? Hurry, shoot at him!' The copilot didn't give a damn whether Zinoviev chose to fire his weapons or not – but what he did care about was that they'd soon be easy pickings for anyone on the ground with a rifle.

'Shut up!' Zinoviev pushed even harder on the helicopter's controls because he didn't know what else to do. He had promised Captain Kollontai and Aleksandra Bukharin that he wouldn't use force unless it was absolutely necessary, but then Boris Ney had pulled him aside just before the takeoff from the *Primorye* and convinced him that there would be great risk in attempting further dealings with the Americans. At the time, what Ney said had made great sense. 'The man down there doesn't have any weapons – none that I can see!'

'The people inside must have rifles – or even portable missiles!'

'But there's no one at the windows!' Zinoviev's voice was unusually high-pitched and pleading as he spoke to the copilot on the helicopter's interphone. He desperately wanted a reason *not* to pull the trigger, *not* to fire on the man on the ground, *not* to keep this senseless war between themselves and the Americans going on at the bottom of the world, going on at a spot that might be the last habitable place on the planet. Boris Ney had made sense to him, but Captain Kollontai and Aleksandra Bukharin had made even more sense.

Since they were now near enough to the buildings at the American Palmer station to be an easy target for anyone inside with a rifle or a large pistol, the copilot hunched himself lower in his seat. He could nearly feel the bullets beginning to whiz past the plexiglass canopy, could nearly feel the penetration of that first round of ammunition as it pushed its way through the canopy and deep into his flesh. 'He's going for a rifle!' The copilot shouted as he pointed toward the man on the ground. The American had dropped to the ground in front of a snowmobile parked near the large blue-sided building. Then he got up and seemed to be grabbing for something out of the snow-mobile. 'Fire, for the love of God! Fire!'

Major Ilya Zinoviev pressed his finger against the machine-gun trigger before he had even realized that he had done so.

Michael Starr had tripped and fallen when he ran across the churned wake that he had earlier created with his snowmobile. He got up quickly and, with a fast glance over his shoulder, saw that the helicopter would soon be on him. His only chance was to run, to get the hell out of there, to go through the main building, out the back door and into one of the smaller sheds until he could re-group and decide what to do next. It was just as he was stumbling to his feet that Starr saw what he had nearly forgotten and realized that there was still time to set it straight.

Snowmobile. Too much of an advantage. If it came to a ground chase, Starr knew he would be helpless if he were on foot and the people chasing him were in a snowmobile. Being chased by a helicopter was bad enough, but once he left the camp there were narrow glacier valleys he could hide in where the helicopter couldn't find him. A snowmobile could.

The snowmobile he had taken on his search for Floyd and the girls was their only functioning unit still at the base, so he needed to disable it. Starr lunged forward and grabbed for the key, his gloved hand making it even more difficult for him to first get a grip on the key and then twist and pull it out of the ignition. Just as the key came loose in his hands, Starr fell backward from its sudden release from the ignition. As he hit the snow, a spurt of bullets passed an inch above his head. The bullets tore viciously into the blue wall of the building behind him, tearing the sheetmetal as if it were no more than a can of baked beans opened for lunch.

Stay down! Get inside! Starr had never been in the army, never in his life been shot at — and he could hardly believe that he was being shot at now. The helicopter, the roar from its engine and its whirling blades creating an enormous bellowing of sound, was no more than a hundred feet horizontally away from him and only ten or so feet above the ground. Its two pilots – who were now nearly at eye level with Starr, he could clearly see the men's helmets, their face visors pulled down – had slowed the helicopter's approach and were trying to realign themselves for another shot. On his hands and knees, Starr pushed and clawed his way into the entranceway. He splashed through the puddle of bloody water and clambered over the dead man's body just as the next burst of bullets tore into the façade.

Out the back. Find a weapon. Starr ran down the hallway, stopping for an instant at the doorways of several rooms while he frantically looked inside each. He saw nothing of use to him. When he reached his own bedroom he rushed in, yanked open the dresser drawers and dumped the contents out on his bed. By the third drawer he had found his hunting knife, which he shoved into his jacket pocket.

Starr looked around the room and saw nothing else of value. He knew that the only rifle at the Palmer station had gone with Floyd and the girls, so he had nothing to defend himself with except his hunting knife. Starr was just about to leave when he spotted something leaning beside the door. His baseball bat, his Louisville Slugger, the one he had brought with him from home more as a joke than for any real purpose, but the one they had actually used a few times when they played softball on the glacier on those few sunny and windless days. The last time they had played, Starr had hit a home run that had traveled so far that the ball landed on a piece of floating ice in the bay and they needed to send out a motor boat to retrieve it. Starr grabbed the bat and sprinted down the corridor, then out the rear door and across the snow toward one of the storage buildings across the perimeter.

Starr entered the small metal building and, after he had caught his breath, he edged up to the window and looked outside. The first helicopter had set down on the snow a few hundred yards away, its machine guns pointed toward the main building. Starr could also see that the helicopter had two rockets mounted below the cockpit on either side. *Christ. Rockets. I'm dead.* His initial impression had been that the helicopter bore Russian markings, and now that he had a moment to look it over, the several sets of red insignia and cyrillic lettering confirmed it.

Russians. World War III. Bastards. As far as Starr was concerned, these Russians were attempting to start World War IV – a limited affair, perhaps, but one that would put him in the same position as his friends in Illinois and California. World War IV. Michael had no idea who had won World War III – nobody probably – but he vowed to himself that he wasn't going to be on the losing side of this one.

Starr turned and scanned the coastline, just in time to catch a last glimpse of the second Russian helicopter as it disappeared in the distance behind the jagged coastline. It was either going back to its home base or, more probably, doing some kind of scouting work. The Russians probably didn't know how many Americans were at the Palmer station, so they intended to do some reconnoitering of the area. That made sense. It also meant that he had ten minutes or less to gain the upper hand or he would be trapped in a crossfire between two helicopters – a less than enviable position.

One of the pilots from the first helicopter had come out of the cockpit and stood beneath the whirling blades. Even from this far, Starr could see that the man was short and muscular. He had taken off his flight helmet and Starr could see that the guy was bald-headed. He held an automatic machine-gun in his hands and moved forward slowly. He was taking absolutely no chances because the helicopter kept its engine running at a good clip and its twin blades whirling rapidly – which caused periodic swirls of powdery snow to cascade around the area.

The helicopter kept turning from side to side on its skids in order to keep the man on foot adequately covered. If anyone fired toward that man as he walked across the snow, the helicopter would then pulverize the spot where that shot had come from. The Russian tactic was to protect

156

the man on foot very well, using the firepower of the helicopter as a sort of battle tank. The Russian tactic gave Starr an idea.

Hit them where they don't expect it. His only chance was to go after the helicopter while the guy on foot went toward the building. Starr watched as the bald-headed man with the sub-machine-gun stepped in the main building, over the body, then disappeared into the interior. Without giving himself time to come up with any one of a thousand good excuses why it wouldn't work, Starr edged out the door of the small storage shed he was in, his baseball bat in one hand, his hunting knife in the other.

Make this quick, he can't hear you anyway. Starr broke into as fast a sprint as he could manage in his boots and bulky jacket, his feet falling heavily on the snow, but the noise was more than covered by the enormous racket from the helicopter. He was headed directly for the helicopter, although he was approaching it from the rear left corner and out of what he expected would be the pilot's normal scan. Starr's plan was to jump on board through the opened cabin door, kill the pilot with his hunting knife, then use whatever rifle or handgun he could find on board to defend himself from the bald-headed guy with the sub-machine-gun.

Almost. Get ready. Fifty yards. Starr could feel his pounding heart as he pumped his legs as hard as he could. Forty yards. He held the knife in front of him, its long silver blade glimmering brightly, even in the dull light of the overcast sky. Thirty yards. *Jump on him. Don't hold back.* Twenty yards. *Shit!* The helicopter had begun to turn to the left, its skids rising slightly off the snow, its long and angular body tilting in the direction of its turn.

He sees me. God help me. But even while he watched the helicopter twist around in order to point its machine-guns directly at him, Michael Starr kept running toward it at full speed. Ten yards. *No chance.*

The front of the helicopter was pointed nearly straight at him, and Starr could see the pilot hunched over the controls, could nearly make out the man's face even though he was wearing his flight helmet with its visor pulled down. The helicopter was fully airborne now, two or three feet above the snow, and white covering of loose powder over the hard-packed ice beginning to blow upward even faster and obscure everything as the man-made wind took hold.

Go for it. Without breaking stride and with a sharp and fluid motion of his left arm, Starr tossed the Louisville Slugger baseball bat toward the core of the twin helicopter rotors which were now no more than fifteen feet away. As soon as he did, Starr broke hard left into the thickest part of the blowing snow, his boots digging in like spikes, his body turning as if he were rounding second base and heading for third.

What he really expected was the helicopter's machine-gun to send a bullet across his spine and cut him down, like a sharp throw from an accurate leftfielder who intended to pick him off on his slide into third. That bullet into his spine would signal the last out for his side – and this was definitely the bottom of the ninth. But instead of the sound of that machine-gun, Michael Starr heard something else.

The sound of the rotors breaking up was unmistakable – harsh, foul, obscene noises of metal against metal, of carefully machined bearings disintegrating, of balanced sections of honed metal breaking apart like twigs. Starr glanced over his shoulder in time to see the helicopter yaw violently to its right, half its rotors already gone, the other half not far behind. The baseball bat had caught the rotors just right, mingling between the counter-rotating blades, causing each to impinge on the clear travel path of the other, causing the two sets of closely-fitted blades to bend enough to knock each other down.

The helicopter, now totally out of control, rolled more as it continued along its original line of motion. The outboard blades were already nicking into the snow, and this caused the disintegration process to speed up. Entire sections of metal and fiberglass were being flung off in every direction. Yet the engine continued to roar, and the hub kept flailing around what little was left of its twin set of rotor blades.

Suddenly, as if the machine had just decided for itself that all was lost, that now was the right time for the *coup de grâce*, the Russian helicopter exploded all at once in a violent flash of pure white, followed by long plumes of red flame that leapt a hundred feet straight up, followed by a mushrooming column of billowy black smoke. The carcass of that helicopter – no more than a hideous scattering of torn metallic skin and bones compared to what it had been half a minute before – skidded into the main building at Palmer

The blue walls and white roof of Palmer's main building collapsed onto the burning wreckage. Starr did not wait around to see what, if anything, would be left of the place where he once lived, of the place where he thought he would be spending the Antarctic winter, of the place into which the bald-headed Russian with the sub-machine-gun had disappeared. Starr knew that the other helicopter would be back shortly – and that meant that he needed to be far, far away.

But even as he turned and ran toward the snow-covered hills and the glacier beyond it that stretched out in front of him, Starr began to realize that things had changed, that the score was adding up differently. As far as Michael Starr was concerned, the Russians had just struck out and his team was coming to bat.

Eleven

IT WAS nearly dark, nearly five o'clock, by the time *Airship Nine* reached a position abeam Cape Monaco and turned down the Bismark Strait toward the Palmer station. The visibility out the cockpit windows had been decreasing steadily, and that condition had forced the blimp lower and lower over the Antarctic sea until they were at the minimum height that Captain Whitaker would allow them to descend. 'Hold it at 300 feet,' Whitaker announced to the second officer who sat in the copilot's seat.

'Yessir.' Steve Galloway made the appropriate adjustments to the autopilot's controls while he continued to monitor the flight instruments.

'I don't want us to get speared by a tall iceberg.'

'Right.'

Satisfied that all was as it should be, Whitaker turned to the people standing behind him. 'If we're in the clouds or in very heavy snow as we approach the beach, we can't risk a landfall. The radar is accurate enough to let us hug the coastline, but we can't do an actual landing with it.' Whitaker tapped his finger on the colored electronic presentation in front of him, the hues of green, yellow and red displaying a portrayal of the land that stretched less than one mile in front of them, all of it invisible through the mounting snowstorm.

'I understand.' Floyd Robinson frowned, then nervously rubbed his hands together. He wished to God that he had more than two cigarettes left so he wouldn't have to ration them so carefully – he knew that he sure could use one now. More than anything, he wanted to be on the ground at Palmer so he could get more cigarettes, so he could get his people together, so he could call the South Pole station on the short-wave radio, so he could sleep in his own bed tonight. 'But I still think we have a chance. Stay as close to the coast as you can . . .'

'That's what I intend to do,' Whitaker answered.

'. . . and we might see enough for a quick landing.' Robinson looked over at Annie, who had drawn one of the long straws to be in the landing party, then over at Julie, who had drawn the short one to remain on board. 'Once you get us down there, we'll be all right. We've got lots of supplies down there, lots of room.'

'Good, because I might not be able to pick you up for awhile. If this storm gets any worse I'll go back out to sea and hover off the coast until it clears – I can't risk being blown into the rocks or into that radio antenna you told me about.'

'Of course.' Robinson looked back at the radar scope, then out the cockpit window again. All he could see was the ocean waves directly beneath them, and not very clearly at that. The captain was right, the horizontal visibility was very low, and dropping fast. 'I'll get the landing party ready to jump out, in case you can find the station.'

'Fine.' Whitaker turned back to the second officer. 'I'll take over, you go back and give them a hand. Be sure to reel in the rope ladder after they leave, so that it doesn't snag on anything.' The last thing they needed was for *Airship Nine* to become a tethered balloon flailing around in a snowstorm.

'Yessir.' Galloway slid out of the right front cockpit seat, squeezed past Julie who continued to stand in the companionway behind the captain, then followed Robinson and the other woman toward the staircase that led below.

'Here, sit down.' Whitaker gestured for Julie to get into the copilot's seat while he fine-tuned the radar again.

'How's the radar working?' Julie asked. She pushed back her long blonde hair and glanced down at the set.

'Good. Here's the coastline, see?'

'Yes.'

'And here's that inlet that you people told me about. That's what we're headed toward. With our engine power reduced to its best-economy setting and also considering

161

the headwinds, our forward speed can't be more than forty knots at best.'

'The Palmer buildings are just beyond that inlet, a few hundred yards.'

'That's probably the buildings on the screen – those little dots of red against the green background – although it's difficult to say for sure.'

'Oh.'

'With any luck, we'll have the landing party on the beach in fifteen minutes.' Satisfied that the radar was working as well as he could get it, Whitaker turned his full attention to Julie. 'I know that you wanted to go ashore with the rest of them, but I needed one of you from Palmer to stay on board. I might need advice on the layout, that sort of thing.'

'Sure, no problem. I'll get to see John and Michael soon enough anyway.'

'Right.' At her mentioning those names, Whitaker felt a strange sensation pass through him, a sensation that he hadn't felt in a good many years – and one that embarrassed him now. It was an unmistakable twinge of jealousy. *Don't be an idiot. Don't let yourself act like a kid, you're forty-five years old.* 'I wish we had a radio on board that had Palmer's frequency. Then we could tell your friends that we were coming.'

'They're pretty resourceful guys. I bet they're more worried about what happened to us.'

'Probably.' Whitaker felt like a teenage boy trying to make a date with someone he was afraid would turn him down. Somehow, time had flashed back thirty years and he was trying to date the prom queen again. He hated every minute of this, yet – just like that first time from so many years before – he couldn't take his eyes off the girl. Spending time with Julie – casual conversations, two meals together when they sat side by side, some private time together in the lounge and then in the cockpit – were the only pleasant moments he had managed to salvage in the last two days. Whitaker also suspected that she knew how he felt, but he had no idea how she did. *Keep your mind on business. Get ready for the landing.* Yet as much as he tried to block out the image of Julie Mathews' presence as she sat a few feet to his right, Lou Whitaker found that he couldn't.

The group assembled in the lower cargo bay were dressed in every conceivable kind of heavy garment they could find, with the quality of jackets, boots and coats ranging from the designer fashions worn by Andrew and Kathleen Sinclair to the soiled workman's jacket of Floyd Robinson. The physical condition of the people ranged as widely, too, with First Officer Ray Madigan the most fit, while overweight Frank Corbi was obviously the least. 'Okay – everyone understand their instructions?' Madigan asked once more as he scanned the group.

'I have a question.' Andrew Sinclair stepped forward, having just finished combing his hair. Everyone waited while he paused to put the plastic comb into his ski-jacket pocket and zipper it shut. 'Even if the visibility picks up enough for a landing, it's probably going to turn sour again. Why can't we just plan on making ourselves comfortable in the station and wait until the weather clears completely?'

'The captain covered that point already, but I'll repeat what he said.' With every passing moment, Madigan felt more sympathy for Captain Whitaker's position in this nightmare – just as he had noticed that Whitaker seemed to be treating him more fairly now, too. Unbelievable as it had seemed, he and Whitaker had even shared a few kind words with each other the night before, after the evening meal. 'With our situation being so unpredictable, the captain felt that we should stay together whenever possible.'

'Why?'

'In case of a sudden change in plans. Obviously, being on board the airship gives us a lot more flexibility than being stuck at any single ground location.'

'That concept is open to debate.'

'No it isn't, Mr Sinclair.' Madigan raised himself to his full height and took a deep breath to help keep his temper in tow. He glanced over at Nancy, who stood near the hatchway door, the rope ladder in her hands, a packet of emergency provisions slung around her shoulders. She had turned out to be a real trouper when things got rough – she had volunteered to go through the landing with him, even though she had reason enough to stay on board if she wanted to – and Madigan was proud of her. He had even told her so the night before. 'This isn't a college debating society, Mr Sinclair, and I'm not the moderator. I'm not asking you if you agree with what the plans are, I'm only asking you if you understand them. Is that clear?'

'Don't get excited,' Sinclair answered flippantly.

'If you think that I'm excited now, wait and see what happens if you keep pushing me.' Madigan allowed the heavy silence in the lower cargo bay to linger for several seconds before he finally spoke again. 'Like we briefed before,' he continued as he turned to the group in general, 'we'll head straight for the main building and assemble there. If there's any need for a search, we'll break into our two prearranged sections.'

'And I'll stay back to guard the fort,' Corbi added good-naturedly. He had been given the assignment of remaining at the main building to coordinate activities. Normally, he would have liked to go into the field – but by staying at the fixed center point as he had been in-structed, he figured that his film clips of the action would be more meaningful. Without even realizing that he was doing it, Corbi cinched up the straps on his backpack still tighter to be absolutely certain that the camera wouldn't fall out.

'Okay, if everyone's ready then all we do is wait.' Madigan joined Nancy at the opened door. He smiled at her, then looked out below at the endless whitecaps that lapped over each other on the Antarctic sea. The wind was picking up, and so was the snow. If they didn't get to land at Palmer very soon, it might be days before the weather cleared enough to let them have another shot at it. But before he could think another negative thought, the sight of the rocky coastline came into full view beneath them. 'There it is – get ready, put on your face masks!'

Each of the people in the landing party began to pull

on the woolen face masks they had made earlier that afternoon. All of the masks were crude and misshapen affairs, although they would work effectively to keep faces from being frost-bitten during the walk from the beach to the station buildings. Frank Corbi's mask, in particular, looked the most hideous because it had too much extra material at its top and its eye and mouth holes were each cut at slightly the wrong spot. Even though hers wasn't much better, when Annie Rizzo looked over at Corbi she began to laugh – and Corbi began to laugh back.

Steve Galloway, who had been standing at the rear of the room, had the ship's interphone pressed against his ear. After listening for another moment, he spoke quickly into the mouthpiece, then hung the interphone up. 'The captain says we're over the beach, descending to fifty feet. This is as close as he can get – throw out the ladder.' Galloway watched as Nancy complied.

'Here I go.' Ray Madigan was the first down, the rope ladder swinging back and forth alarmingly because of the motions of his body in the wind. When he reached the bottom, he jumped off and began to steady the ladder for each of the others who came down. Within just a couple of minutes all seven of them were assembled on the beach – just in time because the flight visibility had dropped again and was now no more than a hundred yards. Even a visual target as big and as near to them as *Airship Nine* was difficult to see, and within seconds of when Galloway had hauled up the rope the blimp had turned away enough to disappear completely into the bleary grey of the snowstorm.

'Follow me!' Robinson had taken the lead as he was supposed to, and each of the others followed behind in close single file. Robinson found what he was looking for by literally stumbling on it and almost falling. 'Here – follow this walkway to the camp!' he shouted to the group behind him. From where he stood at the head of the line, he could see the dark and bundled shapes of the first two people in the procession but no more of them than that. He prayed that none of the other four had straggled off the walkway or they would be long dead before they could be found. The weather was getting worse by the minute.

Robinson knew that what they were doing was extremely dangerous – attempting to find their way across the Antarctic terrain in a blinding snowstorm – but the walkway made it reasonably safe. Still, the history of Antarctic exploring was packed with stories of men dying twenty feet from their huts, unable to find them again in the sudden, driving blizzards.

Finally, Robinson had his first glimpse of the Palmer main building –'and when he did, he doubted the validity of what his eyes were seeing. A mirage, probably, caused by the swirling pellets of snow. But Robinson had changed his mind by the time he had taken two more steps forward. 'Oh, my God!' He began to run toward the decimated, charred structure. 'John, Michael – can you hear me!' Robinson stopped where the entrance used to be, all of it completely destroyed, the frame of the burnt-out helicopter stuck in the middle of the wreckage of the roof and walls.

Madigan, who had been bringing up the rear to prevent anyone from straggling off, pushed his way past the others in front of the wreckage. 'Christ Almighty, what happened?'

'I don't know.'

'Do you know whose helicopter this is?'

'Not ours.' Robinson reached out and touched what was left of the twisted and smoke-stained wreckage.

'It's a military chopper.' Madigan walked slowly around it as best he could considering the debris on the ground.

'Doesn't look like any kind I've ever seen.' Robinson pulled his face mask off and watched as the others in the group followed suit. Even though the Palmer building was totally destroyed, its twisted sections of walls and roof provided some protection from the driving snow. They could function in the area downwind of the building for a short while without their faces being covered.

'I'd say it's a Russian helicopter.' Madigan didn't want to admit even to himself that what was left of that fuselage clearly resembled one of the Soviet machines he had seen

166

in his travels – a Kamov, or something of that sort – because it opened up too many other unanswered questions. Instead, he asked about something else. 'What about your two men?'

'I don't know.' Robinson was getting tired of saying that, tired of not knowing. He scanned the remains of the building. Clearly, if either John or Michael were inside when the helicopter hit – and there was no reason to believe that they shouldn't have been – then they were dead. 'It doesn't look good.'

'Right.' Madigan kicked a small piece of wreckage that lay near his foot. 'It might take hours to look through this wreckage for them.'

'Yes.' Robinson didn't like the idea of not knowing for sure if the bodies of his two men were in the wreckage of the main building or not, but the copilot was right. Hours, at least, probably days, to sift through that enormous pile of debris. 'I guess we should look for them at the other buildings. While we do, we can try to retrieve whatever supplies we can.'

'Makes sense.' Madigan looked up at the sky. The snow had turned to blizzard proportions and he suddenly realized that their group of seven could be in real danger if they didn't get inside one of the other buildings very soon. 'This place is a write-off,' he said as he pointed his thumb over his shoulder toward the charred remains behind him. 'Nothing left worth a damn. Let's go.'

'Follow me. Let's all stick together from this point on.'

'No argument with that.' Madigan motioned for everyone to put their face masks back on, then did the same himself. 'Here we go – and don't lose sight of the person in front of you.'

The group retraced their steps for a short distance, then, following Robinson's lead, they turned sharply to the right to follow a cable stretched waist-high across wooden poles stuck in the snow. The visibility had gotten worse, but no one could tell exactly how much worse because the wind-driven slivers of ice and snow that slammed into them forced them to keep their heads down. Any small portion of their skin that was exposed – the loose areas

167

around their face masks, their eyelids, the tiny openings that a few of them had inadvertently created between their gloves and jacket sleeves – were open to attack by sharp needles of ice and snow. Even though the group reached the next building in the Palmer station array in less than three minutes, it seemed like hours to all of them.

'Incredible . . .' Robinson stood beside what had once been the machinery building – it was as badly destroyed as the main building had been. The walls were blown away, and a fire had gutted the insides completely. 'What the hell could have caused this?'

'I don't know. It doesn't look like an accident.'

'Are you sure?'

'No.' Madigan shook his head. 'But that's what I think.'

'It's hard to tell.' Yet Robinson hadn't been surprised by what Madigan had suggested since he had already begun to think along the same lines himself.

'Where's the next building?' Madigan didn't like what he was seeing. A Russian helicopter had crashed into one building, a separate building had obviously been pummeled by some sort of explosion and burnt to the ground – it had the earmarks of one hell of a battle.

'The next building isn't very far. This way.'

'Okay.' Yet even before they reached the outbuilding that was used primarily for food storage, Madigan knew what to expect. If anything, it was worse than the other two. 'What now?' he asked Robinson, his mouth nearly up against the man's ear in order to make himself clearly heard above the howling wind. The walk to the food storage building – a forced march was a more accurate term for it – had been mostly uphill, and that put them right in the thickest part of the pelting ice and snow.

'There's nothing else at Palmer, except one hut near the transmitting antenna.' Robinson pointed further up the hill.

'How far?'

'Too far for the group. I'll go alone.'

'Too dangerous.' Madigan admired the man's courage, but he couldn't let him do anything suicidal.

'No. The transmitter's antenna cable runs along the

ground from here to there – there's no way to get lost.' Robinson was nearly shouting, even though he stood less than an arm's length from Madigan. The combination of the way his face mask fit him, plus the effects of the weather, made it nearly impossible to hear anything but the damned wind.

'Where is this cable?'

'You're standing on it.' Robinson pointed to the black plastic tubing lying inches to the left of Madigan's foot.

'How long would it take to get up there?'

'I's think's not very long, masser, 'cause I's freezin' my black ass off.' Robinson realized that this was the first time he had used his 'old-nigger' voice since they had been picked up by *Airship Nine* and told about the prospect of the end of the world. Somehow, using that voice had made him feel better, made him feel more alive, more resourceful. 'But the real question,' he said, going back to his normal voice, 'is what you're going to do when I get back. We've got no place to stay now, we need your airship to pick us up.'

'I know, I'm working on it – get going.' Madigan watched Robinson move along the antenna cable until, just a dozen feet or so away, he was engulfed in the impenetrable grey of the snowstorm.

Andrew Sinclair was the first to come up to Madigan after Robinson had left. 'We've got to get inside,' he shouted as he adjusted the fit between his face mask and the designer ski-jacket matching that which his wife wore. 'I'm freezing, we could die out here.'

'I know.' Madigan turned to the entire group, who had assembled around him in a semicircle. 'Everyone lay down on the snow and pull one of those pieces of sheetmetal over you.'

'Those pieces are burnt.'

'Metal doesn't burn – its got some soot on it, that's all.' Madigan gestured toward the pile of debris that had once been the food storage building. 'That'll help keep the wind away from you while we wait for Robinson to come back.'

'Dammit, that's not good enough! We need to get

warm!' Sinclair's voice was a strange combination of a shout and a whimper.

Madigan glared at Sinclair for several seconds before he finally answered him in loud but measured tones so everyone else could hear. *Whitaker is right. Being the guy in charge is sometimes a pain in the ass.* 'I tell you what, Andy. If you don't shut the hell up, I'll put a match to your Yves Saint Laurent jacket. I bet that'll warm us up pretty quick.'

Floyd Robinson had fallen eight times – he had lost count after five – before he reached what he thought was the crest of the hill. The urge to shout John and Michael's names was great, but he resisted the temptation because he knew it would be a useless gesture in the wind. *If they're not at the transmitter hut, they're dead.* Robinson kept his body hunched over for two reasons, to help himself keep one hand on the plastic cable run so he wouldn't lose it and also to make himself as small a target as possible while he moved forward into the fierce and biting wind.

Chicken soup. Honest to God, two gallons of it, five gallons of it. Wait'll I get back to the airship. The powdery snow had gotten deeper as he trudged along the cable run, and now he was beginning to feel the cold dampness as it crept up his legs and sliced through what little warmth was left around his crotch. *Chicken soup.* Robinson's fingers and toes were now numb.

Chicken soup. Chicken legs. Chicken Little. The snow Robinson pushed through was sometimes above his knees. That caused the front of his jacket and sometimes even his face mask to brush against the mounds of cold, white powder. He was forced to hunch over even more in order to keep at least one hand on the cable run as he followed it through the mounting drifts. *Chicken gumbo. Chicken and rice. Chicken tetrazzini. Chicken shit.*

Robinson took one more step forward, knowing that he was nearly up to where the cable run would lead into the transmitter hut and then out to the antenna itself. He had the sudden impression that something was directly ahead of him. Robinson looked up.

The heavily-bundled man was no more than five feet away, both his hands held high above his head, a piece of twisted, charred metal tubing raised as a makeshift axe. For an instant, the appearance of the man's clothes – torn garments wrapped around each other to keep them together, entire sections of excess cloth trailing off his shoulders and hips as they hung into the deep white powder that was half way up his legs, the tattered remains of a red scarf swirled mummy-style around his face – gave him the appearance of a science-fiction monster, a devil reincarnated from snowy grave. 'Bastards . . .!' The ice-covered monster began to swing his makeshift weapon down on the hunched-over figure in front of him.

'Michael – no!' Robinson had seen just a hint of the man's eyes beneath the folds of the scarf around his face, and it had made enough of an impression to cause him to shout out a name.

Michael Starr had already begun his downswing – there was no way he could miss splitting this Russian bastard's skull in half – when he heard his name and realized that the heavily-bundled figure on the snow in front of him was not one of the Russians who had destroyed Palmer and chased him off to die in the snow, but one of his own people instead, one of the people he was certain he'd never see again. *Floyd.* At the last possible instant, Starr exerted enough willpower to pull his arms slightly to one side.

The makeshift axe missed Robinson's head by inches as it buried itself in the snow. 'Michael – it's me!'

'Floyd . . . God . . . Thank God . . .' Starr took half a step toward the man he had intended to kill – and had nearly done so. 'Floyd . . . I looked . . . couldn't find . . .'

'Where's John?'

'Don't know, couldn't find . . . ' The efforts of the last few moments had already drained Starr of what little energy remained in him. His legs slowly crumbled beneath him and he began to fall. Michael Starr was already unconscious before he fell, face down, into the snow.

'Damn.' Robinson grabbed hold of Michael and began to drag him backward through the drifts, pausing every few steps to make certain that he was still straddling the antenna cable that he needed as a guideline to get back. *A few more steps. Just a few more steps.* Even though Michael was heavy, Robinson now had the wind and the downhill grade in his favor. In less time than he might have imagined, he was able to pull Michael down the hill and into what was left of the food storage building where the others waited for him.

'What happened?' Madigan rushed up while the others followed.

'I don't know. He collapsed right after I found him.'

'Let me look at him!' Kathleen Sinclair took off her face mask as she knelt beside the unconscious man, her long red hair blowing straight behind her in the wind. She began to examine him carefully, looking first for signs of bleeding and then for broken bones.

Seeing that Starr was being attended to, Robinson turned to Madigan. 'We've got to get out of here – and fast.' He could tell from his own condition – complete numbness of the extremities, a deep chill that seemed to reach into even the insides of his bones – that frostbite was at hand and hypothermia was not far behind for any of them.

'What about the other missing guy?'

'No chance. Just before he collapsed, Michael said something about not being able to find John – or at least I think that's what he said.'

'We'll have to go with that.'

'Yes.' Robinson shivered again. He was, he knew, close to muscular convulsions from the cold. Killing themselves wouldn't help John, no matter what had happened to him. God rest his soul. 'We've got to get going. Right now.'

'I know.' Madigan shook his head. He had already spoken to *Airship Nine* on the portable radio in his pocket, and neither he nor Whitaker had come up with a workable plan. If only the snowstorm would slack off for ten minutes, then they would have a chance to rendezvous with the airship somewhere on the beach. Madigan looked up at the sky – not only was the snowfall heavier than ever, but now darkness was becoming another factor to contend with. Twenty minutes of twilight left, at the most.

They took a few minutes to place Michael Starr securely on a piece of torn sheetmetal that they used as a sleigh, then positioned him in the middle of the group with the Sinclairs pushing while Corbi, Annie and Nancy Schneider pulled. Again, helped by the wind and the downhill run, they reached the turn where the waist-high rope guide ended and the permanent wooden platform led down to the beach.

'Any ideas?' Robinson asked once, after he had seen the copilot transmitting on the portable handheld radio.

'No.'

They made the turn, then traveled down the wooden platform until they reached the beach. Down there, the smooth snow on either side of the narrow wooden platform gave way to irregular piles of rocks that made their footing difficult, especially with the high wind pushing them.

'Where's the blimp?' Andrew Sinclair shouted as he pushed his way to the front.

'Out there.' Madigan gestured over his shoulder without apparent concern, as if he were discussing what time the next rush-hour bus would be along.

'What the hell is he waiting for, why doesn't he pick us up? I'm freezing to death!'

'You hit the nail on the head, mister.' Madigan, too, was freezing and – he'd admit it now if anyone cared to ask – damned scared. As good a pilot as he really knew Whitaker was, there was no way in hell that the captain could find them along this beachfront with the prevailing visibility less than twenty feet. Their group had become the proverbial needle in the haystack, with the added complication that their bodies couldn't survive more than another sixty minutes out in the blowing snow and driving wind.

'What do you mean!' Even through the muffling effect of his face mask, Sinclair sounded as if he were going to cry.

'What I mean,' Madigan answered loud enough for all of them to hear since he decided it was time to let them all in on the truth of their situation, 'is that unless we either get real lucky with the weather or come up with some other idea, the blimp can't get to us. He can't find us. We're invisible. The goddamned snowfall is obscuring our position. I just talked to Whitaker on the radio and he's going to try to run along the beachline with the rope ladder down in hopes that he drags it right over us. The odds of that happening are small, real small.'

Frank Corbi stepped up and positioned himself between the copilot and young Andrew Sinclair. Sinclair – the Yale graduate, class of '83, as he had reminded everyone repeatedly – had apparently been struck dumb by the news. He stood immobile, his mouth agape. He looked pitiful. 'Close your mouth, Andy,' Corbi said. He felt sorry for Sinclair and wanted to jar him back to life. 'Come on, buddy, shut your jaws. You're eating too much of our snow, not leaving any for us.' Without answering him, Sinclair turned and walked away, still in some kind of trance. Corbi watched him for another moment, then turned to face Madigan again. 'What about a fire?' Corbi asked.

'Fire?'

'Yes. We can set a fire here on the beach so Captain Whitaker can find us.' Corbi was getting enthusiastic about his idea and, for the moment, he had forgotten how painfully cold his shoulders and arms had become. 'We can get this place to look like Atlanta did in *Gone with the Wind*. A real bonfire – and I can get my rear warmed into the bargain!'

'That's a good idea,' Robinson said as he stepped up to the other two. 'But it won't work.'

'Why?'

'Nothing left to burn. When I looked those buildings over I saw that they'd already been totally consumed by fire. We've got nothing to start a fire with, and nothing to keep it going.'

'Damn.'

'Even then,' Madigan added, 'I don't think it would

174

help very much. Visibility is too low to see even a big fire.'

'I see what you mean.' Corbi shook his head as he looked at the snow whirling around them. 'What we really need is a laser beam from a science fiction movie, some kind of light saber like Lucas used in *Starwars*. That's what we need to cut through the snow and reach out to the airship.'

Beam. Reach out to the airship. 'Holy shit, hold on a minute!' Madigan fumbled in his pocket for the portable radio, nearly dropping it into the snow as he pulled it out.

'For Chrissake, be careful!'

Madigan ignored Robinson and the others and began to talk excitedly to *Airship Nine* on the portable radio. After a few quick exchanges, he turned to the group. 'Okay, Corbi, Robinson, Sinclair – follow me. You three stay here,' he said to Nancy and the other two women who continued to huddle over Michael Starr. 'We'll be right back.'

'Where are we going?' Corbi nudged Sinclair and then moved forward, following Robinson and Madigan. They stumbled up the wooden walkway toward the main building, none of them speaking because it took too much energy to muscle their way against the blinding snowstorm.

Once they reached the charred shell of the main building, the four men paused a moment to catch their breath. Finally, Madigan spoke. 'Each of you grab one of those metal sheets.' Madigan showed what he meant by lifting a large panel that had once been a section of the Palmer building roof from under the pile of debris. 'Keep it low so the wind doesn't take it. Get back to the beach as quick as you can.'

With each of them pulling as much of the sheetmetal as they could, they returned to the beach. Without a word, Madigan began to erect the pieces as well as he could. Several times the wind knocked the sheet metal sections down, but after a few minutes Madigan had erected what amounted to a circular wall.

'Is this a windbreak for us?' Robinson asked. He was so exhausted that he could barely speak, yet he was afraid to sit down because he knew that the sweat he had worked

175

up doing the hauling would quickly freeze on his skin. Then he would die of exposure.

Madigan was speaking on the portable radio again. After several seconds he shut the radio down, shoved it back in his pocket and turned to the others. The group had all assembled in front of the metal shield to get what little protection from the wind they could find. They waited to see what Madigan had to say. 'This wasn't intended as a windbreak, although it'll serve as one for a few minutes.'

'What's it supposed to be?'

'Our light saber, our way to reach out to *Airship Nine*.' Madigan gestured triumphantly because he had already been told by Whitaker that his plan had worked. 'A radar reflector shield. By standing the metal panels on end and facing them to the sea, we provided enough of a radar target for Whitaker to find our exact location on the beach.'

Madigan had no sooner finished than, as if to confirm what he had said, a shape began to appear. At first it was nothing but a heavier line in the mist, but it quickly developed into a form that had both a beginning and end, a patch of dark substance, a distinct outline. *Airship Nine* emerged from grey nothingness and hovered motionless above them in spite of the howling wind, the glow from the lights in its warm and comfortable cabin providing a backdrop of illumination for the scene that would follow.

The rope ladder dropped from *Airship Nine* and each of the people on the beach began to climb aboard. A rope harness was rigged for Michael Starr – who still remained unconscious – and he, too, was soon brought to safety. Ray Madigan was the last of the landing party to scurry up the rope ladder and into the cabin. With everyone aboard, Captain Whitaker wheeled his craft around and rapidly headed away from the dangerous coastal obstacles that posed a constant threat to the ship's polyurethane hull. Within minutes, *Airship Nine* was back to relative safety over the open Antarctic sea.

Twelve

THE BRIDGE of the Soviet motorship *Primorye* was crowded. In the center of the expansive, glass-walled room were the ship's First Mate Sergei Timoshenko, Navigation Officer Orlov and, behind them, the helmsman and two other seamen. On the far side were the three remaining members of the governing council: Captain Kollontai, Doctor Boris Ney and Aleksandra Bukharin.

At Kollontai's insistence, the *nachalstvo* had just finished holding their latest meeting – an emergency meeting to review what had happened at the American Palmer station – in full view of the operating crew on the *Primorye*'s bridge. Aleksandra Bukharin had agreed with Kollontai that there should be no more secrets from the people on the *Primorye*, and the two of them had collectively overruled Ney. Holding their meeting in front of the operating crew was the quickest and easiest way to take the secretiveness out of the *nachalstvo*'s plans. Now that the meeting had more or less been concluded, everyone on the ship's bridge stood in silence as the ship plowed on through the icy waves. They all kept their attention focused forward, even though there was nothing out there to be seen.

The shrouded blackness of the snowstorm engulfed the ship and deprived the people on the bridge of their normal panoramic view. All that was visible out ahead was the misty outline of the ship's bow. First Mate Timoshenko leaned forward in an exaggerated gesture of scanning the horizon. He used that action as his preamble to speaking since, theoretically, the conversations he had overheard from the far corner of the ship's bridge were not actually meant for him. 'I haven't seen a snowfall like this since last year's winter cruise,' Timoshenko said in order to break the uncomfortable silence that lay across all of them like a heavy winter blanket.

'Last year's cruise?' Navigator Orlov asked casually. He could hardly believe what he had heard during the past half hour as the three surviving members of the *nachalstvo* openly discussed the facts of the current situation: what had happened at the Palmer station, what the new scientific evidence about the effects of the world-wide nuclear war was and what the possible choices still open to the people on board the *Primorye* would be. After all of that, Orlov was glad to hear Timoshenko's friendly voice as it shattered the tension. 'Where did you go on that winter cruise?'

'The East Siberian sea.'

'Ah, yes.'

'That whole damned area is a frozen hell, from Laptev to Chukchi.'

'I once sailed from Ostrov Vrangelya to Novyy just before the pack ice closed in, and that was the worst weather I'd ever seen.' Orlov looked out the bridge window again. 'The worst I'd seen until this trip.'

'I'd agree with that.' Because it was his duty to do so, the first mate turned to Captain Kollontai. The captain stood silently on the port quarter of the bridge. Timoshenko knew that he had a protocol obligation to let the captain participate in their conversation since he was on the bridge with them, so Timoshenko addressed the captain directly. 'This is certainly one hell of a storm, captain,' Timoshenko said awkwardly. 'Have you ever sailed in worse than this?'

Captain Andrei Kollontai raised his head slightly, although he didn't alter his stance or position. He glanced over at the first mate for a moment, then stared back outside. 'Not that I recall,' he answered in a flat voice that signaled an end to the conversation between them. Kollontai turned back to watch the ship's bow. In the darkness and through the driving, blinding snow that pummeled at them from all sides, he could barely make out the angles of its structure – even though the furthest sections of the bow extended only twenty-three meters from where he stood on the bridge. The first mate was right, this was one hell of a storm.

Per his own instructions, two seamen had been stationed on the forward forecastle and Kollontai could make them out in the diffused glow from the spotlights on the quarter deck. Both of the seamen were hunched over as far below the top of the bull nose as they could get, undoubtedly for maximum protection from the wind. The communications wires that connected them to the two officers on the bridge snaked across the white painted deck. The long black cable trailed behind the men like rats' tails. Kollontai shivered involuntarily as he watched the two men, knowing how damned cold they must be. 'Sergei,' Kollontai said as he addressed the ship's first mate by his given name – something he seldom did when official orders were being given.

'Yessir.'

'Be certain that the forward watch is changed on schedule. In this weather, I can't expect a man to pay attention for icebergs for more than fifteen minutes, it's twenty-five below out there.'

'Yessir.' But Timoshenko didn't bother to communicate the additional order about the iceberg-watch since he had already done so. The first mate coughed nervously into his hand before he turned back to the captain. 'Fifteen minutes on watch, then thirty minutes off. Those were the initial orders I gave to the watch party – I'm certain they'll be carried out.'

'Very good.'

Although he hoped that his expression didn't show it, Timoshenko was worried. For some reason, the captain had begun to repeat himself, had begun to give the same order more than once. Perhaps the point that Doctor Ney had earlier made to him in the strictest of confidence – that Captain Kollontai was showing signs of acute emotional strain – had truth to it after all. If the captain were losing his nerve, his courage, his resolve, then everyone on board could be in real danger.

Doctor Boris Ney, who stood in the rear corner of the bridge, sensed another opportunity to re-enforce his own position. 'Tell me,' he asked the first mate. 'What about the radar? How does that situation look?'

'Perfectly clear,' Timoshenko answered. He looked down at the radar display in front of him, then turned back to the group. 'There's nothing ahead of us for at least the next twenty kilometers.'

'Oh.' Ney looked at the first mate with an expression of feigned puzzlement, then turned to the captain. 'It's perfectly clear up ahead?'

'That's what the radar indicates.' Kollontai could tell which way the conversation was going, but at that point he didn't care anymore.

'Then perhaps we should reconsider.' Ney took a slight step forward in order to close the distance between himself and Kollontai. 'Perhaps we could go a little faster.' Ney couched his words in friendly tones and smiled amicably, his forced grin making a tentative display of itself between the dark folds of his sculptured beard.

'Absolutely not.'

'Why?'

Kollontai surprised himself by feeling more patience toward Ney than he might have imagined himself to possess. 'Because the Americans are not the only ones who can have a *Titanic*. Wouldn't we feel like a bunch of asses if we punctured a hole in the hull of the ship,' Kollontai said as he tapped his hand against the brass fittings around the master control panel in front of him. 'All of that risk, just so we can get ourselves into the next series of senseless battles a little sooner.'

'I guess you're right.' But Ney knew that Kollontai was wrong – he had already learned from several of the ship's officers that the radar was very sophisticated and could easily spot any iceberg large enough to be a threat to the ship's double steel hull. The iceberg watch being conducted on the bow was a futile gesture at best, since by the time the men stationed out there would see something through the blinding snowstorm it would be too late to change course. 'Is that why you've got those two men stationed at the bow?'

'I'm covering every possibility.' Kollontai shrugged,

since he already knew that the men selected for the watch had grumbled about the iceberg duty. Senseless and stupid, he had overheard one of them say. Perhaps it was, but Kollontai felt that he had to do something to protect the people on board the *Primorye* – first from the icebergs, then from the Americans – and this was all that he could come up with at the moment. Any action was better than no action at all.

'A good decision.' Ney glanced quickly at the other two officers on the bridge, making just enough eye contact with each of them to get his message across: the captain was unmistakably becoming irrational, he was showing increasing signs of bizarre behavior. All Ney wanted to do for the time being was to reinforce that notion.

'Let's get back to our main decision – which seems unavoidable,' Kollontai said after a silence of a few moments while he mulled over what had been said. 'The Americans demonstrated once again that they couldn't be trusted – and Major Zinoviev has died as proof of that fact. I'm beginning to think that you're right, Ney, that we have no choice but to launch an attack on the American base at McMurdo. Aleksandra, how do you feel?'

'I agree, too.' She had answered in a hollow voice that was not her own because Aleksandra could hardly believe what she had seen less than one hour before. The helicopter she had been in had remained one kilometer out to sea and had flown up the beachline while Major Zinoviev went toward the Palmer station in his helicopter. To her amazement, the Americans had launched an attack against Major Zinoviev soon after he landed. Aleksandra had seen the results of that attack instantly, as that horrible orange fireball leapt into the sky.

By the time Aleksandra's helicopter had flown the short distance between themselves and the Palmer station, Major Zinoviev's helicopter was nothing but charred wreckage. That was when the pilot of Aleksandra's helicopter had begun his own attack. With machine guns and missiles, he had totally destroyed the Palmer station in less than five minutes. Now, at least, the Americans

181

wouldn't be able to use that facility against them any longer.

'The Americans have escalated the fighting between us,' Ney said to pick up the pace of the conversation. He could see that good luck and momentum had taken events exactly to where he needed them, and Ney knew that a timely shove from him wouldn't hurt. 'As far as I'm concerned, we have no choice.'

'So you've convinced me.' Kollontai shook his head, not knowing how to feel about this turn of events. Crazy, stupid, immoral – yet there seemed no way out of it.

'It's the only logical decision. We need to launch a surprise attack on their McMurdo station or get ourselves locked out of any chance of surviving. Remember what the report says.' Ney waved the sheaf of papers in his hand – papers that told the story about what would happen to the world during the next few weeks.

'Yes.' Kollontai looked down at the papers in Ney's hand. The scientific community on board the *Primorye* had just finished their research and compiled their data. The facts – supported by radio reports from what little was left of the rest of the world – were unmistakable, as their report had indicated. Because of the estimated extent of the battle and the overall number of nuclear weapons detonated, nearly the entire globe would be doomed. Radiation and ozone-layer poisoning would make every civilized land mass uninhabitable.

'It's interesting to note that all the identifiable problem areas are open-ended.'

'What does that mean?'

'That the evidence presented here,' Ney answered as he tapped the paperwork in his hand, 'is a best-case scenario. Everything in this report is the minimum that could fore-seeably occur. The actual outcome should potentially be even worse because of unknown consequences and inter-dependencies.'

'I see.' As Kollontai had read from his brief scanning of the documents, the scientists had unanimously predicted that the Northern and Southern Hemispheres would be cut off from direct sunlight by the circling clouds of debris.

What that meant was that all across the globe – from the temperate areas to even the tropical zones – there would be months and even years of severe cold weather caused by blockage of the sun's direct rays. That, in turn, would destroy all plant and animal life. But the freezing to death of what little life remained would be a secondary consequence of the world-wide nuclear holocaust, after the preliminary effects of radiation and ozone poisoning had run their course. No one had been able to guess what a third or fourth-level consequence of the massive nuclear exchange might be, since the report indicated that those points were probably academic. Most living creatures would be long dead before the third and fourth-level consequences could begin.

'Have you seen the tables of verification?' Ney flipped the weighty document to the proper page and held it out for Kollontai to read.

'I've already seen them.' As further proof of the accuracy of their findings, the scientists on the *Primorye* had conducted atmospheric and seawater samplings that very morning. The tests had confirmed that radiation had already begun to reach even as far south as the Antarctic. Very soon the area where the *Primorye* was sailing would be as dangerous to humans as Gorky Park had become.

'We might be the only people on earth to have this information.' Ney looked down at an illustration in the opened document in front of him, the lines and angles of the graph taking on almost mystical powers. Even Ney had been surprised by how the scientists on board the *Primorye* had managed to make their report so comprehensive, surprised by how nightmarish their conclusions had been. Yet all of it had been measured and calculated. All of it was true. Except for that two-line conclusion on the last page that spoke about the American South Pole station, there was not one ounce of hope anywhere in that volume of words, charts and tables that Ney held in his hands.

'Do you think that the Americans realize that their South Pole station is the only hope?' Kollontai asked.

'That's difficult to say. We don't know how many scientists they have at their McMurdo and South Pole stations, and we don't know how good their testing and communications facilities are. All we know for sure is that we've figured out that fact for ourselves.'

'Right.' Kollontai shook his head, unable to accept in his heart what his rational mind had already taken in as the whole truth: that except for the American station at the South Pole which was expected to be isolated from danger because of its six months of pending darkness, its high elevation and the downslope effect of the mounds of pure and deep-cold air piled above it high into the stratosphere, the remainder of the world was doomed to extinction.

'That brings me back to my original point. As distasteful as this might seem, we need to launch a surprise attack on the American station at McMurdo so we can capture their land vehicles. That's the only way we can get inland, the only way we can get ourselves to the safety of the South Pole station.'

'All right.' Kollontai stepped over to the navigation chart and eyed the symbol of the American McMurdo station, which lay on the coast approximately 1400 kilometers from their current position. The *Primorye* could be abeam that American station in forty-two to fifty hours from now, depending on the extent of the pack ice. Then they would get to eliminate that last pocket of American resistance, the only thing that stood between them and the safety of the American facility at the South Pole.

'What about our speed?' Ney asked as he saw another opportunity to exert his influence. That was an especially important factor now with the first mate and the navigation officer standing so near, since those two would undoubtedly spread the story of Ney's natural leadership to everyone on the *Primorye*. 'Can we pick up our speed?'

'That's still a risky thing to do.' Kollontai looked over at Aleksandra. She had stayed very near to him all through the first part of their meeting, during their lengthy discussion about exactly what had happened at the Palmer station and what was required next at the American McMurdo base. All during that time, Kollontai felt her presence, could hardly contain himself from reaching out to her, from wrapping his arms around her and cradling her tightly. 'Aleksandra, what do you think about the risk of more speed? It's a calculated chance – although I do have to say that Ney is probably right about the exposure factor being pretty low.'

'Andrei, I'm not qualified to give an opinion. I think you've got to decide on that point for all of us.' Aleksandra looked at him with unmasked emotions – admiration, trust, love. For a moment she seemed to be considering adding something to what she had said, but she finally turned away to allow Kollontai to make up his mind without distraction.

'Okay.' *Speed. Risk. Exposure.* Somehow, everything had become an ultimate compromise, a trade-off of extremes. There were no more simple choices, only bad ones and worse ones. Kollontai knew that he was continually being faced with decisions that a few days ago would have been impossible to comprehend – yet now he had no more than a few minutes to make up his mind about choices that would literally determine the survivability of what remained of mankind. Compromises. But one thing he couldn't bring himself to compromise was the safety of those on board the *Primorye* – especially the ultimate safety of Aleksandra. 'It seems to me that our safety depends completely on eliminating the American resistance so we can get ourselves to the South Pole.'

'That's what it looks like to me,' Ney prodded.

'Then I suppose we have no choice.' Kollontai had already lost his wife and daughter to this senseless slaughter, and he now knew that he wouldn't be able to bear up if he somehow lost Aleksandra as well. She had become all that mattered to him. 'It's against my normal methods of doing things, but I see the need to take that slight chance. Since the risk seems small enough, we'll increase our speed by ten knots.'

'Yessir.' First Mate Timoshenko made the necessary adjustments to the master control panel. As he did, the pulsations from the *Primorye*'s diesels picked up their pace.

'But at the first signs of any formidable ice, we drop back to dead-slow.'

'I understand, sir.'

'Very well.' Kollontai looked back at Aleksandra. Every passing moment of this nightmare had an obvious effect on all of them. Even Aleksandra had changed, since she had reluctantly but finally agreed that the Americans seemed to want nothing but fighting, that there seemed to be little choice but for them to meet the Americans at McMurdo head-on.

Kollontai watched Aleksandra a moment longer. She had a neutral expression on her face as she stood beside the helmsman, her attention fixed on his continual motions with the *Primorye*'s steering wheel as the ship picked up speed. Kollontai kept his gaze on Aleksandra, even as he spoke again to Ney. 'But remember that we'll need to be careful. Very careful.'

'Yes, we will. That's a good point.' Ney didn't really understand what Kollontai was thinking of, and he couldn't care less. Ney was satisfied with the overall way things had gone – Zinoviev killed in a fortuitous exchange with the Americans, the second helicopter brought in by its impetuous pilot to attack and totally destroy the American Palmer base – and saw now that he was no more than a few days away from being able to assume total control of their group. *Vozhd*. Events had confirmed to Ney what he had known in his heart all along – that he was certainly a great leader, that he was capable of becoming the world's next Lenin.

Ney allowed a lull to develop in the conversation. Finally, after a few moments, he stepped outside onto the port steering station. Ney leaned against the rail. It was extremely cold outside in the brisk wind, and the sea was beginning to get very rough and choppy – but the entire display of harsh elements was a powerful stimulant, a refreshing break from the warm stuffiness inside. *Nothing can stop me now. Just like nothing could stop Lenin.* As he stood out there in the Antarctic wind, Ney began again to think about that one man from history he had such vivid images of.

Vladimir Ilich Lenin. Lenin as a small boy, Lenin as an old man, Lenin as a leader of a nation, leader of the world. Ney thought about how Lenin must have felt during that historic return to Russia in April 1917 – Lenin's ride in the train back from exile was not so different from Ney's own voyage to the new birthplace of Mother Russia on board the motorship *Primorye*. Lenin had moved decisively to take control in October 1917, just the way Ney was poised to take firm control of the newly-forming Soviet Antarctic State at that very moment. The parellels were overwhelming. It was predestined.

'Ney – come back inside. We've got to work up our schedule for the attack,' Kollontai shouted.

'Of course.' Ney turned and stepped back inside the warm and stuffy bridge of the *Primorye*. As he did, Ney noticed that he had begun to shiver slightly. *Just a few more days at the most. Then I'll be firmly in control. Then no one will dare to challenge my authority.* Ney knew that the shiver that ran through his body had not been caused by the Antarctic cold. Instead, it had been caused by the excitement of anticipation.

Through the continual slow and rolling turbulence caused by the snowstorm, Captain Lou Whitaker stepped carefully into the darkened rear lounge of *Airship Nine*. Julie Mathews stepped in behind him, putting her arm on Whitaker's shoulder to steady herself in the constant back-and-forth swaying. 'How's the hands?' Whitaker asked as he looked down at the man sitting on the corner couch.

'They'll be all right.' Ray Madigan forced a smile through the pain that was constantly traveling up both his arms. 'Rope burns and frostbite don't mix together too damned well, I'll give you that much.'

'Please, Ray . . . sit still.' Nancy Schneider put on an exaggerated scowl, then turned her attention back to the medical dressings and bandages that she was working with.

'What do you think, Nancy?' Whitaker asked as he led Julie to the couch across from where the first officer and the stewardess were sitting. 'Any complications?'

'I don't think so. I don't have much experience in these things, but I think the damage should heal nicely in a few days.' Without even realizing that she was doing so, Nancy raised Ray's bandaged hand and brushed a gentle kiss across his fingertips.

'I'm glad to hear that.' Whitaker coughed awkwardly as he glanced around the lounge.

'Where is everybody?' Julie asked.

'Some went to bed. Some went to the cockpit.'

'Frank Corbi and Annie Rizzo went back to the kitchen,' Nancy added as she finished bandaging Ray's other hand.

'Again?'

'Yes.'

'They're eating again? That's incredible.' Both couples laughed heartily for a few moments. Finally, they lapsed into silence. Whitaker looked back across the room toward the soft grey light that played from the screen of the video recorder. 'Does Corbi know that his movie is still on?'

'Yes. He says it won't hurt it to leave it on – and even if the tape breaks or something like that, his machine has already made two extra copies of the movie. Just turn the sound up whenever you want to hear it.'

'Okay.' Whitaker waited another moment before he began to mention what he had really walked aft for. 'Ray, that was one hell of a job that you did on that beach. I don't have to tell you what would've happened if you hadn't come up with your radar-reflector idea.'

'And if you hadn't been able to fly this big balloon like you did, we'd all be frozen whale meat by now,' Madigan answered. He looked directly at Whitaker. 'The others may not be able to appreciate it, but that was one hell of a flying job, that's for sure.'

'Thanks.' Whitaker waved his hand distractedly, not knowing how to lead into what he wanted to say next. 'There's another thing . . .'

'Yeah?'

'About the problems we've had.'

'Problems?'

'You and me.'

188

'Forget them.'

'No. Just the opposite.' Whitaker moved forward to the edge of the couch. He leaned closer to Madigan. 'What I mean is that . . . you were right.'

'Right?' Madigan had been taken off guard. He didn't know what to say. He glanced first at Nancy and then at Julie, but neither of the women seemed to know what Whitaker was leading up to. 'What was I right about?'

'Right about me.'

'Hell, let's not get into that. Not now.'

.'Yes. Right now, before I change my mind about saying something. I'm not making a big deal about it, I just wanted you to know that the things you said were true. Having standards is one thing, but I was far too rigid, far too demanding. Saint Whitaker you said, and you were right. I didn't mean to, but I see now that maybe I pushed my son too hard.'

'I shouldn't have said anything about him – that wasn't any of my business.'

'That doesn't matter, not now. When Julie and I were alone in the cockpit looking for you people through that snow, I had time to put things into perspective. My ex-wife is dead, my son Allan has been dead a long time – and there's nothing like the idea that the remaining portion of most of the world's surviving population – the eleven people from *Airship Nine* – would suddenly be reduced to less than half for a person to get their own priorities in order. By the time I found you people, my own little hang-ups seemed small, even to me.'

'Nicely put. I wish I could say that I didn't understand you, but I'm here to say that I also had a few minutes out on that ice when my own brand of stupidity seemed pretty transparent.' Madigan picked up his bandaged hand and laid it carefully against Nancy's arm. 'I guess what we're both saying is that each of us screwed up some in the past . . .'

'. . . and now's a good time to start afresh.' Whitaker stood up. So did Madigan.

'You guys are beautiful,' Julie said as she looked up at the two of them. 'I had a boyfriend for years who I loved

189

an awful lot,' she continued as she stumbled slightly on her own words, '. . . loved an awful lot. But he could never get himself to where you two guys just did.' Julie sat there with a smile on her face, although there was a growing flow of tears from the corners of her eyes.

'Maybe he didn't have enough of a chance.' Whitaker reached down for Julie's hand and took it into his own. 'We've had a reprieve, a second chance, that almost no one else on earth has gotten. We're using time that wasn't available to anyone else.'

'Maybe you're right.' Julie squeezed Whitaker's hand. Finally, she released her grip and allowed her fingers to slide free.

'Speaking of available time,' Madigan said to Whitaker, 'how is Michael Starr?'

'He's got some frostbite, bangs and bruises. But most of his problems seemed to be related to shock. He was pretty close to hanging it up for good because of exposure to the cold. He's asleep now. I think he'll be all right.'

'Who's taking care of him now?' Nancy asked as she gathered up the equipment and supplies and shoved them back into her medical kit.

'Kathleen Sinclair and Steve Galloway, mostly. Frank Corbi and Annie Rizzo have also helped. Floyd Robinson has been in and out – but now Floyd is busy with the radio.'

'Radio?'

'Sorry, I guess I forgot to tell you.' Whitaker shook his head, embarrassed by his oversight. 'I'm really sorry that I forgot to mention it, but you were back here with Nancy when I found out. Michael Starr had a portable transmitter stuck in the pocket of his overcoat. It's a short-range transmitter, but the important point is that it has the proper frequencies for both the McMurdo and South Pole stations.'

'Christ, that's terrific. Can we speak to either of those stations?' Madigan glanced outside the lounge window, as if he expected to be able to see one of those American Antarctic bases out there. Instead, he saw nothing beyond the length of the airship's grey hull through the darkness and snow.

'Not yet, because it's a short-range transmitter. But Floyd is trying to rig up something – a coupling to our own amplifier and antenna system – to increase range. He expects to be able to talk to McMurdo sometime before we get there.'

'And what's the estimate of arrival at McMurdo?'

'Difficult to say.' Whitaker glanced down at the calendar bubble on his wristwatch, then back at the first officer. 'It's going to take us two days, more or less. The late afternoon of the ninth or the morning of the tenth, I'd say.'

'Two full days?'

'Yes. Right now the headwinds are so severe that we've gone to minimum power. That's barely enough to keep us from being blown backward.'

'But we're saving fuel, right?'

'Exactly. The McMurdo base isn't going anywhere and I figured we'd be better off conserving fuel and waiting for the headwinds to die down. I've been wanting to talk to you about that,' Whitaker added, since he had wanted to get the first officer's opinion of how they should handle their dwindling resource of aviation fuel. 'What do you think?'

'I agree with you. The Russians who attacked Palmer must've come from the Bellingshausen station. A bunch of crazy men out looking for revenge, I guess. Anyway, we should have no problems from here to McMurdo. Since we've got more than enough food on board, there's no need to rush to McMurdo at the expense of extra fuel against the headwind. Moving slowly until the wind swings around is definitely our best bet.'

'There's one other unanswered question,' Julie said as she joined in on the conversation. 'What about weapons? How are we going to defend ourselves?'

'Frank Corbi had the only good suggestion on that point,' Whitaker said with a smile.

'What?'

'If the Russians attack, we should send Andrew Sinclair out first. He'd talk them to death.'

191

'Or bore them to death,' Nancy Schneider added as she laid her medical kit on the lounge table.

'Right.' All of them laughed. Finally Whitaker addressed the main point again. 'Seriously, though, other than a few hunting knives we don't have a thing on board to fight with.'

'Floyd had a rifle, but in the rush to get on board the airship we left it back in the tent,' Julie added.

'And we sure as hell can't go back for it now,' Madigan said emphatically. The three others nodded in agreement. 'But I don't think it'll make any difference. Santa Claus himself couldn't find us in this snowstorm, and once we get to McMurdo those people are bound to have something that we can defend ourselves with if it comes down to that.'

'So the bottom line is that, for the time being, everything is status quo. We pass time at our current position until the wind dies, then move on to McMurdo. We'll just plan on mooring the airship at the McMurdo station – maybe even deflating it for safe storage if we have to – and spending the winter with them.' Whitaker rose from his seat to stretch the stiffness from his arms and legs. Finally, he sat back down.

'Now all we can do is wait,' Madigan said as he gestured for Nancy to move closer to where he sat on the couch.

'Since we've got nothing to do, we might as well watch the movie,' Julie said. 'I haven't seen very much of it yet and, believe it or not, I've never seen *Casablanca* before.'

'Do you want to rewind the tape back to the beginning?'

'No, just pick it up where it is.' Julie got up from the couch and stepped over to where the video recorder was. The black and white images from the old movie had been playing constantly across the small screen, but everyone had ignored them while the sound had been turned down. Julie turned up the volume control, then went back to the couch to sit next to Lou Whitaker.

They watched the remainder of the scene play out. It was taking place in a crowded, smoke-filled cafe, with Ingrid Bergman sitting next to the piano player, Dooley Wilson. He began to finger the keyboard while she continued to talk. It was obvious from Wilson's expression that he was uncomfortable with their conversation – while Ingrid Bergman made it equally obvious that she had something entirely different on her mind, something personal, something very important to her.

Finally, she asked Wilson to sing *As Time Goes By*. At first he resisted, but after she had hummed a few bars, Wilson reluctantly but obediently complied.

> You must remember this,
> A kiss is still a kiss,
> A sigh is just a sigh;
> The fundamental things apply,
> As time goes by.

Ray Madigan and Nancy Schneider moved even closer to each other, with her head resting against his shoulder and his bandaged hands draped carefully around her body. A few feet further down on the lounge couch of *Airship Nine*, Julie Mathews put her hand back on Lou Whitaker's arm and pulled her body nearer to his. The four of them watched what happened on the small video screen in absolute and rapturous silence.

> And when two lovers woo,
> They still say I love you,
> On that you can rely;
> No matter what the future brings,
> As time goes by.

Thirteen

KATHLEEN SINCLAIR relaxed in the small, darkened state-room of *Airship Nine*. Her feet were up against the fold-down table as she leaned back in the chair beside the bed and, even though it was late afternoon and the sun had finally come out from behind the cloud deck, she hadn't bothered to open the curtains to let the sunlight in. Every now and then Kathleen glanced over at Michael Starr as he lay sprawled across the bunk, just as he had for the last two days.

Michael was still sound asleep, which was exactly what he needed most in order to get his strength back. Kathleen watched Michael's rhythmic breathing for several seconds. Finally, she pushed the strands of her long red hair across her shoulder, then leaned her own head back against the fiberglass wall panel. Kathleen closed her eyes, intending to rest them for just a few moments.

'I thought this was too important for you to have dinner with me.'

'What?' Kathleen opened her eyes and looked up at her husband. Andrew was standing over her, scowling. 'I just closed my eyes half a second ago.'

'A very typical response from you.' Sinclair tapped his foot impatiently. 'Meanwhile, I've been standing over you for a full minute at the very least. Probably closer to two minutes. You've been sitting with your legs spread apart, your head tilted back and your mouth opened. Not too charming for a girl who went to Mount Holyoke. If the truth were to be known, I think you were snoring, too.'

'Sorry.' Kathleen instantly regretted having apologized, but the word had popped out of her mouth before she could stop it. 'You know that I haven't been getting much sleep the last two days,' she added in a low but angry voice as she stood up. Kathleen motioned to Michael and indicated to her husband that he should speak quietly.

'You're damned right you haven't been getting much sleep,' Sinclair answered. 'If you're not baby-sitting in here, you're locked in some kind of endless discussion with that assistant copilot.'

'Steve Galloway is the second officer,' Kathleen said. 'The two of us volunteered to take care of Michael. You were invited to help, but you didn't seem interested.'

'Pardon me. I didn't realize that you were running for the Florence Nightingale award.'

'Keep your voice down.'

'Who died to make you Queen of the Nile? You seem to have forgotten that I'm the one who made the money to pay for this trip. This trip saved your life.'

'No, you're wrong.'

'How?'

'You didn't pay for this trip. Your father gave you the money.'

'That's ridiculous.'

'No, it's true.' Kathleen surprised herself by what she had said, but it felt so good that she couldn't stop. 'I remember very well what happened at that last dinner party up at the club, when you and your father carried on about the evils of Democrats, social programs and job training plans.'

'What in God's name are you talking about?'

Kathleen rubbed her eyes, as much to hold back the tears as to control her fatigue. 'Please give me a chance to explain – and stop interrupting me!' She knew that she wasn't making a great deal of sense – the lack of sleep, the emotions that pulled her in every direction at the same time, the sudden onslaught of feelings toward the people around her – but Kathleen didn't care. 'You and your father said that the marketplace should determine who was worth how much. I had heard both of you say those things often enough before . . .'

'Your memory is a finely-tuned instrument, there's no doubt about it.' Sinclair smirked contemptuously as he

195

indulged himself in the familiar sport of verbally prodding his wife.

Kathleen ignored his interruption. '. . . but that last time you and your father said those things, that was the first time I began to understand what it all represented.'

'You will, at some point in the not too distant future, be so kind as to fill me in on the meaning behind your incoherent rambling?'

'Unearned privilege. That's what you and your father represent. The proper prep school, the proper college, the proper three-piece suit, button-down shirt and those club ties. It's a kind of nobility, practically. You were each knighted inside those Ivy League castles and you then set out to do battle against anyone outside those walls. Even before that night at the club I had some distinct feelings about it . . .'

'I noticed your true feelings about my income every time you'd go shopping to rub the numbers right off your Saks and Neiman-Marcus charge cards.'

'. . . but that last night up at the club with your father made it all clear to me. Neither of you were interested in doing anything besides accumulating wealth, power and status for yourselves. You both talked about how you despised people who didn't earn the things that they possessed – yet the most blatant example of charity that I've ever seen was when your father sent you to Yale so he could have an excuse to make you branch manager.'

'You sure as hell better stop this right here and now, you bitch!'

'And if you don't think that I noticed the stares that you got from the men that worked for you, then you're wrong. You may not have noticed, but I certainly did – even in those few times that I went to the office with you. The men who worked for you – good men, honest men – hated you because you didn't know what you were doing, didn't know how to handle them or the business. That didn't matter to you because you could flaunt your authority anyway. If you made a mistake, then the profits would go down and your father would blame low productivity or high union wages and lay off some of the workers. And

196

instead of learning from the men around you who had lots more experience, you kept reminding them in a thousand little ways that your daddy signed the checks. Your father and his money were your shield and sword to cut everyone down. You wanted to make the men who worked for you jump because that's the only way you were able to measure how important you were.'

'Go to hell!'

Kathleen watched her husband storm out and slam the door behind him. Kathleen closed her eyes and stood quietly for a few seconds.

'You've got courage to tell him that,' Michael Starr said in a thin voice. He picked himself up from where he lay on the bunk.

'Oh, damn. I'm sorry that we woke you.'

'Don't be. Two days of sleep are enough. I feel much better.'

'Good.'

'And I'm being sincere. You really do have courage.'

Michael kept his eyes on her as she sat on the bed beside him. Even after having her beside him for the past two days, Michael could hardly get over what a startling impression she made on him each time he opened his eyes. He loved to look up at her long red hair and her beautiful smile – but most of all, he loved that look of brightness in her eyes, the appearance of alertness and buoyant, bountiful life that radiated from her face.

Whenever she left the room for even a few minutes, he and Steve Galloway would talk about her. Both he and Steve found Kathleen incredibly attractive for the same reasons. Neither of them could understand why she had married her husband.

'No, I don't have any courage.' Kathleen reached down and adjusted the pillows so Michael could prop himself up comfortably. 'If I did have courage, then maybe I would've said those things a long time ago. I would've said it when we were first dating, or when he first asked me to marry him.'

'It's hard to picture him asking you to get married.'

'Now that you mention it, I think Andrew *told* me to

marry him.' Kathleen laughed nervously as she looked down at Michael, who smiled back at her. 'But it's not fair for me to say that. I married Andrew because I wanted to, because I thought that the life he offered me was the only one worth living. It was the life my parents had groomed me for. It was the only life that I had known.'

'Now what do you think?'

'Now I think that it's hideously, insanely funny how the world has been shrunk to almost nothing – maybe just us people down here, stuck in Antarctica for what little might be left of our lives – and yet that world suddenly seems so much bigger to me.'

'It sure has gotten bigger for me, too – ever since you people found me in that snowstorm. What's the old saying? Sometimes less is more.' Michael stopped talking for a moment while he allowed himself to be totally enraptured by the smooth and elegant lines of Kathleen's face. 'When I left Palmer on that snowmobile two mornings ago,' he finally added, 'I didn't realize how much things would change for me. I didn't realize that I'd never see my friend John again.'

'You called his name out a dozen times while you were asleep – especially yesterday.'

'I bet I did.' Michael stopped for a moment, to allow the memory of John to slide back into the recesses of his mind. He would deal with John's memory later. 'But now I'm trying to do nothing but look ahead. Now I've got the people on this airship. Now I've got you and Steve.' Michael reached up and took Kathleen's hand into his.

'And that's exactly the way both Steve and I feel about it, also.' Kathleen held his hand a few moments longer, then gently laid it back down as she stood up. 'Hey, how about a little sunshine in your life?' she suddenly asked as she broke into a big smile.

'Sunshine?'

'The real stuff, what little of it is left out here. Just like the captain had promised, the snowstorm ended a few hours ago and now most of the clouds are gone.' Kathleen stepped up to the window and, with the grand motion of an unveiling, she yanked aside the heavy curtain. A flood of late afternoon sunlight poured into the room and it caused both of them to squint for several moments before they could look outside. Finally Kathleen opened her eyes enough to see out clearly. 'Look at that!'

'Christ.' The view from the stateroom window was magnificent. The clouds that remained were in scattered clumps or wisps, and shafts of brilliant sunlight poured between them in what appeared to be nearly solid beams of connecting white. From a flight altitude of eight hundred feet, it was easy to see the hundreds of icebergs in the foreground that dotted the ocean's surface between *Airship Nine* and the rugged coastline they flew parallel to. The icebergs were composed of alternate shades of deep black and stark white as long shadows played off their varied angles. 'Look at those mountains!'

The coastal ridge that Michael pointed to rose abruptly from the edge of the sea. The tops of the mountains either contrasted markedly against the clear blue background or buried themselves into the patches of cloud that remained. All the mountains were covered with ice and snow, although some vertical areas of rock had shed themselves of their covering of white to expose the colours beneath. Black, mostly, but there were also patches of vivid browns and blues mixed with traces of reflected patterns of gold and silver. Caught just right by the low angle of the sun as it slid below the peaks of the highest of the mountains, the colors of each section of land changed as they watched. Neither Michael nor Kathleen moved or spoke while the scene in front of them held them in utter fascination. Finally, after the sun had sunk beneath the trough of the last ridgeline, Michael cleared his throat. 'That was incredible. Every time I look outside in this part of the world, it's different. I've never seen the same thing twice in the Antarctic.'

'I see what you mean.' But before Kathleen could step back to where Michael lay on the bunk, the door to the stateroom burst open.

'Hey, you're awake!' Steve Galloway rushed up next to the bunk where Michael lay. 'Do you think you'll be able to get up?' As Galloway asked, he offered his hand to Michael to help him.

'I guess.' Michael grabbed Steve's hand and began to move himself upright.

'What's happened?' Kathleen stepped beside Steve and, without another word, also began to help him get Michael up from bed. 'Are we in trouble?'

'Just the opposite.' Galloway smiled at his two friends, obviously happy to be the one to tell them the good news. 'Radio contact. Right now.'

'With who?' Michael maneuvred his legs slowly to the floor. He allowed himself to be propped up by Steve on his one side and Kathleen on the other.

'McMurdo. We're about four hundred miles out, but Floyd managed to get them on the radio using a modification of the portable transmitter we found in your coat pocket.'

'That's great.'

'It sure is.' Kathleen and Steve continued to help Michael as the three of them maneuvred slowly into the corridor of *Airship Nine*. They joined everyone else on board who had pushed forward to be near enough the radio room to hear the ongoing radio conversation.

When the first words from the McMurdo station poured out of the radio speaker of *Airship Nine*, Floyd Robinson dropped the cup of coffee from his hands as he lunged forward to hit the transmitter switch to reply. The cup of tepid brown liquid hit the floor and its contents spilled aft to create a muddy river that tracked diagonally across the soiled carpet of the radio room. Robinson did not notice the mess he had made as he grabbed for the microphone and almost shouted out his response. 'Yes, McMurdo, yes, dammit – we're out here! *Airship Nine* is answering McMurdo, do you hear me!?'

'Airship answering McMurdo, your transmissions are breaking up,' the tinny voice answered. 'But you are readable.'

'God Almighty! Wonderful!' Without letting go of the

transmitter switch, Robinson motioned for Doctor Tucker to go get the others. While Robinson began his explanation to the McMurdo station of who he was, why he was now on an airship and what had happened at Palmer station, Doctor Tucker rushed into the corridor to gather up the people of *Airship Nine*.

'Say again your position,' McMurdo asked just as Captain Whitaker rushed into the radio room. Since he had been doing an inspection of the lower cargo bay when the news was shouted down to him, Whitaker was the last one of the twelve to join the group.

'He wants our position,' Robinson said as he turned around in time to see Whitaker enter.

'Approximately four hundred nautical miles to the east of them,' Whitaker answered from the rear of the radio room. The captain began to push himself past the others and toward the transmitter desk. 'Tell them that we're off the Saunders Coast, abeam Cape Colbeck. I think they'll know where that is.'

Robinson relayed the message, then switched off his transmitter while he waited for McMurdo's reply. He could feel the swelling press of the people behind him as they pushed into the back of his chair and hung over the edges of the radio table, twelve jammed into a room meant for no more than three or four. Yet there was not a sound from any of them as they waited for the voice on the radio – a voice that meant that they had a chance of survival or that they had no chance at all.

After what seemed like an absurdly long time without hearing a thing – Robinson was reluctant to press his transmit switch since that would cut off any chance of receiving McMurdo's reply – the voice from McMurdo again filled the room. 'Airship, what is your estimate of arrival at McMurdo?'

Whitaker looked across at Ray Madigan. 'What's the estimate look like?'

'The wind has died down just like we figured. We'll be there in six more hours, although it'll be pitch-black outside in another forty minutes.'

'Right.' Whitaker looked at his wristwatch. 'Tell them

that we'll reach a point twenty-five miles due north of McMurdo in six hours. We'll hover over that spot for the night. Tell them to plan on our landfall at eleven tomorrow morning, about one hour after dawn.' Whitaker didn't like the idea of being so near to McMurdo without going in at once, but hovering over the open sea was the only logical plan. Attempting a mooring in the dark would be riskier than hell, and the weather looked like it should stay good enough through the night and into the morning.

'Okay.' Robinson relayed the message, then stood by as he waited for a reply. After a few moments of silence from the radio, Robinson turned to the others in the room. 'I hate to be the one to bring this up,' Robinson said, his voice tentative and hesitant, 'but I think there's something wrong at McMurdo.'

'What?' Whitaker didn't want to ask because, deep down, he had begun to feel the same way himself.

'His voice, right?' Madigan said from across the room. Without verbalizing it, the three men had come to the same conclusion.

'Yes, his voice.'

'What do you mean?' Julie asked. She looked to Whitaker for the answer.

Much as he didn't want to, the captain ignored her question for the moment. 'Can you tell from the voice who's speaking?' Whitaker asked Robinson.

'At first, no – but now, yes. Definitely. It's Vernon Hays.' Robinson frowned. 'He's a geologist. We've been together at least a dozen times. He's a nice guy.'

'And did you tell him who you were?'

'During the return transmission after they answered me that first time.'

'I see.'

'What does this mean?' Andrew Sinclair asked in a nervous voice. He was on the other side of the crowded room from where his wife stood with the other two men. Sinclair ignored her and looked directly at Whitaker. 'You've got no right to keep secrets if you know something. Tell us.'

'I intended to.' Whitaker looked at both his first officer

and Floyd Robinson and, seeing that both of them were still in agreement with him, he addressed the group. 'Floyd knows the guy at McMurdo. They've worked together. Floyd identified himself, but the guy hasn't responded in any personal way. He's being very formal, very cold . . .'

'He's acting like a robot. That's not like Vernon.' Robinson held his hand over the transmit switch but couldn't decide what to do. He knew that, in this instance at least, the decision of how to handle their contact with McMurdo was totally on his shoulders.

'That's ridiculous,' Sinclair snorted contemptuously. 'Maybe he's tired or hungry. Maybe he can't tell that it's you because of static or something.'

'That's hard to believe. He's not having any trouble understanding me, so it can't be static. As far as him knowing that it's me . . .' Robinson turned back to the radio and pressed the transmit button. 'McMurdo,' he said as he spoke into the microphone, 'I'z got da' big question now. You'z guys ain't runs too low on da' chicken an' biscuits, haz ya?' Robinson slid his finger off the transmit button and waited.

After a few moments the answer from McMurdo came though the speaker. 'Negative, airship. McMurdo's food supplies remain adequate.'

'Shit.' Robinson turned to Whitaker. 'He knows it's me, that's for sure. Something's wrong.'

Whitaker decided to give his order without hesitation so that he wouldn't have time to come up with any reason why he shouldn't. For the sake of everyone on *Airship Nine*, he had to know right now what was happening at McMurdo. 'Press him on it. Try to force him to acknowledge that it's you.'

'Vernon, what's wrong?' Robinson asked into the microphone.

This time, the reply from McMurdo came back without hesitation. 'Floyd, the Russians attacked us! Go straight to South Pole station, it's your only . . .' A long horrible scream of pain then poured out of the speaker and filled the crowded radio room. Moments after that, the radio link between *Airship Nine* and the McMurdo station was abruptly terminated from McMurdo's end.

With his own hands, Doctor Boris Ney shoved the long blade of the knife into the American's stomach. He had never killed a man with a knife before. During the past few minutes while he stood in the McMurdo radio shack he wondered how it would feel. No matter what happened, Ney had planned to kill this American after the final transmission with *Airship Nine* was complete. All that the radioed warning had done was to shorten the man's life by five minutes at the most.

Ney was surprised to see that killing a man with his own hands had affected him as little as it did – it seemed no different than using a pistol or a syringe. As soon as he had pushed that knife deeply enough into the American, the man had stopped screaming. A moment later his eyes closed and the American tumbled forward as far as the two men holding him from behind would allow. It was as simple as that. All of it had happened slowly, like the exaggerated motions of a carefully orchestrated ballet.

'A real fool.' Ney motioned for the two soldiers to drag the body out to the pile of other bodies. The twenty or so Americans at McMurdo had been overpowered easily enough, and Ney had all along planned to eliminate the last one of the Americans with his own hands simply in order to create the sort of legend that he needed. Just like the stories about Lenin that seemed to grow with each passing year, the soldiers who had been in the radio shack with Boris Ney could be counted on to embellish this tale often enough. That would, Ney was certain, make him the unmistakable choice of the *nachalstvo* to become the leader of their new state. He would then abolish the *nachalstvo* and become the sole supreme commander of Antarctica and, later, possibly of what remained of the world.

'Shore party, do you read the *Primorye*?' the portable radio that hung from Ney's belt crackled.

Ney reached for the portable radio, brought the unit up to his lips and pressed the transmit button. 'Yes, *Primorye*.

Go ahead.' Ney smiled as he released the transmit button because he could easily predict what Captain Kollontai would want to know.

'What's the situation?'

'The situation is under control, although the Americans surprised us by refusing to surrender,' Ney lied. He knew that he could depend on his story being accepted since Ney had already convinced the few soldiers who had seen the Americans' white flag that it would be nothing but a trap.

'Any survivors?'

'The enemy has been totally eliminated.' Ney knew that he was making an important speech since Kollontai and that damned Aleksandra Bukharin had already decided to put all ship-to-shore radio messages directly onto the *Primorye*'s public address system. 'Our proud troops suffered only minor injuries during the battle to control the American McMurdo station. We are now totally in control.' Ney knew that his broadcast from the battlefront would do much to help him consolidate his base of power since his name would now be inexorably linked with this major Russian victory over the Americans.

'What's the supply situation?'

'All the American supplies are intact, we stopped them before they could destroy any.' Ney glanced through the double-paned window of the radio shack and toward the clusters of buildings that comprised the McMurdo complex. There were twenty or more buildings in total, some painted blue, others painted red or green. Most of the buildings contained supplies of one sort of another, since the Americans used the McMurdo station as their main depot during the hectic midsummer exploration season – a time when there would have been upwards of several hundred people stationed here. Ney thanked the heavens that the outbreak of World War III had not occurred a month earlier, before the Americans had pulled out everyone but the twenty who stayed as a wintering-over housekeeping crew.

'And what about the vehicles? Have you had a chance to reconnoiter?'

'Yes.' Checking out the vehicle situation had been Ney's first priority, since he needed that information in order to proceed ahead with his overall plan. 'The Americans have two large snow vehicles that seem to be in perfect working order, plus several smaller vehicles. They also have five other large vehicles in various stages of repair, which our people will be able to get back together in a few days. Until then, however, those serviceable vehicles plus our command helicopter will enable us to launch the attack on the American South Pole station.'

'When do you want to proceed?'

'At daylight. As we discussed earlier, once the South Pole station is firmly under our control, we can then use our helicopter and the repaired surface vehicles to move the remainder of our people from the *Primorye*.'

'Very well. Do you intend to return to the ship soon?'

'Yes, to review our battle plans. But I must tell you that some new factors have come up.'

'What sort?'

'I now have firm evidence of the existence of additional Americans. They are on board an airship.'

'Airship?'

'Yes. At this moment, their airship is a few hundred kilometers to the east of us. The Americans in this airship are the ones who murdered our people at the Bellingshausen station.'

'Are you certain?'

'Absolutely. You'll be interested to know that we nearly had them convinced to come to McMurdo where we could have dealt with them easily enough. Unfortunately, one of the Americans at McMurdo took control of the main radio and warned them at the last moment.'

'Could this airship give us much resistance? Will it be a problem to deal with them?'

'No resistance that we can't contain. I have information that shows that this *Airship Nine*, as it is called, is now en route to the American South Pole station. I probably don't need to point out that since I know its current position and its destination, it won't be too difficult to figure out where to intercept this airship with my heli-copter.'

'And then what?'

'And then I'll be able to deal effectively with this *Airship Nine*,' Doctor Boris Ney continued, his voice moving across his mellifluous tones in careful measure so that all those aboard the *Primorye* would be suitably impressed by what he had to say. 'I intend to deal with this *Airship Nine* in a manner befitting their own style of war-monger barbarism. I intend to use my own helicopter's tactical missiles to eliminate those murderers once and forever. We should feel absolutely no sympathy for them because those Americans are nothing but a blood-thirsty gang who systematically killed our innocent comrades at the Soviet Bellingshausen station – not to mention what they also did at the Palmer station to Major Zinoviev and his copilot. I vow, here and now while you are all my wit-nesses, to avenge once and forever the untimely and unnecessary deaths of our brave Soviet people.'

Fourteen

ANDREW SINCLAIR woke from his fitful night's sleep on the couch in the lounge. The dull grey of the dawn had just given way to the reflected brilliance of full sunlight, causing a harsh glare to bounce off the ice and snow below. Sinclair rose from the couch and squinted out the lounge window. Beneath *Airship Nine*, which flew rock-solidly through the calm air, was the interior region of the Antarctic. It crawled past the window slowly.

Sinclair rubbed his eyes, then looked at his wristwatch. It was ten minutes to noon, yet the sun had just come up. Sinclair expected as much, yet it still amazed him. As Captain Whitaker had mentioned at their meeting the night before – which had lasted until nearly six in the morning on the airship's clocks – the further south they flew, the less daylight there would be. Whitaker had told them that today would provide no more than four hours of sunlight at the most, starting at nearly noon and ending at four o'clock. It was sheer madness.

Sinclair stood up, stretched his muscles and looked around. No one else was in the lounge at the moment, but he did catch sight of someone working in the galley area twenty feet forward. After a few moments Sinclair realized that the person in the galley was his wife.

Damn bitch. Sinclair strode forward and cornered Kathleen. 'I've got a goddamn headache already,' he said, showing that he had no intention of making small talk.

'I'm sorry to hear that.' Kathleen put the tray of food she was carrying back on the stainless steel counter of the small kitchen. She turned to face him.

'Who's the food for?' Sinclair asked.

'Michael.'

'Is that so?' Sinclair waved his hand over the tray of

food. 'That's quite a substantial breakfast for a sick guy.'

'He's getting his appetite back.'

'That so? I don't suppose any of that food is for you, is it?'

'Of course it is.'

'And how about that assistant copilot friend of yours?' Even though he knew it well enough, Sinclair avoided using the man's name whenever he could. 'Is he planning on joining you and sickly Michael for breakfast?'

'Matter of fact, yes.' Kathleen bit into her lower lip as she attempted to glare back up at her husband. *Tell him now. Don't let it go any further.* After that horrible experience the night before with the McMurdo radio transmission and the meeting in the lounge afterward when the decision to turn directly toward the South Pole had been made, Kathleen had gone back to Michael's room. Less than an hour later, Steve had joined the two of them – a bottle of sherry in his hand. A few drinks after that, Kathleen had confessed that she couldn't go back to Andrew, that she didn't want to be married to him any longer.

'What have you turned into, some kind of tramp?'

'If that's what you want to think, then that's just fine.' Kathleen turned away from her husband and reached for the tray, hoping that Andrew would let the subject drop. She felt him grab her shoulder, and she knew then that there would be no easy way out of this. 'Let go of me.'

'If you think that I'm going to let you get away with this, you're damned wrong.' The night alone on the lounge couch had been humiliating enough since several people on the airship had seen him, and at dawn Sinclair had made up his mind to confront his wife. He pulled her around until she faced him again. 'Neither one of your boyfriends is more important than your husband – and don't you forget it. Let them get their own goddamn meals, you're coming into the lounge with me.'

'No.'

'And after we've had our own breakfast, I think it's time that we did something suitable to renew our marriage vows. I'm sure we can find an empty bedroom to use for an hour or so.'

'Andrew, stop this.'

'Bullshit. You're my wife. You stop.'

'What's the problem here?' Michael Starr had gotten enough of his strength back to hobble out of his bedroom and toward the galley on his own. He stood in the corridor adjacent to the kitchen entrance, his body leaning heavily against the wall as he braced himself so he could stand upright.

'None of your goddamn business.' Sinclair reached for his wife again, but she backed away into the corner of the galley too quickly for him to grab her. 'Get into the lounge, dammit. I'm not putting up with your shit any more.'

'Have you told him anything yet?' Michael asked, not knowing what else to say. Even though he tried to sound in firm control, his voice was still thin and shaky – even the short walk down the corridor had depleted him of what little energy he had managed to muster.

'No – he hasn't let me get a word in.' *And I haven't tried, either. Do something, quickly. Stand up to him.* Kathleen looked back and forth between Michael and her husband. She could see that there would be trouble between Michael and her husband, but she didn't know how to head it off.

'Maybe if the two of you sat down and talked things out, then maybe you'd be able to make yourselves more understood to each other.' Starr put on a half smile and fumbled for his words, trying desperately to find some intermediate ground for Kathleen and her husband to compromise on. More than anything else, both he and Steve had agreed that they wanted to see Kathleen happy – and neither of them were certain that what she had said to them the night before about leaving her husband had been thought out enough to be acted on. Not yet, anyway. 'Maybe if the two of you tried to clear the air . . .'

Sinclair looked down his nose at the scrubby-looking guy standing next to him. 'Maybe you should clear the air by keeping your mouth shut.'

'Listen, I'm only trying to help . . .'

'Damned right – and I think we both understand exactly what you've been trying to help yourself to.'

'Andrew, stop this!' Kathleen had allowed this affair to go too far, but she still had no idea of what to do next. 'Maybe I should get Steve. Then we can all talk this out.'

'Like hell we will.' Sinclair took one step toward his wife, but then changed his mind. He turned around and, without warning, swung a clenched fist at Michael Starr.

Starr saw the punch coming. He twisted away as fast as his convalescing muscles would allow. The blow from Sinclair landed harmlessly against Starr's raised shoulder and deflected off it, but the punch had enough energy in it to cause Starr to loose his footing. He stumbled forward and fell heavily to the floor.

'Michael!' Kathleen pushed past her husband and rushed up to where Starr lay sprawled in the corridor.

'What the hell are you doing!?' Steve Galloway had entered the corridor from the cockpit just in time to see Sinclair take a swing at his friend and knock him to the floor. 'You bastard!' The only thing that prevented Galloway from putting Sinclair's face through the galley wall as he rushed toward him was that Michael had stumbled to his feet quickly enough to put himself between the two of them.

'No . . .' Starr attempted to add more, but he was already too much out of breath. Instead, he leaned against Galloway, his arms draped around his friend's shoulders as he hung on to keep himself upright. '. . . no fighting . . . don't . . . no sense to it . . .'

'What's happening here?' Captain Whitaker vaulted up the steps from the lower cargo area two at a time, with Julie Mathews right behind him. 'What's going on?' Whitaker glanced at the three of them, then looked directly at Galloway. 'I want an explanation. Right now.'

'It's my fault.' Kathleen stepped up to the captain before the second officer could speak. She glanced at her husband first, then at the other two men. *Don't back down. It's the only way.* 'I don't want to be married to Andrew anymore. I want to be with Michael and Steve.' Kathleen closed her eyes after the words had popped out. That was it, she had announced to all of them what she had hardly even allowed herself to think.

'Both of them!' Sinclair bellowed. He pointed at his wife, then turned to Whitaker. 'See what I mean? She's become a goddamned tramp.'

'Wait a minute.' Whitaker pulled himself up to his full height of well over six feet, which caused him to tower over Sinclair. 'I'm not going to put up with any name-calling. We're going to hash this thing out here and now like adults. Is that understood?'

Sinclair nodded without answering, then glanced over at the other three. Kathleen had moved to the far side of the galley to be nearer to the two men who had somehow become inextricably intertwined with her life. 'She's my wife, and that's all there is to that. I have no intention of sharing her.'

'That's right, captain.' Kathleen stepped forward. 'Andrew doesn't like to share any of his possessions.' She could feel the tears welling up in her eyes, but she managed to keep them back. 'That's exactly what I am to him, a possession. But I don't want to be a possession anymore.'

'Okay.' Whitaker held up his hand as if to ask for silence, yet none of them had made a sound. He could feel them all watching him as he hesitated a moment. He was holding court in the galley, deciding questions of morality and ethics with a piled-up tray of food on the one side of him and a percolating coffee pot on the other while the harsh morning sun made every detail of the event stand out. It was absurd – but then again, so was what had happened to the world.

'Is this a private meeting, or can anyone listen in?' Doctor Everett Tucker joined them, with Frank Corbi and Annie Rizzo directly behind him.

'No, it's not private. Matter of fact, it's very public. Let's get everyone back here so we don't have to do this again. Frank,' Whitaker said, addressing Corbi, 'you run forward and get everyone but Ray Madigan back here right now. Ray will have to stay in the cockpit, I'll fill him in later.'

'Sure thing, captain.'

'We'll wait until the others show up before we go on.'

'Just tell these two guys to leave me and my wife alone,' Sinclair said in the silence. When no one answered him, he stepped back and remained quiet until the others had shown up.

With the entire group assembled, Captain Whitaker cleared his throat and began again. 'Something that Andrew Sinclair said a minute ago was absolutely correct.'

'Damn right.'

'If you don't mind, I have the floor.' After he stared long enough at Sinclair to make his reprimand as pointed as he could, Whitaker glanced over at Julie. She had become his own lover for the first time during the night before, when they had gone directly to his cabin after the evening's emergency meeting was finished. As soon as they had entered his room, they had begun to make love to each other as if both of them suspected that they would never have another chance. Yet now that dawn had come, it was obvious to each that neither had changed their mind about what they had done, that neither regretted the actions they had taken. Whitaker turned away from Julie and again faced the group. 'One thing for sure is that everyone in this group is going to keep their individual freedom. I don't want to start to sound like Thomas Jefferson or Patrick Henry, but we're sure as hell not going to allow any single person or group to dominate any of the others.'

'Good. You tell them that.' Sinclair pointed at the two men who stood across the galley from him and next to his wife.

'The only logical course we can take,' Whitaker continued as he ignored the latest of Sinclair's interruptions, 'is to create laws among ourselves to protect individual freedom.' Whitaker stopped and looked directly at Julie again. 'Since God has, for some unknown reason, given all of us a second chance at life, I think it's only reasonable that we consider everything in our past as well behind us. Just like the people that each of us left behind, I think we should consider our memories and obligations from the past as also long dead.'

'Now, wait a minute . . .' Sinclair shuffled his feet uncomfortably, a growing sense of dread rising in him. He was losing, and he didn't know how to deal with that fact. 'You've got no right to say something like that.'

'Of course I do.' Whitaker eyed each of the members of the group for a moment. Each of the people assembled in the galley – except Andrew Sinclair – nodded their agreement.

'Then from this point we operate with only one basic assumption, is that what you're saying, captain?' Doctor Tucker took his pipe out of his pocket and popped it into his mouth, at least partially to obscure his growing smile. He knew exactly what Whitaker was leading up to – Tucker agreed completely – and he also knew exactly what to ask to give the captain enough leeway to make the next necessary point.

'That's right. Our only law from this point on is that each individual is free to do whatever they want, as long as their actions don't harm the group as a whole.'

'But she can't do this – we're married!' Sinclair shouted.

'I'm afraid, dear boy,' Tucker added from the rear of the room, 'that those papers went up in the same smoke that the rest of the world did – at least as far as this group is concerned. I gather from what the captain has said that, as a group, we will neither condone nor condemn anyone – as long as their individual actions don't interfere with the overall plans and goals of the group.'

'As far as the specific question that you asked is concerned,' Whitaker continued, after he returned Tucker's smile, 'the ruling on what Kathleen can do is a simple one. If she doesn't want to spend time with you, that's her business.'

'But . . . !'

'And if she wants to spend time with either – or both, for that matter – of the other two men, that seems to me to be strictly between her and the two of them.'

Without answering, Andrew Sinclair pushed his way

214

through the group, his head down. He stormed through the corridor and disappeared down the staircase that led to the cargo area.

'Captain, now that the meeting is over, can I have your attention back here for a moment?' Tucker said.

'Of course.' Whitaker moved aft toward the lounge and, as he did, he put his arm around Julie and took her back with him. Both Whitaker and Julie glanced back in time to see Kathleen walk down the corridor toward her stateroom with Michael Starr on one side and Steve Galloway on the other.

'Here's what I wanted to show you, captain.' Tucker pushed the paperwork around on the lounge table so all of them could read it. 'A historical point, but one that you might find interesting.'

'Historical?'

'Our route of flight since last night, since the vote to head directly for the South Pole.'

'What of it?'

'An important historical route, captain.' Tucker puffed on his pipe for a moment, even though he hadn't bothered to light it. 'You have, of course, heard of the Antarctic explorer Amundsen?'

'Yes, I have.'

'He was the Norwegian who beat Scott to the Pole,' Julie volunteered.

'Precisely.' Tucker tapped the paperwork in front of him, which contained a general chart of the Antarctic. 'Amundsen and Scott were in a race, as you know. Amundsen selected a route straight across the Ross Ice Shelf, across the Queen Maud mountains and up the plateau to the Pole itself. As you can see from the chart, that happens by coincidence to be our planned route to the Pole.'

'I'll be damned.' Whitaker leaned over the chart and took in the details.

'But that's far from the end of it, I'm afraid.' Tucker waited until he had the captain's full attention before he continued.

Whitaker finished studying the chart and looked up. 'Not the end of it? What do you mean?'

'I think I know what he means,' Julie said. 'You're talking about the loser, right?'

'Yes.' Tucker smiled at Julie. He always enjoyed a beautiful young woman, especially one who had a knowledge and appreciation of history. 'I would be most honored if you would explain my discovery to the captain.'

'Here,' Julie said as she turned the chart toward her, 'is the line representing the path that Amundsen took in 1911 on his way to the South Pole. That is, as Doctor Tucker has said, just about the exact flight path that we've been taking with *Airship Nine*.'

'Yes, it is.' Whitaker looked at the scale of the chart, then glanced at his wristwatch. 'How long did it take Amundsen to get from the edge of the ice shelf to the Pole itself?'

'Approximately two months,' Tucker answered.

'Well, if nothing else we've come a long way in transportation since 1911. We've already covered half that route in six hours, and I expect that we'll be over the South Pole station in another five hours at the most.'

'But I think that what Doctor Tucker wants us to look at is this other line,' Julie said as she pointed back to the chart. 'The one from the McMurdo area direct to the Pole. Correct me if I'm wrong, but I think that this is just about the path that explorer Robert Scott took in his attempt to beat Amundsen in their race to the Pole.'

'You're absolutely correct, my dear.' Tucker pointed to the blinding glare outside, the nothingness of the never ending fields of white that they flew over. 'Scott not only failed to win, but he and his men died horribly on the return trip to their base camp as the incredible cold and the harsh terrain wore them down.'

'I'd believe it.' Whitaker glanced outside again. 'Even in this direct sunlight, it's nearly thirty below zero out there. This is not the place for a crash landing, that's for sure.' Whitaker shivered at the thought of being stranded on the rising plateau of ice below them, since it was at least several hundred miles in any direction to anything – even a natural mound of rock – that was even remotely usable for survival.

216

'I'm perfectly thrilled to see that you find history interesting, captain – but I'm afraid that I've digressed. My real point in bringing all this up has to do with the Russians.'

'What about the Russians?'

'The McMurdo base that we've heard has been overrun is precisely the spot where Scott began his ill-fated journey in 1911 – that area is a natural harbor, so that's why the Americans built their McMurdo base at that very location fifty years after Scott's death. Now, unless I miss my guess by a long shot, I'd venture to say that the Russians – who are nobody's fools when it comes to looking out for their own self-interests – have every intention of racing us to the South Pole . . .'

'Christ, I never thought of that,' Whitaker said.

'. . . and – in addition to what undoubtedly our more immediate concerns will be – these additional factors will provide us with the greatest of ironies.'

'How do you mean?'

'Simply this. Either history will repeat itself and we prove once and forever that Amundsen's route is the fastest . . .'

'Or history balances everything out,' Julie added, 'and the Russians make Robert Scott's route the one that works best this time around.'

'I see.' Captain Lou Whitaker stepped to the lounge window and stared outside through the double-thick insulated glass at the hostile terrain a thousand feet below. He looked over at Julie but could think of nothing to say, nothing to add, no way to be reassuring or positive. It was obvious from her expression that Julie also couldn't think of any way to change the subject, to get their minds off what their only concern had become. A race with the Russians to the Pole, a repeat of what Amundsen and Scott had done nearly eighty years before. All they could do now was wait to see what would happen as *Airship Nine* plodded its way due south toward the only safe spot left on earth.

Fifteen

'No, YOU idiot – the other way!' Doctor Boris Ney jabbed a finger in the new direction he wanted the helicopter to take. Since first climbing aboard two hours ago and clamping on a flight helmet that seemed three sizes too small for him, Ney found to his continued annoyance that, once again, he needed to shout every word to make himself heard above the racket of the twin turbines. 'Pay attention, damn you!'

'Sorry,' the pilot shouted back. He quickly manipulated the Kamov Ka-25's flight controls to head in the direction that Ney ordered. They flew directly toward another set of ridgelines in the endless chain of mountains and valleys – a literal maze of vertical rock and ice that they had been methodically searching for more than an hour. 'The airship might stay above the mountains,' the pilot said as he glanced up into the clear blue sky above them.

'Don't be ridiculous.' Ney shook his head contemptuously. 'He's got to realize that we're looking for him. That means he'll stay as low as possible to make himself difficult to find. It's the only chance the airship has.' Ney frowned because, if it hadn't been for that radioed warning from McMurdo, the airship would never have known about them, would not now be on the defensive against them. Ney regretted not having killed that last American even sooner than he had.

'Oh. I see what you mean.'

'I'm happy that you do.' Ney worked hard to prevent himself from telling his pilot that he considered him a complete buffoon. 'Keep it steady. Keep your eyes open.'

'Yessir.'

Ney scanned the mountain range ahead, then glanced down at the helicopter's fuel gauge. It had sunk to the lower quarter of the scale, very near to the mark that meant that they must turn back for the base camp. But the sinking fuel gauge wasn't their major problem at the moment – darkness was. The sun, which had hardly gotten much above the mountain tops even at the height of midday, had already set below the horizon. Ney knew that it would be absolutely futile to continue searching for the American airship once nighttime was on them, so his plan was only a handful of minutes away from being a total failure. 'Wait! What's that?!' Ney leaned forward in his flight chair as he pointed straight ahead.

'I don't see anything,' the pilot answered hesitantly. He fidgeted in his seat, knowing for certain that he would now be in for another barrage of abuse.

'Look, damn you! Open your eyes – it's over there!'

'All I see is a shadow against the ridgeline.'

'Shadow?' Ney peered straight ahead as hard as he could. All at once, the shape and form that he was certain had been the American airship transformed itself into nothing but a splotch of darkness on the rock-strewn vertical surface of a sheer cliff. 'Oh.' Ney sat back in his flight chair. 'Nothing but a shadow. I see what you mean.'

'Should I keep going? This direction?'

'Yes.' In his mind, Ney had already given up. He took his eyes off the horizon and looked straight down for a moment. The surface of the plateau that they flew over was nothing but a brief interlude in the continual upheavals that comprised the Queen Maud mountains. On those sections of the plateau that were covered with ice and snow, the prevailing down-slope wind had created frozen waves that were several meters high and many meters in length. From what little he could see in the enveloping darkness, some of those snow waves were beautifully sculptured. They had long icy tails that streamed behind them, making patterns that pointed to where the cold wind had gone in its rush toward the Antarctic sea several hundred kilometers behind them.

'There's nothing out here. Should I try the next valley?'

'Yes.' Ney held onto the arm of his flight chair as the helicopter rose abruptly. As they maneuevered across the next ridgeline, the air turbulence worsened. Ney put a death-grip on the armrest. 'Why is it so rough?' he said, in a tone that indicated that he was less than pleased with the way the flight was being handled.

'Nothing I can do. The wind,' the pilot shouted back.

'Well, I think that you should . . .' Ney stopped in mid sentence because he had seen something. Something big. Something dark against the contoured pattern of mountains that formed the next grouping in the chain. 'Is that . . .?'

'Yes!' The helicopter pilot nearly yanked the control stick out of its base as he flung the Kamov helicopter toward starboard. 'That's it! The airship!'

There it was, unmistakably. It was still a kilometer or more away, riding low over a saddleback between two mountains, looking like a whale getting ready to dive beneath the surface of the sea again. 'I knew we could find them,' Ney shouted. 'Get ready!'

'Ready.' The pilot concentrated on the pattern he was flying, keeping in mind what he had been briefed to do when visual contact with the American airship was finally made. *Don't get too close, they might have weapons. Don't waste a shot.*

'He's diving into the shadows.'

'Maybe he's seen us!'

'I don't think so.' But even as Ney watched, the bleak grey color of the airship began to blend in with its surroundings. The American airship captain was trying to hide by staying as low as possible in the countless valleys – and Ney could see that there was a distinct possibility that he might succeed. There were only a few moments of diminishing twilight left, then it would be pitch-black – too dark to find which valley the airship was in, too dark to fly a helicopter safely between the ridges. 'Faster!'

'The missiles are ready.' The pilot had already released the safety cover and had activated the other cockpit controls he needed in order to send their two AS-8 self-guiding tactical missiles into the enemy. 'He's in the third valley, right?'

'Yes.' Ney sounded certain, but he wasn't. Flying so low and moving through the overlapping shadows so quickly, the scene in front of him kept changing drastically every few seconds. From their angle and perspective, none of the valleys seemed to be the one that the airship had disappeared into – or every one of them did. 'No, over there!' Ney shouted as he suddenly changed his mind. 'Not this valley, the next one!'

'But I think it's . . .'

'Listen to me, you idiot!' Ney was shouting as loud as he could, leaving no room for his authority to be challenged as he pointed toward the valley that he thought the airship had descended into.

'If that's what you want.' The helicopter pilot shoved on the flight controls to readjust their path toward where Ney had pointed. The Ka-25 hurtled over the top of dozens of mounds of powdery snow, the blasts of air from the whirling blades kicking up a visible trail behind them. When they had crossed the last ridge, the helicopter pilot yanked rearward on his control stick to bring the helicopter into a hovering standstill. 'Now what?'

Ney stared down the broad valley beneath them in utter disbelief. Empty. He had picked the wrong valley from the several around them. 'I . . . I don't know . . .'

Without a word, the helicopter pilot slammed his control stick to the right and then pushed it far forward. The Ka-25 obediently darted up the length of the valley and then crossed the next ridgeline. But the next valley was also empty. 'Damn!'

'Is there any chance . . .?'

The helicopter pilot ignored Ney completely and concentrated instead on his flying. The valleys themselves were now impenetrably black and most of the peaks above them were also deeply washed in tones of dark grey. 'One more chance, that's all we'll get.'

'Find him.' Ney couldn't think of anything else to add. As much as he didn't care to admit it, the ultimate success or failure of his global plan would probably depend on the skill of the pilot who sat to his right, would depend on how lucky that technician got in the next two minutes. 'Hurry.'

The helicopter pilot decided to try something different. He pushed the helicopter far below the ridgeline, then hugged the east wall of rock and snow as he rammed the throttles wide open. Using the contrast of the slightly lighter sky above them, the pilot managed to keep the edge of the cliff in sight despite the near-total blackness in the valley. 'Hang on!'

'Be careful!' The wind that spilled down the face of the sheer cliff was buffeting them. Ney was wide-eyed as he watched the pilot push the helicopter as fast as it would go. They traveled between the narrow valley walls at a breathtaking speed, the images on both sides of them nothing more than a soft blur. It was like watching an out-of-focus film being run in fast motion.

'There!' the pilot shouted triumphantly. Straight in front of them at a distance of less than five hundred meters, was the American airship. It hovered midway between the invisible valley floor below and the pencil-thin horizon line formed by the mountain peaks far above them.

'Fire!'

The helicopter pilot pressed his thumb on the first switch, then on the next. The Ka-25 lurched slightly as both the missiles sped away from their launching tubes, an irregular line of puffy white smoke trailing behind each of them. With the missiles away, the pilot turned his attention back to his flying again. 'We need altitude!' he shouted to Ney as he yanked back on the flight controls. The helicopter jerked straight up and away from the rock and ice walls on both sides of them, clearing the nearer cliff by no more than twenty meters.

Doctor Boris Ney leaned as far forward as his shoulder harness would allow as he attempted to follow the path of the two missiles from his seat in the rapidly climbing helicopter. 'We can't miss the airship – not this close!' Ney lost the trail of the missiles in the blackness but, just as he did, he also caught his last glimpse of the Americans. Both missiles were headed in silhouette against the obscuring darkness of the far cliff. *Airship Nine* was definitely going to take both missile hits dead-center.

*

Captain Lou Whitaker had taken over the controls of the *Airship Nine* just before they had entered the foothills of the Queen Maud mountains. He had earlier slowed their forward speed so that he could time their crossing of the mountain range – the mountains were the last major obstacle between their present position and the South Pole – to occur during the last hour of daylight. As Frank Corbi had suggested a short while before, the shadows created by the low sun angle and the high mountains would do a good job of camouflaging the airship if they could fly low enough. Whitaker had kept *Airship Nine* as low as possible, rising only when absolutely necessary to give them adequate clearance from the terrain.

'How much longer?' Floyd Robinson asked from the back of the assembled group. As the minutes had gone by most everyone on board had, one by one, joined the crowd that was now jammed in the cockpit.

Whitaker nodded to Ray Madigan in the copilot seat to take over the flight controls. He then turned to face the crew and passengers. Julie stood nearest, her hand on his seatback, her fingers occasionally brushing along the top of his shoulder. Behind her were all the others – except for Andrew Sinclair, who had not come forward. 'The charts I have might be sketchy for this region, but so far they've been right. If it stays that way, we'll be through the Queen Maud mountains in fifteen minutes.'

'And from that point to the Pole?' Michael Starr asked. He was against the far wall, with Kathleen Sinclair standing next to him, and Steve Galloway next to her.

'Two hundred and seventy miles.'

'Three hours?'

'No. More like five hours because of the increasing headwind.' Whitaker scanned his flight instruments, then turned back to the group. 'From what I've been told, this kind of wind is normal for this area.'

'Yes, it is. The wintertime mounding of super-cold air over the Pole,' Robinson said as he addressed the group with the same information that he had volunteered earlier to the captain, 'stretches far up into the stratosphere. The pressure of that cold air begins a cascading motion down the slope of the Antarctic plateau. The elevation of the South Pole is nearly ten thousand feet, so it's one hell of a continual drop for that cold air to get down to sea level at the Ross Ice Shelf. The effects of gravity accelerate this cold air on its way to the sea, and this gravity-induced wind is a constant element out here. It's generally steady, and always from the same direction – always from the Pole and toward the ocean, due north.'

'Do you think that's why that poor chap at McMurdo told us to go to the South Pole – that he realized that the downslope wind might help to keep the ill effects of nuclear debris away from the Pole itself?' Doctor Everett Tucker, who was nearly in a state of exhaustion from staying up all night to take notes on their situation, leaned heavily against the bulkhead. There was a pad and pencil in his hand and he occasionally forced himself to jot down pertinent words and phrases, taking special care to attribute each remark accurately to its spokesman.

'I don't think Vernon had enough time to figure those things out,' Robinson said. He paused for a moment while he thought about what must have happened at McMurdo. Everyone on the airship owed Vernon more than could ever be paid. Robinson turned back to Tucker. 'But what you said does make good sense, I was thinking about it earlier. I'm sure the Russians have figured this South Pole business out also. I think that they went after McMurdo because it was the nearest base to get land vehicles from, the nearest camp from where they could launch an assault to capture the South Pole station itself.'

'Then what happens after we get there?' Starr asked. 'How are we going to stop the Russians?'

'One problem at a time, okay?' Ray Madigan struggled continually with the set of flight controls at the copilot's seat as he worked at keeping the airship pointed in the direction that he wanted. 'We've got enough problems right here. The wind is getting worse and I can't see a damned thing. How about it?' Madigan asked as he glanced toward the captain. 'Do you think it's dark enough for us to climb above the mountains yet? I'm not sure I know where this valley is leading to.'

Whitaker looked outside at the darkness. The valley floor

was etched in nothing but shades of black, but the upper portions of the cliffs – which rose hundreds of feet above them on both sides – were still slightly outlined by the faint glow on the western horizon. 'Ten minutes more, just to be sure. But I think you're right about not being able to see enough. Slow up if you think we should – we can make up the time later when we climb above the mountains.' Whitaker turned back to the group. 'Everyone remember now, no lights on for any reason whatsoever – we can't risk taking a chance of giving the Russians a visible target.'

'Do you think they're out looking for us?' Julie asked.

'There's no sense taking any chances, but if you want my opinion – I'd say no.' As he finished speaking, Whitaker glanced across the cockpit and out the side window. A few hundred yards away, hovering abeam the far valley sidewall, was the faint but distinctive shape of a helicopter. Whitaker's mouth dropped open and, as he stared at it in utter disbelief, two plumes of white smoke began to hurtle away from the helicopter and directly toward them. 'Everyone down! Get down!'

Captain Lou Whitaker grabbed for the emergency handles on the cockpit overhead panel and yanked down hard on them, causing the main vents to open on each side of the airship's three integral ballonets and thereby reducing the internal pressure of the airship's helium. A moment later the airship began a rapid descent. But even as they began to fall, Whitaker could see that their descent was far too slow to prevent *Airship Nine* from being hit squarely by the two missiles that sped toward them.

Sixteen

THE FIRST of the Soviet AS-8 missiles to hit *Airship Nine* did so by puncturing the polyurethane envelope a few inches above the horizontal red-painted stripe that crossed the airship from nose to tail. The internal guidance system of the missile, which had actually been designed to be used at a greater minimum range from a target, had not yet locked on because it had not received sufficient internal signal to do so.

But that particular deviation from the designer's criteria made absolutely no difference in the final outcome since the target itself was simply too big and at too close a range to miss. What did make a difference, however, was that while ripping through the polyurethane envelope the impact sensors in the nose of the AS-8s could not discover enough evidence that the missiles had actually hit anything.

Like an arrow going through a piece of cardboard, the first AS-8 missile – followed quickly by the second – tore into the starboard side of the airship's envelope and, within a fraction of a second after that, had torn themselves out through the port sidewall. Since there was no frame whatsoever inside the main envelope of the non-rigid class of airships – the hull was simply a rugged, controllable balloon – the missile's impact sensors never felt a tremor large enough to trigger them. As far as both the AS-8 missiles were concerned, *Airship Nine* did not exist; the missiles were simply still en route, still flying through open skies on the way to some distant target.

After both missiles exited through the far side of the airship's thin hull, they continued headlong toward the vertical wall of rock and ice that lay a few hundred yards beyond *Airship Nine*. Impacting there, at a spot several hundred feet below the top of the ridge, both missiles worked as they had been designed. First one and then the next of the AS-8s exploded in a fiery ball of orange and white as the internal impact sensors in each unit verified for certain that they had indeed met a formidable object.

'Julie, hold on!' When he didn't hear an answer, Captain Lou Whitaker had an overwhelming urge to turn around to see if Julie was still behind, still holding on to the back of his flight chair as she had been. But that was a luxury that Whitaker had no time for, not even the split-second it would take to glance over his shoulder. Instead, he worked furiously – and mostly in vain – in an attempt to maintain control over the collapsing airship.

'We're going down – everyone brace!' Ray Madigan had also focused his complete attention on the flight controls, although he could feel Nancy Schneider's hands pressed hard against his back as she held on to him. Madigan shot a quick glance at the overhead instrument panel to verify with the gauges what his gut feeling had already told him: they were losing their helium – the lifeblood of *Airship Nine* – at an enormous, almost incalculable rate. 'We're torn wide open!'

'I known it!'

'We're going to hit!'

'Get ready!' The only fortunate break for them had come after the missiles had exploded against the vertical wall of rock – it had created enough of a fireball to illuminate the valley floor below for several seconds. It was that glow from the smoldering remains of the AS-8s that gave Whitaker a chance to spot the jagged peak that they would have otherwise hit full-force.

'Pull up!'

'Give me power!' Whitaker pulled back on the sluggish control wheel as Madigan pushed both engine throttles to full speed. The combination of the two inputs gave the nearly-uncontrollable airship one final and desperate change of direction. Like an elephant being prodded by a small stick, *Airship Nine* finally and reluctantly began to move in the direction that Whitaker wanted it to.

The crash into the rock ledge came in slow motion, since most of the airship's forward energy had already been dissipated. The long metal runners beneath the fiberglass gondola were the first to snap off, followed quickly by the grinding, cracking fiberglass panels as the lower cargo deck nearly sheared itself away. Enormous sections of the polyurethane balloon had already disintegrated or been torn from the gondola, and what remained began to fall down around them on all sides, some of the smaller pieces still on fire from being ignited by the heat and exhaust gases of the missiles.

Yet the ripping apart of the remainder of *Airship Nine*'s polyurethane shell had, during the last few seconds of flight, helped by acting as a drag chute to break the fall. By the time what was left of the airship had come to a stop on the rock ledge, the only section that remained visibly intact was the upper deck of the ninety foot gondola with its two rear-mounted engines. Both the engines had already stopped turning, the twin sets of propeller blades grotesquely twisted by the bombardment from the falling sections of wreckage. What little fire remained on fragmented edges of the polyurethane shell was being snubbed out quickly by the wind and cold.

'Can anyone hear me?' Whitaker was lying slightly to one side, still in his flight chair, his left shoulder pressed against the cockpit sidewall. The glow from the missile explosions had begun to fade a moment before and soon they were in total blackness. 'Julie?'

'I'm okay,' Julie answered weakly from somewhere just behind him.

'Ray, can you hear me?'

'Yes.' Madigan shook his head to clear it – he had banged it hard against the sidewall when they hit the ledge and he could feel a trickle of warm blood down the side of his face and across the nape of his neck. The other thing he felt was the enormous cold – even this soon it had cut right through him as if he had never been warm a minute of his life, as if he hadn't been sitting quite comfortably in this very seat less than sixty seconds before.

228

'Can you reach your flashlight?'

'I think so.' Madigan fumbled in the pouch to his right, found the flashlight and clicked it on. What he saw took his breath away.

The carcass of *Airship Nine* was poised on a cliff, with the cockpit hanging precariously over the edge. The terrain beneath Madigan's feet dropped away so precipitously that he couldn't see it – and it dropped away so far that the bottom of the precipice was out of the range of his flashlight. The worst part was that he could feel the gondola teetering back and forth in the wind, rocking dangerously over the ledge and then coming back again. 'God Almighty.'

'Don't anyone move!' Whitaker had finally found his own flashlight. He pulled it out of its pouch and scanned the beam back and forth across the upsloped ledge that they had come to a stop on. 'Don't move – we'll be okay,' Whitaker said, a captain's automatic response. But it was more than obvious to Whitaker that they had never been less okay in their lives. The only thing that had prevented them from careening over the ridge and falling to certain death had been the force of the constant Antarctic wind that pressed against them. That incessant, howling wind was pushing backward enough on the remnants of the hull to keep the cabin in a delicate balance. If the wind faded or, worse, died altogether – then they would go over the edge. They would die when the wind did.

'We'd better do something,' Madigan said in a hollow, frightened voice. 'Right now.'

'Yes.' Whitaker was just about to order everyone to the rear of the airship when he heard a commotion behind him. He turned around and aimed the flashlight down the aisle.

'Stop, don't move!' Madigan knew that any movement now would topple them. But Andrew Sinclair, slightly dazed, numbed by the cold and now in a full-fledged panic to get back with the others, was pushing himself toward the front of the airship. He stumbled and thrashed his way across bits and pieces of wreckage in the aisle, pushing

229

things aside – and, as he did, the airship began to tip over the edge of the cliff.

'Help me – help!' Sinclair was holding his left arm where he had cut it slightly during the landing, a small amount of blood staining one sleeve and a portion of his shirt. 'Someone help me!'

'You imbecile! You coddled, mealy-mouthed braggart!' The voice of Doctor Everett Tucker filled the airship, and, for that matter, seemed to fill the entire glacial valley they had crashed in. 'You dithering fool!' The doctor picked himself off the floor and, in one quick motion that suprised even himself, he lunged rearward. Tucker smashed his body squarely into Sinclair's. The two men stumbled backward in each other's arms as they fell toward the aft end of the gondola.

'Move backward – everybody!' Whitaker kept his flashlight aimed outside as he shouted, although he already could feel that the airship had stopped its forward tilt. The passengers and crew scurried aft in the wrecked cabin as quickly as they could. Even before half of them had gone to the rear, the shifting of cabin weight was enough to turn the trick: the gondola of *Airship Nine* hesitated for a moment, then tilted backward and slid several feet away from the edge of the cliff and toward safety. 'Stop running – we're okay!' Whitaker announced to those who hadn't gone aft yet.

'That was too damned close.' Madigan swept the beam of his flashlight out his sidewindow to confirm what Whitaker had said. 'It looks good over here.'

'Over here, too.' Whitaker turned his flashlight back into the cockpit at the group, aiming it first at Julie who was still jammed into the corner beside his seat. When the beam of glaring light flooded over her, she looked up at him. 'Are you okay?' Whitaker asked again.

'. . . think so.' Julie stumbled to her feet, pushing off pieces of shattered fiberglass and trim that had fallen over her. She had already begun to shiver from the intense cold. 'What happened – did we explode?' It was nearly her turn to move aft, as soon as Michael finished helping Kathleen to her feet and the two of them started

230

down the dark corridor and out of Julie's way.

'We were shot down. Missiles.'

'Russians?'

'Must've been.'

'Why did you move people back?' From where Julie had been, on the floor behind the captain's seat, she had no idea what the two pilots had seen. She motioned with her hand to indicate the pitching and tilting that the gondola had gone through a few moments before.

'We were on an upslope, but at the edge of a cliff,' Whitaker said as calmly as he could considering that all of them had nearly died – and not just once, for that matter, but twice during the last two minutes. 'We finally slid backward a few feet, we'll be all right now.'

'I felt us slide backward. How much of a drop-off was it?'

'You don't want to know.'

'What's behind us?'

'I'm not sure.'

Julie looked rearward out one of the cracked, glazed windows but could see nothing. Michael and Kathleen had already gone aft, so Julie took her first step into the aisle and over a section of door frame that lay across her path. All she could see as she looked back out the glazed sidewindow was utter blackness. 'Hurry back,' she said to Whitaker as she moved toward the rear of the airship.

'I will.' As Julie left, Whitaker took time to sweep his flashlight beam across what was left of the cockpit since they were no longer in any immediate danger. 'What a goddamn mess,' was the only thing he could think of saying.

'Sure is.' With all the others now safely in the back, Madigan also took the time to aim his flashlight at different spots in the cockpit. Everything was in a shambles – instruments, radios, controls. *Airship Nine* was a complete and useless wreck, except for odd pieces that might be helpful in building a shelter for themselves. 'Yeah, we're safe, at least for a while. But we'd better do something to get ourselves warm.' Madigan eased himself out of the copilot's seat while he spoke, his flashlight moving steadily

back and forth as he continued to examine his surroundings.

'Right.' Whitaker, who had seen Madigan and the others
shivering, began to shiver himself as the intense cold finally
overwhelmed the effects of his pumped-up adrenalin. 'At
least we've slid backward far enough from the cliff. The
ground around us looks solid enough.'

'Yeah, this is our red-letter day.'

'Well, it sure beats the alternative.' Whitaker nodded
toward the blackness outside, in the direction of the sheer
cliff that they had nearly tumbled over. He shivered again,
this time more from the thought of the cliff than the cold.

'Yeah, you're right.' Madigan nodded his agreement,
then changed the subject. 'How about if I take Galloway
with me to check outside? We ought to know what's
behind us.'

'What about your cut?' Whitaker pointed to the small
but noticeable gash on the side of Madigan's skull.

'It's nothing, don't worry about it.'

'Okay, go ahead – but be careful.'

'Damn right. I didn't live this long to throw it away
now.'

'That's a good attitude. Keep that in mind after you find
out what's outside.'

'What do you mean?' Madigan reached down and pulled
a blanket out of a pile of wreckage on the floor. He shook
the dust and debris off it, then wrapped the blanket around
his shoulders to use it as makeshift protection from the
biting cold.

'If you want me to keep my good attitude, don't bother
to tell me if the news from outside is bad.' Whitaker
managed a small smile for his copilot. He was happy to
see that Madigan managed to smile back. Finally, Madigan
turned away and began to trudge down the corridor.
Whitaker watched him disappear into the depths of the
wreckage. *He's a hell of a guy, he's got a set of balls. He's
no dummy, either.*

As incredible as it would have seemed even a few short
days before, Whitaker now couldn't think of any other
copilot he'd rather have with him right now than Ray

Madigan. Yet both of them, Whitaker now realized, had changed enormously in the last few days, changed to meet the endless needs of their incredible situation. Both had allowed their characters to change, compromise, become flexible. Those were the traits he knew it would take if they were to have any chance of survival, the traits it would take to deal with the here and now. The here and now was all that there was, except – maybe, if they were incredibly lucky – there still might be a tomorrow. Yet surviving for the here and now was all that any of them could afford to think about.

Whitaker pushed himself out of the captain's seat and stood in the aisle of the wrecked airship that was, technically speaking, still under his command. It took no in-depth inspection or analysis to see that the airship wouldn't be doing any more flying, but Whitaker suspected that it would provide enough protection from the elements to keep them alive for awhile until they came up with another plan for survival – something they would need to do very soon since it was thirty below zero outside, and that was before he calculated the chilling effects of the constant wind. Whitaker took another step aft, then stopped to listen.

The wind continued at its steady pitch and howl, but now he could hear voices. The people in the back, the passengers and crew of *Airship Nine*, had already begun talking rationally, planning, organizing themselves into a new pattern for survival. Survival. Even the word itself now had a mystical ring to it, had a sound buoyant enough to grab onto and bob up to the surface with or, more accurately, to step inside of and be propelled two hundred miles of frozen nothingness to the safety and warmth that waited for them at the South Pole station.

Whitaker shivered, then took another step. He aimed his flashlight to his left. Something caught his eye, something protruding from behind the shattered door that had led to the smashed remnants of what had been the captain's stateroom. There, sticking out from beneath a piece of fiberglass, was a finger. 'Damn!'

Whitaker rushed over to the pile of debris and began to

233

move it as quickly as he could. A hand, an arm. The body of a man, a black man. Floyd Robinson. He was dead. His neck had been broken by one of the cross sections of roofing frame that had collapsed on him from above. Robinson's head was twisted at a hideous angle in reference to his shoulders. The skin around his neck was badly scraped, bloated and swollen.

'I can't find Floyd anywhere.' Julie was working her way forward again in the dark and wreckage-strewn corridor. She slowly maneuvered toward Whitaker as she guided herself by using the reflected light from his flashlight beam. 'Have you seen Floyd? At first I thought he must be with Ray and Steve . . .'

Whitaker held up his hand. Even in the glaring beam of his flashlight he could see the alterations in her facial expression as it went from deep concern to utter dread. She had spotted the body. She took two more steps before she knew for sure that it was Robinson. She took another step before she knew for certain that he was dead. 'Oh, God, no.'

As much as she didn't want to, Julie stepped up to the body and rolled it over. 'Dead . . .' was all she could bring herself to say. Julie stumbled to her feet and began to cry.

Whitaker put his arm around her. 'There's nothing we can do for him,' he said softly. It was a stupid and senseless comment, but he couldn't think of anything else. He allowed her to cry for a few more moments until both of them began to shiver so badly that he forced himself to speak again. 'We've got to get ourselves warm. What's the situation in the back?'

'They've got the rear heater going.' Julie wiped the tears from her face and pulled her body closer to Whitaker's. 'Ray and Steve went outside. We were all patching the holes in what's left of the lounge when I realized that Floyd wasn't around.'

'I should've made a better check. How is everyone else?'

'Everyone seems fine, except maybe Doctor Tucker. After he knocked down Andrew Sinclair, he's been having a hard time catching his breath. He was lying down when I left.'

'He saved our lives. If Sinclair had made it to the front, we would've tipped over the edge.'

'Really?'

'Yes.' Whitaker began to steer her around the wreckage in the corridor and toward the rear of what was left of the airship. They pushed aside a curtain that had been hung across the opening to the corridor to keep in the heat as they entered what had once been the lounge. It now looked like a bombed-out room of a war zone tenement.

'We'll be all right in here.' Julie pointed to what the others had done already to make the lounge into a safe haven for them. The diffused glow from the two overhead battery lights provided the illumination and heat came from a wall-mounted unit that used the airship's fuel supply as its energy source. That fuel supply was, evidently, still intact. The temperature in the lounge, while probably no more than fifty degrees, seemed positively roasting when compared to what it had already dropped to in the cockpit.

As he switched off his flashlight and allowed his eyes to adjust to the dim light, Whitaker saw what he had been looking for. He immediately walked over to Kathleen Sinclair, who was taking care of Tucker. Tucker, still wearing one of his three-piece suits, lay motionless on the floor with his eyes shut. A cushion from the couch was propped under his head, a blanket lay across most of his body. 'How is he?'

'Difficult to say.' Kathleen looked up at the captain, then glanced over at Andrew Sinclair. Just as her husband had done since Doctor Tucker first complained of shortness of breath after their arrival in the lounge, Andrew kept his back turned from the old man. 'I think his heartbeat is irregular. I guess what he did was too much of a strain on him.'

'I see.' Whitaker shook his head; Tucker looked worse than he had imagined from what Julie had said. 'Has he been asleep long?'

'He's not really asleep, he sort of fades in and out on me. Sometimes he hears me when I speak to him. Sometimes he doesn't.'

'That's not good.'

'I know it.'

'Do you have any ideas?'

'I've already done everything I can.' There was an edge of desperation in Kathleen's voice. She glanced at her husband, his back studiously turned from them. *That son of a bitch. No wonder I can't live with him any more. Even if it hadn't been for Michael and Steve, I would've left him anyway.*

'Okay, just do your best. Call me if you need help.'

'Thank you.' Kathleen turned from the captain and back to her new patient as she concentrated on making Doctor Everett Tucker as comfortable as she possibly could.

Whitaker went to the front of the lounge again where Julie and a few of the others were. 'We have another one of these heaters in the lower cargo bay,' Whitaker said as he stepped closer to the gasoline-fired unit to warm himself. 'Maybe we'll be able to find it to use as a supplement.'

'Or to use it as spare parts in case this one breaks.' Frank Corbi handed Annie Rizzo the last of the fiberglass panels they were arranging to cover a split in a wall seam. Once that final panel was propped up and secured in place by a section of metal tubing behind it, Corbi turned back to the captain again. 'Do you want me to try to find that other heater?'

'Not yet.' As Whitaker answered, the other two members of his flight crew entered the lounge from the corridor that led outside. Madigan and Galloway were both shivering noticeably. 'What's it like out there?'

'It's like mid-winter in the Antarctic, that's for fucking sure.' Madigan rubbed his hands back and forth viciously to try to warm them.

'The moon is just starting to come up. If the sky stays clear,' Galloway continued, 'we should be able to see more very soon. We'll be able to see for miles.'

'But could you tell anything so far?' Whitaker hated to bother his two men before they got themselves warm, but he needed to know what was around them. 'Are there any more cliffs? Is there a potential for that kind of problem again.'

'No.' Madigan turned around, stuck his backside toward

236

the heater, then addressed the captain directly. 'We're thirty feet back from the cliff at the very least. It's also several feet up the hill to get there. Behind us is a broad glacial plain that fans out on both sides. There are some outcroppings of rock at the edges, but nothing that would be too hard to get around on the way down. It's sort of an uphill box canyon from what I can see. In other words, there's no big terrain problems – except that there's just too fucking much of it between us and where we need to get to.'

'Then the best thing for us to do right now is sit tight and talk things over?'

'Yeah, guess so.' Madigan looked around the makeshift hovel of a room that had suddenly become their only home, their last chance to stay alive. First the world had been reduced to nothing beyond the Antarctic, and now the airship had been reduced to nothing but the rear lounge. 'We're shrinking.'

'What?'

'Never mind.' Madigan glanced around at the shadowy darkness as he began to count heads. 'Wait a second, who's missing?'

'Robinson. He's dead.' Whitaker waited, stonefaced, but to his surprise no one said a thing. 'His body is up front,' Whitaker finally added. 'He broke his neck during the crash landing.'

'Poor bastard.' Madigan shook his head. 'Robinson was a gutsy and brainy guy. He deserved better.'

'And Tucker doesn't look good, either,' Whitaker said, since the doctor's condition was still very much on his mind. Once again, there was total silence from the group – an understandable reaction since there really was nothing left for them to say. One man was dead, another was in jeopardy of dying. 'So since none of you have any questions for me, then I have a few for you.' Whitaker looked at each of the others in the lounge before he spoke again. 'Where does this leave us? Do any of you have any opinion on what you want to do next?'

'I want to wake up and find that this is has been a bad dream.' Starr shuffled his feet. The only sound in the room was the low hiss from the gasoline heater as it spat out hot air as quickly as it could.

After another long silence, Madigan spoke. 'The only question worth a damn is the most obvious one. Can we make it to the Pole on foot?'

'I was talking to Tucker just before we were shot down,' Whitaker answered. 'The things he told us about Amundsen and Scott were doubly interesting because those two explorers basically did this same trip on foot back in 1911.'

'And Scott's party died,' Starr volunteered.

'But they died on the way back, and nearly made it at that. Amundsen and Scott both went roundtrip, and we've already got a two-thirds head start one way – which is all we'll need to go.' Whitaker tried not to sound overly enthusiastic because he knew how difficult it would be for an ill-equipped group to reach the Pole on foot, but he couldn't stop himself from becoming upbeat. Since it seemed like their only chance, Whitaker was making himself feel positive about it.

'That sounds like a good backup plan, but I think maybe we should wait a day or two before we start out.'

Whitaker gave Corbi a puzzled look. 'Why should we wait? What for?'

'For the Russians.'

'What?'

'You're crazy.' As he spoke to them for the first time since the crash and his ridiculous problem with the old man – it certainly wasn't his fault that no one had told him not to come forward after the crash landing – Andrew Sinclair stepped into the middle of the group. 'The Russians shot us down. They're damn well not going to help us out now.'

'That's right.' Corbi nodded. He was nearly bubbling over with the idea that he had been thinking about for the last few minutes. 'Annie and I were talking it over. The Russians are obviously after us . . .'

'Obviously,' Sinclair replied.

'. . . so what makes us think that they're going to stop now? I think that they might come back to finish us off, as soon as it gets light enough to travel into this box canyon.'

'That seems like an even better reason to get the hell out of here,' Madigan answered. He glanced over at Nancy, who nodded in agreement with him. But Madigan had learned enough about Frank Corbi not to discount the man's ideas without a fair hearing. 'So why do you think we should stay here?'

'If the Russians come after us, we don't stand a ghost of a chance out in the open. It'll be *Gunga Din* all over again – except we won't have Douglas Fairbanks and Cary Grant to bail us out.'

'But we wouldn't stand much of a chance in here, either.' Michael Starr was going to add something about his own experience with the Russian helicopter back at Palmer, but he decided against it, that there was no percentage in upsetting himself and the others. 'We don't have any guns. They'll probably outnumber us,' was all that Starr added instead.

'Damn right. But if you agree with me that the Russians might be back to finish us off, I've got a plan that might work.'

'We're all ears,' Whitaker said.

Frank Corbi leaned forward and began to explain the plan that he and Annie Rizzo had worked out just a few minutes before.

Seventeen

'A LITTLE further to the left, up that valley.' Doctor Boris Ney put the chart back in his lap and studied the details of the terrain that sped by the frost-covered windows of the snow vehicle that he rode in. The big mountain directly in front of them – barely visible in a grey sky that would hardly be getting much brighter since the sun was nearly at its highest point already – was the reference point that the helicopter pilot had marked on the chart when they flew back to their base camp twelve hours before. 'The crash site should be just a few more kilometers.'

'Very good, sir.' The driver of the big snow cat turned the vehicle's controls and then glanced out the sidewindows to see if the four giant treads responded accordingly. They had. Even though they were maneuvering through the deepest powder yet since they left the others in the assault group and turned further into the mountains, the snow vehicle they had taken from the American Palmer station continued to push ahead without a problem. 'This is a good machine,' the driver commented.

'It seems adequate.' Ney looked down at the vehicle's steel treads. He watched the snow kick up behind them in billowy mounds as he sat in silence. *Eliminate problems, leave nothing to chance. That's what Lenin would do.* Even though he was certain that none of the Americans could possibly have survived the explosion and crash – he had seen the orange flames light up the sky and had also caught a momentary glimpse of the airship going down – Ney had convinced Captain Kollontai and Aleksandra Bukharin that he needed to leave the main battle group for a short excursion into the mountains in order to pinpoint and mark the position of the wreckage. There might be, he had told them, something of value in that wrecked airship that they'd want to retrieve later.

'Could you tell what the terrain around the wreckage was like?' the driver asked. He kept his attention focused straight ahead on the clear path that the powerful twin headlights marked across the dark and shadowy snowfield.

'Don't get too close to that ice crevice.' Ney pointed to his right as he ignored the driver's question since he had no intention of committing himself to a definite plan until he saw what lay ahead. Ney's real object in the trip to the wreckage site was to investigate the airship crash by himself. If by some unexpected miracle a few of the Americans had survived, Ney intended to eliminate them before they had any opportunity to tell their side of the story – and Ney knew that he still needed to come up with a rational excuse in order to make that decision plausible to the driver.

'Don't worry, I see that ice crevice.'

'Why can't we go a little faster?'

'If you like.' The driver shrugged, then advanced the snow cat's throttle slightly. The twin diesel engines in the compartment behind the passenger cabin picked up their pace, and soon the giant vehicle was bouncing even faster across the icy ridges.

'Move to the left once we've passed that outcropping of rock.'

'Yessir.' The driver complied and soon the snow cat was entering what seemed to be the throat of a box canyon. 'This looks like a dead end.'

'I know.'

They lapsed back into silence as the roar of the twin diesel engines filled the spacious cabin of the snow cat. While he waited as they slowly climbed the grade toward the first plateau, Ney gave some thought to the plan of attack on the South Pole station – an attack that was certain to succeed. In order to prevent the Americans from destroying any of their equipment or facilities, Kollontai and his men would have to move up slowly in an attempt to get the enemy out into the open. Ney already had an idea about how that might be accomplished, and he had shared that idea with Kollontai shortly after the captain had been flown in from the *Primorye* to their base camp.

'Look – up ahead!'

'Yes, that's it.' Directly in front of them was a partial view of the crash site. They could see evidence of charring on the vertical wall of the far ridgeline and scattered haphazardly across the open fields of snow were pieces of wreckage. 'Keep going as far as that next series of boulders, then stop.'

The driver maneuvered up to the boulders that Ney had pointed to. He throttled the snow cat back until it came to a halt. 'Now what?'

'The main portion of the airship is just beyond that next plateau. You stay here, I'm walking up.' Ney began to zipper up his topcoat and hood.

'But I can drive you there.' The driver looked at Ney in amazement; he had no idea why the man would want to walk the last several hundred meters across the ice and snow – it was twenty-five below zero, the last time the driver had looked at the thermometer – when he could be driven.

'No. I remember from last night that there was a deep depression in the snow between where they had crashed and where we are now. I promised Captain Kollontai that I wouldn't take any unnecessary chances with this snow cat. We've only got two of them, we'll need both of them for tomorrow's attack.'

'How can you get to the wreckage on foot if it's not safe to drive there?'

'It looked to me like there were a few narrow paths through the danger area. I won't take any chances, but on the other hand, I don't want to risk our getting stuck.' Ney turned away from the driver, not knowing how long he could keep up his charade since most of the things he was saying were basically absurd.

'I see your point.' To the driver the reasoning he had just been explained seemed stupid and pointless at best – it was ridiculous not to move ahead cautiously in the snow cat. But if that was what this bigshot wanted,

242

then it was all right with him. 'It's a good idea.'

'I've taken the flare gun. If the snow looks firm enough to be usable, I'll send up a green flare and you can follow these red markers to join me.' Ney pointed to a satchel stuffed with small red pennants wrapped around metal spikes. 'If I need help but it's too dangerous for the vehicle, I'll send up a red flare and you can walk up to help me.'

'I understand.' The driver frowned – when he had volunteered for this duty he didn't realize that he might be leaving the warm cab of the snow cat and marching across the open ice.

'Here I go.' Ney jumped outside with the satchel of markers in his hand. The air temperature alone – the rising sun had warmed it up some, to twenty-two below zero at that moment – was enough to take his breath away. Even with the insulated parka, hood and woolen face mask on, Ney was cold to his bones as he trudged uphill, around the jutting point of boulders, then toward the main section of wreckage.

Stay to the side, stay out of sight. After he had moved forward enough to give himself some perspective, the site of the crash began to take shape. The valley was dark enough to make it difficult to see ahead clearly, but sections of the wreckage were unmistakable against the featureless fields of snow. Only toward the upsloped end of the ridgeline did the pieces of the crashed airship begin to blend in too much with the exposed areas of rock, making it difficult to tell one from the other. Yet all of it was good news as far as Ney was concerned: with each passing step he doubted even more that he would need to take out his pistol or the explosive grenade he had brought along. From what he could see, if any of the Americans had survived the crash itself, they had probably died of injuries or exposure during the long and bitterly cold night that followed.

Ney glanced behind him, to be certain that the snow cat was out of sight. It was. He dropped the satchel of markers in the snow, then began to move forward again. Ney easily pushed aside the mounds of thin and powdery snow as he went forward, the snow offering little resistance. Even then, Ney had to stop twice to catch his breath. Each time he did, he listened – and each time he listened, he thought that he heard something from ahead.

Ney reached an outcropping of rock that was less than a hundred meters from what he had identified as the main wreckage. His target was the airship's gondola. It lay on its side near the shear end of a ridgeline, the remnants of what had once been the massive upper structure of the airship now reduced to little more than odd chunks of twisted metal, ripped plastic and charred rubber scattered in various spots across the snow. *Go slow. Be careful.*

Fifty meters to the gondola. Ney stopped again, this time dropping down his hood and adjusting his woolen face mask so he would be able to hear more easily. Voices floated toward him from the wreckage – someone was still alive! Ney moved ahead to the next set of boulders, then crouched down so he could listen again.

The voices were more distinct now. From what he could tell, there were two of them. Ney was going to listen for more details before proceeding ahead when he spotted a body lying in the snow.

Ney took the pistol out of his pocket and put it in one hand. Out of his other pocket he took the grenade that he had gotten from one of the army officers on the *Primorye*. With a weapon in each hand, Ney approached the sprawled out, face-down body that was ten or so meters from the rear end of the gondola. From the position of where the body lay, Ney assumed that it had been thrown out during the crash. He rolled the body over and saw from the injuries that the crash landing had been as severe as he had hoped for. That told Ney all that he needed to know. The survivors inside the gondola were probably few, and he would be able to deal with them easily enough.

Ney maneuvered ahead slowly. The snow was deeper now than it had been. He took his hood off and listened for another moment: the voices he heard were two, a man and a woman. Ney was on the verge of being able to understand what they were saying, but he could tell from the pitch and tone of their voices that they still had no idea that he was outside and less than ten meters away.

244

Boris Ney pulled the safety pin on the hand grenade, then pushed further ahead through the snow and toward an exposed area of the gondola. The two voices became much clearer as he approached the spot where he intended to throw the grenade from. Just before he tossed it into the gondola, Ney began to understand the words that the man and woman were saying. She was making a comment about never leaving him, while he answered back that he had a job to do that she couldn't be part of.

Now! Boris Ney threw the grenade into the gondola and fell to the snow. A moment later, the explosion rocked the ground that he lay on. A moment after that, Ney lifted his head up. The gondola had been split wide-open. Yet the astonishing part was not what Ney had seen but, instead, what he continued to hear. The voices of the man and woman were going on as if nothing had happened! Ney vaulted to his feet, gripping his pistol, and rushed into what was left of the American airship.

Mounted high against the sidewall and protected by a piece of fiberglass that had shielded it from the explosion was a small television screen. On it, in black and white images, was the outline of a man and a woman standing near to each other, speaking. She had lowered her eyes as if she were about to begin to cry, but the man reached across and gently touched her face. He then made some emotional but nonsensical comment about him looking at her.

Boris Ney rushed outside and saw the big snow cat heading down the hill. He stumbled forward and fell to his knees in the deep snow. The big vehicle was already so far down the plateau that it was hardly more than a dark blot against the snow. 'No . . .!' Ney shouted, his voice carrying a considerable distance in the cold, dry air. But Boris Ney now realized that there was no one around to hear him, no one left at the site of the crashed airship other than himself.

While he lay in the snow and watched the snow cat disappear across the distant horizon, Ney finally realized his situation. 'No . . . No . . .' He was trapped outside in the snow and sub-zero cold, with no way to keep himself warm and no way to get help. Even though he knew that if those Americans in the snow cat did manage to reach the South Pole station – there was nowhere else for them to go – they would meet with certain death during tomorrow's assault, that offered no consolation. Boris Ney now understood that he was only an hour or two away, at the most, from an agonizing end to his own life.

'Would someone in the back check the ropes on that guy?' Ray Madigan shouted over his shoulder while he continued to steer the snow cat down the icy plateau ahead. 'We don't need any problems from him when he wakes up.'

'Sure thing.' Steve Galloway moved from the right rear corner of the snow cat's cabin as he checked on the Russian driver he had knocked over the head with a metal pipe. 'He's still out cold. It would take fifty Boy Scouts to get this guy out of these knots.'

'Good,' Madigan answered. He turned to the man sitting in the seat beside him. 'By the way, I want to tell you again what a hell of an idea this turned out to be.'

'Thanks.' Frank Corbi smiled, then turned to his right and looked at Annie Rizzo. She had finally taken off her hat and opened up her parka. 'Have you warmed up yet?'

'Barely. Maybe I should ask you to sit closer to me again – not only does it warm me up, but it does wonders for my morale!'

Corbi laughed. 'Maybe later.'

'Promises, promises.'

'You middle-aged women are all alike.' Corbi then reached for her hand, took off her glove and held her fingers. 'And I want everyone here to know, for the public record,' Corbi announced in a loud voice that carried back to the people crammed in the rear of the snow cat, 'that Annie gets the credit, too. This was as much her idea as mine.'

'Not really.' Annie smiled back at Corbi, then pulled him closer and gave him a kiss on the cheek. 'But if you're giving credit, I'll take it. You never know where a girl's going to have a chance to run up a charge account these days.'

'True.'

'But I do have something to trade you – and it's not what you think.' Annie unzipped one of the pockets on her coat and took out a video tape cartridge. 'This may not mean much to you now since we left your camera and player behind, but here's one of those copies you had made of *Casablanca* – I grabbed it before we left the gondola last night.'

'Hey, that's real nice.'

'It's sort of an empty gesture I guess, but I'm sentimental and I know what that movie meant to you. Me, too, for that matter.'

'That's what I like about you, you're a real movie buff.' Corbi took the video tape from her, shoved it in his own pocket, then put his arm around her.

For the next few minutes the snow cat continued down the plateau with nothing but the noises from the twin diesels filling the interior. Finally, they reached a broad plain with snow piled high on both sides, some of it sculptured magnificently by the effects of the persistent wind.

'Listen,' Lou Whitaker shouted from the rear of the snow cat where he sat next to Julie, 'the next valley should be a wide one.' Whitaker had remembered to take the navigation charts from the airship the night before when they moved to a hidden temporary shelter they had built out of fiberglass panels between the rocks. Whitaker had spread the charts between his lap and Julie's and the two of them, together, had taken on the job of navigator. 'Make a turn up that valley. That's the route that should take us out of the mountains.'

'How far until we get to the plateau?'

'It looks like maybe twenty miles. Then it should be nothing but clear sailing up the slope to the Pole. Another hundred and fifty miles.'

'Great.'

'How's our fuel situation?' Galloway asked. He moved forward in the snow cat so that he could find the appropriate gauge on the panel and see for himself.

'It looks pretty good.' Madigan pointed to the instrument's needle. 'More than half a tank. From the consumption I've seen so far, we should have more than enough to get to where we're going.'

'And we've still got the gasoline heater from the airship.' There was pride in Andrew Sinclair's voice as he made that observation – it was, for him, the first time he felt like a valuable part of their group. 'And fifty gallons of aviation fuel to run it on, too,' he added. It had been solely his idea to take the gasoline heater with them. Sinclair had been the one to run back to get it, making him the last one to get on the snow cat as it started down the plateau.

'That was a good idea you had, Andrew,' Kathleen volunteered from where she was nursing Everett Tucker in the center of the vehicle.

'Yes, it was.' Michael Starr was being sincere – and he knew that Steve Galloway felt the same way, too, since they had both discussed it a little while before. They were all living in a new world now, and there was no time to harbor grudges or carry along old hatreds. Both he and Steve had agreed that the past should mean nothing and that maybe all of them would eventually be able to work out something that took everyone's feelings into account – stranger things had happened under far less trying circumstances. 'That heater will keep us alive if we have an engine breakdown.'

'Bite your tongue,' Sinclair answered jokingly.

'No, I'm being serious. We could be in deep shit if you hadn't thought to go back for the heater – none of us did.'

'Thanks.' Sinclair paused for a moment as he fidgeted in his seat in the middle of the crowded snow cat. 'How's Doctor Tucker doing,' Sinclair asked.

'Not good, I'm afraid,' Kathleen said. She shook her head.

'Is he awake?' Sinclair asked.

'Sort of.'

'Can I talk to him?'

'I don't know. You can try.' Kathleen moved aside to make an empty spot for her husband to slide into.

'Can you hear me?' Sinclair asked as he touched Tucker

on the shoulder. He could feel a dozen eyes on him, but Sinclair kept his attention focused totally on Tucker. The old man looked pasty-white, drawn, bloodless.

'. . . yes . . .' Tucker opened his eyes and looked up at the young man who hovered over him, the young man he had shouted at and knocked down during those first few moments after the crash. '. . . I hear you . . .'

'I . . . I want you to know . . .' Sinclair shook his head. 'How sorry I am. Really sorry. You were right about the things you said. I wasn't thinking, I was in a panic, I was out of my head. But the important thing is that you understand how you saved all of us. If you hadn't stopped me from getting to the front, they tell me that we would've tipped over the cliff. We'd all be dead now if it wasn't for you.' There were tears in Sinclair's eyes, but he managed to keep his head up. 'I just want you to know that we really appreciate what you did. Me, especially. I appreciate it the most.'

'. . . you're a good fellow . . .' Tucker coughed once, and the exertion from it caused him to close his eyes. Finally, he opened them again. '. . . I'm afraid I shan't be around much longer. That's obvious . . .'

'Don't talk like that,' Sinclair interrupted.

'. . . but I want you to know that I, too, appreciate what you and the others have done for me.'

'What we've done for you?'

'Yes.' Doctor Everett Tucker reached up and grabbed Andrew Sinclair's hand. The old man was suddenly feeling full of energy, as if a floodgate had just opened inside him to wash away all his weakness. '. . . a life is something that a person spends, as if it were so many pounds and shillings. I've spent mine in the diligent pursuit of accurately recorded history. It's been well spent, I assure you, and I've no regrets on that score.'

'Maybe you should lay down,' Sinclair said nervously. The old man's eyes were glazing over and the coloring in his face was beginning to look even worse.

'. . . but what this has all afforded me,' Tucker continued as he ignored Sinclair's comments and he sat up even higher, his trembling hand locked rigidly around the young man's, '. . . is a chance to make a mark, to create balance on the other side of the ledger. For the first time in my life, I've had the good fortune to seize the opportunity . . .'

'Please, lay down.'

'. . . not only to record history but, this time instead, to make it . . .'

As the last words came past Tucker's lips, a tremor began deep inside him and then passed through his entire body. The old man closed his eyes as that last surge of energy drained from him as quickly as it had arrived. A moment later, his hand went limp in Sinclair's grip. Doctor Everett Tucker's body fell backward into the pile of blankets that he lay on; quite still – and now without so much as a heartbeat.

Andrew Sinclair gently laid the old man's hand down, then looked at the others in the crowded snow cat. Not one of them said a word. Instead, they paid their last respects to their fallen companion to whom they owed so much by giving their complete silence. The majestic, pristine beauty of the Antarctic passed on both sides of the snow cat as it bore the ten survivors of *Airship Nine* and the body of Everett Tucker toward whatever lay ahead for them at the American South Pole station.

Eighteen

THE LOW profile of the geodesic dome and the single vertical spike of the lone radio mast were all that Captain Andrei Kollontai could see in the semi-darkness that covered the terrain. 'We should get just a little more daylight, but not much more. This is just about as bright as it's going to get. I suppose it will have to do.'

'Then you're planning on going ahead with it?' Aleksandra Bukharin sat next to Kollontai, the two of them alone in the second of the snow cats. The twin diesels of the big vehicle idled noisily behind them, the hot air pouring on them from the ventilators in the panel grillwork.

'Of course we're going ahead with it. We have no choice.'

'But what about the things I'm telling you?'

'Feelings, that's all. I don't like Ney any more than you do, but at least I don't invent silly reasons to go against the plans – the very logical plans – that we've created together as a group.'

'You're a good man, but you're blind when it comes to him.'

'You haven't given me any reason to think anything else.'

'I knew that would be your response – that's why I've saved the evidence for last.'

'Evidence?'

'Yes.'

'Here.' Aleksandra opened her coat pocket and took out a syringe.

'What's that supposed to prove?'

'It's supposed to prove what I've known in my heart all along – that Boris Ney can't be trusted, that he makes up stories to suit himself.'

'Go on.' Kollontai waved his hand for her to proceed. While he listened to her, he looked outside at the brightly-painted temporary shelter several meters away that they had brought with them from McMurdo and erected to house their troops. Twenty professional soldiers, plus volunteers from the *Primorye*'s crew, to bring the total of the battle group to nearly fifty. Once the last unit of reinforcements was brought up by helicopter to join them, they would launch the attack to capture the South Pole station for themselves.

'I finally realized it a little while ago, while I was unpacking the medical supplies that I had brought with me.' Aleksandra held the plastic syringe toward Kollontai, the sharp needle pointed directly at him. 'Do you remember what Ney said after he returned from the Bellingshausen station where he told us that the Americans had massacred our people?'

'I don't know what you're getting at.'

'Simply this. Ney found one of our people still alive . . .'

'Yes, I remember that.'

'. . . and he told me that he wasn't able to give that dying man an injection of the sedative I had sent along. He said that he was nervous, that he had dropped the syringe. He said that it had broken into a hundred pieces.'

'So what? He's not a medical doctor, he's a scientist . . .'

'Here.' Aleksandra raised the syringe above her head, then flung it down on the metal floorboards of the snow cat as hard as she could. The plastic syringe bounded upward off the floorboards, then careened down from the low roof panel and finally landed on the grillwork near the snow cat's driver's seat. Aleksandra reached out, picked up the syringe and handed it to Kollontai. 'Do you see what I mean? It's still perfectly intact.'

Kollontai examined the syringe without a comment. Although the needle was bent, there was not so much as a scratch on the heavy plastic body of the syringe itself.

'So what do you think of that?' Aleksandra asked after a suitable silence. She didn't care about what happened to Ney – he had failed to meet them at the rendezvous point the evening before and now was presumed to be lost and probably dead – but she felt that she needed to totally discredit Ney's reasoning in order to get Kollontai to change his mind.

'I don't think much of it,' Kollontai finally answered. He handed the syringe back to her as if he wasn't interested in it in the slightest. 'If that's all you've got, then you've got very little. Maybe the syringe you gave Ney was defective, or maybe he was referring to the bending of its needle.'

'Or maybe it shows that he's been systematically lying to us all along!' Aleksandra had raised her voice again even though she didn't want to. To her, Ney's actions had become transparent, the motives behind those actions had finally made sense. Ney had been manipulating them in order to keep control of the *nachalstvo* – and he probably intended to get rid of Andrei and herself as soon as the opportunity presented itself.

'Stop this, it's a pointless waste of our time!' Kollontai attempted to sound angry with her, but his true feelings and his mounting doubts were unmistakable in the tone of his voice. Boris Ney had not returned and had now been missing for nearly fourteen hours. Maybe Ney had lied to them, maybe he had intentionally steered them down some path of his own choice. But no matter whether Aleksandra was right or not, the question of Ney's motives was now far behind them. 'We don't have any options left.'

'Of course we do. We've got to stay flexible, to re-evaluate our thinking.'

'We've got to do what our people expect, we've got to follow the rules.'

'Rules?' Aleksandra couldn't believe what she was hearing, couldn't believe that the man sitting less than an arm's length from her was the same man she had made love to, the same man she had fallen in love with during the last few days.

'That's right. Maybe rules aren't the right word. Expectations is what I really mean. We can't simply change the tide by holding up our hands and deciding to turn it around. It's too late for that.'

'No, it's not.' Aleksandra was getting frantic; the helicopter was due back from the *Primorye* at any minute with the last of the troops, which meant that the attack would be launched against the Americans inside the South Pole station within the next half hour.

'You know as well as I do what the rules of the *nachalstvo* are. The last official plan remains in effect unless we have a meeting and vote otherwise. But now that we're poised on the edge of the American base, you've wavered again and want to cancel the planned attack, to find some other way to deal with the enemy. How's that going to look to our people?' Kollontai turned away from her and looked out the vehicle's sidewindow at the featureless plateau of ice and snow to the rear. 'Maybe Ney will show up after all, then we can have a meeting. Then we can vote on a change of plans.'

'Don't be ridiculous – we both know that he's dead by now. They must have fallen through the ice or gotten hopelessly lost.' Aleksandra had no idea what had happened to Ney and his driver, since the two men had simply vanished without a trace. Timoshenko, the *Primorye*'s first mate, had ranged out several kilometers from their temporary base camp on one of the smaller snow vehicles and so had a few of the soldiers – but none of them had found a thing. 'The helicopter will be back soon.'

'Yes. Perhaps he's found something.'

'I doubt it.' Both she and Kollontai had agreed to divert the helicopter from its last flight back from the *Primorye* in order to have it fly toward the suspected area where the American airship was reported to have crashed. But they had both agreed that finding Ney's body or any other evidence of what could have happened to him would be a long shot at best.

'I don't see why we should consider changing our plans. Nothing has changed. The latest report from the scientific committee on the *Primorye* is even more conclusive.'

'I know.' Aleksandra nodded in agreement because the scientific evidence presented by their technical people was

254

irrefutable: the spot where the *Primorye* was moored several hundred kilometers behind them at the entrance to the American McMurdo station was no more than a few days away from becoming uninhabitable. Yet measurements showed that the atmosphere surrounding the South Pole station itself should remain free of pollutants throughout the long and dark Antarctic winter. Six months from now the contaminated atmosphere would have retreated far enough north to make the McMurdo area and the *Primorye* usable again – and a year after that, possibly even the tip of South America would be cleansed enough of its nuclear contaminants to make a landfall possible. Slowly, these few survivors of the holocaust that had destroyed the rest of the world might be able to work their way back toward a more usable environment in the north, long before the storehouse of supplies at McMurdo and the other Antarctic stations had given out.

'So why should we reconsider?' Kollontai asked forcefully. 'We all agreed that we could only build a new world out of total and complete trust among the surviving people – yet the Americans have shown us that there's no way that we can trust them! How will we ever be able to sleep peacefully knowing that the people in the next bunk from us or in the next hut from us might tiptoe in some night to murder us in our sleep?'

'But it doesn't make any sense that they'd want to,' Aleksandra pleaded. 'There are probably no more than twenty Americans inside that station,' she said as she pointed to the dark blotch on the far horizon that was the only known structure on earth that people would be able to survive in for the next six months. 'So how can they hope to overpower us? Wouldn't it be more reasonable if we just let them live?'

'Do you mean that we should make the Americans our prisoners – have them work for us?'

'No, this is a new world and we won't have any concentration camps here – I won't permit it!' Aleksandra shouted.

'And neither would I,' Kollontai answered quietly. He looked at her directly, his eyes tired and pleading. 'But

255

that's why we have no choice. We can't take the chance on anything else happening,' Kollontai said as he reached out for her hand and took it into his own.

Aleksandra sensed that Kollontai was beginning to open up again, just as he had the other night when they lay together in bed after making love. Andrei was about to tell her what was really on his mind. 'Please . . .'

'No.' Kollontai shook his head wearily. After the explanations and excuses were all laid out in the open, there still remained the biggest reason of all why he couldn't make himself stop the attack against the Americans. 'We have no right to take the chance. We've lost too much already, each of us has.' Captain Andrei Kollontai understood that deep down he already knew what had to be done. Yekatrina and Lidiya were gone and nothing would bring them back. But now Aleksandra was there for him. 'All we have left is each other. There's no way I could vote for a plan that would leave open even the slightest chance that something could happen to any of us in the future – that something could happen to you.'

Inside the giant geodesic dome of the South Pole station – a dome that had been erected to cover the individual buildings of the station itself in order to protect them from the drifting snow – several of the survivors of *Airship Nine* huddled near the main entrance door. Captain Lou Whitaker opened the door slightly to look out again at the Soviet encampment a few hundred yards away. 'Damn. There's still no response from them.'

'Do you think they see it?' Julie asked.

'Of course they do.' Whitaker opened the door wider, which allowed more of the cold Antarctic wind to pour in on them – but it also allowed everyone behind him to see the white flag they had mounted on a metal pole and stuck just outside the door. The big white sheet flapped noisily in the constant breeze, the end of it already shredded from the constant pounding that the light-weight cloth was taking in the wind. 'They see it, all right.'

'Ray is coming back. He's empty-handed.' Nancy Schneider pointed to the group coming up behind them – a dozen people, some from *Airship Nine* and the others from the wintering-over staff of the station itself. Ray Madigan was in the lead of the group as they walked out of the station's machinery building and toward the geodesic dome's main exit.

'No luck?' Whitaker asked.

'None worth a damn.' Madigan's expression told it all, but he put it into words anyway. 'A few metal pipes, a half-dozen knives. I didn't bring any of it, it's not worth defending ourselves if that's the only way we can do it.'

Whitaker nodded, then looked toward the leader of the South Pole station personnel. When the survivors from *Airship Nine* had arrived at the station a few hours earlier – undetected by the Russian camp because of the darkness – the seven men who were wintering-over at the South Pole thought at first that they'd be able to come up with some kind of defense against an attack. They had gone from building to building and literally torn the station apart looking for ways to protect themselves from what appeared to be one hell of a mounting offensive force in the Russian camp across from them. But none of the men had found anything that was useful.

'The only option that I've come up with is that we could destroy the nuclear powerplant.' Madigan looked at Whitaker, then at the others, as he waited for their answer.

'You mean just to stop them from using it?'

'Yeah. A scorched earth policy, that sort of thing.'

'I see.' Whitaker had already made an inspection trip into the central building of the geodesic dome, the one that housed the small nuclear reactor that provided the station with its heat and light. Both he and Julie had commented simultaneously on how ironic it was that, in a world destroyed by nuclear bombs, what had been reported as the last habitable spot on earth had a small nuclear reactor to make it run. 'Well, I think it's something we should vote on.'

'Right.' Madigan turned and faced the group. 'All in favor of destroying the reactor so that the Russians can't

257

have it – raise your hand.' Madigan looked around at the faces as he waited. One man from the back of the group coughed but, other than that, all of them stood in silence. No one said a word, and – more importantly – no one raised a hand.

To a man and woman, the survivors from *Airship Nine* and seven men assigned to the South Pole station had unanimously elected not to destroy the sole powerplant in what they had learned was probably the only usable facility on earth. 'Okay, the motion on the floor gets a resounding boo,' Madigan said. 'You people are as stupid as I am. We're all going to need to learn how to hold a grudge better than this, I'll tell you that much.'

'I'd agree with that,' Whitaker said. He put his arm around Madigan's shoulder and smiled at him, then turned to the others. 'Okay, then it's settled. No more fighting. I think we should walk out toward the Russians with our hands in front of us. Show them that we're not going to keep this stupidity going on any longer. Maybe that'll be enough to make a difference, to change their minds about the attack.'

'And maybe it won't,' someone said from the back.

'That's true.' Whitaker touched his hand against Madigan's shoulder again, then walked back to Julie.

'Look, their helicopter just landed again.' Michael Starr opened the door wide enough for the others to see around him. 'Christ, they've got another ten Gestapo men – and one of them looks like he's carrying a machine gun!'

'I hope he's a good shot,' Madigan said. 'Nothing would piss me off more than bleeding to death on the fresh snow.'

'Okay,' Whitaker announced to the group. 'I guess now's as good a time as any.'

'Wait.' Frank Corbi ran up from behind, with Annie Rizzo trailing behind him. 'I found something we might be able to use.'

'What?'

'In that far building,' Corbi said as he pointed to a dark, squat structure on the opposite side where the roofline of the geodesic dome sloped down.

'That's our recreation hall,' one of the station people volunteered.

'I found a video recorder, same format as mine. I found an amplifier and some big speakers, too.'

'What difference does that make? Don't tell me that you want to take pictures again?' Whitaker asked.

'No. I want to do the same thing we did before. Put on a tape and make it sound like there's more people in here.'

'I don't think that would stop this group.' Whitaker motioned over his shoulder toward the Russian encampment.

'It worked once, maybe it'll work again.'

'I guess it's worth a try, we certainly have nothing to lose.' Whitaker asked some of the others to help Corbi lug up the equipment. While Whitaker stood with his arm around Julie and her head laid against his chest, he watched Corbi get ready.

'That's it,' Corbi announced as he turned on the video tape machine. 'It's all set.'

'Here we go.' With Captain Lou Whitaker leading the way, the people from the South Pole station walked out the entrance to the geodesic dome and began to head slowly toward the heavily-armed Soviet position a few hundred yards across the ice. Fifty or more men, rifles and machine guns aimed and ready, waited behind their snow vehicles and barricades as a ragtag gang of seventeen unarmed Americans marched toward them.

'Here they come – get ready!' Captain Andrei Kollontai already had put his men into position as soon as the helicopter had landed and the pilot had reported that he'd been unable to locate the American airship's wreckage. Boris Ney was lost forever – and that meant that the decision to change the attack plan rested totally with Kollontai. 'Get ready!'

'Please, Andrei, no . . .' Aleksandra walked beside him as Kollontai strode up to his army of fifty men, their weapons drawn. Even though it was thirty degrees below zero, Aleksandra could feel the perspiration rolling down the back of her neck.

Kollontai turned to her. 'Get inside the snow cat,' he ordered. 'We're not taking any more chances, period. This is another American trick and I'm not falling for it. For all we know, they've got another five hundred people inside that dome.'

'That's not even possible, it doesn't make any sense!'

'Don't argue with me, get inside the vehicle. It'll be over in just a few minutes.'

Aleksandra stumbled away, her face wet with tears, some of the tears already freezing as they rolled down her cheeks. The twenty or so Americans who came at them looked like toy soldiers in the distance, all of them marching stiffly in their heavy coats and boots, moving slowly toward the line of extended rifles and machine guns. *No, he's wrong.* As much as Aleksandra loved him, she could still see the truth. She had become the problem, she had become the reason why all those innocent people would soon die. Andrei had been fooled by Boris Ney, made to think that the only way she could be protected was by eliminating the enemy, by eliminating the Americans.

Stop him. Aleksandra yanked open the door of the snow cat and reached inside. Lying on the grillwork was Andrei's pistol. She grabbed it and stepped back out.

My fault. He's doing it for me. Aleksandra knew that she really had begun to love Andrei, that he already meant more to her than any other man ever could. But Andrei Kollontai was totally possessed by the loss of his wife and daughter, totally possessed by the need to protect the woman he now loved. He was not acting any more, he was reacting. Andrei was no longer in control of himself and nothing could change that.

No, no . . . Yet even as she tried to stop herself, Aleksandra found that she couldn't. She took several quick steps to put herself near Andrei, then began to move quietly to get directly behind the man she loved. Her eyes were so filled with tears that she could hardly see. Kollontai did not know she was there, but some of the others in the front line did. The First Mate Timoshenko and other officers in the chain of command watched her and what was happening in profound silence. None of them would say a word, none of them would intercede between the two surviving members of the *nachalstvo*. Yet Timoshenko and the others would readily accept whatever outcome was handed them by the *nachalstvo* – such was the Russian character. It had been precisely that way for the last several centuries, and even more so since the revolution of 1917. It would probably have remained that way for the next several centuries, if it hadn't been for the effects of the nuclear world war.

'Get ready to fire, on my command!' Kollontai ordered. He stood with his back to the snow cat, his back to Aleksandra. Kollontai's attention was focused on the enemy in front of him. Their range was down to less than one hundred meters – when they reached the fifty meter position, he intended to order his men to open fire. Kollontai had no choice and he knew it – he needed, most of all, to protect his own people at whatever cost.

Please, no . . . Aleksandra Bukharin had reached a spot in the snow less than two meters behind the man she loved. She raised the pistol and aimed it at Kollontai's head. For the last time Aleksandra glanced at Timoshenko and the other army officers on both sides who watched her, hoping for any sort of signal to her that they would disobey Kollontai's order to fire. They all stood stone-rigid, offering no hope whatsoever, making it clear that they would do nothing to change the natural and official order of things. Aleksandra turned back to Andrei. This time, without hesitating, she pulled the trigger.

The shot rang out loud through the sub-freezing Antarctic sky. The small bullet hit Kollontai point-blank in the back of the head and threw him forward. Yet Andrei Kollontai had enough consciousness left as he was spun around by the force of the shot to catch one last glimpse of the woman he loved. She stood in the snow with his pistol in her hands, the barrel of the weapon pointed directly toward him.

She watched him fall into the snow and then slowly sank down beside him. She dropped the pistol from her hands and began to sob uncontrollably, the flow of her tears dropping into the mounds of deep white powder and disappearing into it.

Sergei Timoshenko was the first to move. He turned toward the Americans, who had stopped in their tracks at the sound of the single shot. The Americans were no more than sixty meters away, only ten meters from where the firing would have begun. The *Primorye*'s first mate tossed his own rifle into the snow and began to walk toward the first man in the American procession. Others from the firing line quickly followed, and soon all of the Russian troops were walking rapidly toward the Americans. The Russian soldiers had their arms held out, and they had already tossed their weapons far behind them.

Somewhere in the distance, from behind the Americans, came an amplified, electronic sound. At first it was nothing but talking, but soon that dialogue gave way to a combination of music and words. The music was from a piano, and the lyrics were sung soulfully by one man. It was to this background music that the last two groups of world survivors met on a snowy plateau in the Antarctic and began to embrace each other.

> Hearts full of passion,
> Jealousy and hate;
> Woman needs man and man must have his mate,
> That no one can deny.
> It's still the same old story,
> A fight for love and glory,
> A case of do or die.
> The world will always welcome lovers,
> As time goes by.